HIDDEN
DAUGHTERS

BOOKS BY PATRICIA GIBNEY

HIDDEN DAUGHTERS

PATRICIA GIBNEY

bookouture

Published by Bookouture in 2025

An imprint of Storyfire Ltd.
Carmelite House
50 Victoria Embankment
London EC4Y 0DZ

www.bookouture.com

The authorised representative in the EEA is Hachette Ireland
8 Castlecourt Centre
Dublin 15 D15 XTP3
Ireland
(email: info@hbgi.ie)

ISBN: 978-1-83618-587-1
eBook ISBN: 978-1-83618-586-4

This book is dedicated to just some of the teachers who had a positive influence on me in my school years and beyond Fionnuala Aherne, Mary Casey, Joan Farrell and Yvonne Keaveney

PROLOGUE

THE PAST

When her mother died, she was not yet seven years old and she believed it was the worst day of her young life. How naive of her. There were times ahead that would define 'worst' for her in a myriad of ways.

The day her daddy hit her with the back of his hand, almost breaking her nose, she knew things would never be the same again. He'd been in Flanagan's bar all evening, spending the money he'd made at the mart after selling two lambs, and she was at home trying to feed and change the baby. One of her brothers was outside in the yard. The eldest lad was a bit of a waster. She'd heard that said about him, and her daddy had said he would be written out of his will. Whatever that meant.

Her daddy wasn't happy when he arrived home. He was never happy since her mammy died. There was no one to keep him on a straight line. And a straight line of any sort was far out of his ability after spending hours in Flanagan's.

She was frying rashers in a pan on the range and had burned them. The smell was so bad that it clung to her clothes, her skin. She turned around when she heard him kick off his rubber boots on the front step. She knew he was drunk. Badly drunk. She *abandoned the rashers and ran into the side room where the baby, born the day her mother died, was asleep in the cot.*

Her daddy always looked at the baby nasty like, and she feared he could do harm to the little mite. He'd tried it before, and she'd grabbed the baby and ran the whole way to her granny's house across the fields. Her granny sent her home when she asked if she could live with her. No, she'd said, she was not her mammy. Go home to your daddy, she'd said. The little girl pleaded for her granny to take just her and the baby, not her brothers. The boys could look after themselves. Her granny had said she was sorry, but no, and told her to go on home. So she did. She knew she had no one and nowhere to run to.

Her father thundered into the room, the frying pan in his hand, black smoke rolling up to the ceiling like a bad omen.

'What do ya think you're doing?' His words were slurred, his body leaning to one side like he was about to fall over, pan and all.

'I... I was cooking for me and you. There's no milk for the baby. Did you get milk on your way home from the mart?'

'Are you trying to be smart with me, Miss Prim?'

'God, no, Daddy.' She hated when he called her that. It made her disgusted at her torn dress and ripped socks. She was no more prim than the man in the moon. If her mammy was still alive, she would be dressed better.

'Don't you go taking the good Lord's name in vain. He was no use to your mother in her dying days and he's no use to you now either. Come here.'

She knew she had to do whatever he said. She walked slowly away from the cot, thankful that the baby was asleep.

'Yes, Daddy?'

'You need a convent education. The nuns will knock the corners off you.'

'What nuns? At primary?' She hadn't gone to school since her mother died, nearly a year ago. Did he mean she could go

back? She rarely knew what he meant, especially after he'd had a feed of pints.

'Primary? You good-for-nothing hussy.' He swayed then and leaned against the door jamb. 'You need to make a few bob while you're getting a good Catholic education, lassie. I'll be bringing you down to the convent of the Sisters of Forgiveness.'

She had no idea who that was or where they were. And now the baby decided to wake up, and her father, as if suddenly realising he was still holding it, threw the frying pan across the room. The blackened rashers hopped out of it and grease splashed everywhere. She'd have to clean it all up. She thought she'd never be able to look at a rasher again, never mind eat one.

She was not to know that she wouldn't even get the opportunity.

1

COUNTY GALWAY

SUNDAY

'I'm Imelda Conroy, and my radio documentary is dedicated to those who lived through a horrific time in Irish history. A time from the not-too-distant past. A time when young women were shamefully branded "fallen women" by the Church, even though most were just girls who'd been abandoned by their families to be hidden away behind imposing convent walls. Convents with laundries. Magdalene laundries, so called after Mary Magdalene, and you know how *she* was portrayed in the Bible.

'But we won't be talking about biblical times. Instead we will be concentrating on the late nineteen seventies and eighties, even up to the mid nineties. The women you will hear recounting their experiences were painted as modern-day Mary Magdalenes. Fallen women. A misnomer if ever there was one. They did not fall, they were pushed. They were not women, they were no more than children.'

Imelda hit the pause button. She inhaled a breath and scanned her eyes over her notes, though she didn't need them.

'You will hear from survivors. Ordinary young women. Some were just children abandoned by their families because of financial problems. Others were pregnant girls, and at a time that should have been the happiest of their lives, they were ostracised by family, church and community. I want you to hear these survivor stories in order to honour those who did not survive. Women and children who lost their lives behind those high walls. Who knows how many lie in unmarked graves throughout this luscious green island of saints and scholars. Ha. The reputation of this little country was apparently greater than the lives of the most vulnerable in our society.'

Removing her headphones, Imelda sat back in her chair. She'd already recorded and edited some of the episodes. She had one more to do, but for now she was framing the intro for Episode 1.

Having listened to the women speak for hours over the past few months, she felt physically and emotionally drained. She would finish the introduction in the morning. No, finish it now and have a lie-in.

She felt a tingle of excitement. What she had uncovered was about to blow the previous reports and investigations wide open. It could rock the government, might further erode the power of the Catholic Church in Ireland. The last vestiges of respect for the Church would crumble under the words of these brave women. And no one knew of her own emotional link to the story. The truth was, she hadn't yet figured out the whole sorry tale. She was still searching. Seeking to uncover who she was and why her life had taken the twists and turns it had.

She went to fill the kettle and switched it on for a bedtime cup of tea. She was peckish, so she slotted two slices of bread into the toaster and got out the butter and jam. A knock on the door caused her to pause. A glance at the clock told her it was after midnight. Another insistent, quick-fire *knock-knock-knock*.

'Damn.' She stared out the window into the inky darkness.

Though it was June, and warm, the sky was dark, starless. Might be rain tomorrow. What else could she expect? A typical summer in Ireland.

At the door of the rented holiday cottage, she leaned in to listen. There was no spyhole like in her Dublin apartment. But she was safe here, wasn't she? Nothing bad happened in Connemara. Bad things only happened in the past.

'Who's there?' she asked.

'Assumpta Feeney. Let me in.'

'Who?' It was hard to hear through the thick wood. Imelda pulled back the bolt and twisted the handle. As she did so, the door burst inwards and a woman almost fell in on top of her.

'Jesus, Imelda, you'd think I was a murderer the way you're looking at me.'

'I... I don't know...' She wasn't sure if she recognised the woman.

'Assumpta Feeney? Remember? You spoke with me. On the phone and at my house.'

She knew then who her late-night visitor was. 'What are you doing here?'

'To warn you that you're in danger. I want to stop you from making the biggest mistake of your life.' The woman paused, breathless. 'Then again, depending on what you make of it, I could be giving you the scoop of a lifetime.'

With those words, Assumpta sat on a chair and took a bottle of wine from her bag. 'Corkscrew?'

'I'm sure there's one somewhere.' Imelda went to the kitchen, getting ready to record the conversation. Once she had their wine poured, she sat back and waited for whatever Assumpta had to tell her. She was intrigued by her intrusion. 'I'm ready when you are.'

'Before we start, tell me a bit about yourself.' Assumpta drained her glass and reached for the bottle.

Imelda cringed. She never talked about herself to anyone.

She kept her life private while invading the privacy of others. But her quest for the truth did not fill her with guilt.

'Honestly, there's not much to relate. You know I do this for a living, but I'm thinking I might have to take up a new job. It's a struggle to secure funding.'

'When I reveal my story, you'll make a fortune. You'll have Netflix breaking down your door.'

'I doubt that,' Imelda said. 'This is a radio documentary, not television. I don't see how they'd be interested.'

'Perhaps you should make a podcast. Podcasts are huge at the moment.'

She thought it was an idea worth pursuing if the promised finance did not materialise. Assumpta's second glass of wine was almost finished, and though Imelda herself had consumed very little, she felt drunk with anticipation.

'We can start again, if this is new information. Where are you from, Assumpta?'

'I've travelled the world for most of my life, so I hardly know where I'm from or who I am any more. Life has been good to me in recent years. Before that... well, I'd buried it all. I told you some of it already, but I think the time is right to reveal the truth.'

Half an hour in, Assumpta was on her third glass of wine and Imelda was getting antsy and tired because the woman still had to reach the crux of her story. She went to the kitchen and poured her own wine down the sink, then switched on the kettle again.

She went back to the other room. 'I'm making a cuppa. Would you like one?' As she said the words, she froze. Something white, for all the world like a face, had flashed by the window. 'Did you see that?'

'See what?' Assumpta twisted round awkwardly on the chair, spilling wine on the upholstery. 'Oops.'

'There was someone at the window, I'm sure of it. I saw a face. It had to be a face. Did you not see it?'

'It's the wind. The shadow of branches blowing. It's always been spooky out this way. I'm surprised they get anyone to rent these holiday homes.'

'The other two cottages are unoccupied.' Imelda looked out the window, thinking just how isolated they were.

A gate banged.

Gravel crunched.

She felt her throat dry up as she tried to speak. 'Footsteps. I'm sure of it. Jesus, Assumpta, there's someone out there.'

'You're imagining things. I've put the wind up you with my story. There are no ghosts. Just haunted memories.'

A high-pitched sound came from the kitchen. Imelda jumped again, her hands clutched to her chest. 'Did you hear that?'

'Water's boiled?'

She sighed and peered out into the blackness of the night. All was quiet again. What had she heard? She was crazy to rent in such a remote place. Halfway down a hill, the ocean in the distance. The location had played to her romantic and whimsical nature, but now she was regretting her decision. Another shadow moved. Was it just the branch of a tree swaying before it returned to stillness?

'I'm sure there's someone out there.' She could not rid herself of the anxiety in her chest.

'You're so jumpy. I'll go take a look.' Assumpta stood, but fell back onto the chair with a giggle. 'Gosh, I think I'm drunk. Might be time for that coffee. Here, take my bag, there's a packet of biscuits in it somewhere.'

Imelda stood staring out for another moment. 'Must be my imagination.'

She didn't believe it was all imagination, but she didn't

fancy going outside to look around in the pitch dark. They were safe inside, weren't they?

Picking up Assumpta's bag, she switched off her recording equipment and put the USB in her jeans pocket before returning to the kitchen. She could not shake off her anxiety as she switched on the kettle once more.

That was when she heard the front door burst inwards and Assumpta scream.

2

RAGMULLIN

MONDAY

Her early-morning run before work was turning into a nightmare for Maura Carroll. She grimaced as she thundered along the narrow footpath, her feet hurting. Her runners needed to be replaced, though she was hoping to get to pay day. That meant she'd have to last until June thirtieth.

'Damn,' she muttered under her breath.

She paused at the end of the road, a hundred metres or so past the fruit and veg shop, one of only a few retailers in the area. A stone had somehow worked its way in through the sole to irritate her foot.

Leaning on the narrow bridge, she wiggled her foot out of the runner and shook the stone into the River Brosna below. Something caught her eye in the reeds by the riverbank. Was that hair? Her heart almost stopped as she peered over to get a better view.

'What the...? Oh my God!' She recoiled in horror and backed out onto the road, narrowly missing a car.

A body. No! It couldn't be. She'd been running too hard, that was all. She was imagining it. She had to be. Still, she had to look again.

She inched forward and forced herself to gaze downwards, hand clasped to her mouth.

'Shit, oh God. No!'

She tried to concentrate on her breathing so as not to melt into a full-blown panic attack. What was she to do? She worked at the hospital, but her job was in administration, not as a medical professional. She knew basic CPR, but this person was way past saving. She failed at controlling her breaths, and they came out in quick, hysterical bursts.

'Help! Oh my good Lord, help!'

Had she even uttered the words? She didn't need divine intervention. She needed someone to help, but there didn't seem to be anyone else in the vicinity. The solitary car that had passed her was in the distance up the road. The fruit shop was not yet open. What was she supposed to do?

Was there a correct procedure to follow? Perhaps she should go down into the reeds and check for a pulse?

No. No way was she going anywhere near the body. She'd probably slip down the bank and drown. Stupid thought. Even though the river was fast-flowing, it didn't look too deep. No, she needed to call the emergency services.

Fumbling her phone out of the arm strap she used while running, she almost let it drop over the bridge into the water below. It took her another minute to remember her PIN, such was the shock and fright surging through her body. Eventually she tapped in the 999 number and gave the details. She realised she was almost screaming.

A flock of birds rose as one from the trees lining the bank on the opposite side, their crowing louder than her shrieks.

. . .

It took just six minutes for the first of the emergency services to arrive at the scene. In those waiting minutes Maura had sat on the footpath kerb, phone in hand, not knowing what to do. Sit and wait, that was all she was able to do anyhow.

The emergency response teams had to park up along the road and inch their way down the riverbank carrying their equipment. They immediately got to work.

A young garda stood in front of Maura, notebook in hand, asking a barrage of questions. Time of arrival, what she'd done, when she'd noticed the body. She was physically and mentally drained and it wasn't yet 8.30 a.m.

'I can't stay here much longer,' she said. 'Honestly. I need to get to work. I've no annual leave left because I took three weeks to visit my sister in Dubai and ...' She knew she was rambling, but her eyes were glued to the paramedics as they attended to the body in the water. She checked the time on her phone. 'I really need to go. I have to shower and then change into my work clothes... This is a nightmare.' She couldn't halt the hysteria screeching in her voice.

'You're thinking of work at a time like this?' the young garda enquired.

Maura hugged her hoodie tight to her chest. 'I can't process this. Is it a woman that's dead?'

'I just need to confirm all your details. A short statement. Then you can—'

'Look, I gave my details to that other guard over there. Check with him. Can't you call me later?'

'I suppose I—'

'Thank you. I'm so shocked by all this, I can't think straight.' Maura kept her eyes averted from the reeds where the body lay partially submerged. White-suited CSI technicians, or whatever they were called, were attempting to erect a tent on the riverbank.

Once the guard allowed her to leave, she turned and ran, hobbling in her ripped running shoe, not caring about stones getting through to her foot. Life was a whole lot worse for the poor unfortunate in the river.

3

COUNTY GALWAY

The car was warm as Lottie drove behind Boyd on their way to Connemara for his sister's wedding the coming weekend. They'd brought both cars because he had to go home later in the week to pick up his son, who was staying with Kirby and his girlfriend, and Lottie didn't want to be stuck in the wilds with no transport of her own. They'd decided to make a holiday out of the break away. She wondered how that would go.

She hit the hands-free phone. 'Can we stop soon? I need to pee.'

They turned off the motorway at Ballinasloe and parked at an imposing hotel. After using the bathroom, she entered the roomy lounge bar and joined Boyd, who'd ordered coffee and sandwiches.

'It's no more than a two-hour drive,' he said. 'You should have gone to the toilet before we left.'

'You'd think I was a child,' she said, unable to hide a grin.

'You act like one at times.'

She swatted his arm playfully. He was joking, but still, it rankled a little. It had been Boyd's idea to take the time off. Lottie hadn't been sure about being away from her family for an entire week, but they were due to arrive on Sunday, the day of the wedding. And if she was fully truthful with herself, she would miss her job too.

Their food and drinks arrived.

'Grace will be delighted to see us,' Boyd said. 'She wants you to help her with the last-minute arrangements.'

'I'm not sure I'll be any use to her, but I'll try.' She had only met Boyd's sister a handful of times and figured Grace wasn't the easiest person to get along with. Then again, neither was she. 'Have you even met Bryan yet?'

'No, but he sounds grand on the phone. A real farmer.'

'Whatever that means,' she said.

'Down-to-earth. No airs and graces. Nice man.'

'I hope he is, because I wouldn't like Grace to get hurt.'

'Neither would I,' Boyd said. 'He seems sound anyhow.'

She picked at her sandwich, feeling uneasy. 'I wish we'd booked a hotel for the week. I'm a bit iffy about staying with people I don't really know.'

'Grace would be insulted if we didn't stay with them.' Boyd wiped his mouth with a napkin. 'Are you finished? We need to get back on the road. Grace said she'd have lunch ready for us.'

'I'll just use the bathroom again so that you won't be cribbing at me.'

4

RAGMULLIN

With Detective Inspector Parker and Detective Sergeant Boyd away for the week, Detective Larry Kirby had assumed the lead in the office. Maria Lynch had opted to extend her time off with unpaid leave following the birth of her most recent child, and he missed having her around. They'd always had each other's backs. Now he was at the mercy of Detective Sam McKeown. At least Garda Martina Brennan was in his corner, as was Garda Lei, whose first name always escaped him.

The inspector had tasked him with making sense of the budget projections for the next six months, and Kirby found himself sinking into despair at the unfamiliar spreadsheets. He'd rather be out catching and interviewing criminals, or finding a space to have an illicit puff on his cigar. And with Superintendent Deborah Farrell on his case, he was hoping for an investigation to land in his lap so that he'd have an excuse to abandon bloody projections of income and expenditure. He could hardly believe it when his prayers were answered.

. . .

Kirby walked with Garda Lei, who was tapping his notebook against his palm. 'I had to let Maura Carroll go home. Poor woman is an innocent in all this.'

'And how do you know that? For all we know, she could have been involved.'

'Involved in what, though?' Lei said, a plaintive tinge to his voice. 'She was only going for a run before heading into work at the hospital.'

'That's what she told you? Did you check it out before you let her go?'

'Well, no... but I—'

'No buts, Lei. Make sure this Carroll woman is who she says she is.'

'Certainly. I can do that.'

Kirby stared at him.

Flustered, Lei continued. 'Okay. Her story makes sense, and—'

'Story? Let's hope it's not a fictional tale then.' Kirby watched the young guard slouch off, head sagging between his shoulders. He called him back. 'And organise a search of the riverbank, all the way back into town, and upstream to the lake too.'

'What am I looking for?'

'Something that might give us a fucking clue.' Kirby relented as he noticed the hurt on Lei's face. 'The body is naked. I don't think she did this to herself, because why would she take off all her clothes? The water isn't too deep either. If we can conclude she was murdered, then the killer might have disposed of her clothing and belongings in or along the river.' He realised he was assuming the body was that of a woman.

He quickly assessed the surrounding area. 'The buildings and shops need to be canvassed. There's not too many, so that's good. I'll organise that.'

The traffic on the main road was backed up and the link road that ran by the small bridge was now closed. The entire area around the bridge was cordoned off, out of bounds. He gazed around. No CCTV cameras, unless the fruit and veg shop had one, but that was nothing more than a galvanised structure, and anyway it was a hundred metres away with no clear view of the river. Still, maybe they'd strike lucky.

He peered over the bridge as SOCOs carried out their preliminary work beneath the tent that had been erected below. He needed to see what they were seeing, so he pulled on a protective suit, booties and gloves and, after psyching himself up, gingerly made his way downwards. At least the weather had been kind. No rain, so he wasn't slipping and sliding.

Crouching into the tent, Kirby got his first look. The hair was dark, but he noticed grey roots. He had no idea of the age of the victim. Possibly a woman, but long hair didn't tell him anything, and the body was face-down, partially submerged. The narrow, bony shoulders pointed to the body being female. No rings or bracelets. No tattoos that he could see.

'Could the water have wrinkled the skin?' He addressed Grainne Nixon, the SOCO team leader, who was working tweezers through the hair as another SOCO took photographs.

'We will assess all possibilities. I'm doing preliminary work until the pathologist arrives, then we need to get her to the mortuary to discover what happened to her.'

'So it is a her, then?'

'Yes, she is female. Look at this. There's evidence of burning or scalding on her back.'

'Shit.' He studied the blistered skin. 'Can you move the body?'

'Not until the state pathologist does her thing. And just for the record, I don't think this was an accidental drowning, or a suicide.'

'Because she's naked?'

'No. There is evidence of ligature marks on both wrists. She was bound, scalded and most likely killed elsewhere.'

'Christ.' Kirby scratched at his head, only for his gloved fingers to slip on the hood of his suit. 'There doesn't seem to have been any attempt to hide the body. Can you make out anything that might help me with identification?'

'No, not yet. But there are abrasions and indentation marks between her shoulder blades.'

'From rolling down the bank or being pushed down it?'

'I have no idea.'

'How long has she been dead?' He knew better than to ask, but he did it anyhow.

Grainne raised an eyebrow above her face mask. 'You know right well that you'll have to wait for that answer.'

'When will the pathologist arrive?'

Jane Dore, the state pathologist, was based in Tullamore. Normally it was a thirty-minute drive, but with the morning traffic now backed up on the main road, it could take an extra half an hour, if not more.

'Jane is away at a conference, so it will be the assistant state pathologist. It will take them as long as it takes,' Grainne said. 'I'm sorry, Kirby, but like the rest of us, you'll have to have patience.'

He made his way back up the bank. As he divested himself of his protective gear beside the garda technical bureau van, he tried to figure out what needed to be done next. What would the boss do? Damn, why did she have to be away this week of all weeks? His mood didn't improve when he spotted Detective Sam McKeown striding purposefully towards him.

'You found time to join us,' Kirby said, unable to hide his derision.

It was a known fact that the two men did not get on. Hardly anyone got on with McKeown, except for Superintendent

Deborah Farrell. Because of that, Kirby was well and truly stuck with the younger, shaven-headed detective.

'Not that I have to explain anything to you,' McKeown said, 'but when I heard about the body, I decided to take a quick look at the recent missing persons lists and—'

'We don't know anything about her yet. You're jumping the gun.'

'Not entirely. A woman has been reported as missing since Friday. Fifty-three years old. The family were not unduly worried as she's done it before, apparently. Disappeared, then reappeared after a week without explanation.'

'What makes you think that it's her in the river?'

'This time she didn't take money or belongings. One of the reasons for the report being made, apparently. Her handbag was still in the house, her coat hanging on the back of a chair and—'

'It's too warm for a bloody coat in this weather.'

'If you'd stop interrupting and let me finish...'

'The floor is yours.' Kirby rummaged in his jacket pocket for a cigar, then tapped his shirt pocket, without finding one. He needed something to do with his hands or he might just hit McKeown.

'The missing woman may or may not be the person found dead here, but I thought it was suspicious enough to snap her photograph for comparison purposes. It's your funeral if it turns out to be her.' McKeown turned to walk away.

Kirby grabbed his sleeve. 'Show me the photo.'

'Now you're interested?' McKeown sighed, extracted his phone from his trouser pocket and tapped it.

Kirby looked at the screen.

'Edith Butler, known as Edie. As I said, fifty-three years old. Single – maybe widowed, separated or divorced, but that's not clear. She's been living in Ragmullin for the last twenty-odd years. She has two sons, aged eighteen and twenty-five. The elder, Noel, reported her missing.'

'Where are these sons now?'

'How would I know? I only just pulled the report five minutes ago on a hunch.'

'Email it to me.' Kirby handed back the phone and glanced towards the river. 'Edie Butler,' he murmured, 'is that you down there? And if so, what happened to you?'

When he returned to the station, Kirby was glad to note they had at least one piece of progress. The photo of the missing woman matched the body in the river. The fly in the ointment was McKeown, who seemed to think he was in charge.

'Edith Butler,' he announced. 'Known as Edie, so we will call her that. Aged fifty-three. Two sons. The younger lad, Jerry, aged eighteen, has just completed his Leaving Cert and is in Tenerife on a holiday with his friends. Noel, aged twenty-five, works as a mechanic at Maguire's Garage in the industrial estate. He reported her missing. The report says Edie moved to Ragmullin over twenty years ago from the west of Ireland, and—'

'Where from exactly?' Kirby asked, thinking that the boss and Boyd were over west for the week and they might come in handy to delve into Edie's background if it became necessary. Then again, he shouldn't really bother them. This was his rodeo.

'How would I know?' McKeown snapped. 'It doesn't say and I doubt it's relevant, as she's been living here for a long time.'

'Everything is relevant until it's not.' Kirby felt a little surge of glee at his riposte.

McKeown had the audacity to roll his eyes before continuing. 'I've found out that she was married, then widowed. We can ask her sons if she's been in any relationships—'

'Why on earth would you ask two young lads about their mother's marital status? She's just after being found dead.' Kirby threw his hands heavenwards.

McKeown ignored him. 'She drank a lot, too,' he said.

'For God's sake, you're unreal. I suppose you asked the son how many glasses of wine she consumes on a Friday night?'

'No, I did not. I haven't spoken to the family yet. It's written here, recounted from the older son when he reported her missing.'

Swallowing his gall, Kirby said, 'Go on, Sherlock, enlighten me further.'

But before McKeown could continue, Garda Martina Brennan entered the office, sounding breathless. 'Sorry for barging in, but this is important.'

'Go ahead,' Kirby said, loving the darkness that descended on McKeown's eyes when Martina ignored him.

'There's a lad at the desk downstairs. Noel Butler, Edie Butler's son. Says he read on Facebook that a woman was found in the river, and someone commented saying it was her. He wants to know if it is, and if so, why wasn't he informed.'

'You seem to be the boss of this,' Kirby said, pointing to McKeown, glad that it wasn't him having to do the informing.

'Shit, how did that information get out?' McKeown said. 'We only have photographic identification. Come on, Martina, you can sit in with me while I formally break the bad news to her son.'

'Why me?' She frowned. 'If it's because I'm a woman, that's sexist.'

'It's because I need someone with me who has a clear head

and a calm demeanour. Gobshite there is making my blood pressure skyrocket.'

Martina gave Kirby a sympathetic pat on the arm as she followed McKeown out of the office.

This is going to be a shitshow, Kirby thought.

Chloe Parker returned from the shop with the daily newspaper for her gran. Rose Fitzpatrick insisted on having it; said she liked the feel of the pages between her fingers, even though she had access to the radio and television news.

She laid the paper on the table in front of Rose who scrabbled about for her glasses. Chloe noticed how her gran had dressed herself. Yesterday's clothes, despite her having laid out clean fare on the bedroom chair. A slobber of marmalade down the front of her blouse, the collar manky. Dementia was a cruel disease. She felt she was fighting a losing battle, so she switched on the kettle to make a cup of tea.

'There's nothing in here about it that I can see.' Rose rustled the paper loudly. 'It should be on the front page.'

'What should?' Chloe fetched two mugs and took the sugar bowl out of the cupboard. Almost empty. She mentally added sugar to the growing list of groceries needed. Her sister, Katie, could go next time. She was bored of having to do everything. At least her mam would get a little respite this week, being away with Boyd.

'That woman's murder,' Rose said indignantly, as if Chloe

should know what she was talking about. 'I heard it on the midland radio news while you were at the shop.'

'What woman? When did it happen?'

'This morning. Someone found a body in the river.'

'Really? I didn't hear that.' Chloe opened the tea-bag box to find only one bag remaining. It would do for her gran, and she'd have coffee instead. 'There's no way it could be in the paper if it only happened this morning.' Damn. The coffee was rock hard in the bottom of the jar. Gran must have put a wet spoon into it.

'And why not?' Rose's voice was rising. 'It's news, isn't it?'

'Yes, but the papers are printed the night before. You know that.'

'Are they? Oh aye. I forgot.'

Chloe made their drinks – at least they had fresh milk – and brought the mugs to the table.

Rose turned up her nose. 'A biscuit would be nice.'

With an exasperated sigh, Chloe fetched the almost empty packet of biscuits. Another item for the food list. 'You can have the last two.'

'One is fine. Do you want me to get diabetes as well as all my other ailments?'

'Tell me the story from the radio.' Chloe knew this was a good way to stimulate her gran's brain.

After dunking the biscuit into her tea, Rose waited till it was soggy before biting into it. 'Ah, you can't beat a ginger nut.'

Chloe sipped her coffee. She didn't think Rose would remember what she'd heard on the radio. She probably wouldn't even remember what she'd been saying ten seconds ago. However, her gran continued to surprise her.

'A lassie out for a jog saw the body caught up in the reeds. Down by the bridge at the end of the link road. Apparently it had been burned and tied up, or something like that. That's what it said on the radio.'

'Oh.' Chloe put down her mug. She wasn't sure if her gran

was recounting what she'd actually heard or something from an old memory. 'Anything else?'

'Isn't that bad enough?' Rose slurped her tea, and dribbles ran down her chin onto her shirt.

Chloe dampened a cloth and gently wiped her gran's face. 'Do you want to do some knitting?'

'I recall something like this from long ago.'

'Someone wiping your face?'

'No, girl, don't be stupid. I remember Peter telling me about it. Where is he?'

'Grandad Peter died years and years ago. Now how about that knitting?'

'It seems an awful way to die.' Rose stood up so suddenly she tipped over the mug. Chloe watched the milky tea pool on the table before drip-dripping to the floor.

She wished her mam was home because she was losing patience.

She heard a letter drop onto the mat and escaped to get it, hoping against hope that this might be the one she'd been waiting for.

'Well, that was a waste of time,' McKeown said as he returned upstairs with Martina.

Martina didn't think it had been a waste of time talking to the victim's son. She felt sorry for Noel Butler, but she kept her lips sealed because McKeown was in a mood. They'd had a recent enough relationship. She'd fallen hard for him. That was until his wife and kids appeared in the station one morning looking for him. Now she detested him, but they still had to work together. Suffering for her sins, she concluded.

He dropped the file on an unoccupied desk. 'I'm heading out for a coffee.' He left without offering to buy one for her. Typical of the bollox.

At the incident board, she studied the sequence of photographs. The first was of Edie Butler holding a glass of white wine like she was toasting whoever was taking the photo. Her eyes shone red in the reflection of the flash. Her skin was smooth, not puffy like it'd be if she'd been a drinker like McKeown claimed. Her hair was coloured a deep brown. It was easy to see she was thin, even though it wasn't a full body shot. Sunken cheeks, and hollows curved around her eyes. The fingers clutching the glass were long and bony. Nails painted black, or maybe burgundy. Martina squinted but could not make out the colour.

In the photo, Edie was unsmiling, her mouth set in a flat line as if she was indulging the person behind the camera. Martina could see that she had once been beautiful. She wondered if the death of her husband years ago had dimmed that beauty, to give her an air of sadness evident even in a photograph.

The next photo she looked at was in stark in contrast to the first one. It was taken before the body had been moved from its grim surroundings of reeds clogged with discarded bottles and cans. A body disposed of like mere rubbish. So sad, Martina thought.

The following image showed SOCOs laying Edie on the body bag after she'd been brought up from the river. Another had the assistant state pathologist leaning over the body. The next was of Edie lying sideways in the black body bag, her spine misshapen and bruised, skin burned in places, sagging off in others. The indents on her wrists. She'd definitely been bound at some stage, and that pointed to murder.

Finally Martina allowed her gaze to linger on Edie's face in death. She was shocked at the scalded skin of her face and lips, frizzed hair stuck in places to her scorched forehead and neck. Evidence of the horror Edie had endured made her turn away to look instead at the photos of the woman alive.

'What do you think happened?' She knew it was Kirby even before he spoke. The odour of cigar smoke lingered on his clothing.

'Whatever happened,' she said softly, 'it was cruel.'

'It was definitely that.'

'It was planned,' she murmured.

'Why do you say that?' Kirby moved forward to study the images.

She turned to him. 'If it was spur-of-the-moment, whoever did this would not have taken the time to strip her naked.'

'True.'

'And she isn't wearing any of her jewellery. In each of the photos her son supplied, Edie has the same silver stud earrings, a thin silver bracelet on her right arm, a similar chain with a small cross around her neck, and a watch on her left arm. She is wearing none of those in death.'

'Good point,' Kirby conceded. 'So the killer took them as trophies?'

'Or to muddy identification? Maybe to send us down the wrong track.'

'We haven't got *any* track to follow yet.'

'I know.' Martina could feel his desperation. 'But it's obvious she was burned, maybe scalded with boiling water going by the type of blisters on her skin. I believe someone wanted her to suffer.'

'That's a bit above my pay grade.'

They were standing side by side staring at the photos, and Martina felt heat rise in her cheeks.

'I'm currently taking an online course. The psychology of murder.'

'Wow. That sounds deadly.'

She laughed. He did too, and it relieved some of the tension in her shoulders. She watched him drag forward two chairs, their legs scraping the floor.

'Sit, please,' he said, in a nice way, not the way McKeown spoke to her. 'Let's talk this through.'

Gratefully she accepted the offer.

They sat in silence, searching for answers while staring at the images of Edie Butler in life and then in death.

Noel Butler knew he had to contact his brother, Jerry, who was abroad with a gang of lads, celebrating their end-of-school exams. He needed to tell him before he saw it on Facebook, or before some goon posted it to TikTok.

His head was fried. He needed a drink. After leaving the garda station he hurried along Main Street then turned down Gaol Street to Cafferty's. He sat alone at the bar and messaged his girlfriend but knew she wouldn't reply. She was teaching until three.

With the phone still in his hand, he scrolled through his photos trying to find a better image of his mother than the ones he had given to the guards. He noticed his nails were embedded with grease and oil from being at work that morning before he'd hightailed it to the guards. He felt an urge to dunk his hands into hot water to scrub them clean. He couldn't stand being dirty. His mother had instilled this need for cleanliness in him and his brother.

'Another half one, Noel?' Darren asked.

'Go ahead then,' he told the barman. He hadn't realised he'd already drained his first drink. He must be careful. His mother always warned him of the dangers of alcohol, a disease she had worked on controlling.

He had very few recent photos of her. The camera roll was full of selfies taken with his girlfriend all around the country. They went away most weekends. Both lived at their respective parental homes and worked in town, and weekends away offered them an escape.

Darren put a whiskey on the counter in front of Noel. 'Sorry for your troubles, man. Knew your mother. Kind lady. Sort of sad in herself, wasn't she?'

'She was always sad.' Noel swirled the whiskey in the glass. 'How did you know it was my mother they found dead?'

The barman blushed. 'Someone posted about it on Facebook. About a body being found tied up. In the river, you know. Then they... there was a comment saying it was Edie Butler.'

Scrunching his eyebrows together, Noel shook his head. 'The guards never said she was tied up. Jesus, how are people allowed to get away with that shite? Her death was only confirmed to me by the guards not five minutes ago. And I still have to tell my brother, who is abroad, and I've to formally identify my mam's body.'

'It's a hard world out there. Keyboard warriors make it worse.'

Darren went out to the lounge, leaving Noel alone with his thoughts about his mother. They were mainly good thoughts, even though they'd had it tough. He did not want to dwell on those days. For a few months this year things hadn't been too bad. His mother had found a boyfriend, a prick Noel didn't like, but she'd been more settled within herself for the first time in a long, long while. Until she wasn't.

Her latest disappearance had been unusual only in so far as it was the first in over a year. Noel felt the anger swell inside him again, even though she was now dead.

He hadn't been worried initially on Friday evening when he'd arrived home for his tea and she hadn't been there. It must have been around 6.30. He never minded rustling up food for himself, but he had a niggle of unease because recently she was always home in the evenings. Then he'd become angry when her ex-boyfriend, Robert, called to take her out. He didn't like him, but the thing was, she still wasn't home. Most of all Noel was furious because he believed his mother had slipped back into her old ways. When she'd disappear for days and then come home dishevelled, disorientated and silent.

Now she was silent for ever.

8

Standing in line, Martina eyed Robert Hayes, Edie Butler's ex-boyfriend. He was working behind the carvery, serving the queue at Danny's lunchtime rush. He wore a white tunic, black and white checked trousers and a chef's hat. He looked the part of a Michelin-starred chef, but here he was serving food in a bar. The smell of the cooked food assailed her and she realised she was starving.

'What can I get you, love?' He grinned, a lopsided one that made her think he'd practised it in front of a mirror. He was older than she'd first thought.

'What's the chef's special?'

His smile slipped for a moment as he gave an exasperated glance over his shoulder at the chalkboard menu on the wall. She read that the special was a choice of beef stroganoff or boiled ham.

'Tough luck for vegetarians.' She attempted a joke.

'You asked what the special was, love, but as you can see laid out in front of you, we also have pasta dishes, battered cod, a selection of salads. You name it.'

'Sorry.'

'No bother. You're not the first to ask.' The smile returned.

She reckoned he was in his early sixties, and he had a worn look about him that even his fake smile could not disguise. His hair, streaked with grey, was tied back in a ratty ponytail.

'I can't make up my mind.' That was the problem with such a choice. It complicated things.

'There's a long line behind you, love, so do you want to stand to one side while I serve this gentleman?'

'No, it's okay. I'll have the cod and chips.' She watched while he dished up her food. She didn't like the way he squinted at her ample waistline before adding an extra scoop of chips.

She found a free table and waited for Kirby to join her. He'd chosen the stroganoff.

'Smells divine,' she said, feeling a little jealous.

'I could eat an old boot. I'm starving.'

He dug into his food and she picked at her chips, keeping an eye on Robert Hayes.

'He's a bit smarmy for my liking,' Kirby said with his mouth full, a dribble of sauce curling on his chin. 'The way he was calling you *love* and sizing you up made me want to thump him.'

'And what would that have achieved?'

'Satisfaction.'

'We don't want to spook him. Not yet, anyhow.' Martina maintained her surreptitious glances towards the chef.

'What exactly did Noel Butler say about him?' Kirby asked, chewing while talking.

'Hayes is the most recent guy his mother dated, and she was doing fine up until a month ago. That's when Robert dropped off the face of the earth. Then he called to their home on Friday night wanting to take her out, but she wasn't around.'

'Has her phone been found? It might confirm if she was still communicating with that prick over there.'

'Shh. This place is jammed.' Martina lowered her head, moving closer to Kirby. 'No phone found yet. Search is still ongoing in the area where her body was found, and upstream. Her son says it's not at the house. She left her handbag at home, the one she normally uses, according to Noel.'

'We should search her house for the phone.'

'McKeown said he'd organise that.'

'Another prick,' Kirby said under his breath. 'Well, we'll have to question Noel again.'

'Would he even know if his mother was still meeting Robert during those weeks when he thought it was all off?' She swallowed a chip before continuing. 'She was slipping back into her old ways. His words, not mine.'

Kirby wiped his mouth with the back of his hand before taking a slug of his beer shandy. 'If someone you'd been going out with for a few months had died, even if the relationship had run its course, wouldn't you be a bit more forlorn than he is over there?'

'Maybe he doesn't know yet.'

'Everyone knows. It's all the town is talking about.' He spread his hands wide, taking in the lunchtime crowd.

Martina shook her head. 'You're great at generalising, aren't you?'

'What do you mean by that?'

'Forget it.'

Kirby said, 'You've changed since you used to go out with that bollox McKeown. You've got more cynical and too serious. I fancied you myself at one time, you know?'

'I know, but then you met Amy and you're happy with her. Aren't you?'

'Happier than a pig in shite.' He filled his mouth and munched loudly.

She had to laugh. Kirby could be obnoxious and adorable at the same time. She liked him, and she liked his partner, Amy, even more. All she felt for McKeown was disdain, and disgust at herself for ever having fallen for him. If that experience had given her a cynical view of mankind, so be it.

'What's our next move?' she asked.

'We need to talk to him.' Kirby pointed his fork towards the chef.

'I'll have a word and see what time he finishes.'

Kirby held up a side plate. 'Ask for an extra portion of chips for me while you're at it.'

9

CONNEMARA

The drive to Galway was fine until they'd skirted the city and passed the seaside towns of Salthill and Spiddal. Then, as they turned to head for Bryan O'Shaughnessy's house, the road gradually narrowed to little more than a lane, with the sea to their left.

'It's at the end of the world,' Lottie said to herself, peering through the windscreen at Boyd's car ahead of her. She hoped that if her car disappeared into the ocean, he'd miss her before it was too late.

She slowed as a windswept farmhouse came into view. Pebble-dashed, with two storeys and ancient-looking sash windows, it didn't hold out much hope for comfort.

Once they'd parked in the yard, she took her small suitcase and followed Boyd in through the back door. Grace greeted them dressed in a mid-length green cotton dress. With her hair tied back, face devoid of any make-up, she looked fresh and healthy.

'Mark, it's so good to see you.' She filled the kettle and, seemingly as an afterthought, glanced at Lottie. 'And you too. Tea? I baked scones this morning, and there's our own honey. I thought you'd be here earlier. You must be starving.' The last comment she addressed only to Boyd.

Lottie wondered if this was to be a portent for the days ahead. She hoped not or it was going to be a very long week indeed. She was about to say they'd stopped for coffee and sandwiches, but she caught Boyd's warning look just in time.

'That would be great, Grace,' she said. 'Thank you.'

'Sit at the table.'

'Can I help?' All Lottie wanted to do was take a long shower and a nap.

'I'm well able to make a pot of tea and butter a few scones.'

Stifling a sigh, she did as she was told. Joining her at the table, Boyd took her hand and squeezed it.

'It's great to be here, Grace,' he said. 'I hope we aren't putting you out too much. We could have stayed at a hotel.'

'Why would you do that? There's room for everyone here. I made up the two spare rooms.'

Lottie felt her jaw drop. Did Grace think they were teenagers? No way was she letting that pass, despite Boyd gripping her hand tighter.

'We'll share a room,' she said. 'Less washing and cleaning for you.'

Grace pierced her with a look. 'Fine then.'

One–nil to Lottie.

10

RAGMULLIN

If Robert Hayes was hoping to portray himself as a Michelin-starred chef, his house let him down badly. It was a mid-terrace, 1950s or maybe earlier, just down the road from Ragmullin army barracks.

Kirby shook his head and looked at Martina. 'Some mess, isn't it?'

He noted the front gate hanging off its rusted hinges, paint peeling with more rust beneath. The iron bars in the fence were corroded, bent and twisted, some even missing. He walked up the short cracked-concrete path to find the bottom panel of the PVC door patched up with cardboard. Might have been kicked in. Recent, he thought.

Robert opened the door and led them straight into what looked like a cramped living room. There was no hallway. With the three of them standing in the space, it seemed even smaller.

'Welcome to my humble abode,' he said, picking up two empty wine bottles from the floor beside a chair. 'Sorry about the mess. I didn't get a chance to do my recycling yet.'

'Do you actually recycle or dump them in the river?' Kirby

asked, as if it was an innocent question, though his interest was piqued because of the bottles he'd seen caught in the reeds.

'Ah, you're clever. I see what you're after doing there.' Robert walked to the galley kitchen that led off the living room. From where he stood, inside the front door, Kirby could see into the tiny area. Something caught his eye, and he made a mental note to find an opportunity to explore it further.

Robert continued, 'You're trying to tie me to the body found this morning.'

'She had a name,' Martina said. 'Edie Butler.'

Kirby threw her a look, then concentrated on Hayes. 'As we explained earlier, we want to talk to you about Edie.'

'It's shocking. Will ye sit down?' Robert pointed to the two hard-backed dining chairs at the table under the window while he settled himself in the only armchair. It sported faded floral polyester, worn away at the arms, and was situated beside a stove that appeared well past its best too. Ashes lined the floor in front of it.

He looked weary without his chef's regalia. He'd untied his hair and it hung loose around his shoulders. The open collar of his checked shirt revealed a scrawny wrinkled neck. His trousers were stiff dark-indigo denim, cheap, and on his feet he wore fake Ugg slippers. Kirby thought Amy had a pair just like them. He recoiled at this comparison.

The room emitted an unusual smell. Not from cooking, nothing stale really, but Kirby couldn't put his finger on it. Possibly incense of some sort, though he couldn't see anything like that, no candles or diffusers. He'd ask Martina later.

'How long had you known Edie Butler?' he asked.

'Known her? Or how long did I go out with her?' Robert's brown eyes had a glint, and the corner of his mouth turned up as if to say, *I know something you don't.*

Kirby sat back on the uncomfortable chair, his buttocks flopping over the edge. 'Now isn't the time for playing silly buggers. A woman is dead, a woman you knew, so I'd appreciate it if you could answer the questions in a straightforward manner.'

'If you asked your questions in such a manner, then I might be able to answer them.'

'Go on then. When did you first meet Edie Butler?'

'Might have been sometime around the early to mid eighties.'

'That's a long time ago,' Kirby exclaimed.

'You do the maths, I can't be bothered.'

'Yeah, and you don't seem particularly bothered about her death.'

'I was fond of Edie, but she was her own worst enemy. A lovely woman, who drank. A lot. She was probably on one of her binges and fell into the river. Are you sure it's not a suicide?'

'Certain.' Kirby knew he was pre-empting the pathologist's findings, but Hayes was making his skin crawl just a little bit too much for comfort.

'May God have mercy on her soul.' Robert blessed himself.

'Do you believe this was an accident?' Kirby probed.

'Wasn't it?' A raised eyebrow.

'She was badly burned. Looks like she was scalded. Perhaps intentionally.' He wanted to shock the man but decided he'd said too much. 'We have to wait for the post-mortem to confirm cause of death.'

The eyebrow dropped as Robert leaned forward, his hands dangling between his legs. 'Are you saying she was murdered?'

'It's early in our investigation. Nothing has been confirmed as yet.'

'How long was she in the river? I can't get my head around this at all.'

'She was reported missing on Saturday afternoon by her son. Last he saw her was Friday morning. He said you called to the house Friday evening looking for her. Why was that?'

'After we'd been meeting for a few months, she suddenly ghosted me. That was the situation until last week.'

'What do you mean?' Kirby hadn't a clue what the man was on about. He patted his shirt pocket for the reassurance that he had a cigar for later.

'She didn't answer my calls or texts. She blocked my number.'

'Why did she do that?'

'Why did Edie do anything? She was a complicated soul.'

'Aren't we all,' Kirby said. 'What did you do when you were, eh, ghosted?'

'I let her be. You see, Edie has... had a lot of demons, alcohol being only one of them. As I said, I left her alone. But she rang me last week out of the blue. Said she'd love to go out Friday night. That's why I called to her house. That idiot son of hers said she wasn't home. I thought he was just being pig-headed. He never liked me. Possessive of his mother, you know. Anyhow, I was in no mood for a row, so I left.'

'Tell me when you were actually with Edie last.'

'Must be a month or more. We went to Rosco's for a meal and drinks afterwards in Cafferty's.'

'Did you speak with her by phone or text after that?'

'No. She ghosted me, I told you.'

'Did you have a row that night?'

'No, everything was grand. We got a taxi and I left her to her door. I was rarely invited in, especially if the Noel lad was home.'

'Did you ever bring her here?' Kirby couldn't imagine a romantic tryst occurring in Robert's dingy abode. 'To your home.'

'No, never.'

'So it wasn't a sexual relationship?'

'It was more... companionship, I suppose you'd call it.'

'Who kicked your door in?'

Robert's face darkened. 'The Noel idiot. Yesterday morning. Shouting and ranting for his mother. He went off with himself when I didn't answer the door. She wasn't here anyhow, never has been. And that's the truth.'

Kirby wasn't sure whether to believe him or not. He tried to think of further questions. 'Why do you call Noel an idiot?'

'That boy is too old to be living with his mother, having her wait on him hand and foot. I know I said Edie was a bit soft, but she should have been able to stand up to him.'

'You never said she was soft.'

'Well, she was. She was too nice. She liked to take care of people, that was her nature. Because of that, she'd sometimes let them walk all over her. Noel was protective of her, but she did too bloody much for both those boys.'

'Did you have a run-in with Noel other than the front door yesterday?'

Robert said, 'He came into my place of work two weeks ago, shouting and roaring to stay away from his mother. It was embarrassing. He wouldn't listen to me when I tried to tell him I hadn't seen her. He's a psycho, so he is.'

Kirby ignored Robert's slur on Edie's son. 'Did he give any reason as to why he was verbally attacking you?'

'He did not. You better ask him yourself, because I won't risk going anywhere near him now that his poor mother is dead.'

'You said earlier that you first met Edie in the eighties. Where was that?'

'Galway.'

'You from there?'

'No. She was, but I was just working there.'

'What were the circumstances of that meeting?'

'It isn't relevant.'

'Let us determine if it is or not.'

Robert looked uncomfortable. He stood, opened the stove door, then shut it again before sitting back down.

'It was a long time ago. We were young and foolish. I hadn't seen her in decades, but then she walked into Danny's one lunchtime about six months ago and smiled at me, and I felt the time was right for us. Back then, it wasn't right. But of course, with Edie, no time was ever right.'

Kirby scratched his head. 'Can you be more specific?'

'I think I was a little bit in love with her years ago. But she didn't want to know me. And even when we met up again, she was distant. But I was smitten and ignored the warning signs.'

'What signs?'

'I don't want to speak ill of the dead.'

'She can't hear you.'

'No, but if her son ever got wind of anyone saying a bad word about her, life would not be worth living. Anyway, I had a feeling that she was just using me. For what or why, I don't know.'

'Do you think Noel is dangerous?'

'That's a mild way of putting it. I think he's a bloody lunatic.'

11

Kirby lowered the window, lit his cigar and leaned his elbow out into the warm sunshine.

'What do you make of it all?' he asked.

Martina let her own window down, fanning away the smoke. 'He wants us to concentrate on Noel, but it might be a diversion tactic. He could be hiding something.'

'Got that impression myself.' He took a long drag, coughed, doused the cigar between two fingers and slipped it into his shirt pocket. 'Did you notice anything in his kitchen?'

'Like what? We weren't in the kitchen.'

'No, but I could see into it, the place is so small.'

'Go on.'

'There were a few stains at the sink, on the tiles. I thought they looked like blood spatter.'

Martina turned to look at him. 'You're joking me. I didn't notice that.'

'And I thought there was an underlying earthy odour. I know smoking cigars blunts my sense of smell, but...' He stopped. 'Shit, Brennan, it could have been from meat. Human?

I don't know, but I should have inspected it while we were there.'

They drove in silence away from the house.

'He is a chef after all, but do we get a search warrant for his house?' Martina asked.

Kirby's racing imagination had calmed a little as he drove. 'He might have cut up a side of beef to store in his freezer.'

'His house is so small. I didn't notice a freezer.'

'Might be outside in a shed. Does he even have a shed?'

She shook her head. 'I have no idea.'

'I didn't notice any blood or cuts on Edie's body, but she was partially submerged in the river. I'll have to think about how to proceed.'

He indicated to turn off Main Street and drove up towards the station. At the top of the street, Ragmullin Cathedral stood in all its magnificence, imposing its stature on the town. So much had happened over recent decades to destroy the power that the Church had held over the people, he thought, and he for one wasn't sorry about that. Others might not think the same.

'I wish Inspector Parker was here,' Martina said. 'She'd know what to do next.'

'And I don't?' Kirby took the turn into the station yard a bit tight, and Martina squealed.

'I'm sorry for saying that,' she said. 'It was disrespectful to you. You're doing just fine.'

'Nah, it's okay. You're right. I could do with the boss's guidance.'

'Don't fret. You'll do what you can.'

'Let's see when the post-mortem is scheduled and we can take things forward from there.' He parked but didn't switch off the engine. 'Where did Edie work?'

'In a hair salon in town. Happy Hair.'

He shook his head. 'Jesus, who comes up with those names? I'd prefer a Happy Meal or a happy hour myself.'

After making a sharp U-turn in the station yard, Kirby drove back out again. 'I think we need to have a chat with Noel. I want to get a sense of him as a person.'

'He's just a kid.'

'You call twenty-five a kid?' He caught her eye. 'You're not much older than that yourself, Martina, and I'd never class you as a kid.'

'I know, but still...'

They drove in silence down Bishop Street and around the back of the town to Miller's Road, which was located close to the greyhound stadium. The Butlers lived in a duplex apartment, one of sixteen nestled behind an open gate and low wall.

'You sure he's here?' Kirby peered over his hands on the steering wheel as he parked the car.

'He said he wouldn't be going back to work when he left the station this morning and he'd be at home if we needed him.'

She walked to number 11 and pressed the doorbell while Kirby eyed the carwash down the road. He wondered if he should get his car cleaned, but then the door opened and he clapped eyes on Noel Butler for the first time. Tall and lean, with shining shoulder-length black hair, he wore a faded black T-shirt and denim jeans ripped at the knees. His skin was clear and, like his hair, smooth and clean.

He invited them into the apartment. It didn't appear to be much larger than Robert Hayes's house. Snug and cosy was how Kirby would describe it. When they'd settled onto faux-leather armchairs with Noel sitting on the edge of the two-seater couch, Martina took out her notebook.

'Thanks for seeing us,' Kirby said. 'I want to offer my condolence on the death of your mother.'

'Her murder, you mean.'

'Edie's cause of death has not been confirmed as yet, but foul play has to be a contributing factor.'

'Of course it's murder. That prick killed her, dumped her body in the river like she was a piece of trash and then walked away.'

'And who are you referring to?'

'Her ex-boyfriend. Robert fucking Hayes. He's a nutter.' Noel paused. 'What do you mean by foul play?'

'Her death is currently classed as suspicious,' Kirby said. 'We need to wait for the post-mortem, but ...' He stopped. The brutality of Noel's mother's death was not something he liked sharing.

The lad shook his head. 'Don't worry about upsetting me. Social media has already described it in gory detail.'

'That's all hearsay. I'd advise you to stay off social media for the time being.'

'Yeah, right.'

'Is your brother coming home?'

'Not yet. I told him to stay there until I know more. I'll have to organise her funeral, won't I? I've no money saved and I doubt Mam had either. I'll have to get a credit union loan. Mam was a hairdresser and I never saw her with much.' He paused and picked at a perfectly manicured cuticle. 'Then again, she was saving a bit to put Jerry through college, that's if he did well enough to secure a place. She did her best for us, she was a good mother and I'm going to miss her so much.' He sniffed, but no tears fell.

Martina said softly, 'It might be better if you had someone here with you. We can appoint a family liaison officer.'

'Don't want or need one of those. I'm not a child.'

'I know, but someone being here could help. Have you any other family? Relations?'

Noel scrunched his eyebrows, thinking for a moment. 'As far as I know, there's just me and Jerry now.'

'What about your dad?'

'He died. When we were little.' He tugged at his ear lobe and his eyes seemed to have hardened.

'And is your dad Jerry's dad too?' Kirby butted in.

'What sort of question is that?'

'Can you answer it?'

Another ear tug. 'I can't remember when Mam was pregnant with Jerry, as I was only a child, but Dad died and then there never seemed to be a man in her life. Not until that prick Hayes muscled in on her.'

'You really don't like Robert, do you?' Kirby said. He caught Martina eyeing him with some sort of veiled message. He had no notion what she was trying to imply.

'No,' Noel said.

'He says you called to his work a couple of weeks ago, shouting at him. Why was that?'

He raised his shoulders as if to deny it, then his body slumped. 'Because Mam got into real bad form after a phone call. Wouldn't tell me what was going on, but I knew it had to be something to do with him. Warned him off. That's all I did. She was too good for the likes of him.'

'But I thought you said she had stopped drinking, bingeing or whatever, once she met him.'

'Yeah, okay. Doesn't mean I have to like him, and I never did. He has this weird smile that kind of says he knows something you don't. Do you get me?'

'Like he's hiding a secret?' Martina leaned forward. She'd noticed that too.

'Yeah, exactly.' He smiled at her. 'I asked Mam, but she never noticed it. So she said.'

'He told us he knew her in Galway,' Kirby said, 'in the eighties.'

'What?' Noel jumped up but sat back down as quickly. 'He's a liar. She never said anything about knowing him before.'

'Okay, that's grand. Where and when did they meet when she started going out with him?'

'It might have been about six months ago. After Christmas maybe. Think she met him in a pub.'

'Okay.' That tallied with what Hayes had said. Kirby tried to straighten his back, but the soft cushions had him trapped. 'Now, we want to ask you about your mother's belongings.'

Martina took his cue. 'Noel, in all the photos I've seen of your mother, she's wearing jewellery – stud earrings, bracelet, a silver cross on a chain. They weren't on her when she was found. We haven't located her phone either. Do you think the jewellery or phone could be here somewhere?'

'What good will it do anyhow?'

'Her phone might have tracked her movements.'

He shook his head. 'She always had her phone with her and I haven't seen it here. But she wore that jewellery constantly. Why would it be missing?'

'We don't know yet.' Kirby didn't want to say Noel's mother had been stripped naked and even her stud earrings had been removed from her ears. 'When you came home from work on Friday, were there any signs she'd left in a hurry?'

'What do you mean?'

'Maybe a cup of tea left on the table? An upturned chair? Clothes dragged from her wardrobe?'

'She didn't even bring her jacket or handbag. Doesn't that tell you she left in a hurry?'

'Where is her handbag now?' Martina asked.

'In the kitchen. Will I get it?'

'Did you move it?'

'Of course I moved it. It was in the middle of the...' Noel paused, tugged at his ear lobe again. 'Look, it was on the hall floor. Like she had put it down for some reason and then went off without it.'

He left the room, followed by Martina.

Kirby rubbed his back, took in the sad little room. Its sparseness and old furniture was a mirror of Robert's room. He felt a deep sorrow for Edie, a woman he'd never known. It was like she'd done her best for her boys but had somehow put herself in danger.

When they returned, Martina held a black, possibly fake-leather handbag in her gloved hands. 'We will have to send SOCOs in. Just to see if there's anything amiss. And Noel, we need your fingerprints and DNA.'

'Yeah, well surprise, surprise, that will be all over the house.'

Kirby didn't enlighten Noel that he wanted to see if his DNA and fingerprints were all over the area where his mother was found.

What had happened to Edie Butler on Friday evening? And where had she been until her body was discovered almost three days later? He scratched his head, unable to fathom it. He really missed having Lottie Parker around.

12

'So what did you make of him?' Martina asked Kirby as she put Edie's handbag into an evidence bag and locked it in the boot.

Kirby leaned against the car, inhaling the freshly lit stub of a cigar. 'He never shed a tear while we were there with him.'

'Neither did Robert. Are all the men in Edie's life cold and heartless?'

'That's a very hasty observation to make, but thing is, I agree with you in regard to Robert. There's something we're missing. As for Noel, he's in a state of shock.'

Martina thought for a moment. 'He's a mechanic, isn't he? So why is he so bloody clean? I mean, I like clean, but he had been at work this morning before the news broke. There wasn't a speck of grease or oil on him. Even his nails were spotless. The grooves around his nails and whorls of his fingers would have some trace, wouldn't they?'

'I get it, but he probably had a shower before we arrived. He may just be very conscientious about his appearance.'

'Or he was washing away all traces of murdering his mother.'

'God Almighty, Brennan, you are leaping so far in the air on this your name should be Mondo Duplantis.'

'Who?'

'I was watching pole vaulting on television over the weekend. Some athletics thing. This Swedish lad broke the world record. Amazing stuff.'

'I'm sure.' Martina always wondered how Kirby's mind worked, and she was no closer to reaching a conclusion with his latest statement. 'Where to next?'

'I'll get Edie's handbag to forensics and then make sure McKeown has organised the search of her home. I can let you out at Happy Hair, where Edie worked.'

'Thanks,' Martina grumbled, feeling he'd undermined her because she was female by having her go to the hair salon. But then she was only a uniformed guard and Kirby was the detective. She let it ride.

The Happy Hair salon was located at the top of Gaol Street, on the left-hand corner after the market square. The outside walls were painted black and the lettering was metallic silver. Inside it seemed to be a slow day. One stylist sat behind the desk. There were no other staff or customers present.

'How can I help you? Do you have an appointment, or do you need to make one?' The young woman tapped the screen with a pen.

Martina was in her garda uniform with a hi-vis equipment vest over it. She took off her cap and automatically touched her hair. Did she look like someone who was in for a cut and colour? 'I'm here about Edie Butler.'

'Oh.' The woman, make-up pristine, false eyelashes fluttering – they had to be false, Martina thought – got off her stool and stood. She was small, about five foot, in her twenties and dressed in a black work tunic over trousers. 'Terrible news. Do you know what happened?'

Without answering the question, Martina took out her notebook. 'I've a few questions. Can I have a minute?'

'Not sure how I can help you, but fire ahead.'

'Your name?'

'Margaret Woods. Everyone calls me Marge, and don't start the *Simpsons* jokes. I've heard them all.' She giggled, a little hysterically. Nervous? Maybe.

'When did you last see Edie Butler?' Martina asked.

'Edie? Friday. She only worked Wednesday to Friday and she was on the rota from ten until three. She had to finish off a colour and cut Friday afternoon, so I'd say it was about three thirty by the time she left. And that's the last I saw of her.'

'How did she seem?'

Marge appeared to hesitate.

'What sort of form was she in?' Martina clarified.

'Huh, I don't know what to say. It's...'

'Go on,' Martina coaxed, 'you can tell me.'

'Was she murdered?'

'We're looking into the circumstances surrounding her death.'

Flicking her gel nails – maybe acrylic, definitely not natural – the stylist sighed. 'Edie wasn't the easiest person to get along with.'

'How so?'

'She was grumpy at times, sullen I think is the word. You'd have to remind her to smile at the clients. And she'd let herself go, too. Turning up for work with grey roots in dark hair wasn't an ideal image for a hairstylist.'

'I suppose not.' Martina realised she could do with getting her own roots done, but no one had commented on her appearance. They wouldn't dare. 'Was Edie unhappy?'

'Probably. She was a loner as far as I could tell. I felt a bit sad for her.'

'I heard she had a boyfriend. Did she talk about him?'

Eyes widening, accentuated by a lorryload of kohl, Margaret said, 'That's the first I knew about it. Wait a minute. Some guy turned up here on Friday looking to speak to her. When he walked in, it was like she saw a ghost or something.'

'What do you mean?'

'She got all flustered. Nearly dropped the scissors. Said she was taking five minutes. In the middle of a haircut? I said no way. She had to finish the cut first. She told the guy to wait outside.'

'Did she join him?'

'She finished the cut, then ran outside. She was back in a few minutes to do the blow-dry.'

'Did you recognise him?'

'No, though I thought he looked a bit familiar. She didn't tell me who he was, either.'

'Were you not curious?'

'Of course I was, but me and Edie never had that kind of relationship. Her private life was always off limits. I knew very little about her.'

'How long had she worked here?'

'Two years give or take.' Marge turned up her nose.

Martina thought she would be grumpy too if she had to work here. 'What did he look like?'

'Who?'

'This man who called to see Edie?'

Marge thought for a moment, chewing her lip. 'Hard to say, really. I only got a glimpse of him. Why did I think he was familiar, though?'

'You tell me?'

'Give me a minute and it'll come to me.'

'Okay. Did her mood change after that?'

'Not really. Same old Edie, always with a puss on her.'

Martina felt sorry for Edie, who didn't seem to have had anyone fighting her corner. 'So she didn't talk about him or mention any personal information?'

'Edie? Never.'

'Did ye ever go for drinks after work?'

'We did.' Mock surprise, as if it was the most natural thing in the world to do. 'But Edie rarely joined us. We hardly ever asked her, to be honest. Who wants a killjoy at drinks? And she was a good bit older than us, like way older.' Marge seemed to think she'd said something wrong and added, 'Not that it made any difference, but still. It'd be like having your mammy out drinking with you.' She laughed. Martina thought it was plain sad.

'Did she ever say that she felt afraid of anyone?'

'What do you mean?'

'Did she feel threatened?'

'I've no idea. She may have done, but she didn't say.'

'Okay. Thanks, Marge. We will have to interview all the staff at some stage, but if you think of anything at all, please phone the station.'

'Will do. The boss will be back from her holiday on Wednesday. God, it's hard to believe that Edie is gone. It's awful.'

Martina headed for the door, mulling over everything the young woman had told her. She imagined the staff now had a new topic to gossip about with their clients.

'Hey. Hold on.'

'Yes?' She stalled with her hand on the door as Marge came up to her. A waft of hair products and cheap perfume preceded her.

'I know why the guy looked familiar. I think he's the chef in Danny's.'

13

Happy wasn't a word Martina would use to describe her mood after her visit to the Happy Hair salon. She mulled over how Marge Woods had reported Edie as being sullen and grumpy. Maybe unhappy or sad would have been a nicer description. Why was Edie like that, though? What had been bothering her? Okay, so she had battled addiction, but she'd been fine recently if her son was to be believed. But then again, Martina felt there was something about Noel. Had he put on an act, or was it really shock? And then there was Robert and his omission about having seen Edie on Friday afternoon.

She dragged a chair over to Kirby's desk and told him about her visit. 'And she said the man who came to talk to Edie on Friday at the salon was probably Robert. He neglected to tell us that.'

'Maybe he forgot about it. Being distraught at news of her murder.'

'Yeah, pull the other one. That man was positively stoical.'

'What?'

Martina shook her head. 'You need to switch off the television now and again and read a book. Anyhow, Edie left the salon around three thirty on Friday, not long after Robert's visit.'

'How did this Simpson woman know who he was if Edie didn't share anything personal with them?'

'Simpson? Stop, Kirby.'

He grinned. 'Sorry.'

'Her name is Margaret Woods and she recognised him from Danny's.'

'Okay, so we need to go back and talk with Hayes to see why he omitted this piece of information. First, though, I'll have to update the team, including McKeown.'

'Good luck with that.'

Garda Lei had teamed up with a small group of guards scouring the shallow waters of the Brosna and the surrounding riverbank. They worked in a grid format, moving left and right from where Edie Butler's body had been found.

As he trawled through the reeds, his wellingtons sticking in the mud, he looked up at the accumulation of bottles, jars, cans and even some scraps of clothing that had been discarded. They now lined the top of the bank. So far they'd discovered nothing suspicious. Nothing they could link to Edie or her murderer.

'This is a waste of time,' McKeown said, folding his muscled arms, doing nothing other than spouting orders down at them from the bridge. He'd yet to get his hands dirty, taking on the unofficial role of supervisor.

Lei climbed up with his latest find. A black plastic bag. He began laying out cans and dripping pieces of cloth on the tarpaulin that had been spread on the ground. God knows what diseases he might pick up in the river. He was glad that he'd been given a white forensics boiler suit, though it made him sweat like a pig.

'Why do you say it's a waste of time?' he asked.

McKeown snorted. 'Surely her killer wouldn't have been stupid enough to throw any of her belongings into the water.'

'Maybe if he burned them first.' Lei held up a strip of wet canvas material with scorch marks down one side. 'Why would someone burn this?'

'Tell me, Einstein.' McKeown had a nasty streak, but Lei didn't let it bother him.

'To destroy their DNA, perhaps?'

'Why throw it in with the body, where it could be found? Come on, man.'

'Well, if it's burned it's useless anyhow.' Lei returned to concentrate on his work and found more remnants. These he laid to one side, then he called over a SOCO.

Detective McKeown's eyes bulged and his mouth circled into an O when Lei held up the handles attached to what might have been a tote bag. It was badly singed, but some of the words on it were identifiable.

'Looks like it says Happy Hair,' Lei said. 'That's where she worked. It has to be hers.'

'For fuck's sake,' McKeown muttered under his breath as SOCOs began putting the charred scraps into evidence bags to log them. 'Good work, Lei,' he said grudgingly. Then he stomped off.

Lei grinned, but then became sombre. It was a hollow victory over the detective, he realised. Because those burned fragments surely belonged to Edie Butler. Dumped in the river as unceremoniously as her poor damaged body.

14

Kirby gathered the team for a briefing, which McKeown attended under protest. Kirby knew a turf war with his colleague was developing. He didn't care. He'd been stationed in Ragmullin longer than the blow-in. Anyhow, Superintendent Farrell had appointed him SIO, senior investigating officer, until Lottie's return. Perhaps Farrell had seen the light after all.

'We need to trace Edie Butler's last movements,' he said, 'in order to get a handle on whether she went with someone willingly or unwillingly. Last known sighting was around three thirty on Friday, when she left her place of work.'

Martina filled in the team on her interview with Marge Woods at Happy Hair.

Garda Lei informed them of his find in the river: what could be a tote bag from the salon.

McKeown found his voice before Kirby could comment. 'There's no CCTV along that stretch of river. There is a camera on the opposite side of the fruit and veg shop, but guess what?'

'It doesn't work?' Kirby said.

'Bingo. So that's a dead end. We are still checking out other businesses in the vicinity, though none are located close to the river. SOCOs are still on site, and a couple of them have gone to Edie's apartment to do a sweep there.'

'What about Robert Hayes's house?' Martina asked.

Kirby caught her eye. 'I asked Grainne to call round there. Hope he admits the SOCOs without need for a warrant.'

'Why do you want to search there?' McKeown asked.

Kirby said, 'I thought I saw what looked like blood spatter on the kitchen counter and tiles.'

'There were no visible wounds on Edie's body,' McKeown pointed out.

'I'll follow up with the assistant state pathologist,' Kirby said, 'and see what she has to say.'

'Yeah, do that.' McKeown was now as adamant as Kirby about who was in charge. Martina ducked her head from the incoming fire.

Kirby puffed out his chest like a turkey cock. 'You need to work on whatever CCTV footage is available from around the town.'

'I've already had a glimpse at what we've got so far. It picks up Edie at various locations, all on her route to Miller's Road, where she lived. It seems she went straight home.'

'There's a carwash down the road from her apartment. Maybe check their cameras, if they have any.'

'They've no CCTV there and none at the apartments. We're canvassing her neighbours, and if any have doorbell cameras we will gather that footage. But I wouldn't hold my breath.'

'Where is the last place we have sight of her?'

'Walking by the greyhound stadium at three forty. It's about a ten-minute brisk walk from the salon to Miller's Road.'

'We can assume she reached home, because her handbag was found on the floor there,' Martina said.

McKeown gave one of his derisive snorts. 'Maybe she left it there that morning. You heard Garda Lei. The remnants of a tote bag were found at the scene. Did you ask this Marge woman if Edie had a handbag or a tote bag?'

'Did you see her with either bag on the CCTV?' Martina asked.

McKeown fiddled with his iPad. 'She has a handbag strung over her shoulder. No tote bag.'

'Then she got home. Got inside her front door,' Kirby said. 'So did she drop the handbag then, or was she about to leave when someone came to the door?'

'Perhaps she was just untidy,' McKeown said.

Martina shook her head. 'I don't buy that. Her home was neat as a new pin. No, it was dropped there and she had no time to pick it back up. Someone surprised her.'

'Did she let them in? Or leave with them?' Kirby tapped his shirt pocket.

'Is there a back door?' McKeown asked.

'Yes,' Martina said. 'I went to the kitchen with Noel to fetch the bag. She could have grabbed the tote and left that way.'

'Doesn't matter which way she left, we have no eyes on her after three forty. But someone out there knows where she went.' McKeown slammed the cover of his iPad shut.

Kirby's phone buzzed and he answered it.

'Grainne, hope you have something for me. I'm putting you on speaker.'

He heard the lead SOCO sigh. 'I hate being on speaker. Anyhow, I don't have good news, I'm afraid. It seems Robert Hayes is gone.'

'What do you mean, gone?'

'We called to his house and the door was ajar. We entered, having first identified ourselves. Not a sign of Mr Hayes. And his bedroom appears to have been ransacked. Either someone broke in or he left in an awful hurry.'

· · ·

On the path outside Robert Hayes's house, Kirby scratched his head, tapped his shirt pocket and walked in small circles. 'If this isn't the sign of a guilty man, I don't know what is.'

'We've issued an alert on his car,' Martina said. 'We should find him quickly enough.'

'He's had a head start. He could be anywhere by now.'

'Try to be positive. We'll catch him.'

'Has Noel Butler been brought in yet? I bet any money he has bloody knuckles.'

'McKeown went with Garda Lei to get him. Show of force, he said, or some such shite.'

'I wish the boss was here,' Kirby said quietly, as he crossed the threshold.

A SOCO worked diligently in the kitchen. There wasn't much room for more people. Kirby couldn't see any evidence of a disturbance or even a scuffle. Just the visible blood drops or spatter on the counter and wall tiles.

He went through the tight galley kitchen and out the back door. A small shed took up most of the tiny garden, almost flush to the house. He opened the door to find a narrow chest freezer the only item inside. Making sure his gloves were secure, he lifted the lid. Meat in clear bags. All dated. It seemed to be lamb. The top bag was the freshest; frost had yet to gather on the outside. Chops, dated that morning. He'd leave the freezer for SOCOs, but from what he could make out, it was all animal. A dead end.

Back inside, he went up the wobbly stairs to find the house had one bedroom and a bathroom. Wire hangers hung empty in the single-door wardrobe. The drawers hung open in the locker, a similar story to the wardrobe: empty. The bed covers were ruffled, but the bed was made up. He looked out the window at the busy road.

'Where did you go, Robert Hayes? And did you go willingly?'

THE PAST

He was two years older than his girlfriend and he'd wanted to do the right thing. To marry her. He loved her and he was sure she loved him back. Okay, it was wrong that they had had sex before marriage, but they were committed to each other. Young love, his mother had scoffed. Love won't put a crust on the table. And then his mother went and died.

He realised that she had been the one keeping the farm ticking over, because as soon as she was no longer around, his father had the freedom to drink in earnest. And the farm suffered. The family suffered. He was the eldest, and with few skills other than shearing sheep and digging the fields, he was left with no money, no income. And a burning hunger. Robbing a loaf of bread and a packet of Mikado biscuits, which had fallen out from under his jumper as he ran from the shop, had been his biggest mistake. He didn't count getting his girlfriend pregnant a mistake; that was love. This was stupidity. And it wasn't the first time he'd stolen. The guards had plenty of evidence of all that. The punishment for his many misdemeanours saw him being sent up to Knockraw, a school for wayward boys. An industrial school, it was called.

That was when his real nightmare began.

He knew he should never have been sent to Knockraw. Now that he was trapped, he had to make plans to survive. The second he entered through the imposing tall door, he realised he was too soft, too young, too naive to outlive his sentence. Stealing to keep his hunger at bay had landed him here, but before long he would know a hunger like no other. A hunger to escape the horror.

The other boys were stronger and meaner. He didn't like them. But he didn't fear them either. Not like he feared those in charge. One was a chaplain, but he'd heard he wasn't really a priest yet, just studying to be one, and this was like work experience. That made him laugh. As if any experience in Knockraw could compare to the real world. Though he supposed if you could survive Knockraw, you could survive anything, anywhere.

As the days bled into months, he noticed a strange bond developing between the chaplain and one of the boys. That was when he came to know the meaning of true evil. And when those two got together, they were the devil incarnate.

Life became so bad that he almost forgot about his girl and their unborn child. Almost. Not quite. But by then it was too late.

15

CONNEMARA

He came up behind her as she stood at the sink, scrubbing a plate in the warm soapy water.

'We do have a dishwasher, you know.' His voice was soft and his words, whispered at the nape of her neck, brushed the hairs there. She felt his hands snake around her waist, the gentle squeeze, and then he turned to switch on the kettle.

'I like the feel of the water,' she said. 'By using my hands I can clean better than any dishwasher can.'

'Whatever floats your boat,' he said with a smile in his voice. 'You aren't going to change now, are you?'

'Don't suppose so.' She tried to add a little laugh at the end of the sentence, but the 'so' came out as if she'd asked a question. Too high-pitched. Too shrill. Too bloody nervous.

She found it increasingly hard to endure his touch. He tried to be loving and gentle. Too gentle. Too much. She couldn't help her feelings, how she shuddered and squirmed in on herself. She realised she was too broken. Too damaged. She thought she'd overcome it all – that she'd 'moved on', as people said – but with everything resurrected again, with inquiries and podcasts and this Imelda Conroy radio documentary being made, it had bubbled back to the surface. She feared she'd explode with the memories, the emotion, the hate. Terrified that everything she'd locked into the darkest corner of her mind, deep in the recess of her soul, would resurface and she wouldn't be able to control it. If she lost control, she might destroy all she had gained. Her husband, her home, her comfort.

He made tea and left a mug for her beside the draining board in their newly renovated bright kitchen, then went into his study to work. Work? More likely to scroll the GAA scores. But that was fine. She loved him. As much as she was capable of loving anyone. She supposed what she meant was that which passed for love.

With the last of the dishes piled and drying naturally, she wiped her hands with a towel. Rubbing harshly between her fingers, right up to her wrists, before throwing the cloth into the laundry basket in the utility room. She noticed she'd forgotten to take out a wash she'd put in earlier, so she set it to go through another cycle with fabric softener so that it wouldn't have a fusty smell.

Back in the kitchen, she opened the wall cupboard that contained every sort of condiment on earth and took out the frosted glass bottle from the back. Her secret stash. She rationed them because it was so hard to get her GP to prescribe them. Narcotics, he'd said. Lifesavers, she'd countered with a nervous laugh. They got her through the day. That was why they were addictive, he'd insisted. But he'd lost that battle when she cried and sobbed. Six miserable pills, he prescribed. Better than nothing.

She needed one now but couldn't afford to waste it. She broke one in half and swallowed it with her now cold tea. She no longer experienced the immediate hit she used to get at the start, but she'd be able to work and then sleep tonight, even though her dreams would be nightmares. Nightmares from the memories of what had been done. How she'd escaped one hell and found herself in another. That unending loop of horror that she could never forget no matter what she did or what she took. And six miserable pills weren't enough to take in one go to end it all. She really should save them, get more and... Stop!

She deserved to be punished.

She had to live her waking hours with the memories and stare at the ceiling in the sleeping hours remembering the barbarity of what she'd gone through and what she'd done. Or more importantly, what she hadn't done. Silence was sometimes worse than action.

'I am not worthy. I am useless. I am dirt. I should be dead.' The mantra as clear to her now as it was back then. And she smiled sadly, because she believed it all to be true.

16

The cottage was quiet enough in the early afternoon sunshine, despite the echo of his knocking on the door reverberating through the small living room inside. The garda put his booted foot over the threshold, having pushed in the door with his hand because it was already open. He paused at the scene before him.

A wooden kitchen chair lay on its side, the armchair was twisted askew and the fire in the stove had long since burned to embers. A myriad of papers littered the table, which was pushed up beneath the window, and some pages had fluttered to the floor. This disarray along with the open door had prompted the walker who'd looked through the window to call the guards, believing the cottage had been burgled.

Now that he was inside, he wasn't sure that was what had happened. Okay, it appeared a skirmish of some sort had taken place, but as to a burglary having occurred, well, he'd leave that to others to determine.

He edged inwards, shouting out, 'Hello? Anyone home?'

His voice echoed in the stillness right before he heard a soft scuttle above his head. Mice in the attic, most likely, he thought as he ventured further into the tight space.

Tugging open an inner door, he peered into a narrow kitchen.

Toast was popped up in a toaster, a plate and knife beside it. Mugs and a wine glass were on the draining board, and the narrow counter held a sliced pan, a jar of jam and a carton of milk out of the fridge. He touched the side of the toaster. Cold. Stepping backwards, he wondered if he was gatecrashing someone's solitary weekend away. No kettle. Odd. Maybe they, whoever they were, boiled the water in a saucepan on the two-ring hob. But there was an electrical lead dangling from a socket. Weird.

Two more rooms to check, then he was out of there. Write up his report. Head home. His shift was almost done, so he opened the first door quickly.

A bedroom. Bed made. Clothing on a chair. No sign of a struggle. Good.

The last door must be the bathroom, he told himself. The cottage was cramped, leaving him, a big man, little room to turn, but he edged forward. That was when he noticed the water pooled by his feet.

Slowly and warily he pushed the door, and was immediately hit with an odour he had smelled only once before in his career. That had been a suicide victim who hadn't been found for four days.

Without taking another breath, he leaned forward, thrusting his head and shoulders inside. He wasn't about to contaminate a crime scene, if that was what this was. But once he had visually assessed the horrific spectacle before him, he had no doubt that that was exactly what it was.

The body was naked, blistered and burned. Lying in a bath overflowing with water that had spilled onto the floor before some of it had seeped under the door.

His eyes were drawn from the body to the kettle on the ground in the corner. Likely the one he'd missed from the kitchen. No way did the person in the bath do this to themselves. He figured the kettle was too far away from them. His gaze returned to linger on the body, his mind a jumble of questions he knew he could not answer.

He backed away from the stench-filled space and retraced his steps to the front door. Standing on the stoop, he dry-retched before gulping a few deep breaths of clean air. He listened to birds noisily chirping in the trees, to the swish of the wind through the leaves and the roar of waves on the ocean nearby.

When his hands stopped shaking, he unclipped his radio and called in the murder.

17

The cold Atlantic wind tore into Lottie's skin, prickling it like thrown darts.

'Should have worn a jacket,' Boyd said as they walked.

'Wise words, but it's June not November,' Lottie replied.

'That's the west of Ireland for you.'

'Glad I live in the midlands, then.'

'You're always giving out about the weather there too.' He stopped walking and smiled at her. 'Let's just enjoy the few days' break. Grace would want us to do that.'

'Sure. Once I warm up.'

'Here, you can have my jacket.' He began to take it off.

'And have you complaining?' She laughed. 'No, I'll be fine. Thanks.'

Grace and Bryan's house was located on a hillside, sea in the distance, fields all around, long reeds and worn wooden fences stuck into gaps in dry-stone walls. Lottie stood at one of those walls, features of the western landscape, and watched the bog cotton blow in the breeze. The sea was rough and green, and the waves turned over quickly and crashed onto the rocky expanse of an inclined shoreline. She smelled seaweed and freshness. It was beginning to permeate her brain, lightening it, slowing her pulse, and she felt calmer than she had in months. Months of debating where they should live and how they would finance a house move to benefit both their families.

'What do you make of Bryan?' She tightened her arms about her in an attempt to ward off the cool air.

'First impressions? He's lovely. But he seems a little withdrawn, don't you think?'

'At his age, I suppose he's seen it all. He can't really be sixty-four, can he?'

'He's actually in his fifties. Grace got his age wrong, either intentionally to rile me, or unintentionally because she didn't know for sure.'

'She isn't underhand, so I'd go for the latter,' Lottie said with a grin. 'I'm surprised she's having a civil ceremony wedding and she doesn't seem too excited about it.'

'Her lack of enthusiasm is Grace just being her usual self. She loves him in her own way.'

'She never gets excited about anything, does she?'

'Grace is Grace. One of a kind. A rare person.' Boyd buried his hands in his jeans pockets. 'Neither Bryan nor anyone else will change her. That's the beauty of my sister. She is her own woman.'

A soft mist gathered across the fields, blowing up from the sea, and Lottie wished again that she'd worn a jacket rather than the light quilted gilet she had on.

'I got an odd vibe from him,' she said. 'Like he was keeping something from her.'

'He kept staring at you when Grace was dishing up lunch earlier.'

'What do you mean?' She scowled in the face of the rising wind and turned to him.

'It was like he was waiting for an opportunity to get you on your own. To talk to you.'

'I didn't notice.' She had, but didn't like to say so.

'My observation skills must surpass yours then.' Boyd sat on the wall, and a small stone dislodged and rolled down to his feet. 'At least they've started to build their new house, not that I see much wrong with Bryan's old one. They've had more progress in the last four months than we've had.'

'Don't start that argument, Mark. I'm saving for a trip to see Leo in New York about finance, and until that is done, we have to park it.' Her half-brother was playing silly buggers again, and she did not want to think about all that while having a rare week off work.

'While your whole family develops asthma from the damp in that creaking old house. Why don't we take Grace up on the offer of Bryan buying a house in Ragmullin and us renting it? She said he has the money and wants to invest in property.'

'What did I say about not starting an argument?'

'Okay.' He smirked, and she caught the mischievous gleam in his eye.

'We're here for your sister's wedding and we are going to enjoy it.'

'Sure thing. You're the boss.'

'I am.' She grinned and grabbed his hand, and they made their way towards the edge of the field to take in the magnificence of the Atlantic Ocean.

With Tess, his Border collie, racing ahead of him, Bryan O'Shaughnessy walked his land counting his flock. He rubbed his furrowed brow with one finger and wondered if he had made the right decision. He couldn't dislodge the nagging feeling that he was a fraud. The sensation woke him in the middle of the night and scratched away at the anxiety spots that flared the closer he got to the wedding.

He *was* a fraud.

Who did he think he was, marrying a young woman almost half his age? What in God's name had he been thinking? The way people looked at him and sniggered behind their hands. Did he care? Not for himself, no, but he did care for Grace. He loved her deeply.

She was a beautiful, complex human being, and vulnerable in a manner few understood. She was innocent in some ways, but in others she was wily and wise. A good foil to him and his rugged country style. But what bothered him most was what he hadn't told her. Hadn't told anyone.

The arrival of her brother was bothering him too. Mark Boyd was a detective. Maybe he should talk to him. Share the load. But no matter what, he didn't want Grace to know. Why not, though? She'd understand. The thing was, she might not understand why he had kept quiet about it. It was so long ago now, but it felt like yesterday, the memory weighing heavier on his soul the closer he got to marrying her.

'Come on, Tess, we're done here.' He waited for his dog to join him, then set off again.

THE PAST

The morning started like every other in the cold and damp of Connemara. That was until Mary Elizabeth felt the weight of her parents, grandparents, ancestors, all of them, like sacks of potatoes on her shoulders. The first wave of nausea hit her as she got ready for school, bending over to pull on her white knee socks.

She sat back on the hard wooden chair in the corner. She was never sick.

Mentally she went through the little she'd eaten the evening before. Boiled potatoes, bacon and cabbage. Maybe it was the cabbage. But she knew deep down. She knew what was wrong, and that was why the weight settled on her and she would never again be able to remove it.

The second wave had her pulling the door open and racing to the only bathroom in the house. Her brother was inside. Typical.

'I need to go to the toilet,' she said calmly. 'Open up.'

He didn't answer, or didn't hear her with the flow of water. She imagined him dunking his drunken head under the tap. He'd been out the night before and she could smell the stink of stale alcohol wafting through the slats and door jamb. It'd take more than water to rid him of the smell of pints of Guinness. The very thought had her retching right there on the landing, bent in two, holding her stomach as if it was about to fall out of her body.

'What's all that racket?' her mother shouted up the stairs, a woman who rarely lowered her voice. 'You'll have your father running in from the field thinking something is wrong, and you don't want that, do you?'

She was below in the kitchen stirring porridge, and the smell rose and mingled with Joseph's overindulgence. Another retch tore through Mary Elizabeth with such force that this time she couldn't hold it in. Bile dribbled through the fingers of the hand she'd clasped to her mouth, and she thought she would surely die with the force of it.

The door opened, and bare-chested, green, her brother came out and stalled at the sight of her. 'Jesus, you look worse than I feel. What'd you drink?'

She couldn't answer him. She ducked under his arm and skidded on the moist floor, dropped to her knees and puked into the rancid toilet. Her brother still had to learn to flush. Another wave. More expulsion. Then she felt her hair being gripped and gently held back.

'Sis, what's wrong?'

She didn't have to say it. She knew by the look on his face that he understood.

'Daddy will kill you. He'll put you in the convent. You have to run away.'

'I can't do that. I have to tell them.' The enormity of her predicament hit home, and it scared her. But she couldn't bring her brother into it. 'Leave me be.'

And he did.

He fecked off to America two weeks later, leaving her totally alone.

She curled up into a ball on the floor and sobbed into her arms.

18

The hypnotic crash of the waves was soothing with a hint of danger. Lottie looked over the wall and breathed in the freshness of the sea air.

'It's amazing,' she whispered. The sound of the waves calmed her brain and she felt her body loosen and relax.

'We could ask him for a site,' Boyd said. 'Build here and move.'

'Don't start, please. But we could take a holiday here sometime.' She gazed out at the grey sea glittering with the silver and white of the waves. A familiar sound in the distance caused her to lean her head to one side. Listening.

'Yeah, a six-month holiday would—'

'Shh, Boyd. Do you hear that?'

'It's thunderous.'

'Not the sea.' She turned around and hurried back across the field towards the dirt track they'd walked from Bryan's house. 'I hear sirens.'

She broke into a run.

'Hey, Lottie, slow down. Whatever it is, it's nothing to do with you.'

She didn't answer. Just climbed over the fence and jumped out onto the narrow road with grass and weeds growing along the centre. Shading her eyes, she squinted. Down the hill from the house she saw them. Blue strobe lights, flashing.

'I have to see for myself.'

He reached her side, breathless. 'Bryan will know what it's about. Let's find him.'

'You can talk to him. I'm heading down there.'

'It has to be a good mile away, maybe even more.'

'What's there anyhow?'

'Holiday cottages, I think.'

'Something bad happened,' she said. 'I feel it in my bones.'

'Someone probably had a heart attack. Or something like that.'

They walked in sync.

'All those vehicles arrived simultaneously,' she said. 'That tells me there's a death, and not from a heart attack.'

'All that's wrong with you is that you're missing the job and wishing for a murder.'

She looked over at him. 'I would never wish that on anyone.' She thought for a moment and grinned. 'Maybe on McKeown.'

'You're evil, Lottie Parker.'

'I'm honest.' She paused at a fork on the narrow road. From where they now stood, she couldn't see the strobe lights or any activity. 'Go talk to Bryan. I'm heading down to the holiday cottages.'

'What are you going to do?'

'See if I can help.'

'Even if it's something suspicious, it's not our jurisdiction.'

'Okay, then I'm just being nosy,' she said. 'Find out what you can, and if you want, you can meet me there.'

'You're the boss,' he sighed, repeating his earlier words as he slouched off.

As Lottie walked along the road that sloped downwards, she could feel a knot tightening in the pit of her stomach.

Something awful awaited her at the foot of the hill. She knew it as if she was already there.

19

The wind shifted. It was as if the three cottages commanded stillness. Everything stood inert, while at the same time everything moved. An uncanny phenomenon that Lottie experienced whenever she walked onto a crime scene.

Was this a crime scene? It must be, she thought, holding her hand to her stomach, where her gut emitted warning signals.

Surrounded by trees, the cottages were lined up side by side with a small front lawn bordered by pebbles and stones. Wooden fences separated them. Each had a gate with a cobbled path leading to the door. Two patrol cars and an ambulance were parked out on the narrow road beneath the trees. A uniformed garda in shirtsleeves and a hi-vis vest complete with radio stood guard at the gate, clipboard in hand.

'Sorry, you can't go any further, madam,' he said, his tone all official. 'You'll have to leave.'

Lottie wished she had her badge. Not that it would do her much good in Galway. She had a business card containing her details, though. No harm chancing her arm. 'I'm Detective Inspector Lottie Parker. I was wondering if you could do with a hand here.'

'Did they send you over?' He examined her card, apparently interested now.

Lie or truth? Maybe just dodge the question. Whoever *they* were. 'I want to see if I'm needed.'

'Only person needed here is the state pathologist, and she's been notified.'

Jane Dore, the state pathologist, was located in Tullamore, well over two hours away, without allowing for the gridlocked traffic that needed to be navigated to get out to Connemara.

'I'm good friends with Jane,' Lottie said. 'Can I speak to the senior investigating officer?'

'Who? Oh, you mean Matt? Detective Sergeant Mooney is inside.'

She made to skirt around the guard. 'I'll have a word with him so.'

The man sighed long and hard before thrusting the clipboard and a pen towards her. 'Sign in first. I hope you don't get me fired.'

She signed a scrawl and rushed down the path before he changed his mind. At the door, she was handed a mask, booties and gloves, which she pulled on before entering. She noted how rural the setting was. No chance of CCTV out here like you'd find in a town. Then again, she knew how unreliable it was no matter where you lived. The cottage also had no visible cameras or security system.

A man with a shock of red hair and a struggling beard showing beneath a mask commanded the centre of the small living space. An aura of cigarette smoke clung to his skin, otherwise the atmosphere appeared neutral. He was the only one in there.

'Who the fuck are you?' He pulled off his mask to reveal a seen-it-all-before face. 'Did Delaney let you in?'

She wondered who had rocked his boat. 'I'm Detective Inspector Parker.' Time for the truth. 'I'm based in Ragmullin but visiting Connemara for the week.' He didn't seem too impressed, just tugged at his beard with a gloved hand. Bad practice, she thought, but said, 'I have a vast amount of experience and might be able to help you.' She had no idea what he was dealing with, but it had to be suspicious if the state pathologist had been called in.

'Are you insinuating I have no experience?'

'Not at all. Just saying I can offer assistance if it's needed.'

'I think I've heard of you.' He inhaled deeply, then exhaled. A nicotine breath hit her. She could almost see the anger leaving his body as he deflated into a shroud of defeat. 'It's not lawful to have you here, Inspector, but I could do with another pair of eyes on this. Matt Mooney's the name. Detective Sergeant.'

Inexplicably, she felt sorry for him. He appeared to be out of his depth, weariness lodged in the curved lines around his eyes.

'Where's the body?' She wanted to see it for herself.

'Paramedics declared her dead and we haven't touched anything since. The forensic team should be here soon.'

'I can take a look, give you my observations.'

'It's not pretty.'

'Murder rarely is.'

'It could yet be ruled a suicide.'

She caught the doubt in his tone. 'You don't think so?'

'No, I don't. See for yourself.'

He led her to a door to one side of the fireplace. A bathroom. Her skin itched with apprehension as she stepped forward. She looked in without entering the room. 'This is...' She was lost for words. 'It's...'

The woman in the bath was dead, very dead. Her skin burned, perhaps scalded.

'I know,' Mooney said. 'I've never seen anything like it in my twenty years on the force.'

She raised an eyebrow. He didn't look old enough to have served that long, but she sensed a career weariness about him.

'It's b-brutal,' she stammered. 'I can't believe someone did this to another human being.'

She noticed an electric kettle on the floor, without its cord. Too far away from the body in the bath. The woman did not scald herself. Someone did this to her. How? Why? Who? Too many questions crowded her brain. It was difficult to determine the woman's age, such was the damage to her face and body.

'Can I move a bit closer?'

'I'd prefer to wait for SOCOs and the pathologist.'

'Sure. You're right. I need some air.'

She backed out. He followed. They stood on the outside step and took deep breaths.

'I reckon she's not been there too long,' Lottie said, pulling off the mask and gloves and wiping her nose with her hand, as if that could get rid of the smell now lodged there. 'But decomposition is setting in, so it's hard to tell.'

'Definitely less than twenty-four hours,' Mooney said.

'When was she last seen?'

'We don't know – we don't know who she is or if she was here alone. My guys are contacting the owner of the cottages to get a name. This time of year people come and go. Short-term lets, weekend breaks, Airbnb and the like.'

'The other cottages...' She pointed to the two similar dwellings.

'Unoccupied.'

'It's so remote.' Stating the obvious. Maybe she should just leave. But the dichotomy of the tranquillity outside against the horror within the walls numbed her. She was intrigued. 'Did you search the rest of the rooms?'

He turned and gave her a look that asked if she thought he was an idiot. 'Of course I did.'

'Sorry, just checking.'

'It's okay. There are some clothes in a rucksack. There's also a laptop lead in the bedroom, but no sign of a laptop anywhere in the cottage. No phone either. Might be a burglary gone wrong.'

'The way she was... tortured seems a bit extreme for a burglary.'

'I know that. But even if she was targeted, nothing could warrant such barbarism.'

The clipboard garda came over to them. 'Got a call from the owner. The woman who rented the cottage is Imelda Conroy. A documentary-maker. You can google her. She does freelance stuff for national radio and television. Lives in Dublin.'

'What was she doing here, then?' Mooney asked. The guard shrugged. Mooney continued. 'Find out more for me, Delaney.'

'Will do.' Delaney scuttled off.

'Did you find any equipment other than the laptop cable?' Lottie asked.

'Not yet, but there were some pages disturbed, all blank and might be from a new ream. And a chair overturned. Whoever did this took her stuff.'

'You need to find out what she was working on. It may have been something the killer wanted, or didn't want exposed.'

Mooney straightened his shoulders and narrowed his eyes at her. 'It's probably totally unrelated to her work. Thanks, Inspector. I can take it from here.'

She heard the annoyance in his tone. Feck. She'd insulted his intelligence.

'I'd really like to help.'

'Give your number to Delaney over there, and if I need your input, I'll call you. Good day.'

He marched back inside the house.

Damn. With her curiosity piqued, she itched to be involved. She debated following the surly detective. No point. Instead, she breathed in the fresh air, smelled the countryside, listened to the waves in the distance and wondered why someone had brutally murdered Imelda Conroy. Then another thought struck her. Imelda may have rented the cottage, but it might not be her lying dead in the bath.

She wanted to impart this scenario to Mooney but figured she'd belittled his professional character enough for one day. It wasn't her case. She was on holiday, here for a wedding. She had to keep her nose firmly out of this.

As she walked back across the fields, she knew that would be impossible.

Lottie showered, unsurprised at the low water pressure. The house was old and situated on a hillside after all. Grace had shown them the plans for their new house, and Bryan had promised to bring them to the site to look at the progress being made. She no longer had any interest in seeing it.

She pulled on light-blue jeans and a white cotton blouse as Boyd came into the compact bedroom.

'Have you time now to tell me what went on?' he asked.

'Sorry about rushing up the stairs like that, but I had to wash the stench of death out of my hair. I needed to decompress.' She sat on the edge of the bed, brushing her damp hair. 'It was so harrowing. It was as if someone scalded that poor woman to death.'

'Is that the official line?' He sat on the bed beside her.

'No, she may have died of a heart attack from the shock of being doused with boiling water. Whichever way it's ruled once the post-mortem is conducted, it's obvious to me that she suffered. Suffered horribly.'

'Who was she?'

'They say the cottage was rented by a documentary-maker

Imelda Conroy, and Mooney, the detective in charge, is running with that. He strikes me as diligent, so I'm sure he will conduct a proper investigation.'

'Sounds shocking,' Boyd said. 'And for it to happen in such a beautiful place – you don't expect that.'

'I wouldn't expect it anywhere, to be honest.'

'Do you know what the woman was working on?'

'No idea.' She left the brush on the bed, giving up on her hair. 'But I'd love to find out.'

'Now, Lottie.' He held her hand and turned her round to face him. 'It's not your case. You're here for my sister's wedding. Leave the murder to the local team.'

'I offered to help.'

'What? You have no jurisdiction here.'

'I can assist, can't I?'

'Stop.' He stood. 'I don't want you to ruin this for Grace.'

'I'd never do that, Mark. Honestly.'

He eyed her sceptically. 'Dinner is ready. Come down and eat.'

'I don't think I can stomach food.' She caught his look, one that said Grace would be insulted if she declined. 'Go ahead then. I'll be there in a minute. Have to dry my hair first.'

'Five minutes, then I'm coming to get you.'

'Sure.' She kissed his cheek.

Then she was alone. With her thoughts. With the images from the cottage. With the horror of what that woman had gone through. She knew she couldn't walk away from it.

After a cordial dinner, Bryan decided he couldn't talk to Grace's brother. It was obvious he was very close to her, so instead he decided to have a word with Lottie. She seemed interesting. A little intimidating, if he was being truthful, but he was used to dealing with stubborn animals, so she should be easy to handle. He felt himself blush at the thought, wondering if it was inappropriate.

Getting her on her own was the problem. He could hardly ask her to come out and corral the sheep with him. Or could he?

In the end, Lottie was happy to accompany him outside, leaving Boyd helping Grace with the dishes.

'I wanted to talk to you about something,' Bryan said as they walked around the rear of the house. Tess, his dog, led the way.

Lottie could still hear the waves crashing on the shoreline not too far away. The sound swathed them like they were in an echo chamber.

'I know you've had an eventful day,' he said, 'but there's been something on my mind that I hope you can help me with.'

'Go on,' she said, looking at him from under her eyelids. Bryan was a tall, handsome man. A bit rugged and square-jawed, if she was being picky, but then again, it added to his farmer image. Dressed in a clean light-blue shirt and dark denim jeans, she thought the wellingtons kind of ruined his image.

'Grace can't know about this, and if she is to be kept in the dark, her brother will have to be kept that way too.'

'Oh.' She wondered where the conversation was leading.

'Do you agree?'

'I need to hear what you have to say first.'

He ran a hand through his thick greying hair. 'I suppose I'll have to accept that.'

They'd reached the boundary wall, with a vast barren field before them.

'What is it you want me to do?' Lottie asked.

'Listen to me first of all. Then see if you can help.'

He leaned against the old stone wall and folded his arms. She felt awkward standing beside him, but was intrigued to hear what he had to say.

'When I was a boy, I was sent to a place called Knockraw. One of those industrial schools. I was only a young teenager at the time. It was an all-boys institution, run by the Christian Brothers and a couple of priests. It's closed down now, could even have been demolished, but it remained open until the late eighties, maybe even into the early nineties. Anyhow, it's been said that over a hundred boys died there and at the infamous Letterfrack industrial school.'

'I've read about Letterfrack. And you were in a place like that?'

'Aye, I was. Whipped raw, I was. There was physical and sexual abuse, and death. Aye, too many boys died. No words for it other than it was barbaric treatment.'

'I'm so sorry.' She felt genuine pity for the boy this weathered man had once been.

'Not your fault.'

'Why were you sent there?'

'My mother died, and then didn't my father take to the drink. My other brother didn't want to have anything to do with me, so I was left to my own devices. I was always starving with the hunger and started stealing. Mainly food and cigarettes. But that sort of carry-on landed me in Knockraw. I thought when my mother died that it was my worst nightmare. But the real nightmare began the day I was led through those doors. I was subjected to all sorts of abuse for three years.'

'That's terrible, Bryan.'

'When I got out of that hellhole, the country was in the middle of a recession, so I took a few jobs to get enough money for a plane ticket to America. Wanted to make my fortune there. A pipe dream. But I worked hard on the building sites in and around New York, and when I'd made a good few bob, I came back.'

'What has all this to do with me?'

'It's complicated, and I don't want Grace to know about this. Not yet, anyhow.' He patted Tess, who was circling his legs in silence.

Once the dog was settled at his feet, he went on. 'I had been seeing this girl. Mary Elizabeth O'Dowd. She was younger than me, might have been sixteen, a gentle soul, and we had a connection of sorts. Long story short, I got her pregnant. It was around that time that I was packed off to Knockraw. I heard she was sent to a convent, one of those horrible laundries. That place was nothing more than a Knockraw for young girls. I never saw nor heard from her again. I don't know what happened to the baby, or if Mary Elizabeth is even alive. Maybe they both died in that place. I'm sorry for putting you to trouble, and say no if you want to, but would there be any way you could find out what happened to them?'

She knew she should say no, walk away, but it was not in her to do that. 'Where was this convent?'

'Not far from here. People talk about the laundries in Dublin and Cork, but this one was in Galway. They did the laundry for all the hotels and businesses in the city, and for the industrial schools at Letterfrack and Knockraw, if you can believe it.'

Lottie was puzzled by his request and also his need for secrecy, which worried her a little.

'Bryan, there's been a commission of investigation into the industrial schools and the laundries. I'm not sure what you want me to do.'

'I want to know what happened to that girl and what happened to our baby. He or she would be an adult now – that's if they're not buried in an unmarked grave somewhere.'

'Have you tried to find them yourself?'

'I wouldn't know where to start. I fled to America and tried to forget about that time in my life. But now I need your help. I'm getting married and this secret is weighing heavy on my heart.'

Against her better judgement, Lottie felt inclined to help him. Mainly because she was intrigued by his story. 'Tell me about this convent.'

'It was a big building with a massive basement where the equipment was housed. You know, the old-fashioned washing machines and rollers for drying linen, but on an industrial scale. I've seen the photos online. You can check them out.'

'Is the place still standing?'

'Yes, though it's been abandoned and neglected. Not far from here at all and not that far from Knockraw either, as the crow flies. The graveyard is still there. You can see it for yourself. But I believe a lot more died who didn't get a headstone.'

'A dark time in our history,' she said, feeling some of that darkness fall as a cloak around her shoulders. She shuddered. 'What was the convent called?'

'It bore the name of the order of nuns that ran it. Sisters of Forgiveness. If you can get your head around that.'

'And you haven't told Grace any of this?'

'No. I couldn't bring myself to tell her. I had put it all behind me and hadn't thought of it in years, but then Grace started saying she's still young and wants to have a family. The thing that haunts me is that I might already have a child out there somewhere, and if he or she is still alive, I want to know about them. And if they were born and died there... I also need to know what happened. Do you get me?'

'I do, but I'm not sure what I can do for you. As I said, there have been investigations, commissions, reports. Have you read those?'

'A little. But they didn't help me. You could look for the records. I read how you uncovered what happened to your brother in that St Angela's place in Ragmullin. How you found his bones buried on that land. You could find out what happened to Mary Elizabeth and our baby.'

'Bryan, I think you have to speak to Grace about this.'

'I will, maybe. First, though, I need to know that you'll help me find out what happened.'

'I can't promise you a good result, but I'll see if I can dig up anything.'

'That's good enough for me. *Go raibh míle maith agat.* Thank you.' He shook her hand, formally, as if they had sealed a deal, then turned and walked slowly back to the house.

She looked over the wall at the fields falling away to the sea below. A massive seagull swooped over her head, its huge webbed feet and harsh squawking causing her to duck reflexively.

Was that an ominous warning?

She hoped not.

She knew full well what happened when you stoked the fires of the past. Usually it wasn't good.

THE PAST

This was not how she'd imagined giving birth to her child. Within cold, bare walls. Surrounded by iron-faced nuns with stiff wimples, ratty veils and camphor-smelling gowns.

Despite everything, she wanted her family by her side.

She wanted him too. He had promised. Hadn't he?

Another pain ripped through her and she felt the urge to push the child out of her body.

'Not so fast,' one of the nuns said. She had no idea which one. They all looked the same.

'It's coming!' she yelled.

Unable to hold on for a second longer, she gritted her teeth and pushed with the little strength she had left.

Then... relief. The pain was gone. The child was out. She could fall into a restful sleep. But there was pushing and shoving around the bed. Heads bowing and looking, and then she felt towels or sheets being bundled up under her legs.

Where was her baby? Was it a boy or a girl? She wanted to ask these questions, but all her strength seemed to have left her body.

They wouldn't tell her anything, just whisked the baby away from her after cutting the cord. She thought she would die from the heartache.

But a fate worse than her baby being stolen from her awaited in the not-too-distant future.

21

RAGMULLIN

TUESDAY

Kirby was thrilled that his girlfriend, Amy, was caring for Boyd's son while Boyd was in Galway. She seemed to love having the boy around and ferrying him to and from school.

He was keen to get stuck into the murder investigation. His first as lead detective. The task had scared him yesterday, but today he was full of renewed energy. By the time he reached the office, though, his spirits were depleted and anxiety trickled down to his feet, slowing his pace.

Their main suspect was AWOL. Yesterday afternoon, an alert had been issued for Robert Hayes and his car. And if he wasn't found, it was on Kirby's head.

'Don't worry, it might never happen,' Martina Brennan said as he entered the incident room.

'No word on Hayes, then?'

'Nope. And Edie's son, Noel, is in the clear. His girlfriend has vouched for him for the entire weekend. McKeown will corroborate it with CCTV from where they said they went, but it seems he checks out.'

'What have we got to go on?'

'The tip line has been active, but I've read through the reports this morning and it's mainly cranks and crackpots.'

Kirby studied the board covered with photos of Edie Butler, both alive and dead. 'Do you think I should call the boss for advice?'

'You *are* the boss. Be confident in your own ability. In the team's abilities. We can work through this.'

'You're right. Where's McKeown this morning?'

'Gone back to the river where the body was found. He wants to recheck everything that was done by SOCOs yesterday.'

'And Garda Lei?'

'He's at Danny's Bar interviewing Robert's colleagues. I was thinking of returning to the salon where Edie worked to see if I can get more from Marge Woods.'

'Yes, do that.'

When he was alone, Kirby checked his email and discovered that the preliminary post-mortem results were in. He read quickly.

Edie Butler had been subjected to sustained scalding by boiling water. Her hands had been bound tightly at some point, and she was dead before being put in the river, according to the assistant state pathologist. Investigation was ongoing to discover what had made the indentations on her back, but it was possible they had been caused by bath taps. Alcohol was found in her bloodstream and a myriad of samples had been sent for toxicology testing. It was estimated she had died some twenty-four to thirty-six hours before her body was found. So where was she from Friday evening?

He pulled Lottie's number up on his phone. To call or not to call? No, Martina was right. He had this. He could do it himself. Couldn't he?

22

CONNEMARA

Tuesday morning, Lottie hadn't heard anything from Detective Sergeant Mooney, and that irked her, but she had to accept it was not her investigation. To occupy herself, she decided to do a little sleuthing based on Bryan's request. She studied the handwritten directions he'd given her. Sisters of Forgiveness. What type of name was that?

She drove up to the old rusted iron gates and idled the engine. The gates hung open, bent and twisted, and a gravel path, interspersed with weeds, led the way beneath a tree canopy. Keep driving, or get out and walk up?

According to Bryan, the convent had been abandoned for decades, but why hadn't it been sold and reused as something else? A Google search had provided her with no clues, except it appeared the religious order that had run the laundry no longer existed. Interesting in itself, because did that mean there were no records to be found?

'To hell with it.' Deciding to drive on, she pointed her car up the weed-strewn avenue. Rounding a corner, she gasped.

A forbidding-looking building loomed before her, appearing mysteriously from behind the trees. Still intact, and from her vantage point in the car, she was certain it was uninhabited. Obviously. With its shattered windows, it looked like it had been vandalised, but the main door appeared to be chained and locked.

After parking the car, she grabbed a fleece jacket from the back seat and wrapped it around her shoulders, put her handbag on cross-body and made her way up the concrete steps to the door. Definitely locked.

She stood back and craned her neck, looking up.

Shadowed against a grey-clouded sky – summer flitted between seasons in one day here, she mused – she could see three storeys punctured with narrow pointed windows. It certainly was a menacing-looking place.

She could only imagine how terrified young teenage girls would have been when they were abandoned at the front door. She thought of her own girls. How could a family do such a thing to their own flesh and blood? She suppressed a shudder. From the outside, the convent was so big and imposing it was like a giant mouth ready to gobble them up, strip them of their identity and eventually spit them back out, broken and battered.

Were they the lucky ones? Those who got to walk away rather than those whose bones were buried somewhere on the surrounding land? Or were they for ever scarred by their experience? She could ask Bryan if he knew of any women who had survived and were still living in the locality. If so, had they talked to the commission of inquiry, and if not, why hadn't they come forward when it was ongoing? Or did this building house a darker secret than the other institutions? Too dark to make its way to the official investigation pages.

Her interest was sparked, not just because of what had happened to her own brother in a not dissimilar institution, but because this was an unsolved mystery of sorts.

She made her way around the side of the building. The

windows were so high up that the ledges hung like bulging lips above her head, mocking her. As she moved to the rear, the trees seemed to shiver around her as birds took flight en masse.

Having picked her way through thistles protruding from the cracked and broken flagstones, she noticed a dip in the ground, like a moat circling the walls. Peering down through the long grass and weeds, she saw barred windows. Below ground. Her body shivered and shuddered. The cellar.

As she approached the steps to the back door, she could see that there was no lock on it. Or rather, the door hung open, the chain snapped by bolt-cutters or some such tool held by opportune burglars. Or maybe she wasn't the first to come investigating. No, it had to be vandals or burglars. Only one way to find out.

She climbed the steps, turned the handle and entered into the hallway of an abhorrent, unforgiving history.

Perhaps she should have asked Boyd to accompany her. But he was busy with Grace, both of them mulling over what should be in or out of the wedding ceremony. At least Grace was at last showing some enthusiasm for her big day. Lottie hadn't said exactly where she was going. Just out for a drive. Yeah, and what if she fell through rotting floorboards? Who would come to help her if no one knew where she was? But it didn't stop her.

Ignoring her anxiety, she scanned her surroundings, her eyes becoming accustomed to the indoor gloom. She was in a dark corridor. Hooks nailed to the walls. Wrought-iron shoe racks lined up beneath them. At least she assumed they were shoe racks and not some antiquated method of torture. This made her think of the dead woman in the bath at the holiday cottage. She wondered how the investigation was proceeding. Not her concern. She moved further inside the old convent in search of answers for Bryan.

The high ceiling reminded her of St Angela's, where her brother had been incarcerated all those years ago, and a sudden disgust filled her with unbidden nausea. Glancing back towards the door, she felt like fleeing the building. Running out into the fresh air. Not opening any more ancient doors hiding cans of worms wriggling to break free. But as she was here, she convinced herself that she might as well continue.

On one side was a large room that might once have been an industrial-sized kitchen. It was stripped bare of all copper piping, sinks and anything that had a value. Scavengers had been and gone over the years. Easing out of the room, she noticed a door to her left. She turned the ancient black knob. A dark stairway led downwards. Stairway to hell? She hoped not.

Scrabbling around for a light switch, she found a string above her head. She pulled it, but no light came on. Of course the electricity would have been cut off years ago. It puzzled her as to why the place had been allowed to rot. Why hadn't the nuns sold it? If it became necessary, she'd get someone to check it out, but she figured the convent was something people would prefer to forget rather than resurrecting old wounds. Another thought struck her: if the religious order was no longer in existence, who actually owned the building? Probably the bishop and the diocese. And she didn't fancy having a confrontation with a bishop. Been there, done that, she recalled.

It was ebony dark below. She remembered she had a slim penlight in her bag. By some miracle, she found it nestled among the detritus. When she flicked it on, a thin beam revealed concrete steps leading downwards.

'I'm here now, I might as well see what's down here,' she said aloud, more to reassure herself than to alert anything or anyone that might be lurking beneath her feet.

She had no idea what she was about to encounter. Her breath lodged in her throat as she stepped off the last stair. The basement room opened out as she swept the light around, casting unnatural shadows.

Ransacked was too nice a word. Decimated might be more apt. It was as if someone had taken a sledgehammer to the huge old washing and drying machines. They lay in shattered, rusting pieces. Vast rollers, perhaps for ironing sheets, were still secured to the walls but were criss-crossed with a multitude of slashes. Why such wanton destruction? Teenagers with nothing else to do with their time? Or someone who had been consigned to the convent and later sought revenge on the inanimate objects? It was not her role to question.

An eerie sense of dread settled on her shoulders. It felt like a wet towel weighing her down, and her entire body shuddered. Even her toes curled.

Scratching and shuffling sounds echoed in the darkness. The tiny hairs rose on the nape of her neck, and she balled her hands into fists. Fight or flight? She had no idea, but she was unnaturally fearful. Lottie Parker did not scare easily, but she had a massive phobia of four-legged creatures that skulked in dark corners, skittered in walls and attics.

'Now I'm frightening myself,' she said, and twirled around on the ball of her foot.

Nothing moved in the thin beam of her penlight.

The hoot of an owl somewhere seemed to rattle the rafters. But it was the scurrying of tiny vermin that spurred her into action.

She wasn't waiting around.

Taking the stairs two at a time, she fled.

He'd watched her park her car from his unintentional hiding place, huddled beneath the overhanging branches of the large oak tree. It had stood there for over two hundred years. He had heard that said somewhere, though there was no one alive who could possibly know if the nugget of information was true. He himself felt two hundred years old betimes, but today he felt surprisingly buoyed by a stirring of internal electricity.

Who was this tall woman with straggly hair and a freckled nose? She didn't appear to be dressed for the wind that was rising from the ocean, ready to blow in from the seashore and up over the fields. A tourist? Lost? No. She seemed to know where she was going and what she was doing. Peering in through the cracked windows, trying the front-door handle and then skirting around the back. What was she hoping to find? He mulled this over in his head and decided he needed to do something.

Leaving his shelter, he crept forward in her footsteps. She'd gone inside. He knew there was nothing left there worth stealing. He'd commanded that operation. Maybe he should report this interloper to the guards. But then he'd have to provide a reason as to why he was there too. Best to wait and see.

Still, he itched to follow her inside. To accost her. To demand what her business was. If she didn't come out in the next five minutes, he was going in. This decision consoled him somewhat. He kept his eyes on the old silver watch with the worn black leather strap.

'I'm counting, lady,' Mickey Fox muttered.

23

Sitting on the top stone step, Lottie waited for her pulse to stop racing. Definitely should have brought Boyd along. He knew about her phobia. One she had been unsuccessful in overcoming. She could stare down a maniac with a lump hammer in his hand, stand her ground before a knife-wielding thug, but the scuttling of mice or their larger cousins always caused her to run.

Maybe she should have a quick look around upstairs to ease her fears. There the windows allowed more light in, so she'd no longer be dependent on a narrow torch beam.

Moving out of the basement, she closed over the door. That was when she smelled something rancid and heard harsh laboured breathing behind her. She turned, ready to accost whoever had followed her.

'Hey, lady, not so fast. I'm not here to hurt you.'

'Jesus, you scared me. You shouldn't creep up on people.'

The man held up his two empty hands. Pleading? Or demonstrating to her that he held no weapon? He licked his lips through his white scruffy beard, which did little to help her determine his age.

'What are you doing here?' His voice was as gravelly as his skin.

'Snooping.'

'I can see that.'

'And can I ask what *you* are doing here?'

'Keeping an eye out for snoopers.' There was no trace of mirth in his tone. She reckoned he was deadly serious.

'Do you have some claim on the convent?' She walked a little away from him. He smelled bad. Unwashed.

'Used to be the gardener here, back in the day.' He grinned, one tooth and blackness.

'Oh, so you were here when the convent operated as a laundry?' She retraced her steps towards him, now interested in this strange man.

'Aye. The nuns were good to me. Not so good to others. None of my business. And I don't like people ferreting around in places they have no right to.'

'I just wanted a look. It's part of our country's history.'

'That's what the other one said.'

'What other one?'

'No one pays a blind bit of heed to the convent for donkey's years, and then two of you appear out of nowhere within a week of each other. Are you working with her?'

'With who?'

'That's a no, then.' He lit up an unfiltered cigarette, and the distinctive waft of cannabis hit her in the face. 'You should be on your way, lady.'

'Okay, I'm leaving, but I'm interested in who else was here recently.'

'None of your business if she has nothing to do with you.'

Should she play the detective card? Scare the shit out of him? No, it would take a lot more than the threat of the guards to scare this man.

'I'm Lottie.' She braved holding out her hand, half hoping he wouldn't accept it. 'Who are you?'

He paused as if debating making physical contact. He moved his smoke from his right hand to his left and eventually took her outstretched hand. His was cold and hard. Like the eyes she found staring back at her.

'Mickey Fox,' he said. 'Pleasure, I'm not sure. Why are you here?'

'I told you. I was just snooping. What about you?'

'Worked here for forty years and the nuns pay me a retainer to keep an eye on the place.'

'But the order is no longer in existence.'

'The order might not be, but some of the nuns are still around and the bishop has deep coffers.'

'Would you be able to give me details? I'd like to talk to them.'

'Private and confidential.' His grin bordered on salacious, which she found disturbing.

'Are there any records still here?'

'Records? The other one asked that too. There's nothing left. Place was stripped to its floorboards. And even some of them were taken too.'

'What did you tell... the other woman?'

'Same as I'm telling you. She was more of a snoop, though. Didn't pay any heed. Took off up them there stairs.' He pointed to the stone staircase behind her. 'I followed her, of course, in case she stole something.'

'Thought you said there's nothing left.'

'Might be something I missed.'

She smirked. 'So it was you who stripped the place bare.'

'Only returned things to their rightful owners.'

'Those who no longer exist?'

'You said that, not me.'

She tried to follow his cryptic logic. 'When you followed the woman around this place, was she scared?'

'Not a bit. A right amateur sleuth Mel was. I made her tea in my caravan back in the woods. Told her a few lies and off she went, happy as Larry.'

'Was she a detective?' She banked the woman's name.

'Not at all. But I'd say you're one. That makes me wonder what you're doing out here. Did Mel send you?'

'Who's Mel?' Draw him out, she thought.

'Come on, lady. You know right well, don't you? She sent you here. All talk of a grand exposé on some documentary. Silly girl. Nothing left to expose. All the secrets are out in public. Hounded the nuns away. Inquiries and commissions did me out of any respectability I may have once had.'

Now Lottie was silent, her mind in turmoil. His revelations were both enlightening and sickening, because she believed the Mel he was talking about was Imelda Conroy, documentary-maker. And she had been brutally murdered in a holiday cottage not far from where Lottie stood with this strange old man.

'Can you tell me exactly when Mel was here?'

'Last week sometime. I don't keep a diary. Hardly know what day it is most of the time.'

'Did you report back to the nuns? The ones who don't exist?'

'Now you're pulling the mickey.' He laughed, a bawdy sound that reverberated in the hollow space. 'My name may be Mickey, but I haven't had it pulled for a long time. Don't suppose you'd—'

'Mr...' What was his name again? She hid a grin at his attempt at a joke. 'Mr Fox. I take offence at your crudeness.'

'That's the trouble with the world today. No sense of humour.'

'And I suppose your nuns had a great sense of humour.

Laughing all the way to the bank while poor unfortunate girls, through no fault of their own, were incarcerated here into a life of hard labour.' She paused to take a breath, her mood darkening suddenly with her rage-fuelled words.

'No fault of their own? You're deluded, lady. Those girls were sinners. Each and every one of them. And they got what they deserved.'

Despite his words, Lottie felt there was a lack of certainty in his tone. Was he trotting out what some might refer to as a party line?

'Did Mel get what she deserved?'

'What do you mean? She was satisfied once I showed her the basement laundry. And off with her she went.' He hesitated as if he'd caught the unspoken words in her question. 'Did something happen to her?'

'You could say that, Mr Fox. Good day to you.'

She sidestepped, needing to get away from him. To put a physical space between them.

With a final glance at the oppressive building, the walls leaning over her, she scooted by him.

She had to talk to Detective Mooney.

24

Walking quickly to her car, Lottie was glad to escape from the desolation she'd felt oozing from the convent walls. A prison. That was what it reminded her of. Not a modern one like Castlerea, with stainless-steel fittings and plastered walls, but something from the novels of Dickens. Newgate or Dartmoor. Or the old Irish prisons like Spike Island.

After driving down the weedy avenue, she turned onto what constituted the main road. It was little more than a lane. At last she could breathe normally. Mooney. She had no contact number for him. Damn. He was probably based in Galway city. Bryan might know him. Then again, Bryan O'Shaughnessy was a Connemara sheep farmer, so how or why would he know Mooney?

Her phone blared loudly in the silent car, and she leaped in her seat. Unknown number. She pressed the hands-free button and waited without speaking.

'Is that Detective Inspector Lottie Parker?' A semi-familiar gruff voice.

'I was just thinking of you, Detective Sergeant Mooney.'

'Great minds and all that.' He laughed, and it was a joyous sound compared to Mickey Fox's raspy tones.

'How can I help you?' She drove on a little before stopping at the side of the narrow road, at a field gate. 'Just pulling in the car. The audio's coming and going. Bad coverage.'

'Lucky to get any coverage at all out here.'

'Are you at the scene?'

'Just came back to it an hour ago. Look, I could do with your insight. This is more complicated than I first thought.'

'Being scalded by kettles of boiling water in a bath isn't complicated enough?'

'It is, but there's more. Can you come by the holiday cottage?'

'Sure. I can be there... Shit, I actually don't know where I am. I'll have to get my bearings.'

'Give me some idea of your location and I can direct you.'

'I've just left a convent. Used to be a laundry. One of those—'

'What were you doing there?'

'Doesn't matter. Where do I go?'

He established her general whereabouts and spouted directions.

'See you in fifteen minutes,' he said. 'Oh, and by the way, you're still only here in an advisory capacity.'

'Got it.'

She drove on, and the call dropped.

A thick mist rose from the sea, giving an eerie atmosphere to the three whitewashed stone cottages. She had to park a good way down the tree-lined lane, such was the number of parked garda cars and the forensic technical van.

Delaney, the clipboard guard, had been replaced by an enthusiastic young female garda, who allowed her through once she'd checked with Mooney. The only proviso was that she wasn't allowed to enter the cottage.

Lottie signed in and stood on the stoop. Waiting was not one of her stronger points, but she couldn't argue. It wasn't her crime scene.

Mooney came out and, without divesting himself of his protective gear, wordlessly indicated that she follow him.

She trudged behind him as he rounded the cottage. The small, square garden was enclosed by low stone walls, greening patio slabs on the ground and a weatherbeaten wooden table with chairs. He pulled one out and sat. She did likewise, hoping SOCOs had examined them.

'It's okay,' he said. 'Nothing of note was found out here.'

He rustled a cigarette pack from inside the folds of his Teflon boiler suit, and a lighter appeared with it. Lighting up, he inhaled, then exhaled a cloud of smoke. He coughed but didn't speak.

'Look, Sergeant Mooney, I haven't got—'

'Matt, call me Matt.'

'What's going on, Matt?'

'It's not her.'

'Who's not who?' She scrunched her eyes. He had her confused. 'The dead woman?'

'Aye, it wasn't Imelda Conroy in that bath.'

'Are you certain?'

'Hundred per cent. We checked online. Passport, driver's licence, her website. All that shite. Wrong age demographic. Conroy is in her thirties, and according to the pathologist who attended at the scene, the dead woman is possibly in her fifties. It's not her.'

'Then where is Imelda Conroy?'

'No idea.'

'Car?'

'She had a car. Registration number was on the cottage rental form. Matches vehicle licence records. But no car here.'

'And it's not her body. Shite, this is a curveball.'

'You're telling me.' He stubbed out his cigarette under the sole of his shoe. Glancing over at her, he caught her staring. 'Told you, it's okay. SOCOs have been and gone from out here.'

'And inside? Did they find anything?'

'Apart from the lead for a laptop, they also found a phone charger plugged in beside the bedside locker. No phone, though, like I said. A few blank pieces of paper scattered around, giving me nothing to go on. A lone hoodie hanging in the wardrobe. Few bits of clothing in a rucksack. Other than that, zero.'

'Fingerprints, DNA?'

'All gathered and being analysed and fed into the system. Takes time for results.'

'Any idea who the victim could be?'

'No one reported missing. Not yet, anyhow. So no, I've no idea.'

'You need to interview the neighbours, if there are any, and—'

'Being done as we speak. I'm not a total amateur.'

'I wasn't implying that. Sorry. I'm just working through what I'd do.'

'Can I ask you a question?'

She knew he would ask anyhow. 'Sure, fire away.'

'What were you doing up at the old convent?'

She didn't think it would do any harm telling him why she'd been there. Yet she was apprehensive. Too soon for confessions or revelations.

'I don't think my reason for being there is relevant to your investigation. It was a private excursion. Curiosity. You know yourself.'

'But it's a coincidence, and I don't like them.'

'What do you mean?'

'We've learned that Imelda Conroy was making a radio documentary about the laundries.'

She digested his words. According to Mickey Fox, Imelda, aka Mel, had been at the convent the previous week. Should she inform Mooney? Perhaps she'd wait a while. 'There've been loads of podcasts, television shows, documentaries made over the years. I don't see what any of it has to do with me having a gander around an old convent.' But then she felt the hairs stand up on her arms. She knew what he was going to say before he said it.

'Imelda was making a documentary with particular emphasis on the Sisters of Forgiveness.'

'Who are they?' She stood, then sat again, trying to get her thoughts in a straight line. She wasn't any good at lying. And it wasn't right to keep information from Mooney, but she was loath to divulge what she'd learned.

He said, 'The same nuns who ran the convent you were at earlier.'

'Okay. But why did you ask me here?'

'The post-mortem is taking place shortly. I'd like you to observe with me.'

'Is that even allowed?'

'It is now.'

25

Professor Jane Dore had had to deal with her fair share of unusual deaths over the course of her career. As the country's state pathologist, she handled unexplained fatalities. Murders. Grisly cases. Torn bodies. Crushed bones. Also, those that at first appeared to be unexplained. A perfect body. Unblemished. A mystery contained within the shroud of skin. Those were the cases she craved, where her skills as a pathologist thrust her into the heart of an investigation.

Today she was in the mortuary at Galway University Hospital. The location was familiar to her, as she'd worked on suspicious deaths there before. She was in Galway to speak at a conference, and her assistant was covering for her in Tullamore. Being in the locality, she felt obliged to accede to the Galway gardaí's request.

The body laid out on the stainless-steel table told its own story before the pathologist even took up the cold scalpel in her gloved hand. Lottie suspected that Jane was a little surprised to see her arrive with Mooney, even though she'd been given permission to be present. She eyed the pathologist and waited anxiously until she spoke.

'Age is hard to determine. Like I told you at the scene I'd say this woman was somewhere in her fifties. You can verify it once you identify her. The hands were thrust into boiling water.' Jane paused before continuing. 'Skin is blistered, and in places it's slid off. Third-degree burns. Her face has suffered similar injuries.'

'Is that what killed her?' Lottie asked.

'Short answer – I don't know yet. The shock could have led to a heart attack, but until I open her up...'

'What can you tell us now?' Mooney asked.

Lottie studied the unfortunate victim, avoiding the face, and felt her breakfast rise from her stomach to her throat. She swallowed down the acidic taste, but it lingered in her mouth.

The scene she'd encountered in the bathroom of the cottage was one of the most horrific she'd ever walked into. And looking at the victim laid out on the steel table, it was difficult to figure out if the woman had been flayed or scalded. Blisters had sprouted in places, but in others the skin had sloughed off completely. No identifying features. No eyebrows or lashes. The pathologist would have to determine the cause of death; SOCOs would forensically sweep and analyse the scene. Then Lottie could... No, she couldn't do anything. It was Mooney's investigation. But he'd asked for her help. That was something at least.

She couldn't tear her eyes away from the woman's hands. Long, slender fingers. Blistered where the skin remained, otherwise they were skinless. Just bone and sinew.

'You okay?' Jane asked her.

'Not really. How could someone do this to another human being? This was torture.'

'You think?'

'Do you not?' Lottie raised an eyebrow.

'I have no idea what happened to this unfortunate woman. But it was painful, that's for sure.'

'There was an empty kettle on the bathroom floor,' Mooney said.

'I noted that,' Jane said. 'Too far away from the body. Someone did this to her.'

'She could have brought it in herself. It might have fallen...' Mooney argued, but he looked doubtful.

'Yesterday you didn't think she killed herself, but now you do?' Lottie asked incredulously. 'There are less painful methods to—'

'No, I don't think she did this to herself,' he said gruffly.

Jane cut in. 'Neither do I. There's bruising on the upper arms. She was held. Tightly. And the boiling water was applied more than once. I had a quick look at her back before we turned her over again. Someone stood over her and poured boiling water along her spine. She was badly scalded.'

'But she hardly stood or lay there and let someone do that, did she?' Mooney was getting more animated.

'I have to run toxicology,' Jane said.

'You think she was drugged?' Lottie asked.

'I don't *think* anything at the moment. I'm only pointing out what I can see.'

'Sorry, Jane. I'm shaken, that's all. Human nature continues to horrify me.'

'And me. This is one of the worst I've come across.' Jane walked slowly around the table, and Lottie watched as she stopped at the woman's feet.

'There was a wine bottle and glass in the cottage. Maybe she'd had a few. That would impair her, wouldn't it?' Mooney asked.

'You'll have to wait for toxicology results.' The pathologist looked up along the body from her vantage point, then back down again. 'The soles of her feet are blistered too. Don't quote me, but this may have come first to keep her from fleeing. Then the hands, to stop her fighting back, and there's evidence they may have been bound. Then all that was followed by the burns to her back. When I examine her lungs, I'll know if she drowned. If that isn't the cause of death, then she died as a consequence of the burns. Shock? Heart failure? You'll have to wait until I have all my tests completed.'

'Sure, thanks,' Mooney said. 'So what kind of a sicko am I looking for?'

As Jane moved to the other side of the table and picked up a scalpel, Lottie could see the pathologist had been wondering the same thing. 'The most dangerous person one can face. Someone with no fear.'

Mooney gulped.

Lottie digested this nugget. Jane had been unusually candid. After all, providing her personal opinion was not part of her brief.

'Send your report as soon as you can. Thanks again.' Mooney made for the doors. It seemed he couldn't escape fast enough.

Lottie took a last look at the woman's body and gave Jane a sympathetic nod. 'I've faced a lot of murders in my time, but this seems to be one of the cruellest.'

And as she let the door swing shut behind her, she wondered how Mooney would go about identifying a woman with no face.

26

Feeling a bit shell-shocked, Lottie joined Mooney at his car, where he was smoking a cigarette.

'Coffee?' she asked, delaying having to go back to the house and talk to Boyd, Grace or Bryan.

'I need a stiff whiskey. I'll buy you one.'

'I don't drink.' She'd love one. 'But I won't say no to a coffee.'

'I'll drive.'

She sat into his car, leaving hers at the University Hospital. He drove through the city to a hotel. Traffic was mental, but he flashed the blue lights on the front grille and bustled his way through.

The bar was old-style, perhaps with tourists in mind. It was a world away from Cafferty's in Ragmullin, where drinking was more important than aesthetics. Whatever about the decor, it was a welcome place to sit down.

Mooney came to the table with his whiskey and a pint of lager. She'd have taken him for a Guinness drinker, but when he sculled the pint in three gulps, she figured he hadn't the patience to wait for a Guinness to settle.

'Your coffee is on the way.' He tugged off his sports jacket, revealing a short-sleeved navy cotton shirt with underarm sweat marks. His hands were as tanned as his face, and a shade darker than his arms. He nursed his tumbler, sniffed the alcohol and put it back on the table without drinking. 'Connemara whiskey. You can taste the peat. The finest.'

'Is it distilled here?'

'No, it's from your neck of the woods.' He picked up the glass again. 'What do you think of it all?'

'The whiskey?'

He eyed her over the rim. She knew right well what he meant.

'It's hard to know what to think,' she said. 'Still no sign of Imelda Conroy? Or her car?'

'Not a thing. We issued an alert on social media. But if she did the deed, then I'm sure she's gone to ground, or maybe she's airborne and on her way to somewhere without extradition.'

'But why do that to another woman? I can't understand the barbarity of it. It kind of freaks me out.'

'You and me both, sister.'

She didn't like the *sister* bit, but let it go. 'This documentary she was making, did you find out if it was for national radio? Who was funding it?'

'All we've discovered to date is that she was operating on a freelance basis. I don't think she had any takers for it. None that we've been able to locate so far.'

'The laundry story has been covered numerous times... unless she had a new angle. Something that got this woman killed.' Lottie waited while a waiter brought over her coffee, then leaned towards Mooney. 'What if Imelda is a victim too and not a killer?'

'All possibilities are on the table until we find her. The only thing we have so far is a kettle with a heap of fingerprints that could belong to anyone – we've had no hits as yet. Plus the cottage is a rental, so it will be a massive job to trace people.'

'Who's to say the killer didn't use the kettle, but left it for you as a red herring?'

'Something was used to pour the boiling water over her,' Mooney said. 'But I take your point. It was very obvious.'

'Maybe the killer is making a statement.' She realised she'd uttered her thoughts out loud.

'What do you mean?'

She didn't know what she meant. 'Whoever did this could kill again. Your priority has to be to identify the dead woman. Otherwise you'll be too focused on this Imelda and her documentary and it may have nothing to do with it at all.'

'I get that, but I'm issuing a request for anyone who was interviewed by Imelda Conroy.'

That was what Lottie would have done, despite her doubts about its relevance. 'I wonder should you take a look at what she worked on previously? You could go down a rabbit hole on the laundry and get yourself plugged down there. Like I said, it might have nothing whatsoever to do with this murder.'

'It's a starting point.' He gulped his whiskey. 'Another coffee?'

'No, I'm fine, thanks. I should get going.' She rustled up her handbag.

'Are you on your own? On your mini-break, like.'

She thought that the less he knew about her, the better. But then again, he was a detective. 'I'm in Connemara for a family wedding. There'll be an SOS out for me.' She smiled at him.

He returned it. 'Take care, Lottie Parker. I'll be in touch. Enjoy the wedding.'

She sensed he wouldn't be in touch; that he would sideline her. Which was what he should do. But she was intrigued and curious about the horrific murder. She wanted to know who the victim was, and who had killed her. And most of all, why. Why such torture?

'The wedding isn't until the weekend. I'm free to help. Honestly, I'd like—'

'If I need input, I'll be on the phone to you. Appreciate your help so far. Now I'm going to get another pint, and this time I'm going to take my time.'

She wanted to stay with this young but weary detective. She wanted to pick over the bones of the investigation. But it wasn't her case.

'See you then.' Reluctantly she left him heading to the bar to call for his pint.

Outside, she realised her car was back at the hospital. Mooney was on his third drink. She couldn't ask him to drive her back. She checked Google Maps. It could take an hour to walk. The fresh air might diminish some of the horror she'd felt while she'd watched Jane naming the wounds on the unidentified dead woman. Or she could just get a taxi.

27

Bryan was working in the barn when Lottie returned to the farm. Though it was constructed of old stone, it was warm inside. The air hung heavy. He was mucking about with a wheelbarrow and straw. She had no idea if he was putting it into the barn or taking it out. His broad shoulders moved up and down beneath his shirt, muscles rippling, his head bent over, intent on his work.

'Bryan?' She came up behind him.

He jumped. 'Jesus, Mary and Joseph.' He clamped a hand to his chest. 'You could give a man a heart attack creeping up on him like that.'

'I'm sorry. Didn't mean to startle you.' She wondered why he was uneasy. Had she really been that silent in her approach?

'It's okay.' He wiped grimy fingers over his forehead, brushing his sweaty hair out of his eyes. 'I was in a world of my own.'

'Can I give you a hand?'

He looked at her as if to say, *You're joking me.* 'You don't think I can manage a job I've done all my life? Ha.' She noticed some of the tension leach from his face as he leaned on his shovel.

'Got time for a chat?' she enquired. 'When you're done here?'

'This can wait.' He threw down the tool and wiped his hands on his jeans. She still found it difficult to believe he was in his mid fifties. He appeared to be even fitter than she was. Which wasn't hard, she figured.

'Is this a private talk,' he asked, 'or do you want to go inside to chat over a cup of tea?'

'It's private, I suppose.'

'Let's walk to the top field. I want to check on the flock anyhow.'

She followed him, wishing she'd taken time to change her footwear. She had on a pair of once white trainers, not the best for trekking through a field. At least it was dry underfoot.

The dog ran ahead of them, and they stopped at one of the many dry-stone walls that traversed the landscape.

'What's going on, Lottie?' He smiled at her and she could see the charm that had more than likely seduced Grace.

'I'd like to ask you some more about your time in Knockraw?'

'Go ahead.'

'Was it very violent?'

'Aye, it was.' He gazed into the distance. 'We were kids, but we were treated like criminals. Savage behaviour. I still have scars on my back and arse from being beaten with a belt.'

'And was it as bad as that in the convent? The Sisters of Forgiveness or whatever they were called.'

'More so, I'd say. Being forced to work in that place was nothing short of child slavery.'

'Can you recall any particular cases of extreme brutality in either establishment?'

'Institutions, you mean.' His eyes had a faraway look. 'Don't like talking about it much. Haven't ever expressed my feelings to anyone. We were locked up, and by the grace of God, some of us survived.'

'Did many die behind the walls that you know of?' She shivered, remembering her own brother's bones, undiscovered for decades.

'In Knockraw, I knew a few. One lad was beaten to death by a fucker of a Christian Brother – or maybe he was a priest, I can't recall. Another lad died of pure hunger. They starved us. Not that you'd think looking at me now.'

She thought he was actually quite lean, but then he was a farmer who worked on the side of a hill. A monster of a seagull flew low over their heads, and she ducked reflexively. The beggars were everywhere. Of course they were, she thought. The ocean was their habitat, not hers.

'You get used to them,' he said without humour, looking skywards. 'You can get used to anything, even torture.'

His choice of word made her heart beat a little faster. 'What sort of torture?'

'Why are you asking these questions? I only wanted you to see if you could find out what happened to Mary Elizabeth and our child.'

'I know, but...' What did she really want to ask him? 'Did you know someone had started making a documentary about the nearby laundry?'

He remained silent, his face like the stone walls around him. He gazed fixedly out over his land. The seagull squawked overhead again before disappearing down to the sea.

'Bryan?' A cool breeze fluttered over Lottie's face, and she found herself shivering.

'Is it this documentary woman that's dead then? Up at the cottages?'

'No, it's not her, but she may have been there.'

'I heard there was someone renting one of the cottages and asking a lot of questions.'

'Did you talk to her?'

He shifted as if the question made him uncomfortable. 'I don't think I ever seen sight nor sound of her.'

'What did you hear then?'

'That she was interviewing people.'

'Okay.' She kept her eyes on him, saw the tremble on his chin, his Adam's apple wobbling. 'There's something you're not telling me.'

He was mute again.

'Bryan? What else? I need the full picture if I'm to find out about your girl.' She didn't add that she wanted to find out anything he might know about the murdered woman or Imelda Conroy.

'She was trying to link the goings-on at the convent with what went on in Knockraw.'

'The woman making the documentary? That seems logical enough.'

'It may, now that I've voiced it. But it was the first time anyone had come here with evidence.'

'Evidence? Of what?'

'I don't rightly know, but she talked about things I hadn't heard spoken of in years.'

'Go on.'

He turned to face her, and she noticed an ashen hue on his weather-beaten face.

'This Conroy woman, Imelda, she did come to talk to me.'

Lottie felt her mouth hang open. 'Ah Bryan, why didn't you say so at the start?'

'I don't know how it can be relevant if it's not her who was murdered.'

'What did you talk about?'

He continued his steely glare towards the horizon as he

spoke. 'She asked me if I knew of a man who'd been in a religious order back then. She thought he was a priest, or someone who masqueraded as one. That's what she said, and it reminded me...'

He paused for a moment, sucking air into his lungs before continuing. 'He was maybe early twenties, but to us lads, being nothing more than kids, teenagers, he was an auld fella. He was based at Knockraw, but this is the thing... he used to take girls from the convent at night.'

'He rescued them?' Lottie shook her head, trying to make sense of it all. She'd heard stories about some of the laundries where locals had helped girls escape and get to England.

'No.' His tone turned as sharp as a shard of broken glass. 'He did not rescue them.'

'Tell me, Bryan.' She spoke in a whisper, dreading what he was about to say.

'He abused them. That's what he did. The prick. Him and others. The older lads and the wardens or whatever they were called. It was rumoured the girls were passed around and they had their way with them.'

'That's shocking.'

'But one fine day... I don't know how true this is, but it was said that one of the men was attacked up at the convent. I suppose the girls had had enough.'

'The priest was attacked?'

'No, another lad.'

'What happened to him?' She balled her hands into fists, with an urge to beat the attacker of young girls herself.

'Like I said, there were rumours, none consistent. But I heard that they threw buckets of boiling water over him and damn near boiled the skin off him. He almost died. Pity he didn't.' Something of a crooked smile curved one side of his mouth.

'Holy fuck. Jesus Christ,' Lottie said.

He flinched at the shriek of horror in her swear words. 'Aye, it was bad. You'd think they were too weak to rebel, but those young girls were heroes.'

'Why has this not come out before now?'

'The question should be why did so much of the horror not come out? Very few know what really went on behind those massive walls and closed doors. All anyone knows who didn't experience it first-hand is just the tip of the proverbial iceberg.'

'But it needs to be made public. All of it.'

He shook his head, weary now. 'No one believed it at the time. Those of us who were eventually let out, or escaped, wanted to leave it all behind us. Like I said, I hightailed it to the United States. It wasn't and still isn't something anyone wants to talk about.'

She heard it then. In his tone, the nuance of his words. Those men, whoever they were, had abused more than the girls. She would let him tell her about that in his own time. And she had to find out who the others were too.

'I'm so sorry you had to go through it, Bryan. Do you have any idea who this person was? His name?'

'I can't remember it, and I don't know where he went or if he's even alive today.'

'But you do believe he survived that boiling water incident?'

'I presume he did, or I would have heard it in the rumours. This documentary woman seemed to know something about the incident and I reckon she asked the wrong person the right question and that's what got her killed.'

'But I told you, it's not Imelda's body up at the cottage.'

'Well it may not be her that's up there, but I reckon she's as good as dead. And if that bollox is back looking for revenge, it won't be the last murder.' His gaze returned to the horizon, his voice so low she had to lean in to hear him say the words she had thought of herself only a little while ago. 'Lottie, this might only be the start of it.'

28

'It can't be true, can it?' Boyd said.

Lottie could see he was astounded when she told him Bryan's story. They were sitting on the bed in the tiny guest room.

'I believe him.' She picked at her nails, wishing she could let them grow.

'How did this Imelda know to talk to him in the first place?'

'I didn't want to press him too hard. That time, long ago, it was all coming back to him. Hurting and haunting him. The poor man.'

'Lottie, I hate to say this, and I know he will soon be my brother-in-law and I'm just being hypothetical, but maybe it's possible he should be considered... No, that's silly.'

'You think Bryan could have killed the woman in the bath? Do you think he killed Imelda too and hid her body? Gosh, Boyd.'

'I was only thinking out loud, I don't mean it. Not really.'

'It did cross my mind,' she said. 'However, at the moment I see him as a victim, not a perpetrator.'

'Those girls in the convent were victims, and if we're to believe Bryan, they became perpetrators.'

'Yes, but they had good reason.'

'You're absolving them of their crime?' Boyd asked.

She thought about that for a moment.

'They were abandoned through no fault of their own. If it's true and not just hearsay or rumour, then they meted out their own sort of justice and I for one make no apology for it.' She caught his askance glance at her. 'Yes, yes. I know it goes against everything we believe in, but I was down in that basement, that dungeon of a place in the convent where they were forced to work, to slave day in and day out. Young girls called sinners and whores. Subjected to misery and torture. Yes, Mark, it *was* torture. Nothing short of slavery. And then some fucker comes along and sexually abuses them. Good God Almighty.' She couldn't stop the anger as it rose like a sudden tropical storm within her.

'Okay, I get it,' Boyd said calmly, as if he was talking her down off a ledge. 'And now someone is torturing and killing... who exactly?'

She relaxed a little. 'I don't know, but Mooney needs to identify that dead woman in order to progress his investigation.'

'Do you think you should tell him everything Bryan said?'

This made her stop and think. Could she betray Bryan's trust in her? 'No. I can't even verify it.'

'I know that, but Imelda contacted him. That's important for the investigation team. They might be able to find out who else she was in contact with. Those she interviewed.'

'Maybe.' Lottie stood, then paced in the confined space, conflicted emotions in every step. 'I don't want to get Bryan in any trouble. It will highlight his past when it seems he doesn't even want Grace to know about it.'

Boyd stood too. 'You mean Grace doesn't know?'

'That's what he told me.'

'Shit. That's some way to start a marriage. He's already keeping secrets from her.'

'I'm sure he'll tell her in his own time,' she said, not sure at all. 'I think he'd suppressed the bad memories and it's possible Imelda Conroy resurrected them.'

'How did she even know to find him? Someone had to have told her about him being in Knockraw. And that someone could be a killer.'

'We are going round in circles here.'

Boyd touched her arm. 'Talk to Mooney.'

Galway Garda regional and divisional headquarters looked like one of those American tech company headquarters. Contemporary and imposing, and totally out of character with its surroundings. Seagulls swooped, then squawked and soared into the sky. The smell of the tide reached Lottie as she stood outside the building.

'Holy shit, this is a monster of a place.' She looked up at the height, took in the frontal dimension with the evening sun behind it. 'You work here?' She was a bit frazzled. It had taken her well over an hour to get there in the awful Galway traffic. It never seemed to abate no matter what time you tackled a journey.

'I'm based here in the city,' Mooney said, 'but I cover the Connemara district. A lot of the local stations have been downgraded over time.'

'I suppose loss of manpower helps pay for this monstrosity.'

'It does have an indoor firing range,' he countered.

'Great for dealing with murderers quickly. Bypassing the justice system?' She grinned. 'Why did you want me to come here?' When she'd phoned him, he'd asked her to meet him at HQ. She'd had misgivings but had come anyhow.

'To make a statement so as to classify your informal information as formal.'

She halted outside the main door. 'No way. I was told it in confidence. It's hearsay. Nothing concrete. A burned man who may or may not be dead. Another man who may or may not have been a priest. One or both may or may not have something to do with the woman's murder in some sort of revenge attack. But we're talking a gap of decades. Have you even identified her yet? Have you found Imelda Conroy?' She talked herself into silence.

'You know how these things work,' Mooney said. 'It takes time. Yours is the first solid piece of information I've got.'

'The only thing you've got, you mean. What about forensics?'

'Nothing yet. No hits on fingerprints. DNA will take a while.'

'It's a murder. Fast-track it.'

'It's not that easy. You know that.'

'And the post-mortem on the dead woman? Anything new from Jane on that?'

'Nothing. Not yet, anyhow. But the preliminary report states there was evidence of old scarring on her arms. She may have been one of those incarcerated in SOF.' He caught her puzzled expression. 'Sisters of Forgiveness. The convent you were snooping around.'

'That reminds me, there was an ancient-looking man there that day. He used to be a gardener. Mickey Fox, he said his name was.'

'And you're only telling me this now?'

'I forgot all about him.'

'Well, don't forget important information in future.'

'Mooney, you are not my boss and I've no authority on this investigation. I'm a civilian, and now I'm exercising my right to walk away.' Which she duly did.

'Hey, I can arrest you for impeding my investigation,' he called after her.

'I know you won't do that.'

'Okay, stop. I'm sorry, right? Come back, Lottie.'

She stalled, turned and looked up at him.

'I need you on my side,' he said.

'I will help in any way I can, but I'm not making a formal statement. Bryan may do so in his own time, if it's deemed necessary.'

'Okay, fine.' He threw his hands heavenward, admitting defeat. Then, as if realising something, he pointed a finger at her. 'You better not go all private eye on me, trying to solve this on your own.'

She wondered if he had read her mind.

That was exactly what she intended to do.

THE PAST

'Your name is Gabriel from now on,' the nun said.

'I don't understand.' And she didn't. How could her name be changed just like that? Her mammy had named her and said it had a special meaning. She'd be so mad. If she was alive. A lump formed in her throat and she tried not to cry.

'We take holy names in here, saints and angels. Yours is anything but holy, just like you're not a saint or your poor father wouldn't have had to bring you to us. Hard work and prayer will knock the corners off you. Come along, Gabriel.'

The seven-year-old had no idea why she was there or what was going on. She wanted to turn around and run after her daddy, but he was gone and she was alone in the huge room with the nun clad in black.

The nun had been all smiles and sweetness when he'd been there, taking her hand and stroking it while telling him she would personally look after the little one. The girl was a bit put out by that, as she didn't see herself as little. She was tall for her age. But she kept her mouth shut. Knowing when to remain mute might have to become her safety net for however long she had to stay here.

She decided that if the nun wanted to call her Gabriel, she could live with it.

The dormitory she was brought to was so big and had so many beds that she almost turned and ran. It was cold, too. Not cosy like the room she shared with one of her two brothers and the baby. She felt tears bubble at the corners of her eyes, but she brushed them away. She already sensed crying would be frowned upon.

Of course she learned that there was much worse to contend with than a few wayward tears.

The first morning in the convent, she was sure she'd be shown into a classroom to begin her 'good Catholic education', as her father had called it. Instead, she was led along the dorm corridor and down the stairs to a hallway, where a door was opened and a set of stone steps rose to meet her. The air grew thick and her throat tightened, and she thought she might faint.

Worse than the lack of air was the steam. She couldn't see a thing. It was like the thick fog she'd often seen roll in from the sea and slip across the fields at home. Don't cry, she warned herself. Don't think of home. She felt a shove between her shoulder blades from the nun standing behind her.

'Now, Gabriel, this is where we do the laundry. You're a scrawny thing, so one of your jobs will be to climb into the machine when the sheets and towels become stuck to the sides and untangle them. Whatever you are instructed to do, you will do it. You will be shown other jobs too. And don't burn or scald yourself. The steam is like fire and I don't want to be calling out the poor doctor because of your stupidity. Do you understand?'

'Yes, Sister.' She didn't understand, but she was clever enough not to admit it. She hadn't a clue what was expected of her. Where were the school books? Her education?

The nun turned and stomped back up the steps, and Gabriel was left there.

Girls were working in groups in the small, clogged space. Not one of them had halted their tasks when she'd arrived, and they didn't stop now that the nun had left. They were like working ants with damp hair, their grey aprons and slip dresses stuck to their bodies with the heat. They were either putting sheets into machines or taking them out and feeding them through massive rollers. Gabriel had never seen anything like it in her life. She didn't know what to do.

'You're the new one, are you? You're a bit thin.'

The voice came from behind her. She was afraid to turn, but a poke in the shoulder told her that was what was expected. So she turned.

The woman – no, she was a teenager, maybe fifteen or sixteen, with skin like leather – held out a blistered hand. Was she to shake it? She did.

'I'm called James, but that' s not my real name. They love giving us holy names.'

'I'm Gabriel.'

'The archangel. Ha. You've no wings, so you're stuck here like the rest of us. Just do what you're told and you'll be fine. Ask no questions, you'll hear no lies.'

She had no idea what that meant.

'Well, get on with it then.'

The teenager dragged her by the hand towards a long table. It was covered with sheets and a group of girls were ironing them. Behind them, along the far wall, were the massive washing machines. That was when she knew what fear was.

29

WEDNESDAY

After a restless sleep, Lottie left the house early, telling Boyd she might do a bit of shopping. She had no intention of travelling into the city. Instead, she headed back out to the convent.

She found Mickey Fox's caravan on the outer edges of the convent grounds, in the midst of a copse of trees. Smoke billowed from a barrel, which, like a beacon, led her to the clearing where he had his abode. Apart from the burning embers, there was no sign of the old man. The caravan door was open. Standing on the step, she looked inside. Surprised to find it tidy but sparse, she debated going in. A shout from behind halted her.

'What do you think you're doing?'

She quickly backtracked down the step. 'Mr Fox.'

'It's yourself, is it? Snooping again, I see. There's nothing in there to interest you, unless you can fix a bastard of a blocked toilet.'

He held a plunger in one hand and a sturdy container in the other with a toxic warning symbol emblazoned on its side.

Nothing that could be used as a weapon, she thought, though the toxic liquid was probably as good as anything. Calm down, she warned herself. She was the trespasser here, not him.

'I apologise,' she said. 'I was looking for you. Thought you might be inside when I saw the fire over there.'

'Snooping, that's what you're at, and that's no word of a lie, missy.'

The 'missy' reminded her of her mother, and a wave of guilt flowed through her. She needed to ring her girls to see how Rose was doing. She had toyed with the idea of bringing her mother to Connemara for the week, but then ruled it out. Katie and Chloe had asked if they should bring her when they were coming to the wedding, but Lottie vetoed that, saying the event would be confusing for her. She better ring later to see how they were getting on.

'I was after some information, Mickey. About your time working for the nuns.'

'A cop was here last evening. Mooney. String of misery, giving the impression of carrying the weight of the world on his shoulders. He should try living out here in the heart of winter. That'd give him something to worry about, so it would.'

She grinned internally at his take on Mooney, but outwardly she maintained a stoical expression. 'Did you ever hear of a time when someone got burned at the convent?'

'They were always getting burned, little souls. Between irons and boiling water and steam, sure there was always accidents.'

'Any time when it wasn't an accident?'

He moved towards her. His white beard seemed darker, his froggy eyes bulged and his grip tightened on the plunger. 'What is it you're not saying?' he growled.

'I heard someone got burned, scalded on purpose. No accident.'

He seemed to draw in his eyes, or maybe his bushy eyebrows shaded them. 'Never heard of that.'

'Really? I'd have thought you'd know everything that went on here.'

'You're being smart with me now.'

'I'm not being smart. I really think you were the eyes and ears of this place. I believe you can help me.'

'You're working with that Mooney detective, aren't you?'

'I'm helping him, when he lets me.'

He put down the plunger and the container, picked up a long stick and began shifting whatever was burning in the barrel. 'You should talk to that woman who was a nun back then. She was young enough and did a bit of nursing in the convent too. Assumpta, her name was. Never knew her full name. I imagine the girls had a nastier one for her.' He chuckled, but Lottie didn't find anything funny in his words.

'She wasn't a nice person then?'

'She was good as a nurse, far as I knew, but she didn't do anything to help. If you get my meaning.'

Lottie wasn't sure what he meant, but she banked the information and ploughed on. 'I heard the girls were abused.' She wanted to say more, but held back. Hadn't Fox called them sinners and said they deserved what they got? She had to tread carefully, knowing Mooney would skin her alive for intruding on his investigation.

She waited.

Mickey was quiet, stirring the ashes. What was he burning? She moved closer to the old oil drum. He didn't seem to notice.

'There were a lot of rumours back then,' he said. 'No truth in most of them.'

'But the ones that did have some truth, can you tell me about them?'

'What is your role in all this?' He wasn't as dumb as he made out to be.

'I'm a detective, but not from round here. And I'm curious as to why there's been a murder. I suspect it could be related to what went on here years ago.'

'Have you proof of any wrongdoing?'

'Not yet.'

He continued to stir. A few sparks flew into the air, spluttered and died. He remained silent.

'What are you burning?' Lottie asked.

'Branches and sticks.'

'If you're doing it to keep warm, it's not that cold.'

'Who said why I was doing it?'

She hesitated. 'Are you burning evidence?'

'And what evidence would that be?'

Time to fudge the truth. 'Things went missing from the cottage where the woman was murdered. A lot of research on the convent.'

He stopped his stirring and the sparks died down. 'I had nothing to do with that. I am a law-abiding citizen.'

'That's what they all say.'

'Who?'

'Those with something to hide. What have *you* to hide, Mickey?'

He said nothing, resumed stoking the dying fire.

'Okay,' she said. 'I'll have to tell Detective Sergeant Mooney about this, and I'm sure he'll be sending out his forensic guys to sift through those ashes.'

'You will do no such thing. I'm living a quiet life here. Minding my own business. I did nothing to nobody. Never have. Never will. Leave me alone.'

She heard it then. In his tone, in the quiver in his voice. 'Who are you afraid of, Mickey?'

He stopped his seemingly mindless task and kept his back to her as he said, 'You'd be best served to not ask too many questions. Questions get you into trouble.'

Mickey Fox was scared, not dangerous.

She was almost certain of that.

Almost.

30

Back at the house, Boyd told Lottie that Bryan was outside somewhere and Grace had gone to the village of Spiddal for a dress fitting. He was drinking a mug of tea with a sulky face. Oh-oh, she thought.

'She's a bit annoyed at you,' he said as she filled her own mug with tepid tea from the pot.

'Grace is? Why?'

'She wanted you to see the dress or something.'

'She never said.'

'I think she expected you to go with her. That you were here to help her make final decisions. Or something like that.'

'If she'd asked me, I'd have gone. I'm not a mind-reader.'

'No, but you're getting yourself involved in things that don't concern you.' Boyd was definitely not impressed with her. She wasn't letting him get away with it.

'Bryan asked me to find someone for him.'

'He didn't ask you to investigate a murder.'

'I'm not investigating a murder,' she said. 'That's Mooney's case.'

'Yes, and you met him yesterday and told him what you had to. So you're done with it now.'

'But he wanted me to make a formal statement. I refused. I'm sure he'll contact me again.'

'You do know this is the first time we've had a week away together in like for ever? I left Sergio with Amy so that we could enjoy ourselves without work. So tell me, where were you all morning? And don't tell me you were shopping in the city.'

She hated lying to him, but she could do without another row. 'I was going into the city, but you know what the traffic is like. I had to turn and come back.'

He sighed. 'You're deflecting from the truth. As usual.'

She sat opposite him, nursing her mug of tea. He was right, of course. 'Okay, so I went to the convent. To see Mickey Fox, the gardener who worked for the nuns.'

'Why would you even do that?'

'Because he might have known this old girlfriend Bryan asked me to find.' Shit, she hadn't even asked the old man about her.

'And did he know anything?'

'He was busy burning stuff in an oil drum. I was trying to find out what it was, because it looked suspicious.'

'Did you discover what was he burning?'

'No. But he was scared. Genuinely petrified.' Not quite, she thought, but near enough.

'Leave it, Lottie. Go to the dressmaker's and meet Grace. Have a coffee with her and chinwag.'

She grinned. 'Have you ever known Grace Boyd to chinwag?'

'No, but there's a first time for everything.'

'Tell me where she is and I'll join her.'

'Not so fast. Finish the conversation about the gardener.'

She knew she'd have to tell him something to pacify his

interest. 'The only thing he mentioned was a nun called Assumpta. I'll pass it on to Mooney.'

'Do that, then walk away from it. It's not your case, Lottie. Nothing to do with you.'

'But it might have something to do with Bryan.'

'Don't go there. Leave it to Mooney.'

'Sure. Did you make this tea?'

'Yes. Why?'

'It's rotten.' She brought the mug to the sink and poured the tea down the drain. 'I'll find Grace and have a coffee with her.'

She kissed his cheek and left the house, with absolutely no intention of going anywhere near a dressmaker's.

She drove back to the convent to do what she should have done earlier. She had to ask Mickey about Mary Elizabeth, Bryan's teenage sweetheart. That was the reason she'd gone there in the first place. Not that an empty shell of a building had given her any answers. It had only thrown up more questions.

She parked out front and made her way through the maze of trees and bushes. It was a hazy kind of dark, with nature's canopy blocking out daylight.

As she approached the clearing where his caravan was located, the trees seemed to shudder all around her before coming alive as a flock of birds rose like a black cloud into the sky, cawing and squawking. A tiny trickle of fear travelled the length of her spine. They're only birds, she told herself. But it wasn't the feathered friends that made her stop.

There was no smoke from Mickey's clearing. No sound other than the birds flying away, leaving a breath in their wake. She sucked it in, held it. Listened. On high alert.

'Don't be daft,' she said aloud, exhaling, and her words echoed in the silence.

Inching forward, she wanted to shout out Mickey's name, but some inherent instinct held her back.

In the clearing, the barrel had ceased its smouldering. The caravan door stood wide open, the plunger and container on the ground by the step. He mustn't have got to unblock the toilet yet, she thought.

It was quiet. Too quiet.

'Mickey? Mr Fox? I'm back.' Silly. Of course she was back. But there was no sign of the man.

Stealthily, her gut now on high alert, she crept forward into the clearing. She smelled it before she saw it. Burning flesh.

He lay on a bed of grass and leaves. His eyes wide open, staring heavenwards through a gap in the foliage, his mouth a silent scream.

'Mickey!'

She made to run forward, but stopped. This was no accident. She knew that deep in her heart. It was a crime scene, and she must tread carefully. She had no gloves or any other protective clothing, but she had to check if he was still alive.

Crouched by his side, she held two fingers to his throat. No pulse. She'd known that already. His upper body showed evidence of burning. Blood on the grass around his head. Someone had knocked him out, maybe. Or perhaps the blow to his head had killed him. Why, though? Why do this to an old man? Because he knew something? Something the killer didn't want being made public? Did the killer know Mickey had been visited by the guards? A lot of questions, and then the one she had dared not think.

Had her visits to the convent put Mickey Fox in the cross hairs of a killer?

Surely not.

Whatever the answer, she knew Detective Sergeant Mooney was not going to be pleased with her.

. . .

After phoning Mooney, Lottie sat on the caravan step. Her gaze fell on the container the old man had been holding earlier. She poked a stick through the handle and shook it slightly. Empty. Her eyes travelled back to the body. Some bastard had poured the toxic drain cleaner over the old man. First there was the body in the bath burned with boiling water, and now this. More barbarity. She leaned her head against the door and tried to stem the rising panic taking a tight grip in her chest. Squeezing the breath out of her. She took small, insistent gasps of air. Allowed the silence to wash over her. Tried to infuse calm into her brain.

She'd thought the forest had settled into quietness since the birds had taken flight, but now she heard the sounds of nature: the rustling of leaves, the drip of sap, the shiver of a breeze. Then something else. Footsteps. Moving away.

'What the hell?' she whispered.

Leaning forward without otherwise moving, she tried to determine where the sound had come from. Once she had it pinpointed, she wondered if she should stay with the body, but then Mickey was going nowhere. Making her decision, she set off in the direction from which she'd heard the retreating footsteps.

Winding her way through the branches, she followed what seemed to be a well-worn path of dry earth and trampled leaves.

Who was she following? Where were they going? Was she being led into a trap? That nearly stopped her pursuit, but not quite.

The trees gave way and the convent walls loomed up ahead. She thought she saw a flash of colour, maybe blue. Had someone ducked in through the large rear door? Should she stop now? Or carry on and see what happened?

Her breath caught at the back of her throat as she paused, trying to decide what to do. She could be putting herself in danger, and thoughts of her three children and her little grandson, Louis, flashed before her eyes. They'd be grand if anything happened to her, wouldn't they? Boyd would make sure they were looked after. Her thoughts carried her inside the old building.

Oppressive darkness. Silence.

Then a bang.

A door swung shut somewhere above her head and the sound bounced off the walls. She took to the stone staircase and ran up it. Breathless, she found herself in a long corridor. Someone had tried to rip the mosaic tiles off the floor at one time, but seemed to have given up. She wasn't giving up.

With no idea which direction to take, she turned left and made her way to a door at the end. Pressing her ear to it, she knew she'd chosen correctly.

The sound from inside puzzled her.

Crying.

Someone was crying?

Without fear for her safety, she turned the old brass knob and shoved the door inwards.

31

RAGMULLIN

Kirby knew he was on a hiding to nothing when Superintendent Farrell called him into her office. Her words flew high above his head.

No suspects.

No witnesses.

No clue.

What was he at? Was he even a detective?

Bring me results.

Her words resounded heavily through his brain as he made his way back to the incident room. He couldn't dispute any of what she'd said.

'I'm useless,' he said to Martina.

'No you're not. You were landed in at the deep end. You just need to think what the boss would do.'

'She'd chew my arse out for lack of results.'

'Our prime suspect has fled the town,' she said. 'We have issued alerts for him and his car. McKeown is going through every bit of CCTV we can lay our hands on. All interested parties have been interviewed. What more can we do?'

He raised his shoulders, then let them drop, defeated.

'There has to be something to throw a light on this murder. Have you got anywhere with Edie's background?'

'It's a bit of a dead duck really. There's plenty to learn about her in the almost twenty years she's lived in Ragmullin, but before that there's barely anything.'

'What about her husband?'

'She was married for a few years. Fred Butler. He's definitely dead. Car accident when the younger boy was a baby. That seems to be when she moved here. She had lived in Galway for a time. Not much to report really.'

'What brought her to Ragmullin?'

'Maybe she wanted a fresh start.'

'Did Marge Woods have anything to offer?'

'She's more concerned with the latest fashion trend in false eyelashes. The salon owner is due back today from her holiday in France. I'll go have a chat with her.'

'Do, and please come back with something to keep the super off my back.'

She laid a hand on his shoulder. 'I'll do my best.'

32

CONNEMARA

The woman was wearing a blue half-zip fleece top and dirty denim jeans. Ripped black trainers with the laces undone. Long dark hair swept down over the arms that clutched her knees up to her face. Shoulders rocked, then stilled as the sobs diminished.

Lottie waited, unsure whether she should speak now or delay the inevitable. Maybe she could wait a few moments...

'Who are you?' she said, confirming her lack of patience.

'Leave me alone.'

She'd been expecting a teenager, but the voice sounded older. Someone around her own age, perhaps. Or younger? It was hard to know.

'What were you doing at the caravan?' she asked, bending down, not wanting to be looming over the woman.

More sobs broke free, and she could see the woman's hands turning white where they gripped her knees beneath the long hair.

'What's your name?'

Silence.

She edged forward. 'I need to know your name so that we can talk.'

'Fuck off.'

'I'm not going anywhere.'

The woman lifted her head, hair still masking most of her features, but Lottie could make out dark-circled eyes; maybe brown irises, though they seemed black from crying.

A hiss issued from pale lips, 'You really don't want to be anywhere near me.'

'Are you going to harm me?'

'Harm you? No, I won't. Can't speak for whoever killed Mickey, though.'

'Did you hurt him?'

'Are you for real, woman?' A high-pitched moan. 'I tried to *warn* him. To protect him. But the old fart wouldn't listen to me. Now he's dead and they're after me, and I want you to leave me alone or you'll be next.'

'Who is after you?'

'Go away.'

'Why are they after you?'

'Are you deaf, or what?'

'Did you know the woman who died at the cottage?'

Silence once again. Broken only by sobs. A heart-wrenching sound. Guttural. Those were the only words Lottie could think of to describe the cries. She had no idea if the woman was genuinely broken or just putting on a damn good act.

'Listen to me,' she urged. 'You're not safe here. If I found you, anyone can. Come with me.'

'Who are you anyway? A cop?'

'Kind of, but I'm on holidays, so I can't arrest you or anything.' She didn't say she could phone Mooney and he'd do the deed.

'Where can you take me that will be safe?'

She hesitated before saying, 'I'm staying with my...' She

couldn't think what to call Bryan or Grace. 'My sister-in-law. It's a farm. Not far from here. I have a car. I think you could do with a cup of tea.' Jesus, she was turning into her mother. Tea to solve the troubles of the world. 'And some food.'

The woman surprised her by standing up quickly, nodding her head furiously. 'I'm starving.'

For the first time, Lottie got a good look at her. Tall and slim. Thin even. Hair unwashed, hands filthy. And her face, dirty, weary and worn as she looked up from under short lashes to reveal mournful eyes. It was still difficult to pin an age to her. Thirties? She should have asked Mooney for a photo of Imelda Conroy, because it was possible that was who this woman was.

Lottie put out her hand and the woman took it, before collapsing into her arms.

33

Boyd invited Mooney in when he arrived at the door asking for Lottie. He made a pot of tea, mainly to keep from having to look at or answer the detective.

They sat at the kitchen table, where he'd sat earlier with Lottie.

'She went into the village to see the dressmaker,' he said once the tea was poured and milk added and he'd nowhere else to hide. 'I told you that on the phone.'

'She's not there. I met your sister. Grace, isn't it? She seemed annoyed with your fiancée.'

'I'm annoyed with her myself.' Boyd sipped his tea, deciding on what to say. 'But with Lottie you learn to let her off to do her thing. You'd never win otherwise. You never win anyway.' He tried to inject some humour into a situation that was anything but humorous.

'Feck that.' Mooney shoved back his chair with his legs. 'Tell her from me that I don't want her interfering in my investigation.'

Now was the time to stand up for her, thought Boyd, even though he was mad as hell at her and actually felt like throwing her under the bus. 'You asked for her help. You asked her to attend the post-mortem with you. Whether you like it or not, you've whetted her appetite, and I've never known Lottie Parker to let a juicy bone drop.'

'Jesus, you're just like her. Talking in riddles.'

'It's catching.'

'I better not bloody well catch it.' Mooney tugged at his excuse for a beard, a surly scowl darkening his features.

Boyd grinned. 'She's one in a million, though. You seem a bit stretched on this investigation. What's going on?'

'Holiday time. Cutbacks. Stress. Who knows? No sign of the bigwigs cutting back on themselves, though.'

'Same everywhere.' Boyd gulped his tea, not really needing it after having had some earlier, but it allowed him time to formulate his next question. 'Did you know that Lottie went to visit the old gardener at the convent this morning?'

Mooney straightened his back. 'Do you know why she was there?'

'No, but she said he was burning something in an oil drum. I reckon if she's not with Grace at the dressmaker's, then she returned to talk to the old man.'

'She's a fucking loose cannon, that woman.' Mooney stood, then sat again, defeated.

'Why do you say that?' Boyd smirked behind his mug. Mooney had his assumption dead right.

'Because that's where I was before I went looking for her. Mickey Fox is dead. She phoned to tell me about it. Looks like he was murdered, as far as I can tell. Suspicious anyhow. Damn suspicious. Blow to the back of his head. A lot of blood spilled. And, for good measure, he was doused in some sort of toxic fluid. Burned the shit out of his chest. He hardly did that to himself.'

Boyd felt the blood seep from his face. 'Lottie could be in danger.' Panic began to set in. 'The killer might have taken her, hurt her. Or she could have followed him. Jesus, man, why are you here drinking tea? You should be out searching for her.'

'She phoned in the incident. She was still there at that stage, as far as I know. Sounded cool as a fucking cucumber.' Mooney slammed his hand on the table. 'If she's off doing a Miss Marple stint, I'll lock her up.'

'Good luck with that. But I really think she might be in trouble.'

'She's in trouble all right. Interfering with an ongoing investigation. I should arrest her.'

'You have to find her.' Boyd felt the blood rush back to his face. Knew he was getting angry. At Mooney or at Lottie? Both, probably. 'I'll help you look for her.'

'Christ Almighty, that's all I need. Two fucking mavericks traipsing all over my crime scenes and mucking up my investigation. Forget it.'

Mooney stood.

Boyd paced. He'd gone through every emotion, and now a deep-seated worry took root. 'Christ, if anything's happened to her, her kids will never forgive me.'

The back door opened and Lottie walked in. Dusty and sweaty. She looked from one to the other. 'What's going on?'

'I was about to ask you the same question,' Mooney bellowed.

'Jesus,' she said, 'you'd wake the dead.'

'Aye, and that might be no harm.' He mellowed a little, just a little. 'The dead might tell me more than you do. What were you doing at Mickey Fox's caravan?'

'I wanted to see what he'd been burning when I'd been there earlier. Not that I found out. He was dead when I arrived.'

'For Christ's sake, why didn't you phone me?'

'I did.'

'When it was too bloody late. You should have called me

when you were there before. And when did you decide to not stay at the scene? It makes you look guilty as fuck.'

'I didn't kill the old man, Mooney.'

'Yeah, well, I have no idea what you did or didn't do, sister.'

'Don't you "sister" me,' she said.

Boyd watched the interaction with interest, glad he wasn't on the end of either of their wrath. Lottie was losing her cool – that was if she'd had any to begin with.

She said, 'There's someone you should talk to.'

'And who might that be?' Mooney raised an eyebrow. Interested now. Anger dissipating. Boyd sagged with relief.

Lottie hesitated, as if debating what to tell him. 'She's outside, in my car. Asleep. Traumatised. She won't tell me who she is. I'm not sure if she has anything to do with the murders, but she's terrified and told me she had tried to warn Mickey.'

'Warn him about what?'

'Maybe that someone was about to kill him? Who knows. She wouldn't say.'

'Where did you find this mystery woman?'

'She was in the trees surrounding the clearing where Mickey's caravan is situated. She took off when she noticed me. She might have heard me on the phone to you. I followed her to the convent. Brought her back here. Look, Mooney, I promised her I'd keep her safe.'

'In our business, we don't make promises we can't keep. You should know that. I want to see her.'

'I don't want you scaring her off.'

'At the very least, she's a witness.' He moved towards the door. Stood into Lottie's space. 'At worst, she's a cold-blooded murderer.'

34

Mooney went outside and Lottie caught Boyd shaking his head.

'What?' she said.

'What's what?' He folded his arms.

'You. Standing there as if you don't care about anything.'

'Maybe I might care if I knew what the hell was going on.' He sighed, unfolded his arms, dragged a chair out from the table and sat. 'Do *you* care enough to explain?'

'I will explain, but not until Mooney's gone. I'll bring the woman in here. Will you ask Bryan and Grace if she can stay the night? I've a feeling it might be Imelda Conroy.'

'Don't, Lottie. Don't get involved. You'll ruin everything for Grace.'

Before she could reply, the door opened and Mooney loped in. 'Are you having me on?'

'Huh?' Confusion knitted her brow, and she could feel a permanent furrow taking root there.

'There's no one in the car. Did she even exist in the first place?'

Her heart dipped in her chest. She ran out past Mooney.

He was right. The car was empty.

She was surrounded by vast fields cut by stone walls, the seashore at the edge of the horizon. No houses as far as the eye could see. Sheep grazed nonchalantly, and she realised the bleakness of this existence. Barren landscape, sheep and the roar of the ocean. Though human life was close, you couldn't see it, feel it or hear it. She'd lose her mind. Like she'd lost the woman.

The barn loomed to the side of the yard. Maybe she had taken refuge in there. Lottie raced over and pulled back the door. It shifted noisily on its rusted wheels.

She yelled, 'Come out...' She didn't even know the woman's name. 'We have to talk.'

Rustling came from the hay. Not loud enough for an adult. Probably rats. She shivered violently. Her phobia froze her blood, and she turned tail and ran. Mooney could look in there; no way in hell would she venture any further inside.

As she returned to the farmhouse, she saw Mooney and Boyd standing in the yard.

'I'm taking your car for a forensic examination,' Mooney said. 'We might get her fingerprints or DNA from it. Maybe link them to the kettle in the cottage or to something on Fox's body or in his caravan.'

'I need my car.'

'I'm sure you can use your brother-in-law's.'

'He's not my brother-in-law,' she said, sounding pettish, and this made her cringe. She'd have to use Boyd's car, because no way did she want to be isolated in this desolate place. Not with a murderer stalking around the vicinity.

'He's not mine yet either,' Boyd said. 'Might never be, by the look on Grace's face.'

Lottie turned to see Boyd's sister getting out of a car, slamming the door and waving off the driver.

'Thanks a bunch, Lottie,' she said, marching in by the three of them. She banged the door behind her.

'I'll talk to her,' Lottie said, making to follow.

'You'll be coming with me.' Mooney grabbed her by the elbow, but dropped his hand when her eyes bored into his. 'You have to make a statement,' he added. 'I need a description of this mystery woman.'

'I can do that from here.' She was adamant.

'Do I have to arrest you?' He leaned his head to one side and scratched his beard.

She figured he'd love to do just that. She scrubbed her shoe on the ground, dislodging the grit beneath it. Maybe she deserved his scorn, but she couldn't rid her mind of the abject terror she'd seen in the woman's eyes earlier. She had promised her safety, then she'd lost her. The only thing she was guilty of was irresponsibility.

'I don't think she killed anyone,' she said quietly. 'She was terrified.'

'Terrified she'd be arrested for murder,' Mooney scoffed.

'No, it wasn't that.' She shook her head distractedly. 'Something or someone made her unbelievably scared. It's possible she might have seen who killed Mickey Fox.'

'Or she killed the old man herself.' Mooney voiced her worst fear. He continued, 'Are you coming with me, or do I have to read you your rights?'

She put out her hand to Boyd. For reassurance rather than comfort. He hesitated, and she thought she might cry. But then he relented and gave her a quick hug.

'Just cooperate, Lottie,' he whispered in her ear.

'I will,' she muttered. 'As soon as I figure out what Mooney knows that he's not telling me.'

'Not your investigation.' Boyd shook his head, warning her.

'I know, I know. But I'm involved on the other side now. You and Bryan carry out a decent search of the area. She's out there somewhere. I'm worried for her safety.'

'And I worry for yours. Be careful.'

'I will.'

She followed Mooney to his car.

Mooney drove in silence. Lottie hated silence. Hated his silence anyhow.

'She can't have gone far,' she said, needing to hear a sound other than the roar of the car engine. 'She's on foot. We should have searched more carefully. That's if she's just fled and hasn't been abducted.'

He said nothing.

'Come on. Matt?'

'Detective Sergeant Mooney to you. And for your information, I've asked my people to search the locale. Where's your brother-in-law? Bryan whatshisname'

'O'Shaughnessy.'

He drummed his fingers on the steering wheel as he drove. 'Where do you think he is?'

'How would I know? I've hardly been in the house since I arrived.' She thought about it for a moment. 'He's probably out tending his sheep.'

'You make him sound like a fucking shepherd.'

'Isn't that what you call a person who tends sheep?' She was well aware that he wasn't amused.

'I've done a bit of digging on your Mr O'Shaughnessy.'

'He's not my anything.'

'It was you who came to me with his cock-and-bull story.'

'Why do you call it that?'

He shook his head. No way was he telling her anything more, which made her wonder what exactly he had found out about Bryan.

'Do you think he's hiding this elusive woman?' she asked tentatively, not really wanting to hear his affirmation.

'What I think doesn't matter. But what I know is this. You

lost her, that's if she even exists, and Mr O'Shaughnessy is seemingly nowhere to be found.'

'We weren't looking for him, were we?'

'Don't be so pedantic. With all the activity around his house, wouldn't you think he'd come running out of the shadows to see what was going on?'

She mulled that over. 'Maybe he did.'

'What do you mean?' Even with his eyes on the road, she still had the uneasy sensation that he was staring at her.

'Maybe he came up to the house and...'

'Jesus. You think he took her? The woman?'

'At this stage,' she said, 'I honestly don't know what to think.'

35

Boyd was drinking a glass of tap water because he'd already had more than his daily quota of tea. By the stove, Grace stood rigid and tall, slapping meat onto a pan. Her mood warned him not to say he wasn't hungry.

'I cannot for the life of me believe you're with that woman. She only thinks of herself.'

'I thought you liked Lottie.'

'I did. From a distance. Up close, I'm not so sure. Why are you even with her?'

'I love her,' he said.

'Hmph, whatever love is.'

'Don't you love Bryan?'

Without hesitation, she said, 'I like him, and he keeps me safe and makes me happy. If that's love, then I do love him.'

Boyd wondered about his attraction to Lottie. He loved her, of course he did, but she rarely thought of her own safety, let alone his. He was happy. Wasn't he? He missed Sergio and couldn't wait to see him again at the weekend. He'd give Amy a ring later and ask to talk to his son. He helped ground him like no one else could. Not even Lottie.

'And another thing,' Grace said, 'I don't know what your Lottie said to my Bryan, but he's been too quiet since she arrived.'

'Don't you think maybe Bryan said something to her?'

The meat sizzled and she smacked it with a spatula, grease bubbles splashing upwards. The smell of burning caught in his lungs.

She said, 'What do you mean by that?'

'Nothing, Grace. Forget it.'

He saw her lower the heat on the range. She turned around, the spatula a menacing weapon in her hand. 'You started this, Mark, so God help you, you better finish it.'

'No, you...' The look she gave him made him sit up straight. 'I think you need to speak with Bryan. There's something on his mind and it's none of my business.'

'Oh, but you think it's Lottie Parker's business, do you?' This was a side of Grace he'd never seen before.

'It's Bryan's business, not hers. The thing is, he made it hers.'

'Explain.' She sat at the table and laid down the greasy utensil before hastily lifting it again, eyeing the stain on the wood.

'I can't. I just know there's something on his mind and he may have spoken to Lottie about it.'

She seemed to mull this over. 'Why wouldn't he talk to me?'

'I don't know.'

'It must be police business then.' A line of worry creased her forehead. 'Did he do something awful that I should know about?'

'I don't think so.'

'But you're not sure? I'm marrying him, Mark, I have a right to know.'

'Not certain it works that way, Gracie. Talk to him.'

'Where I am concerned, it does work that way.' She got up and returned to her cooking. 'Now the mince is burned.'

Her shoulders were slumped, shoulder blades trembling.

And he couldn't think of a thing to say to reassure her.

She knew she couldn't trust that woman. She was a cop. Whether on duty or on holidays, they were cops twenty-four/seven. She would never trust them no matter how kind or caring they pretended to be. They were all the same. Wanted to squeeze you dry. Leaving you without a drop of self-esteem in your system. They hadn't helped people like her and her family before, and they wouldn't help now.

When she'd opened her eyes in the car and seen where she'd been brought, she almost had a heart attack. O'Shaughnessy's place. Why the woman had brought her there, she had no idea, and she had no intention of hanging around to find out. Seeing Bryan O'Shaughnessy was not on her agenda. She felt that that bridge was well and truly burned. Just like poor old Mickey Fox.

She'd got out of the car unseen and unheard, and crept back down the road a little bit before climbing over a wall into a field. She'd crawled like a fugitive along the inside of the stonework.

The cottage ruins she'd come upon had no roof and little shelter from the elements, but it might allow her time to get her thoughts straight. The waves crashing in the distance, far below on the rocky seashore, didn't scare her. She welcomed the sound. It calmed her. But she couldn't become too relaxed. She had to make a plan. Seeing the aftermath of what had happened to Mickey scared her more than anything that had gone before. She was tough, but not so tough that she did not fear the evil she'd witnessed.

The wind made it feel cold, even though the sun was beaming. She wished she had more than her fleece jacket to warm her up. She'd have to make do. Make a plan. Huh, look where her plans had got her so far. Nowhere.

She was still in danger.

She'd been hunted into a corner, and here she was.

But she was a fighter. She would not give up. Not yet.

She tried to settle herself in the ruin. But she felt as if old ghosts were rising from the walls with the wind. And she shuddered violently.

36

Mooney didn't bring Lottie straight to the station, and she was glad of the respite.

He parked up at the old convent and they walked to the clearing. A small forensics tent had been erected over Mickey Fox's body.

'Put these on.' Mooney handed her gloves and booties.

'You are aware that my DNA is all over this place?'

'Do you always have to argue the point? Just do as I say.'

'Why bring me here? What do you want me to look at?'

'I want you to show me exactly what Fox was doing when you were here earlier, and where he was situated.'

'I told you. He'd been burning something in that oil drum.' She pointed to it.

'Were there flames?'

'I remember smoke. Then some sparks flying as he stoked it.'

'Someone threw water all over it.' He glared at her pointedly.

'Not me, if that's what you're insinuating.'

'What about this imaginary friend you found here?'

She sighed loudly. 'She was not imaginary. And I didn't see

her here. I heard her running and followed her to the convent. That's where I found her. You *know* all this.'

'I know that's what you told me. I'm just not sure whether to believe you.'

'What reason would I have to lie?'

'Bryan O'Shaughnessy, for one.'

'Bryan? Come on, Mooney. The man only wanted me to find someone he knew long ago. Don't forget he was a victim in Knockraw. He'd have no reason to hurt anyone.'

But he would, she thought, wouldn't he? Her mind was a jumble of inconsistencies. Imelda Conroy had spoken to him. He said he'd told her about the burned man. Was that even true? Had there been a man who'd abused young girls? Girls who'd taken their revenge by throwing boiling water over him. How had they over-powered him? Where had the nuns been? Were they involved too? Shit, why hadn't she asked Bryan all those questions? But then he'd only heard rumours. That was what he'd said. But was it the truth?

'I checked O'Shaughnessy out,' Mooney said. 'He may not be all that innocent.'

'What do you mean?'

'Ask him yourself. When you find him.'

He marched over to the oil drum. A SOCO stood there carefully rescuing damp fragments of paper and placing them in an evidence bag.

'Anything?' Mooney enquired.

'It'll take some time to dry out, and most of it is destroyed. But we'll try.'

'Good. Let me know as soon as you can.' He walked over to the caravan.

Lottie followed, averting her eyes from the activity around where Mickey's body lay. The woman had said she'd tried to warn him. Warn him about who or what? She needed to find that woman.

The caravan was too small for both Lottie and Mooney to move freely inside. She found herself pressed up behind his back. She smelled cigarettes and his strong aftershave, or maybe he used cologne. Red hairs sprouted along the back of his neck, and she felt like telling him to take a razor to them.

'Not much of a life, was it?' he said.

'He seemed content.'

'But why did he remain here? That's what I'd like to know. The convent was gutted by thieves. Fox didn't do anything to stop that.'

'He must have been eighty years old.'

'He didn't even report it.' The resonance in Mooney's voice showed he wasn't for swaying. 'No, either he was involved in the thefts or he was here for some other reason. If you ask me, it was no good reason.'

'I didn't ask you,' Lottie muttered under her breath. Mooney was irritating her, but she was grateful to him for bringing her along. Even though she sensed he had an ulterior motive.

'Were you in here with him?' he asked.

'No.'

'Someone was. Two mugs in the basin.'

'Maybe he didn't wash his dishes after every use.' She was apt to doing that herself at times. Most of the time.

'You sure you didn't have a cuppa here?'

'I'm certain.' She suspected it might have been the woman in the blue fleece but didn't utter this aloud. Or maybe the killer. That would mean Mickey knew the person who had murdered him.

'Your friend, then?'

'What friend?'

He sighed tiredly. 'The mysterious woman you said was in your car and then she wasn't.'

'It's possible she was here. She told me she tried to warn him but said he wouldn't listen.'

'She whacked him over the head and doused him in toxic drain cleaner. He couldn't listen after that, could he?'

'No need to be so cynical.' Lottie backed out of the cramped space. She'd had enough of Mooney's conspiracy theories. Not that she didn't partially agree with his reasoning, but she'd never admit it.

'The woman acted suspiciously,' she said when he joined her, 'but she deserves the benefit of the doubt.'

'Why run then?'

'She was scared. She might have seen Mickey being killed.'

'But why wait around for you to arrive? And if she wasn't abducted, then she ran from your car. Guilty until proven innocent.'

She considered his words. 'You've that the wrong way round.'

She knew he was aware of what he'd said. But she was thinking the same thing. Why did the woman leave the car? Had something or someone spooked her? Again.

Bryan couldn't concentrate on his farm, his work, his sheep. Or even Grace. Ever since the visit of Imelda Conroy a few weeks ago, memories had been awakened. Memories he'd suppressed for most of his lifetime. They were invading every waking hour, and his sleeping time too, even though sleep had become rare.

Mary Elizabeth had been his first love. His only love until he'd found Grace. But now it felt like he was cheating on the woman he was due to marry. If he knew the truth about what had happened all those years ago, he might be able to move forward with his life. Imelda Conroy had stirred a pot that perhaps had been best left alone. Best for everyone concerned.

He rounded the corner where the old homestead had stood decades earlier. It was now derelict. Moss-covered stones, the roof caved in. He usually avoided going anywhere near it, but today he walked around it.

Something seemed to have caught on a nail in an upright timber. The old door frame. He hadn't counted the sheep that morning, he'd been so distracted. Could a ewe have wandered over here and got herself entangled? Unlikely. They tended to keep to the hilly inclines that bordered his land. Still, he had to take a look.

As he neared the ruins, old memories that had been buried for decades surfaced and threatened to choke him. Images of his brother. His dead mother, of whom he had little recollection. His young sister. And of course his bastard of a father. He blamed that man for all that had happened, but in more forgiving moments he knew his father had had it tough too. No excuse, though, for not rescuing him from Knockraw.

The cloth he'd seen from a distance was some sort of fleece all right, but it wasn't a sheep that had got caught on the old stone ruin. Blue material. He tugged at it and it came away in his hand. It was stained with what looked like blood.

Holding the scrap of fleece, he entered the ruin and went from room to room. There was no one there.

In a corner he spied a plank of timber with a nail embedded in its crook. He lifted it up to inspect it. A trail of blood was smeared all the way down the side of it. It looked like it might have been one of the old rafters. But the stain wasn't old, it was fresh. He let the plank fall to the ground, then turned and walked across the fields towards the farmhouse, moving quickly away from what had been his childhood home.

Something was going on. He had no idea what it might be. Only that it was dark and brutal.

And in his hand he still grasped the blue material saturated with blood.

37

At Galway Garda HQ, Lottie finished her statement, then sat back and looked at Mooney.

'The woman could be Imelda Conroy. You have to find her,' she said.

'We are trying our best. We also need to find out what she was up to. She seems to have opened up this tin of slugs.'

'Can of worms,' Lottie corrected.

'Whatever you want to call it, but in my opinion she let loose a trail of slimy slugs that has me going round in circles. I have two dead bodies, one I have yet to identify, a missing documentary-maker and a nameless escapee who may well be said documentary-maker. What else? Oh, right. No suspects.'

'And a mysterious scalded or burned man from decades ago,' she added.

'That could be a figment of Bryan O'Shaughnessy's imagination. Shit, I have a meeting with my superintendent in an hour.'

'Rather you than me.'

'And the local councillors are up in arms. Councillor Wilson is a thorn in my side. He's on some sort of policing committee at the council. He wants this thing put to bed asap. Says it's bad for tourism. More likely he wants to grandstand when the culprit is caught.'

'Human life has been taken. These people should keep their mouths shut.' Lottie despaired of human nature.

'Agreed, but when have you ever known politicians to do that?'

She was slow to stifle a yawn as tiredness seeped out. 'Can you get someone to bring me back to O'Shaughnessy's? Seeing as you've impounded my car.'

'You realise that I had to do that?'

'Correct procedure, but don't keep it too long. I don't relish being isolated out there in the back of beyond with a killer stalking his way around the countryside.'

'I'm sure O'Shaughnessy will allow you to borrow a tractor if you need to go to the shops.'

'Not funny, Mooney.'

'I don't suppose it is.' He scrubbed at his eyes, and she saw the tension etched there, along with his own tiredness and frustration. All revealed in the motion of a hand on his face.

'One thing I will ask of you,' he said.

'Go on.'

'See if you can get anything from O'Shaughnessy about that woman you lost from your car.'

'I didn't lose...' She threw up her hands, but then relented. 'Show me a photo of Imelda Conroy.'

'This is from her website. Could be an old one.'

She squinted at the pretty young woman. 'I'm not sure. The woman I met was very dishevelled. It might be her, but then again it might not. I'll describe her to Bryan and see what he says. Did you have any luck trying to find out about the nun called Assumpta whom Mickey Fox mentioned. I texted you about it.'

'And when do you think I had time to do that?'

'Sorry.'

'It's on my list. You can wait out front and I'll get someone to bring you home.'

'Home? I wish,' she muttered, suddenly feeling lonely for her ramshackle house in Ragmullin. She wondered how they were getting on without her. No desperate phone calls so far. That was good, wasn't it?

———

They are all looking for me. They'll never find me. I know that with a surety born of years of staying so far back that my true self is barely a shadow. My dark alter ego does not walk around in plain sight. That persona prefers the murky gloom. Lurking in dark corners of the mind. Jumping out when it's time. Taking my prize, my prey. They thought they'd got the better of me all those years ago. My outward scars have healed somewhat, but internally I have become strengthened and watchful, and patient. They succeeded in emboldening me to await my time. And now is my time. To strike. To get my revenge. To take back what was mine. My true self.

As I think these thoughts, I subsume myself back into my manufactured role. The one everyone knows and recognises. It has taken years to cultivate and I'm not going to let anyone take it from me. I am too smart for that.

38

By the time she was dropped back to Grace and Bryan's house, Lottie felt the exhaustion of the last few days paralysing her body, chilling her bones. She could sleep for a month. She'd grab an hour, if she was lucky.

No such luck.

'Where were you?' Grace said accusingly as she scrubbed a plate in the sink.

'I had to make a statement at Garda HQ. They impounded my car and I had to wait for a lift.' Why was she even explaining all this?

'I had to have my dress fitting alone. You were supposed to help me. I am annoyed with you. I'm disappointed in you.' The water splashed up on Grace's apron and onto the floor.

'All I can do is apologise. I got caught up in the murders and totally forgot.' She didn't like to tell Grace that she had no recollection of being asked to go to any dress fitting in the first place. No point in aggravating an already volatile situation.

'Murders that are none of your business.' Grace slammed a plate onto the draining board and picked up a tea towel. 'What has Bryan told you?'

'Bryan? Told me about what?'

'I wouldn't be asking if I knew. It's something to do with him that I don't know anything about. I want you to tell me what it is.'

'It's not my place to say. You will have to ask him.'

'Is it a big secret, Lottie? I hate secrets.'

'I do too. Speak with Bryan.'

The door opened and a breathless Bryan almost fell into the kitchen. 'Grace...'

'You better tell me what's going on,' she said, wet hands on hips, 'or I'm walking out of here and there will be no wedding.'

'I'm sorry, Grace, but I need Lottie to come with me.'

'Is she more important than me?' A childlike expression came with the pout.

'No, but I found blood. Up at the old homestead.' He turned to Lottie. 'You need to take a look.'

'Call Detective Sergeant Mooney in Galway HQ,' Lottie said. 'I can't get involved.'

'You are already involved.'

'They've taken my car. I've been warned off. Honestly, Bryan. Just phone Mooney.'

He took out a piece of blue material from his pocket and showed her. 'I found this.'

'Oh shit. You've handled it. Your DNA could be on it now. You shouldn't have touched it. Leave it on the table until I get something to put it into. Any freezer bags?'

'No,' Grace said, but she took a roll of cling film from the cupboard under the sink, all business now. 'Will this do?'

'Yes. Thanks.' Lottie quickly wrapped the material in the cling film. 'Will you phone Mooney, Grace? I'll go with Bryan to see where this was found.'

'I'm coming with you,' Grace said.

'No, stay here,' Lottie said, more harshly than she'd

intended, but Grace seemed not to notice. Her attention was on her fiancé.

'You owe me an explanation,' she told him.

'I do, but later.'

Lottie could see by his demeanour that he was close to admitting defeat.

'What was this place?' Lottie asked as they approached the derelict house.

'My family home. The place I left when they threw me in Knockraw.'

'Who lived here?'

'My mother died after the baby was born. So then it was my father, myself, my brother and sister. And the baby, of course.'

'Why was the house allowed to decay?'

'Decay is a strong word.' He paused. 'The house I live in now was my grandmother's.'

'This is your land. Was it all left to you?'

'I inherited it, yes. It's a long story.' They had reached the ruin. 'That's where I found the material. And that's the board with the blood.'

'And you took the material and touched the piece of timber?'

'Aye. For my sins.'

'Stay here.'

She made her way through the ruin. Sheep dirt underfoot and weeds to her knees. The smell of the sea was never far away. She wondered what had happened to the rest of Bryan's family. She returned to him.

'There's nothing and no one here.'

'I told you that.'

'But why would she come here?'

'Who? The person whose blood that is?'

'Yes,' she said. 'Is that where the board was when you arrived?'

'Aye. I lifted it up to inspect it before I put it back down.'

'Forensics will have to examine it.' She peered skywards through the roofless space. 'I hope it doesn't rain.'

'Clouds are gathering at sea. Might only be sea fog. Shouldn't be much rain in any case.'

'A little is enough to wash away evidence,' she mused. She hadn't noticed any more blood. 'Someone had to be following her.'

'Who are you talking about?'

She realised Bryan had been out working all day and might not know about the woman she'd found at the convent. And subsequently lost, according to Mooney's take on things. He could explain it when he arrived.

'You mentioned you had a sister. Is she still alive?'

Bryan bowed his head. 'I don't know.'

'How can you not know? She was your sister.'

'After my mother died, I heard that my father put her in the convent, the laundry. I never saw her again, so I'm not sure if that's even true.'

'Jesus, Bryan. Did you look for her?'

He shook his head. 'Life was complicated back then. I was more concerned with my own survival than worrying about my scut of a sister. As I said, I fled to the US when I got out of the industrial school.' Large tears pooled in the crevices around his eyes. 'I was selfish. Maybe I still am. Selfish for not seeking out my family and my girlfriend. For not sharing my past with Grace.'

'What age would your sister be now?'

'I can't think straight.' Bryan shook his head wearily and wiped his tears. He turned away and walked back across the fields.

Lottie wondered what it was that he was afraid to share with her. Why all the secrets?

She snapped photos with her phone and gazed around at the stone ruin again. She wondered if she should bring the plank of wood with her but decided to leave it. The scene had already been disturbed enough.

As she followed Bryan's footsteps, she felt the leaden weight of his ancestors, his family, his siblings resting on her shoulders.

Mooney came as soon as he could. Grace reluctantly made him tea, sporting a scowl. He accepted the drink along with a thick slice of home-made brown bread slathered with country butter.

'Haven't eaten a thing all day,' he said.

Lottie realised she hadn't eaten much either. 'Any update on the identity of the dead woman at the holiday cottage?'

'No one has been reported missing.' His mouth was full, melted butter at the corners of his lips, in his beard. 'Do you really think the woman you lost from your car could have been Imelda Conroy?'

He was never going to let her forget it.

She said, 'I've only seen the photo you showed me, which is a professional shot, and I don't know if it's the same woman. She was terrified and crying with her hair over her face most of the time. It's possible it was her but I wouldn't swear to it.' She shook her head at her own contradictions. 'I honestly don't know.'

He wiped his mouth with the back of his hand and took a gulp of tea. 'About this Assumpta that Mickey Fox mentioned. We found a record of a nun who was at SOF. Assumpta Feeney. She was early twenties back then so must be in her fifties now. She left the order and studied as a nurse before going to Australia. She returned to Ireland a year ago. She's not at her address in Galway city, and no one has seen her in a week.'

'Maybe she's the woman I found at the convent.'

'Don't know, do I? I didn't see her and I didn't lose her.'

She bristled, then decided not to let it bother her. If she was in Mooney's position, she'd be caustic too. 'Have you any more information on this Assumpta Feeney?'

'Nothing to interest you, and I shouldn't be telling you about her anyhow.'

'But you are. Why?'

'I got a bollocking from my super. Told me Councillor Wilson is on the phone to him twenty-four/seven demanding this be solved immediately. Talking more shite about the damage it's doing to tourism in the area. Pfft.' He blew out his cheeks, cartoon-like, and crumbs lodged in his short beard.

'You seem to be a one-man band, Sergeant Mooney.'

'I've a full team working round the clock, but the thing is, we aren't getting anywhere.'

'Any word on what Mickey Fox was burning in the barrel?'

'Not yet. It will take time, but we might never know, and anyhow it might have nothing to do with anything.'

'If I hadn't left him... if I'd stayed with him, he might be alive now.'

'You're lucky you didn't stay, or I could be investigating your murder too.'

That sentiment sobered her. 'I need to find that woman—'

'Stop right there.' Mooney wagged a finger at her and she bit down a retort. '*You* don't need to do anything. This is my case and you are to stay away from it. I should never have confided in you in the first place.'

'But you did.'

'Much to my consternation.' He picked at his teeth with a fingernail. He was reminding her more of Kirby with each passing moment. All he needed was a paunch and a cigar. She realised then that she missed Kirby, missed her team and the buzz of being in the middle of an investigation, rather than being on the outside looking in. Mooney continued, 'Where's this ruin you mentioned?'

'I have to tell you something. You're not going to be happy.'

'I haven't been happy since I met you.'

'Bryan brought this back from there.' She laid the blue cloth wrapped in cling film on the table. 'He also says he handled the board with blood on it. You'll need to swab him for DNA and fingerprints.'

'Very opportune of him to touch all this. For fuck's sake. Where is he? Hope you didn't lose him too.'

'Don't even start.'

'I'm bringing him in for questioning.'

She shook her head slowly in an attempt to distil the swirl of emotions rising in her chest. She didn't want to get Bryan in trouble, but she had an awful feeling he was landing himself in it head-first. 'He's outside waiting for us.'

39

Councillor Denis Wilson liked to project an image that warned people he was not someone to be messed with. Image was everything in his line of business.

He was tall and slim, his neat hair feathered with grey, and he was vain enough to dye it, but not yet. Fine-boned, and handsome – this he'd heard muttered in bars when he bought the pub a drink. Slick-suited, he normally wore navy or grey, though for a funeral he wore ebony black, always dry-cleaned and with impeccable creases.

High-profile was the name of the game. He insisted on wearing a red cravat with everything, even though his advisers told him it distanced him from the ordinary people. The ordinary people had voted for him to become a councillor, so he knew his cravat didn't make a blind bit of difference. Getting potholes filled, that was what they wanted. And grants for lights and community groups. Hedges cut and roads surfaced. All that parochial shit. A necessary evil he had to endure for now. His focus was set on the bigger picture. He was going to go far in politics and relished the day he'd leave potholes behind for ever.

The murder of the unidentified woman in Connemara was

a blessing for him. It gave him a platform with the wider media. At first he praised the competence of the local gardaí and expressed his faith in them. Now he was switching his stance to criticism of the cutbacks and how they were impacting rural forces. A soapbox ready made for him. And he was grabbing it with both hands. No one was going to stop him now. No one would dare stand in his way. And that Mooney detective bloke better get his finger out and do a bit of work. Wilson phoned the superintendent again. Keep the pressure on, because he could not let this opportunity slip through his fingers; no bungling rural guard was going to fuck it up.

He took off his red cravat and selected a similar one from the drawer.

'It's the same as the other one,' said a voice from behind him.

'Oh, I know it looks the same but I like the feel of this one better.' He'd almost forgotten about the other thing that could fuck everything up for him. His wife.

'Don't worry about it, darling,' she said. 'You wear what makes you comfortable.'

'You know I always do.' He hadn't meant to sound sarcastic, but the undertone told her that he didn't need her input. And he didn't like it when she called him *darling*.

'Do you want me to come with you to that gallery opening this evening? I can be ready in no time.'

Dear God in heaven, fuck no, he swore silently in his head. That was all he needed. 'I thought you had your book club this evening?'

'I can cancel. The ladies won't mind.'

But I do, he thought. 'It's okay. I'll manage just fine. My advisers will make sure I don't put a foot wrong.'

'Or a word wrong,' she said.

He caught her image behind him in the mirror. She had that look, that half-smile that wasn't a smile at all. He could never get to the bottom of what really made her who she was, because he sure as hell was failing in making her who he wanted her to be.

After the next general election, as soon as he was elected to government, he'd set the divorce in motion. She was a liability. And those with liabilities did not get to sit at cabinet.

40

Lottie lay on the bed beside Boyd. It had been a tiring, odd sort of day. It was too early for bed. She couldn't sleep. Not when her mind was working overtime.

'Want to talk?' She focused on the ceiling, fully aware that he was annoyed. She dreaded the conversation they needed to have.

'You have to leave this to the locals,' he said. 'It's getting messy.'

'You mean messy in that Bryan might be involved?'

Boyd leaned up on his elbow. 'He's not involved in any murders, even though Mooney brought him in earlier for a statement. But his past might have something to do with what's going on.'

She felt his eyes on her, but she continued to stare at the ceiling. 'He brought me out to the old ruin. The place where he lived as a boy. He had a family. A brother. A sister. He said she was put into the laundry. Can you believe the cruelty of that?'

'Oh God, that sounds horrific. Poor girl.'

Now she turned to him. 'What's more awful is that I don't think he even remembers her name. He never searched for her.

He doesn't know if she's dead or alive. Just like his girlfriend, Mary Elizabeth. How can someone be so damaged by their past that they bury it for decades?'

'Pot and kettle come to mind.'

She caught the grin in his words. 'I searched for my brother. All my life. And I found him.'

'I apologise.'

She plumped up the pillows and sat up. 'Are you sure you want your sister marrying someone that cold, that heartless?'

He turned quickly and sat up too. 'That's an awful character assassination you've just made. I thought you were on his side. Lottie, you know nothing about the man. You only met him a few days ago.'

'I know, but—'

'No buts. Don't ruin this for Grace.'

'I'm not going to ruin anything.' Was she, though? 'But I do think we should dig into your prospective brother-in-law a bit deeper. Mooney mentioned something, but didn't expand on it. I wonder—'

'Leave it. Stop.' He blew out his cheeks and she could feel the cold exasperation on his breath. 'He's a hard-working man, and he makes Grace happy. Allow him to continue to do so.'

'But what if he's involved in all this?' She wasn't going to tell Boyd that he'd changed his tune, but that was what it sounded like.

'Involved in all what? The murder of an unidentified woman in a holiday cottage? Or the murder of an old man who lived in a caravan in the middle of a forest? Or do you mean the disappearance of a mystery woman you claim you found wandering around an old convent?' His voice rose with each question. 'Which of those do you think Bryan is involved in?'

Throwing back the covers, she pulled on her jeans and tugged a hoodie over her head. 'You are impossible when you're like this,' she snapped.

'I reiterate, pot and kettle.'

'Oh, shut up. I'm going for a walk.'

'It's nearly dark out.'

'I'm a big girl. I'm not afraid of the dark.'

A furious rage bubbled beneath her skin, and she knew the only way to contain it was to escape. Otherwise she might just permanently damage her relationship with Boyd.

She left him sitting on the bed with a *what did I do now?* look on his face, and went out into the stillness of the night.

Hugging her arms around her body, Lottie walked over to the barn, then back again.

It was dark here at the edge of the world. Darker than in Ragmullin, where light pollution coloured the sky a shitty yellow. At her own house, located in the countryside by a lake, the moon often reflected off the water. Tonight, it wasn't yet high enough in the sky to sprinkle its magic dust over the land and sea, casting a light to follow. It was too dark. Like her mood.

The Atlantic Ocean, crisp and rowdy in the distance, sounded like the turmoil raging in her chest. Her opinion had changed over the last twenty-four hours. She wasn't sure if she trusted Bryan O'Shaughnessy. She had yet to be convinced about his true intentions, and she sensed that something sinister could be afoot.

God, she sounded like a character out of an Agatha Christie novel. If only she could enlist the help of a current-day Poirot to do some digging on her behalf. No way was Boyd going to help her out, and she understood that. Didn't she? Not really, if she was being honest. If it was her sister, she'd want to be sure the girl wasn't making a mistake.

Yes, she was worried for Grace Boyd. The young woman was an open book. Vulnerable, despite her best attempts to prove otherwise. Easy to manipulate. To take advantage of. To lie to. Lottie could not stand by and watch her be deceived.

She moved around the outside of the house. Leaning on a low stone wall, she gazed out into the dark void of unfamiliar land. Pulling out her phone, she made a call. It was answered straight away.

'Boss?'

'Kirby, how are you doing?'

'Up to my lugs. Good to hear from you. Amy spoke with Boyd earlier and he had a chat with Sergio. That lad is a dream of a child. He has helped Amy so much. You should see them every evening sitting at the table doing his homework.'

'Amy is doing his homework?'

'Nah,' he laughed, 'she's helping him. He's a bright spark, that boy.'

'Not a bit like his dad then.' She was half joking, half in earnest.

'Uh-oh. Trouble in paradise?'

She didn't reply to that. 'Kirby, can I ask you to do something on the quiet for me?'

'Sure, if I can.'

'It has to be between us two only.'

'Of course. Goes without saying.'

'This man Grace is marrying, Bryan O'Shaughnessy, can you run a background check on him?'

Kirby paused, silent for a moment. 'Does Boyd know about this?'

'No. I'm just worried... I don't want her to make a huge mistake.'

'Do you think she might be about to?'

'I'm not sure. Something is off. There's been a couple of murders here and—'

'I get the picture. Don't worry, I'll be discreet. I'll tread with tippy toes.'

She grinned at the image. No way could Kirby do that even if he tried. 'See what PULSE throws up anyhow. And send me a text when you have it done. I'll ring you when I can.'

'All very clandestine.'

'Clandestine? Jesus, Kirby, you swallow a dictionary?'

He coughed, and she kicked herself. She could almost see his cheeks burning. 'No, boss. Just listening to a few audiobooks Amy gave me. Anyhow, I better tuck this lad in. I'll let you know how I get on with PULSE.'

'Thanks. And remember to tell no one.'

'Mum's the word.' He laughed, then coughed again. She could hear the years of smoking in his lungs.

That sounded more like the Kirby she knew.

She is standing out there by the wall, talking on her phone, when I raise my head from my hiding place in the shadows. It felt like a good idea to keep an eye on the house. When this all started, I hadn't allowed for two detectives to be staying there, but it kind of makes everything a bit more exciting. The male cop's not a danger; he's probably making floral bouquets with his halfwit sister. I stifle a laugh. No, the real danger lies with the woman. She's even wheedled her way into the investigation. Interesting. Dangerous.

Things have gone a little awry. The old man wasn't part of the plan, but someone warned him, so needs must. Listening to Mickey Fox's skin sizzle was exhilarating. Even if I couldn't hang around for long, it was a genius idea. Opportune, too.

For the tall, wild-haired woman, it might be too risky to wait for an opportune moment. I have to plan carefully for her demise if she gets too close to the truth. A bath of boiling water might not be enough to put her down. Poisonous drain cleaner? Perhaps.

It needs to be thought through quickly. Things are taking on a pace that I hadn't anticipated. I need to be in control of the narrative. I thrive on control. Then I think of the other woman. A witness. She will have to meet the same fate as nosy Mickey, the sly old fox. I grin at this joke, and the exhilarating mood surfaces again.

Another glance across the field. The woman has finished her call and is heading back inside. No, not now. It's time to finish one task before beginning another.

41

Imelda Conroy believed... no, she *knew* she had been wrong.
Mistaken in everything she'd done and thought. After all her
work and scheming, she'd gone about it illogically, deviating
from her rough plan of action. The big reveal that she'd thought
would shake the system awake would have been nothing but a
damp squib compared to what had really gone on. No one, not
even her – particularly not her – could have predicted what had
happened. Her erroneous delving into the past had roused a
monster, someone more dangerous than she could ever have
imagined. And the worst of it – some of the worst of it – was of
her own making.

The pain had eased in her head, but she felt a scab beginning to form on her neck. She'd snagged her hair on a nail as
she'd run into the derelict house earlier. And as she tried to free
it, another nail had dug into the back of her neck. The bleeding
hadn't stopped for ages. She couldn't remember when she'd last
had a tetanus jab, but she had worse things to fear.

She shivered in her new hiding place. An old barn on an
abandoned farm that seemed to be situated at the end of the

world. It was perhaps five kilometres from the O'Shaughnessy place, and even more remote. The sea roared its anger in the distance as if it wished to swallow up part of the land.

She was bloodied and her clothing torn. Her spirit worn out but not yet broken. Was that how those girls had felt? Locked up through no fault of their own. Made to work in inhumane conditions. All to hide what the Church called a sin. Society had given its blessing by its silence.

Darkness enveloped her. Tonight there were few stars, and cloud seemed to have obliterated the moon. It was like being in a coffin. She sensed she was experiencing the same intense feeling those poor women had suffered when they'd been abandoned behind the doors of the laundries. Those monster convents had acted like coffins within which live bodies slowly decayed. Those who escaped were marked, stained by the experience.

Whose fault had it been? Really?

Not the girls' or their babies', definitely not.

Their families'? Maybe.

What about her own family? They must shoulder some of the blame. That was what she'd been trying to do. To mete out justice with her documentary. But someone else had their own idea of what justice should be, and she was suffering for it.

She'd been told a myriad of stories but she'd never really grasped the true story of her own birth. There were a lot of mixed-up tales. Of girls being locked in the convent, where they'd found comfort and strength in each other and forged a link that bound them for ever. There they'd also discovered degradation and humiliation. Discovered hate. And eventually, they'd discovered how to retaliate. Would Imelda ever get to confront the remains of her family with what they had done?

At the moment, she was consigned to her fate in a miserable, dark place.

She cried bitter tears of failure. By morning, she knew she

would once again be filled with hope. Like those who survived life in the convent with the Sisters of Forgiveness.

Hope kept you going.

Hope kept you alive.

But sometimes hope destroyed you.

42

THURSDAY

The morning light peeked through the thin curtains at around 6 a.m. Boyd was already up and had gone downstairs. Lottie hadn't heard him rise, such was the soundness of her sleep. She supposed it was because she'd offloaded some of her worry by asking Kirby to check out Bryan O'Shaughnessy. Boyd would be mad, but she felt no guilt. She could deal with him if he became incandescent because she needed to be sure about his future brother-in-law. After that, she would let love take its course, and all that shite.

Her phone blared as she stepped out of the shower. She wrapped a large towel around her body and sat on the bed.

'Mooney. Good morning. You're up early.'

'We got the DNA results for the dead woman at the cottage. It's Assumpta Feeney.'

'You're sure?' She tried to hide her surprise that he was once again confiding in her.

'Don't even go there.'

'Shit. Why was she murdered?'

'If I knew that at this stage, I'd be chief inspector.'

'Sorry. So according to Mickey Fox, she's linked to the convent. What about the other woman?' She qualified this by adding, 'The woman who fled my car.'

'It has to be Imelda Conroy. She had the cottage rented in her name, though the owner never met her. All online.'

'Have you got any DNA from my car to match to—'

'We got a preliminary result. And yes, there is some that matches to Imelda Conroy. We believe it's her DNA on the computer cable and phone charger that were left at the cottage. It's possible that she killed Assumpta and went into hiding or on the run.'

'I don't buy that. She told me she tried to warn Mickey Fox. God, it's all very confusing.'

'You're not wrong.'

'And why are you telling me all this?'

The silence dragged down the line like a vibration. She waited him out.

'I honestly don't know,' he said softly. 'Maybe I just want to share with someone who understands how an investigation develops. Someone who is on the outside looking in.'

'I get that.' She thought of her call to Kirby last night. 'What can I do to help?'

'I don't want you involved, but I'd appreciate if you could try getting more out of O'Shaughnessy. He wasn't saying much yesterday when I brought him in. He said he knows nothing about any murders, but he did consent to a DNA swab and fingerprinting. That was something at least. It's gone into the system and I'm awaiting the results.'

'Surely you don't think he is a killer?'

'He could be. His DNA will tell a tale.'

'He told me he lifted up that piece of timber at the ruin. There will be transference on it.'

'I know all that. Yeah. But what if he was at the cottage where Assumpta Feeney's body was found?'

'Now that you've identified her, you need to backtrack, check out her movements. Why was she at the cottage? Had she something to tell Imelda? Or did Imelda draw her there. And where is Imelda? Did she kill Assumpta, but then what about Mickey Fox? And—'

'Yeah, yeah, my team is over all that. Anyhow, talk to O'Shaughnessy and see if you can learn more from him than I did.'

He ended the call before she could say anything else.

She shivered, tightened the damp towel around her and peered out at the beautiful day that had dawned.

She should feel happy and contented in this serene place.

All she felt was a growing sense of doom.

43

RAGMULLIN

Kirby was loath to get up. He rubbed his hand over his eyes, feeling the strain of working a major case without Lottie's steady hand to steer him. His sleep had been intermittent, and he'd felt Amy's elbow in his ribs more times than he could count. She was a restless sleeper too, but somehow managed to always wake up with a smile on her face. As he watched her get dressed in a light pink cotton summer dress, he thought there was a slight strain in her jaw, dark circles round her eyes.

'You doing okay, Ames?'

'Yeah, just a bit tired. You twisted and turned all night.'

'You too.'

'You kept waking me. Anyhow, doesn't matter. It will be a good day.' She zipped up the clunky boots she had to wear. Even though the weather was warm, since her accident these boots were the only footwear she could walk in. 'I'll get Sergio his breakfast and bring you up a cuppa before I drop him to school.'

'I love you, Amy.'

He put out his hand and she leaned in and kissed his cheek.

'What brought that on?' She smiled, and it gave him that warm feeling he could not explain to anyone.

'Well, I do love you. But the conversation I had with Lottie last night made me wonder about some people.'

'What do you mean?'

'It's all hush-hush. Confidential. She asked me to check out Grace Boyd's fiancé. Bryan O'Shaughnessy.'

'Are you serious? Their wedding is this week!'

'I know.'

'Bit late in the day to check him out.'

'Better late than never,' he said.

She leaned in for another peck, and as she left the room, he thought her brow was furrowed deeper than he'd seen it in a while.

He felt a frown crease his own forehead. He had no idea how to advance the investigation into the murder of Edie Butler. A picture of her life was developing as they delved deeper. All so sad. He felt immense sorrow for her, and for her sons' loss. Edie had been an inoffensive woman, working hard, providing for her boys. A typical good mother. Why had she been murdered? He felt there was a story behind her life he had yet to uncover. He could not fathom it out. Plus, there'd been no sightings of Robert Hayes. It was all a dead end.

He should have discussed it with Lottie.

44

CONNEMARA

After she'd pulled on her jeans, Lottie searched her suitcase for a clean top. She hadn't packed enough clothes for the week. She'd ask Grace if she could do some laundry later. She went to Boyd's suitcase and found it empty. Of course. She opened the old pine wardrobe. His clothing was neatly hung. She selected a black M&S T-shirt and slipped it over her head. It would do. Clean. Smelled good. Her trainers would be grand once she gave them a rub of a cloth. Feck it. She put them on and stood.

A sharp knock on the door.

'Come in.'

Grace plunged into the room in that awkward way she had about her. Hair at the nape of her neck neatly tied with a pink ribbon. Black trousers with an ironed seam, and an immaculate white shirt that cast Lottie in the poor-relation category. She wasn't even related, but anyhow. She was in awe at how Grace seemed transformed in her natural environment. So different from how she came across whenever she visited Boyd in Ragmullin. Which wasn't often, she had to admit.

'We need to talk.' Grace's face was severe today, lined, with downturned lips. Her eyes, though, were burning embers.

'Sure.' Lottie sat on the bed and tapped the spot beside her.

Grace wrinkled her nose, childlike.

'Ugh. You and Mark slept in that bed. I'm not sitting there. I will stand, thank you very much.'

Now Lottie was sorry she'd sat down. Boyd's sister towered over her like a doomsday shadow.

'What can I do for you?' Jesus, she sounded too officious. She had to rescue this. 'Is there something wrong, Grace?'

'You need to stop interfering in my life.'

'I haven't interfered in anything.' Oh, shit.

'You're telling lies and it does not surprise me. Not one little bit.'

'What do you mean?' She had an urge to stand, but she sat on her hands – just in case.

'You're interfering in that murder business. And you're trying to break up myself and Bryan.'

'Gosh, no, Grace, I'm not trying to do anything of the sort.'

'Sure you are. Making out like Bryan did something wrong. Spouting lies about him to that detective sergeant, the Mooney man. You have to stop. And stop it immediately.'

Now Lottie did stand. No way was she going to take this tirade sitting down. Grace might be Boyd's sister, but Lottie had done nothing wrong, so why should she take the blame? And then she wondered, why was Grace blaming her?

'Grace, you need to speak with Bryan.'

'I have done. And I believe him.'

'Believe what?'

'That he asked you to check something out for him, and the next thing he knows is that detective had him in Galway Garda HQ making a statement and taking his fingerprints.'

'I think there's a few gaps in that story that Bryan needs to fill in for you.'

'It's not a story, it's the truth, and I believe him, not you.'

'Then you need to rethink what he told you.'

Grace raised an eyebrow. 'Are you being smart with me?'

'No, I'm being truthful.' Lottie made to approach the other woman, but the fire in Grace's eyes halted her. 'Listen, Grace, I don't want you making a huge mistake. This—'

'Don't you dare treat me like a child.' Grace stamped her foot, exactly like a child would do. 'I am a grown woman and I can make my own choices. If they're wrong, it's my funeral.'

Lottie grimaced at her choice of words. 'Okay. But I didn't do anything to hinder your wedding. Bryan asked me to look into something from his past. That's all I was doing.'

'Look into what? He didn't mention anything in particular.'

So what *had* he mentioned? Lottie wondered. 'Talk to him again. He asked me to keep it private and I can't break his confidence.'

Grace seemed to physically pull in her horns. Her head and shoulders drooped, as did her mouth, a slight quiver trembling her lips. Uncertain, maybe? Then she raised her head and took a step towards Lottie, regrouping, wagging her finger in the air.

'I don't need you snooping around behind my back, Lottie Parker. And you can forget about us helping you and your family with somewhere to live in Ragmullin with Mark. That deal is off the table.'

And then she was gone.

Lottie found Boyd drinking tea with Bryan and Grace in the kitchen. Awkward.

She poured a cup from the teapot. You could trot a mouse on it, she thought, then shivered at that image. She would have loved a cut of brown bread, but there didn't seem to be any left. Her stomach rumbled and she placed a hand there to quell it.

'I'm sorry,' she said.

'You should be,' Grace snapped, indignation seeping out of her pores.

'That's enough.' Bryan stood, mug in hand.

'Sit down,' Grace said, but he didn't. She glared at Lottie. 'You try to destroy everything that's good in life, so you do.'

'What do you mean?' Lottie looked at her, bewildered.

'You won't destroy me and Bryan.'

'I have no intention of doing any such thing.'

'Enough,' Bryan repeated hopelessly. He ran a hand through his greying mop of hair and held his empty mug hooked in one finger by his side. 'I don't want anyone falling out. I'll talk to you later, *mo ghrá*.'

'We talked last night,' Grace replied frostily.

'I know, but I need to tell you about something else.'

'Tell me now.' Her voice was laced with a touch of hysteria.

'Later. I've sheep to see to.' He put his mug in the sink, his shoulder brushing against Lottie as he passed.

She stared after him. Was that a signal for her to follow him outside? Did he want to talk to her? She felt Grace was angry enough at the moment without adding further fuel to that particular fire. Whatever Bryan wanted to say, it could wait.

She took a seat beside Boyd, raging that he hadn't stood up for her, and spoke to his sister. 'I'm sorry for any confusion I've caused. I had no intention of—'

'Whether you intended it or not,' Grace interrupted, 'I am properly confused.'

Boyd took his sister's hand in his own. 'Bryan asked Lottie to look into an event from his past, when he was a teenager. I don't think it's up to her to tell you about it. It's up to him.'

She snapped her hand out of his. 'Might have known you'd abandon your own sister in her hour of need.'

Lottie thought it was Bryan who had abandoned his sister, and his girlfriend, years ago, by not searching for them, but before she could retort, she caught Boyd's eye. He was trying to defuse the situation and didn't need her making it worse.

'I love you, little sis,' he said. 'I will always look out for you, but this thing, whatever it is, is between you and Bryan.'

Folding her arms petulantly, Grace sniffed and said, 'I'm calling off the wedding.'

Before she could utter another word, the door burst open and Bryan ducked into the kitchen. 'Mooney is outside. Plus a squad car.'

'Is it me he wants?' Lottie asked, rising.

'No, it's me.'

Shit and fan came to mind as she followed him outside.

45

They took Bryan away without any explanation. He went quietly. A quick arrest for questioning only, Mooney had said. No cuffs. Bryan claimed he'd done nothing wrong.

'Get a solicitor,' Lottie whispered in his ear as he grabbed a jacket from the back of the door. 'Say nothing until they join you.'

'Can you help me?' he'd asked.

'I don't know. I'll talk to Mooney later.'

When the commotion had died down and Boyd had brought a sobbing Grace to the living room to console her, Lottie mulled over her earlier phone conversation with the sergeant. He must have got a DNA hit. So what? Bryan had admitted to lifting the board at the ruins, so that wouldn't warrant him being taken in for more questioning. It had to be something else.

Damn. She hated not knowing. Or only knowing some of it. She wasn't sure which was worse.

Her phone buzzed in her pocket. She checked the caller ID, then scanned the room to make sure Boyd and Grace had definitely left her alone before answering.

'Morning, Kirby. What have you got for me?'

He was slightly breathless. Probably after puffing on a cigar.

'Sorry, boss, I haven't looked at that yet,' he said. 'I wanted to run something by you.'

'Fire ahead.' Anything was better than mulling over Bryan O'Shaughnessy and his irritable bride-to-be. She'd love a cigarette, but she pushed that thought away. She hadn't smoked in ages.

'Have you seen the news this week?' he asked.

'Not really. I'm out in the arsehole of nowhere, supposed to be on a break from work.' She'd been too distracted to listen or watch the news. 'There's been a couple of murders around here, so it feels like a busman's holiday, if I'm honest.'

Kirby laughed. 'Why does that not surprise me? I'd say you've inveigled your way into the investigations.'

She felt a grin creep onto her face. 'You know me too well. Unofficially, I'm giving them my tuppence worth.'

'I'd like to tap into that tuppence worth if you don't mind.'

'What's up?'

She listened while he explained about the discovery of Edie Butler's body in the river. Her post-mortem, which indicated she'd been bound and brutally scalded. That toxicology results were being awaited.

'Jesus, that's almost as grotesque as the first murder here. A woman was scalded with kettles of boiling water.'

'What the fuck is wrong with people in today's world?' Kirby spluttered.

'If we could answer that question, we'd be millionaires. How can I help you?'

'I think I just wanted to speak to someone outside of the investigation. Someone with experience. I'm not used to this running-a-team lark.'

'Is Sam McKeown giving you grief?'

'Of course he is. But anyhow, the guy that Edie had been

seeing, he's a chef in town here, so he is, and he seems to have disappeared.'

'Disappeared? Was he a suspect or a witness?'

'Not sure he's anything yet. But why did he make a run for it? He knew the victim. He's not on PULSE, so he hasn't come to our attention before. The thing is, he said he originally worked in Galway and that's where he first met Edie, years ago.'

'Oh, and you thought I could search for him around here?'

'No. Yes. I don't know, boss. He might have gone back there.'

'What's his name?'

'Robert Hayes.' And then he told her more about the missing chef.

She finished the call just as Boyd returned to the kitchen.

'Who was that?' he asked.

'Kirby.'

'Is he missing you?'

'He has a murder case. Another gruesome one, by the sound of it.'

'Another?'

'There's two here, and he has one in Ragmullin. The circumstances seem similar. I'm wondering if they could be connected.'

'How could they be connected?'

'I don't know. But Kirby told me about a guy who's missing from Ragmullin. He knew the victim there and he originally met her years ago in Galway. He's a chef by the name of Robert Hayes.' She hesitated, wondering at the absurdity of what she was about to say. 'I think maybe he should be looked at in connection to the murders here.'

Boyd shook his head. 'You can't fix everything. I know you

try, but it's not good for you. Nor for us. And I'm not saying that to be selfish. I worry about you.'

'I know all that, but when someone presents me with a mystery, I have to at least attempt to solve it.' She tried not to look defeated. She had to accept that Boyd was only concerned for her. Putting her best interests first. Or his own?

'Run it by Mooney,' he said, relenting.

With his change in direction, she began to doubt it was the right move. 'I don't know. Kirby already has a nationwide alert issued for this Robert Hayes. I might be making links where there are none.'

'What does Kirby expect you to do? You're on leave this week.' He grinned at her. 'Or as much on leave as you can be when you're not poking your nose in where it's not wanted.'

'I take offence at that comment, Mark Boyd.' She smiled, knowing he was joking while also being truthful. In a way, she was glad that even with everything going on, he seemed more relaxed than he had been in a long time. More relaxed than she was, which, come to think of it, wouldn't be hard.

'I know you well, Lottie. You're loving every minute of it.'

'Two people have been murdered here in Connemara and I take no joy in that. I just relish the challenge of walking in the footsteps of a killer and tripping them up. I miss that buzz when I'm not working.'

'Do you seek out these weirdos, or do they follow you around?'

'Shut up.' She smacked his arm playfully, then took his hand. 'We need to find out what Mooney has on Bryan.'

'I can't get involved. I'm too close to the situation, because of Grace. Talk to Mooney if you think you'll get anything out of him. Then leave it up to him. I really don't want you being involved at all. Keep your distance.'

'I'll try,' she agreed. 'How is Grace?'

'Distraught. I sent her back to bed to rest. Which reminds me. She wants a cup of cocoa.'

'Do people still drink that?'

'Grace does.'

'Doesn't surprise me in the least. Will you make it for her? I'll head into Galway and try to find out what Mooney is up to.'

'You've no car, and I might need mine.'

Catching sight of Bryan's keys on a hook by the door, she smiled. 'I've always wanted to drive a Range Rover.'

46

Bryan O'Shaughnessy wasn't afraid of being arrested for murder. There was no way they could charge him because they had no evidence that he'd done anything wrong. Or had they? He'd been upfront with them and admitted his fingerprints were on the piece of timber found at the old homestead. He had a legitimate excuse because how was he to know that picking it up could land him back in the station to be grilled. He had nothing to worry about. Everything had an explanation.

'Mr O'Shaughnessy,' Mooney said, and sat down opposite him, slapping a thin file on the table.

'I'm waiting for my solicitor.'

'That's your prerogative. I'll just get things started while we wait.' He studied the buttons on a recording machine.

Bryan wondered if this was allowed, but he wasn't informed enough to object.

'Who is your solicitor?' Mooney asked.

'A firm called Ward and Gavin. Not sure who they'll send.' They'd rejigged his will late last year when he'd decided to marry Grace. That was the only reason their name was to the forefront of his mind when he had to make the call.

'You'll probably get Norah Ward. She's like a bulldog.' Mooney must have caught Bryan's amazed look, because he tugged at his beard and added, 'Not in looks, I mean. She's a fighter. She'll fight your corner. That's all I mean.'

Bryan couldn't help smiling. Good to have the detective rattled before they began.

The door opened and in walked a young, petite woman. Hair scraped back from her face, dressed in a black skirt suit with a red power blouse beneath. She slapped a new-looking brown leather tote bag on the table and extracted a yellow pad along with a silver-coated Cross pen. Bryan almost groaned. She looked like she'd just finished secondary school.

'I hope you haven't been interrogating my client in my absence.' Her voice was strong and sharp. Perhaps he needed to revise his opinion, which he'd based solely on her appearance.

'I'd never contemplate doing such a thing,' Mooney said. 'Welcome, Norah.'

She threw him a look that told him she knew he had no more welcome for her than a storm at sea.

'Proceed,' she said.

While Mooney did the tape introductions, Bryan studied his solicitor. They hadn't met before, had never spoken. How could she represent him?

'Mr O'Shaughnessy has not been charged with any crime yet,' Mooney said. 'But I do have a few questions for him.'

'Why arrest him, then?' Norah asked.

'He was already in for questioning yesterday, and rather than him becoming a flight risk, I arrested him this morning.'

'Arrested him for what exactly?'

'We suspect he was involved in the murder of Assumpta Feeney.'

'What?' Bryan said. 'That's ridiculous.'

'The royal *we*? What evidence do you have?' Norah was more like a terrier than a bulldog, Bryan decided.

'DNA,' Mooney said.

'How did you get my client's DNA?'

'He voluntarily provided it, along with his fingerprints, yesterday evening.'

She seemed to be working hard not to glare at Bryan. 'What reason did you have for requesting that from my client, Detective Sergeant Mooney?'

'Mr O'Shaughnessy told us he'd handled a plank of timber that had blood on it. It was found on his property. It may have been used in an assault.'

'Is this the property where the Feeney woman was murdered?'

'No, she was found dead at a holiday cottage a few miles away. The board was discovered at an old ruin of a house on Mr O'Shaughnessy's land.'

'Hmm.' Norah tapped her chin with her shiny pen. 'What is the relevance of that piece of timber to the murder at a different location?'

'We have not established a connection yet. But it will be relevant. Can I ask my questions now, Ms Ward?'

'I'm not stopping you.'

Mooney exhaled loudly, puffing out his cheeks. He outlined the discovery of the body at the holiday cottage and how they had identified Assumpta Feeney. 'Her DNA was on PULSE. She'd been involved in a minor demonstration in January where a guard was injured. The lab was able to make the match. We are attempting to trace her relatives, if she has any. She was aged fifty-five and lived in Galway.' He opened his file and flicked through a few pages before extracting one. He slid it over the table.

'What's this?' Bryan asked.

'A DNA profile.'

'What has that got to do with me?' He felt Norah tap his arm and turned to her.

She whispered, 'No comment. That's your answer to everything.'

'Good question, Mr O'Shaughnessy,' Mooney said, ignoring the fact that he'd heard the solicitor's instruction. 'I thought you might be able to tell me what it has to do with you.'

Bryan shrugged.

Mooney sighed. 'Okay. I'll tell you what it is.' He indicated the page. 'We found this DNA profile at the holiday cottage. It's a match for you.'

'Sure didn't I help renovate that place a few years ago.'

'No comment,' Norah hissed between her teeth.

The smile on Mooney's face told Bryan he'd made a mistake.

'You told me yesterday when we had our chat that you'd never set foot in it.'

'You misunderstood me. I was talking about recently.'

'Will you stay quiet? Please?' Norah said, like an irritated schoolteacher.

'Ah sure, let the man speak,' Mooney drawled. 'We might get to the bottom of this "misunderstanding" quicker.'

'My client has explained he was in that cottage at some stage.'

'Okay, let's say I accept that. Now look at this.' He slid a second page across the table. 'This is another DNA profile taken at the scene.'

'Go on,' Norah said, and bit the inside of her lip. Bryan was beginning to think she was sorry she'd been landed with him.

'It belongs to a woman called Imelda Conroy. The documentary-maker who was in Galway doing some sort of thing about the laundries.'

'And?'

'And she rented the holiday cottage.'

'What has this got to do with my client?'

Pushing the two sheets of paper side by side, Mooney then

laid a third on top. 'Our preliminary analysis shows that Imelda Conroy and Bryan O'Shaughnessy may be related.'

Bryan felt his jaw drop and forgot all about his solicitor's instructions to keep his mouth shut.

'What the hell are you saying? That's totally untrue. I don't know the woman. I don't know either woman.' He felt such a surge of anger that he couldn't stop himself lunging across the table at Mooney. 'You're a fucking bollox. You're making this up. Trying to frame me.'

He sat back down at Norah's insistence. Luckily Mooney had leaned back and no contact was made, but Bryan caught sight of the flashing red light up high on the wall in the corner. He was on camera. Shit.

'DNA does not lie,' Mooney said, calm as you like.

'What sort of relative are you talking about here?' Norah asked, and Bryan noticed some of her stern composure slipping away.

'Could be father and daughter. Brother and sister. The lab is carrying out further analysis as we speak. So, Mr O'Shaughnessy, tell me this. Where is Imelda Conroy?'

'How would I know?' His mind was a riot of questions. One kept leaping to the forefront. Could Imelda be his and Mary Elizabeth's child? 'What age is this Imelda?'

Mooney ignored the question. 'We extracted DNA from the blood on the piece of timber, the one you handled. It's a match for Ms Conroy.'

'How did you determine her DNA?' Norah asked.

'I don't have to answer that, but I will.' Mooney folded his arms. 'We initially got DNA from a laptop cable and a phone charger at the cottage. Then we extracted some from clothing left in a rucksack with her name on it. Mr O'Shaughnessy, where is Imelda Conroy?'

Bryan was speechless. He felt a nudge on his elbow from his solicitor. He turned to look at her and read her lips.

'No comment.'

'Have you enough to arrest my client?' she asked.

'I would like a confession.'

'You're not getting one.'

'Then I want time to build a case. I can hold Mr O'Shaughnessy for twenty-four hours. I can also ask my superintendent to extend that time. Okay?'

'No, it's not okay,' Bryan blurted. 'I only met Imelda Conroy the one time, when she wanted to interview me about the laundries.'

'And why would she want to interview you?'

Time to take his solicitor's advice. 'No comment.'

'Right then, Ms Ward, your client will be taken to a cell. You can have ten minutes to talk to him before then.' Mooney spoke for the tape and switched off the machine.

The red light went out in the corner above his head and he left the room.

'Start talking,' Norah Ward said.

Bryan felt his mouth go dry, and all the words he might have wanted to utter disappeared.

47

They left Lottie sitting in the fancy Garda HQ reception area for twenty minutes before Mooney came out to her.

'I need a decent coffee,' he said. 'And air. Let's walk.'

They headed in silence to the hotel they'd been at before. He ordered coffee for them both, and they sat at a table by the large window. It would have been overlooking part of Galway Bay if the sweep of buildings across the road hadn't been there.

'Don't ask me anything about Bryan O'Shaughnessy,' he said. 'I'll be giving you the same bloody answer he's been giving me for the last half-hour.'

'It was a "no comment" interview then?'

'Here and there. What did you want to see me about?'

She waited for her coffee to cool, took a sip and set the cup back on the saucer. 'There was a murder in Ragmullin earlier this week.'

'Yes, I know. Awful business.'

'A man who knew the victim is now AWOL. Robert Hayes. He's a chef in a local Ragmullin eatery. The thing is, it's believed he was originally from Galway.'

'A lot of people are originally from Galway.'

'I'm trying to help you here.' She wouldn't rise to his sarcasm.

'And how can this help me, pray tell?'

'You're an arsehole, Mooney. You know what, forget it.' She stood.

'Sit down and drink your coffee. I apologise. I'm stressed and getting nowhere.'

'Bryan isn't a viable suspect, is he?'

'Nice try.'

'Can't blame me for that.' She sat back down.

'Tell me more about this Ragmullin chef.' He sipped his coffee. Froth lingered on his moustache.

'As I said, he's from Galway...' She paused, trying to think what Kirby had told her. 'Or maybe he just worked here at one stage. I thought he might be worth looking into.'

'Any more details that I should be aware of?'

'I can ask Detective Kirby to talk to you. You might also need to compare the MO of the Ragmullin murder with those in Connemara.'

Mooney slurped his coffee, wiped his bearded chin and leaned back in the chair. 'Okay, but I'm up to my lugs, so I can't spare anyone to look for this Galway chef.'

'Just ask around. Someone might remember him.'

'I know there's been an alert issued for him, and I'd have heard if anyone remembered him.'

'But you and your team have been up to ninety with the murders here. It might have slipped under the radar. Robert Hayes might have too.'

'Okay, okay. I'll talk to your detective. What's he called again?

'Larry Kirby. Thanks. About Bryan...'

'Don't go there.'

'I figure you must be keeping him a bit longer. I hope he's secured a good solicitor.'

'He got a fucking bulldog.'

Lottie laughed. She knew exactly what Mooney meant. She was glad for Bryan and fully expected him to be released without charge before long.

After Norah Ward left him to go fight his corner with the custody sergeant, Bryan leaned his head against the cold wall of his cell. He wondered how he'd get out of this mess. He had to hope his solicitor would help. Why hadn't he remembered the crucial bit of information the first time? Of course he'd been in the holiday cottage. A few years ago. That's why he'd forgotten. Helping a friend to paint a room and move in a few sticks of furniture. Was his helpful nature about to be his undoing?

He thought of Grace and felt an immediate gush of sorrow for her. He didn't know how she would cope with all this. She was a good soul, a kind and gentle person. This – whatever it turned out to be – would have a detrimental effect on their relationship. He had to convince her that he was an innocent bystander. Then there was his past. He was not an innocent in all that. Lottie was right. He should have looked for his sister, and for Mary Elizabeth, all those years ago. A bit late in the day to try to right a wrong now. Look where it had got him.

He noted his stark surroundings while trying to avoid the thought of Imelda Conroy burning in his brain. This was not a good place to be for a man used to wide-open fields and the angry ocean crashing on the rocks. His sheep. God, they'd need to be fed. Would Grace remember? And then his poor dog, Tess, would be pining for him. He'd have to tell his solicitor to remind Grace about the sheep.

Thoughts of the solicitor brought him back to Mooney and the cavalier way he'd thrown the page with the DNA results on the table. He really had to think about Imelda Conroy. She was related to him. DNA didn't lie, did it? His mind was in turmoil. Could she actually be his daughter? The child of the girl he'd asked Lottie Parker to trace?

He recalled when Imelda had arrived on his doorstep. Afterwards he was glad that Grace had been at a fitting for her wedding dress that day. Or perhaps if she'd been there, he might not be in this mess. Would she have been more probing with Imelda's questions than he had been? Or would she have sent the woman off with her tail between her legs and that would have been the end of it? He thought he knew Grace well, but apparently not well enough, because he had no idea what she'd have done.

Imelda had not given him any hint that they could be related. None of her questions were along that line. She'd talked mainly about Knockraw. He'd had no suspicions that she might have had an ulterior motive for speaking with him. With his loyal dog at his feet, he'd sat on the back wall with the young woman and answered her questions. That's what he'd tell Mooney when asked.

Enough of this 'no comment' shite.

He'd talk, but whether he'd be believed or not was debatable.

Whether he told the truth or not, that was also debatable.

48

When Mooney left the hotel to return to work, Lottie ordered another coffee. She scrolled through the bullet-point information Kirby had sent her about Robert Hayes. It included his old Galway address, which had yielded no result when the local guards had investigated it at Kirby's request.

No harm in having a second look. She finished her coffee, then used the bathroom. She caught a glimpse of her face in the mirror and was pleased to note that she looked a little healthier than usual. The Connemara sunshine was good for her. Or perhaps it was the sea breeze. Whatever it was, she knew she looked good, and that elevated her mood. It returned to sombre when she answered a call from Boyd.

'Grace is so upset,' he said. 'I know I told you that you can't fix everything, but is there any way you can get Bryan released?'

'I spoke with Mooney. I reckon they have something on him or they wouldn't still be holding him. Mooney wouldn't budge. But Bryan's got a good solicitor, so he should be out soon.'

She finished the call and made her way to Bryan's Range Rover. It had dried mud splattered on the doors, bonnet and tyres. The filthiest car she'd seen in a long time. She punched

Hayes's old address into Google Maps and made her way there. Slowly. Glaring sunshine blinding her. And traffic, damn traffic.

Robert Hayes had once lived out on the Moycullen Road according to Kirby's notes. Up a leafy hill and at the end of a row of old two-storey detached houses, she came to one that bordered a small stone church. She parked and checked it was the correct address. Yep.

Beside the solid wooden door was an old wrought-iron bell with a piece of rope attached. She pulled the rope and waited.

A stooped, grey-haired woman who only came to Lottie's shoulder appeared, squinting against the blinding sunshine.

'You the police again?'

'Erm, I am, but—'

'Told the last lot and I'll tell you the same. He's not here. Been gone years. No point in asking me again. I can't change what's true.'

'Okay, Mrs...?'

'If you're police, you will know I've never been married. Gave my life to God's work. I'd like you to leave and not to be disturbing me again.' She made to shut over the door. Lottie put out a hand.

'I apologise. I'd like to talk to you. I'm Detective Inspector Lottie Parker, but I'm here on holidays, so I'm off duty. A friend asked me to look up Robert Hayes.' No harm in bending the truth a little.

'What friend would that be? Another cop?'

Lottie figured the woman watched too many US crime shows, but she was sharp. 'Would you mind if I came in? I could do with a glass of water. It's so hot outside.'

The woman laughed. 'Do you think I came down in the last shower? I'm not falling for that old trick. Say what you've come to say, then leave me in peace.'

'First off, I'd like to know your name.'

'Brigid Kelly. What do you want from me?'

'I want to know where I can find Robert.'

'Father Robert, you mean?'

That threw Lottie. Kirby's missing man was a priest? Why hadn't Mooney told her? Shit. 'Erm, yes, Father Robert.'

'He hasn't been around in a long, long time. Father Phillip Lyons is here now. But he's been in Lourdes the last few days. What else do you want to know?'

Lottie still felt like she'd been smacked. Robert Hayes was a priest. Or used to be one. Jesus. 'When did Robert leave the priesthood?'

The woman wrinkled her nose in distaste. 'He didn't leave. The bishop kicked him to kingdom come. And good riddance to bad rubbish, I always say. I reckon he must have dirtied his bib again, otherwise I wouldn't have the guards calling to me after all this time, would I?'

'What did he do?'

'You are a nosy one.' The woman shielded her eyes and appraised Lottie. Seemingly not finding any threat – or maybe she felt sorry for her – she said, 'Come in. I didn't tell the others much, because they seemed satisfied with the little I gave them. But I kind of like the look of you. You're smart. Come on. We can go to the kitchen if you don't mind watching me peel a few spuds.'

'I can help, if you'd like?'

'I'd like that very much.' The woman held up her curved hands. 'Arthritis is a curse.'

49

The kitchen was smaller than Lottie had been expecting. She had an image in her mind of what a priest's housekeeper's domain might look like. This tiny cramped room didn't cut it. It smelled of lemon, which she figured was used to dampen down unpleasant odours.

She wondered how many kitchens she'd been in over the course of her career. Too many. Delivering bad news. Interviewing family members. Arresting suspects. Interfering in people's privacy, their past, their future. Upending everyday lives. Part of the job. But today she wasn't on the job, and she felt a slight tinge of guilt for disturbing the arthritic housekeeper.

'I've been keeping house for priests for nigh on... well over thirty-five years. I worked in another parish before here. I know I must look eighty to a young one like you, but I'm in my sixties, as far as I know.' She gave a wry laugh. 'I've had a hard life. And my arthritis is chronic.' Brigid thrust a small black-handled knife towards Lottie. 'This here is the knife I use for peeling the spuds. I can't manage those scraper yokes. Not that I can manage this too well either.'

Lottie took the knife and squeezed her way towards the work counter in silence. A red plastic basin with a few small potatoes sat in the sink. A saucepan on the draining board held two already peeled potatoes. She was stunned to think Brigid might only be in her sixties. The woman had the body and demeanour of a much older woman. A hard life did that? Or a cruel one? She summoned up her voice. 'How many more will I peel?'

'Whatever fits in that pot. Only myself here for dinner today. Father Lyons is home tomorrow.'

'Take a seat, Brigid, and when I've these finished, I'll make you a cuppa.'

'I'm not an invalid, you know.'

'I know, but there's not much room for the two of us to stand here.'

'The kitchen used to be bigger, but Father Lyons got builders in to divide it. He wanted a separate dining area. For who or what, only God himself knows, because no one uses it and the place was fine the way it was. Men.'

Lottie smiled, keeping her back to her. 'Has Father Lyons been here long?'

'Must be fifteen years or more. Due a move soon.'

'And Robert, Father Robert. How long was he here?'

'Probably for around the same length of time. But my old brain isn't what it used to be.'

'Before that, where was he based?' She took her time peeling the potatoes, now that she had Brigid talking.

'He was out in the field. That's what he used to call it.'

'Oh, what does that mean?' She took a quick look over her shoulder.

'He was a chaplain to the Sisters of Forgiveness. He was a young man then. Oh, he was also chaplain at Knockraw at the same time.'

'Really?' Lottie scraped her thumb with the knife in shock.

Shit. She kept peeling. Slowly. Concentrating on the words as well as the knife. Brigid's revelation connected Robert Hayes to the murders in Galway, albeit historically. A man who was also Kirby's suspect. 'How did that work out for him?'

'You ask a lot of questions.'

'Nature of my job.'

'Well, I don't think I'm telling tales, because if you ask anyone from that era they will tell you the exact same. Folks around here weren't one bit pleased when he moved in as parish priest. Lock up your daughters and sons became the mantra. Mass numbers dropped off. The bishop left him here for too many years. Probably didn't know what else to do with him. Father Lyons is a breath of fresh air. We'll be sad to lose him, when he's moved on.'

Lottie dropped the last of the potatoes into the pot and turned around, drying her hands on a tea cloth. 'I'm assuming from what you've implied that there were rumours about Robert's time at Knockraw and the convent. Can you tell me about them?'

'I don't like to gossip, but...' Brigid blessed herself, as if asking forgiveness for what she was about to say, 'it's said that he interfered with the youngsters.'

Sitting on a wooden chair, Lottie folded the cloth onto the table. 'And he was allowed into a parish after that?'

'They were only rumours. I never heard any hard facts. But there's hardly smoke without fire, is there? He did something bad. Mark my words.'

Wondering how she could elicit more information, she said, 'Both the convent and the industrial school closed down. Where did their records end up?'

Brigid shook her head. 'You'll discover nothing in them, even if you find them. I'm a good Catholic, a God-fearing woman, but I can tell you this with absolute certainty: if there was anything untoward in those records, it's not there now.'

'Even so, where could I have a look at them?'

'You might want to talk to the bishop.'

Lottie had had previous dealings with bishops, so she was inclined to believe that there was no use searching the records. 'Why did Robert leave the priesthood?'

'I told you, he had to leave. Complaints were made, by some of the parishioners whose kids went to the youth club he ran. Inappropriate behaviour, I heard. I think the bishop persuaded the parents not to make a formal complaint to the guards once he agreed to get rid of Father Robert.'

'Where did Robert go after that?'

'No idea. And I can tell you this, I don't want to know.'

'Was he good at cooking?'

Brigid raised an eyebrow as if asking how she knew that. 'Couldn't get him out of the kitchen. Always asking me to buy fancy veg, stuff I'd never heard tell of. Concoctions, I called what he cooked. Tasty, I have to admit, but I never told him that. The kitchen's my domain. And he invaded it.'

'You were glad when he left, then?'

'I was, and I'll be more glad when you boil the kettle for my cup of tea. There's a fruit loaf in the cupboard and butter in the fridge.'

Lottie set to work and laid the table. Brigid's face appeared grey and drained, as if talking about Robert Hayes had sucked the life out of her.

'How did you come to work as the housekeeper here?'

'I was born in the laundry. My poor mother was raped by some bastard – that's the story I heard from the nuns, which may or may not be true.' Brigid blessed herself. 'What is true is that she worked herself to the bone in that horrible place. Fought tooth and nail so that I wouldn't be taken off her. She died in there. I don't even know where they buried her. The nuns made me cook and wash and sew for them. Eventually they sent me to work for parish priests. Housekeeping's the only job I've ever known.' A solitary tear escaped her eye and tracked a lonely trail down the crevices in her drawn face. 'She was a good woman, my mother, and the nuns treated her like a criminal.'

Lottie poured the tea. 'And still you have your faith. How do you do that?'

'I have nothing else. I used to pray to be saved, to have a life. That didn't happen. Now, I pray for all sinners, especially those bitches who professed to be daughters of God, sisters of forgiveness. Give me strength. They were hard and mean and cruel. I often wonder if that's how they were brought up. If they knew no different. But then I think, evil like that lives in the soul. It's rooted there by the long claws of Satan. I was one of the lucky ones.'

'Brigid, I wouldn't call what happened to you and your mother lucky. I think it was cruel.'

'Worse fates befell children in those places. No, I was lucky, but my mother wasn't. They called her names. Those upright religious bigots said she was a whore and a sinner. No mention of the man who got her pregnant. Was he absolved of his sin? The sin of impregnating a teenager? What about the sin of her parents for abandoning her in her hour of need? The sin of the nuns keeping her captive, working her as a slave in a laundry? No. My mother paid the price for others' sins.' She stopped, breathless, then sipped her tea.

Lottie knew Brigid was not the woman Bryan had asked her to find, but she still wanted to know more.

'What was your mother's name?' she asked.

'I only knew her by the name they gave her in the convent. They called her Paul.'

'You never found her grave?'

'No. They said she was buried in a pauper's grave, but they probably threw her in a septic tank, like they did all the little babbies over in Tuam. Unfortunate women didn't survive the hardship meted out.'

Lottie felt a deep sense of remorse and pain at the memory of what had happened to her own brother in such a place. 'Who were these people who treated humans so much worse than animals?' She discovered her voice was choked with tears. She put her hand on Brigid's. The woman squeezed hers back.

'Satan's brood,' she whispered. 'That's what they were. Each and every last one of them. Not a decent bone among them.'

'Do you know where any of the nuns are today?'

'Rotting in unmarked graves, I hope.'

'Can you recall any of their names?'

'They'd all be dead now.'

'The more recent ones, from Robert Hayes's time there?'

'You can ask him, if you find him.'

'I believe he became a chef and worked in Ragmullin for a time. A woman was murdered there this week and Robert has disappeared.'

'The other guards who called here mentioned something about that. What was the woman's name?'

'Edie Butler. She was a hairdresser in Ragmullin.'

Brigid's face drained of all colour.

'What is it? Do you want some water?' Lottie thought the older woman was about to pass out. 'Put your head between your knees.'

Brigid gave a strangled laugh. 'I would if I was able to.' Then she sobered. 'What do you know about Edie Butler?'

'A colleague is investigating her murder. He asked me to see if anyone could locate Robert Hayes. I don't have all the details, but I think he was her boyfriend at one stage. Other than that, I know very little about her.'

Brigid took a gulp of tea. 'I remember Edie from the laundry.'

Lottie felt her heart lurch. Edie's murder in Ragmullin must be connected to the two in Galway. Brigid was still talking.

'I was assigned to housekeeping in the convent and Edie was in the laundry. I remember her well. She was much younger than me. Her real name stood out when I first met her. Not many Edies in my time. They were all Marys, Anns, Ruths. Bible names, and the nuns gave saints' names to those whose own names they deemed not holy enough. There was one young lass they called Gabriel after the archangel. Poor little thing couldn't understand why she had to bear that name. They called Edie something like Joseph, or maybe James. Yes, I think she was called James. Dear God, do you think Robert killed her?'

'I don't know, Brigid, but one thing is certain. He has to be found.'

50

Lottie stayed on to fry a lamb chop, and when the potatoes were boiled, she mashed them with butter and milk, under Brigid's watchful eye. The older woman had been silent for a long time, and Lottie left her alone.

'Will you not have some yourself?' Brigid enquired when the plate was in front of her.

'No thanks,' Lottie said. 'I need to be getting back. But can I ask you a few more questions?'

'If you have to. I've not been so upset in a while. The memories...'

'I'm sorry.'

'Go ahead. Ask away.' Brigid dug into her dinner.

Lottie debated the order of her questions. She decided on asking the last one first. 'A man was murdered out in the woods behind the convent this week. Mickey Fox.'

'He was the gardener. They treated him badly too.'

'How so?'

Brigid took a sip of water, passing her cutlery to one hand.

'He tried to help. He once got a woman out the gate and was about to put her in his car when Father Robert appeared and chastised him and took the woman back inside. Mickey had got the lass a boat ticket to Liverpool. I don't think he chanced it again after that. And now he's dead? May he rest in peace.' She blessed herself, knife and fork still in her hand.

'A woman was found brutally murdered too, out at a holiday cottage in Connemara. You might have heard it on the news?'

'I try not to listen. All you hear is bad news. Father Lyons always has a radio on somewhere, and this week I've had such peace without the hum and noise. Who was this woman then?'

'Her name was Assumpta Feeney. I believe she used to be a nun at the convent at some stage. She would have been quite young.'

'Her name rings a bell, but I can't be sure.'

'What about Imelda Conroy?'

'Is she dead too?' Brigid scrunched up her eyes, brows knitting in the centre.

'I hope not. She was making a documentary about the laundries and the industrial school at Knockraw.' Lottie added the last bit even though she wasn't sure about it.

'I remember a young lassie being at the door a few weeks ago. All biz she was. Wanted to interview Father Lyons. He sent her packing. Don't think he'd have had any knowledge of that time. He's only in his late thirties.'

'Did this woman talk to you?'

'She didn't pay any attention to me at all.'

Lottie stood. 'This is my card in case you think of anything. I'm not on duty here, not my jurisdiction, but if you'd rather talk to me than the Galway guards, please contact me.'

Brigid took the card and propped it against the sugar bowl in the middle of the table. 'Of course I will. You're a good person.'

Lottie smiled. 'I'll rinse the pot and pan, and then I'll be off.'

'And you're a gem of a woman. The man that gets you will be lucky.'

'I don't think he feels too lucky at the moment. His sister is due to get married on Sunday.'

'Must be a civil ceremony if it's on a Sunday.'

'It is and her fiancé is currently in custody. The detective in charge thinks he might have had something to do with the murders.'

'Good God, that's terrible. Terrible altogether.' Brigid blessed herself. '*Did* he have anything to do with them?'

'I don't think so. But he was in Knockraw back in the day. He also got his girlfriend of the time pregnant. He believes she ended up in the laundry. His sister did too. He asked me to see if I could find them.' That wasn't strictly true. Bryan had only asked her to see if his girlfriend and the baby had survived and could be found.

'Any luck with that?'

'Not a bit.'

'What's his name?'

'Bryan O'Shaughnessy. He's a sheep farmer out in Connemara.' Lottie turned from the sink to see Brigid bless herself again. 'Are you okay?'

'May the Lord grant you strength.'

'Why do you say that?'

'The mission this O'Shaughnessy man has given you. It will be like searching through a den of iniquity.'

Lottie sat in Bryan's Range Rover for a good five minutes mulling over Brigid's words before she could bring herself to turn on the engine. Did she know more than she'd revealed? Would she be the type of woman to help a man who had been a priest? Not by the way she'd spoken of him, but then again, the power of the Catholic religion ran deep, especially in the older members of the community. Lottie sensed that no matter how

Brigid had been harmed by those in religious orders, she would not turn away a man of God.

She'd tell Mooney what the woman had said, then she needed to concentrate on the task Bryan had set her. To discover what had happened to Mary Elizabeth and the child she'd been carrying.

The records from the laundry were a good starting point, but it would be impossible to get her hands on them, even if they still existed. She had a feeling Imelda Conroy would have sourced them. So where were all Imelda's documents and recordings that she'd have used for her documentary? Nothing had been found in the holiday cottage as far as she knew. Had the person who'd killed Assumpta taken them, or had Imelda hidden them somewhere? And why was Assumpta in the cottage and not Imelda? Did Imelda kill her?

Then she realised that she'd never asked Brigid if she remembered a man being burned or scalded at the convent. Shit. She didn't fancy further disturbing the woman today. She'd call in again tomorrow.

A curtain twitched in the large bay window.

A soft mist started to fall. The windscreen clouded over and the parish house, shaded by the leafy trees, faded into the background as the curtain fell back in place.

51

By the time Lottie had navigated her way through the miserable misty rain over bog roads and arrived back at the house, Bryan was home.

'Mooney let you go, then?' She joined him in the living room with Boyd. No sign of Grace. 'Did he have any evidence at all? He arrested you, so there must have been something...' Her voice trailed off. Wait for him to talk, she told herself. He will tell you in his own time.

Bryan stoked the fire in the open grate and sparks flew out onto the wooden floor. He stamped them down with more force than was needed. Did they even need to have a fire lit? It wasn't her house. Not her call.

'He showed me some DNA results. Said they needed further analysis because of...' He laid down the poker and fell back into the well-worn leather armchair. 'What's the word?'

'An anomaly?'

'Could be that.'

He appeared to have aged in the few days since Lottie had arrived. The strain of being hauled in by Mooney? Or was it because of something he'd done? She didn't know what to think.

'Can you tell me about it?' she asked.

'It will probably be talked about as far away as Clifden by now, so you might as well know. Sit down.'

She took up a space beside Boyd on the couch. He sat ramrod straight and she figured he already knew what was about to be revealed to her. Bryan lit a cigarette. She hadn't seen him smoke before now and wondered if Grace knew about it. Probably not, or he wouldn't be blowing the smoke up the chimney in his own house.

'Mooney tried to tell me that this Imelda Conroy is related to me.'

'What?' Lottie hadn't expected that. 'Related how?'

'He wouldn't clarify. Said the lab needs to do more of whatever it is they do with DNA. Anyhow, he said it could be brother and sister, or father and daughter. I can't believe I actually might have spoken with my daughter.'

'Oh.' She sat back, a flurry of dust motes flying into the air. She wondered if Grace ever came into this room. It was probably Bryan's domain, otherwise she would have it sparkling clean like the rest of the house. Why these idle thoughts? Deflecting from the DNA bombshell?

'Bryan,' she said, 'did you know Imelda Conroy?'

'Never laid eyes on her before the day she arrived here with her questions. I don't know where or how she got my name, but she seemed to know I'd been in Knockraw. Can you believe all this?' His voice was breaking.

Lottie had to tread carefully. 'You set me a task when I arrived. Do you truly think she could be linked to that quest?'

He looked up at her, his face grey, lines furrowed deep on his forehead. He twirled the cigarette around in his fingers, allowing it to burn down. 'The truth is, I don't know.'

'Did you see any resemblance? To yourself or Mary Elizabeth?'

'I don't know. I wasn't thinking along those lines at all.'

Lottie found Imelda's photo on her phone. It was the one Mooney had shown her, taken from social media. It bore little resemblance to the distraught woman she'd met hiding at the convent. She turned the screen to show him.

'She could be anyone,' he said.

'Did she hint at the fact you might be related?'

'No, not a word. Just asked general stuff about my time there. She was going on about the chaplain. Seemed like she wanted to find him.'

'Robert Hayes was the chaplain, and is a person of interest in a murder that took place this week in Ragmullin. Did you know about that?'

'No, I didn't, but it doesn't surprise me. He was a cruel bastard back then.'

'He ended up being a chef in Ragmullin. What can you tell me about him?'

'I already told you. He's the guy who... Listen, he wasn't much older than I was then. He was only a deacon or something while he was there, before he became a priest. And now he's a chef? Seems that man didn't know what he wanted to be.'

'You think he wasn't a priest when you were at Knockraw?'

'Not sure what he was. He always wore black and a white collar. God knows what he belonged to. The devil himself, I'd say.'

His words mirrored Brigid Kelly's. 'Is Hayes the guy you told me about? The one who used those young girls from the convent.'

'He was part of it. Sex trafficker before it was a thing. Bastard.'

'What do you mean?'

'As far as I recall, the rumour was that he ferried young girls in his car between the convent and Knockraw in the dead of night. Those unfortunates were abused and I'm sure the nuns benefited in some way. Probably got paid for allowing it to happen. I know no more about it. But I can believe it wasn't just a rumour.'

His vehemence startled Lottie.

'You told me before about a man who was burned in the convent. Was that him? Hayes?'

'I can't be rightly sure. It was a long time ago. I'd put that era behind me. I wanted to forget it for ever. Now it seems it has followed me into middle age.'

Boyd said gently, 'You've been through a lot. Maybe later when you've had something to eat you might remember more.' He gave Lottie a look that warned her to back off.

'I'm sorry, Bryan,' she said. 'You've been interrogated by Mooney and now here I am doing the same. If you think of anything that might help us understand what is going on now, please tell me.'

'All I know is that Imelda Conroy stirred a pot and now it's overflowing.' Bryan threw his cigarette into the fire and looked at her pointedly. 'This DNA thing Mooney had, do you think it could be wrong?'

'DNA is usually very accurate. But if he's having the lab conduct further tests, it might indicate that it's not complete, or they need to sort the anomaly.'

'Then it could be true that this woman is related to me? I need to know, Lottie. I need to know for definite if she is my daughter, the child of Mary Elizabeth, who was thrown into that hellhole of a convent. Find out for me. Please.'

The door opened.

'Find out what?' Grace strode into the room. 'Bryan! I never knew you smoked. I'm beginning to think there's an awful a lot about you that I don't know. You need to start telling me the truth.'

Lottie stood. 'I agree with Grace. We'll leave you both alone. I'll muster up some food. We'll be in the kitchen when you're done here.'

She inclined her head towards Boyd to follow her. Few marriages could survive on lies. Bryan had to be truthful. As she closed the door, she felt genuine pity for Grace. What she was about to be told would be difficult to understand. Lies were not easy to forgive. And once secrets were out of the box, they could never be locked back in.

She knew from experience that the past rarely remained secret.

52

Matt Mooney had been sure his day couldn't get any worse, but he was wrong. He'd had to release Bryan O'Shaughnessy with assurances from his solicitor that he'd return when or if needed. The man had no current passport, so he wasn't a flight risk. There wasn't enough evidence yet to charge him with murder. The DNA at the scene was inconclusive. DNA on the wooden plank could be easily explained as he had readily admitted to handling it. Mooney needed more. What he didn't need was to be dragged in front of the super to talk to Councillor Denis Wilson. The man had high ambitions of becoming a member of the Dáil in the next election, and he let everyone know every chance he got.

When he arrived at the super's office, he was told that his boss had been called away unexpectedly but that the councillor was in the meeting room, waiting for him.

Here we go, he thought.

If he could detest someone based on appearance alone, it would be Denis Wilson. The man tried too hard to be something he was not. Too fit-looking, too damn handsome, and what was he like with those red cravats? Gimmicks, Mooney believed, could not make up for shallowness.

'Mr Wilson, how can I help you?' He plastered what he thought was a welcoming smile on his face. He probably looked tortured, but he didn't care.

'It's Councillor Wilson.'

Fuck you, Mooney thought. 'I'm very busy. *Councillor*.'

'I reckon that could be true if you were out there hunting a killer.'

'I am extremely busy, but apparently I have to talk to you.'

Wilson's face darkened at the slight. 'I want to know if you're close to charging someone with these brutal crimes.'

He could deny knowledge of what the man was talking about, but that would just be wasting time. Time he did not have. 'We are following a number of lines of inquiry.'

'I saw a man leaving as I entered the building. Norah Ward was with him.'

'So?'

'I heard reports of an arrest having been made. Was it him?'

'I can neither confirm nor deny that.'

'Well, if he was arrested, why did you release him?'

'*Mr* Wilson, if you have nothing to offer to assist me in my investigation, I have work to do.'

'I recognised him. From when I was canvassing. Bryan O'Shaughnessy. Lives out past Spiddal, doesn't he?'

Mooney raked a hand over his mouth and shook his head. 'When you have information to help me, I will gladly talk to you. But for now, I have to go.'

'Not so fast.' Wilson made no move to leave the sunlit room. He leaned back against the windowsill with both hands behind him. The light caught a hint of dandruff on the shoulder of his otherwise immaculate suit. That imperfection made Mooney smile. Wilson continued. 'I heard stories about O'Shaughnessy.

He was once incarcerated in Knockraw. I make it my business to know about people, and he is a bad egg, mark my words.'

'Do you have evidence of any wrongdoing?'

'Well, if he was in Knockraw as a boy, he must have done something wrong.'

Mooney sighed loudly, despairing of the human race. 'A lot of people ended up in the industrial schools through no fault of their own.'

'But his sister was sent to the convent.'

'To be a nun?' He knew right well what Wilson meant.

'The laundry. She was just a child. God only knows what she did to be put in there. Or maybe he did something to her, if you get my meaning.'

Mooney felt his blood beginning to boil with red-hot anger. He had no time for bigots, no matter who they proclaimed themselves to be. He presumed silence might be his best option. Let Wilson burn himself out with his diatribe.

'And there was a rumour that O'Shaughnessy got a local girl pregnant and she was sent to the laundry too.'

He could remain silent no longer. 'Where are you headed with all this supposition?'

'Just saying he's one to carefully consider. These murders only happened when that reporter, a documentary-maker, started asking questions about the laundries.'

'Oh, and did that documentary-maker speak with you?'

The question must have startled him, because Wilson started fiddling with his cravat, twisting the gold stud that was pinned in its centre. 'She did. I have a great local knowledge. She thought I could help her find her way through all the shit.'

'Great at stirring the shit too,' Mooney said under his breath.

'What's that?'

'I said you must have been a great help to her.'

'Of course I was.'

'In what way?'

'Told her a few home truths about the people living around here.' He looked daggers at Mooney.

'Explain.'

'I don't have to explain anything to you, Sergeant. It's your job to do the investigating.' He'd dropped the 'detective' tag. Probably peeved because Mooney refused to address him by his title. Title. Hah.

'If you are withholding information that proves critical to my case, I could arrest you for impeding the investigation. You're familiar with the term "perverting the course of justice"? If you know something, you need to tell me now.'

'I am not impeding or perverting anything. I'm here to help. I know you had O'Shaughnessy arrested and released without charge. You need to watch him very carefully.'

'Why do you say that?'

'I've already told you about his past.'

'I'm sure you have a past too, Mr Wilson.' He saw Wilson's torso stiffen. Good.

'We all have a past, but the reason I'm warning you to watch that man is that Imelda Conroy mentioned him to me when we spoke.'

'Are you sure it wasn't the other way around?'

'I don't like your insinuation. I am a respected member of the community. I also run a very powerful radio station. You don't want to be in the news headlines for making a big mistake, do you?'

'Are you threatening me?'

'Warning you, Sergeant. You need to charge someone with these murders, and in my mind O'Shaughnessy fits the bill.'

'In my experience, personal vendettas are no way to run an investigation. I don't tell you how to run your radio station or manage a council meeting, so I would appreciate it if you don't tell me how to run my—'

'He did it. He killed the old gardener and he killed the nun.'

Mooney frowned. How did Wilson know anything about Assumpta Feeney? Her identity had yet to be released. Unless the super was one step ahead of him and had issued a press release. Or they had a leak on the team. Then again, he himself had consulted – for want of a better word – Lottie Parker. Damn.

'And how do you know all that?'

'When the Conroy woman spoke with me, she had nothing. No local names. I gave her three. Now two of them are dead. The third was O'Shaughnessy.'

'How did you link him to the others?'

'I linked him to the laundry.'

'Thought you said he was in Knockraw. That wasn't a laundry.'

'Do your work, Sergeant. I'm not doing it for you. You can find the link. I think Imelda found it. And now she is missing. Probably in hiding, fearing for her life. And if she turns up dead, I will personally broadcast your incompetence to the world.'

As if. He thought of Wilson's local radio station with its few thousand listeners. Then again, the man was a pompous ass. People might listen to him. More fool them. But he didn't like that Wilson seemed to possess inside information about the investigation. That was something to worry about.

'When did Ms Conroy meet with you?'

'Oh, must be two months ago now. She was researching the subject matter at the time.'

'And why did she contact you?'

'Initially she was sourcing funding for her documentary. The nationals had told her they'd done all they could about the laundries. She was on her own.'

'And did you?'

'Did I what?'

'Fund her?'

'Not then. But I told her that if she ran the demos by me and if I thought they contained anything new, then yes, I would procure the necessary funding to get her radio series broadcast.'

'Did you get to hear the tapes?'

For the first time, Wilson appeared uneasy. He stopped fidgeting with his cravat and ran his hand through his glistening hair. His eyes seemed to dart this way and that, as if searching for someone hidden in the room.

'No. I hate to admit it and it's much to my regret. But I think whoever your murderer is has the content. Or has destroyed it.'

'Why would you think that?'

'Why else did he go to kill Imelda in that cottage?'

'You think Imelda was the intended target?'

'Of course she was.'

'And was she there that night?'

'How would I know?'

'You appear to know everything else about Ms Conroy. I think it's time you made a formal statement.'

'Why on earth would I have to do that?'

'Because you are one of the last people I now know of who met with Imelda Conroy.' He didn't know if that was actually true, but neither did Wilson. He tried hard to hide his inner dance of glee as Wilson went into meltdown mode.

'I want to speak with the superintendent to make a formal complaint about you.'

'I'm afraid the super tasked me with talking to you. Come along now. I'll try to find a nice cool interview room. Councillor.'

'And if I refuse?'

'That is your prerogative. But as I said earlier, if I believe you have information pertinent to my investigation, I can arrest you. I don't think that would do your run for the Dáil any favours. Do you?'

He knew Wilson might not consent to an interview, but he didn't care. He just wanted to witness him squirm.

53

RAGMULLIN

'Where's Peter?' Rose asked.

Chloe rolled her eyes. It was the fifth time in less than two minutes that her gran had asked that question. She waited for the question that she knew would come next, after she'd told her that her husband had died decades ago. She wished Katie would hurry up and come back from the supermarket. Chloe had to get to the pub for her evening shift. Her sister knew that, but was probably browsing the clothing section at Dunnes Stores before she even bought the groceries.

'Where's Lottie?' Rose added.

After answering by rote for so long, Chloe felt her words were stuck at the back of her throat, and frustration and annoyance bubbled. It wasn't her gran's fault. Dementia was a cruel disease. Her poor gran was stuck in a loop of forgetfulness, even though she did experience small windows of clarity. At times she became more frustrated than Chloe.

Taking a deep breath before she replied, she spied her gran's knitting basket in the corner. Distraction might work. 'Gran, you told me you'd show me how to knit.'

'Not now. Later.'

'I'd really like to learn. Come on, it will pass the time.' She gathered up the basket and extracted the wool and needles. The scarf they'd been working on yesterday – not that Rose remembered it – looked like moths had got to it, such was the number of holes in it.

'What is that?'

'A scarf.'

'Looks too narrow. And there's a dropped stitch.'

More than one, Chloe thought. 'Will you fix it, Gran? I don't know how to do it.'

'You youngsters are all the same. Give it here.'

Chloe gratefully handed over the knitting and made to escape the room.

'Where are you going?'

'To put the kettle on.'

'I'd love a cup of tea. Don't know when I last had one.'

'Five minutes ago,' Chloe whispered. Aloud she said, 'I'll make one for you.'

'Don't leave me on my own.'

'I'm in the next room.'

'Leave the door open so I can hear you.'

'Will do.'

'Where's Peter?'

Chloe kept going. She could manage a few hours with her gran, of course she could, now that she knew she had something exciting to look forward to.

She took the letter out of her jeans pocket. She had got it by email, but they'd posted it too, which saved her having to print it off. This was something she'd been wishing for. Something she wanted to do. But the idea of having to tell her mother was a whole lot worse than spending another hour listening to her gran's repetition.

She had no idea how Lottie would react to her news. But she knew it would not be good. There was a time she'd have asked her gran to put in a word for her. That was no longer an option. Or was it?

How could she go about planting a seed in Rose's mind? One that would take root and not wither before it was allowed to grow. Put your thinking cap on, Chloe Parker. Listen to your gut. Her mother was always harping on about that. Maybe she should try to use her initiative. God knows she'd need it where she was headed. If her mother let her. Well, tough. She was old enough to map out her own life, and no one was going to stop her.

Kirby had just returned to the office after speaking with the owner of the Happy Hair salon following her return from holiday. Martina had told him he needed to talk to her himself as she had some interesting things to say. It had been an informative meeting and he was about to update the team when McKeown shouted out.

'Got him.'

'Got who?' Kirby asked, looking over his shoulder at the screen shot of a CCTV still.

'Robert Hayes's car has been located in the car park at the train station—'

'I thought that was checked already.'

'Ragmullin station was checked. This is in Athlone.'

'It's still there?'

'Yes.'

'Let's go, then.'

Kirby felt a spurt of excitement as he pulled into Athlone train station car park. He sent McKeown off to get the actual CCTV footage while he inspected the grey car.

It was an old Mercedes model. Very old. The doors were locked. He peered through the window. He could not see anything incriminating on display. A yellow clamp was fitted to the wheel and a sticker was plastered to the driver's window. The car had been there since Monday. Hayes would have a huge fine to pay. The least of his troubles, Kirby mused. Why had the man fled if he was innocent? It pointed to one conclusion in his mind. Robert Hayes had murdered Edie Butler.

He caught up with McKeown in the cramped ticket office.

'Find anything?' he enquired.

'The car's been there since Monday.'

'Yes, it was clamped. I read the notice.'

'I've just found him on the security footage,' McKeown went on. 'He got on the Galway train. God knows how we'll find him in the city.'

'We will find him. We have a nationwide alert issued for him, but now we can concentrate it on one county.'

'Fat lot of good the alert has done so far. But you're right. We need to focus our efforts on Galway.'

'I'm putting it in motion,' Kirby said, miffed that he was being told how to do his job. 'Secure that footage and we'll head back.'

'We should go to Galway,' McKeown insisted.

'I've asked the boss to check if Hayes has turned up there.'

'She's on leave. You had no right to—'

'McKeown, I'm in charge, now do as I say. I'll meet you at the car.'

Kirby stomped out of the station office and patted his pocket for a cigar.

Outside, he lit it and inhaled, then coughed. Amy would kill him if she knew he was still smoking. He had to admit there was some merit in McKeown's suggestion. The boss had asked him to see what he could find on PULSE about this Bryan O'Shaughnessy. He had a nugget of information to share with her, but he hadn't found it on the central database. It had come to light while investigating Edie Butler's murder.

He would tell Superintendent Farrell that he needed to go to Galway in his search for Robert Hayes. But he had to do it in a way that meant McKeown couldn't feel smug at it being his suggestion.

CONNEMARA

Brigid Kelly was slow getting to the door. She figured the nice detective woman had forgotten something, though she couldn't see any coat or bag lying around the kitchen.

The bell clanged again.

'Give me a minute. I'm coming.' She made her way painfully down the tiled hallway, cursing the lifetime of hardship that had made her old before her time. Granted, Father Lyons was good to her and helped where he could. Not Father Robert before that. He'd been a mean man and she hadn't liked him, but he was one of God's chosen ones so she'd been inclined to give him the benefit of the doubt. He was no longer a priest, she recalled. A chef, no less, according to the detective. He'd always been giving her orders in her kitchen, so she was not surprised at his change of profession.

She pulled back the lock and slowly opened the door.

'Oh!' She clamped one hand to her chest and the other to her mouth. 'I thought it was someone else.'

'Hello, Brigid. Bet you didn't expect to see me here.'

No, she didn't. She tried to close the door on him. But his hand was on the thick timber and it was no problem for him to push it inwards. He stepped inside, shut the door and walked by her.

'How about a nice cup of tea and a cosy chat.'

She couldn't stop him. He was already in. He knew exactly where he was headed. She followed his loud clipping footsteps towards the kitchen. Before joining him, she slowly made the sign of the cross on her forehead, chest and shoulders.

'Help me, dear Lord,' she prayed.

55

FRIDAY

Father Phillip Lyons's early-morning flight into Knock airport had been comfortable and on time, but the journey down the N17 was disrupted by a road accident. The detours were badly signposted and he got lost twice. By the time he parked outside the house, the good mood he'd nurtured in Lourdes was in shreds.

'I'm home, Brigid,' he shouted as he shoved his carry-on case inside the door.

Not a sound. He checked his watch. It was only breakfast time, and she always kept hot food for him. But there was no smell of anything recently cooked.

'Brigid?'

She rarely went out unless to the shops for something, and that wasn't a regular occurrence. They did online groceries with delivery added. He thought it was the best invention yet. He was so looking forward to a full breakfast of rashers and sausages and eggs. He sniffed again. No, he couldn't smell it.

He sat on the bottom step of the stairs and kicked off his

shoes. His socks were wet with sweat, so he tugged them off too. He found his slippers on the floor under the coat stand. It was good to be home.

He looked into the parlour – the good room, Brigid called it. Empty. Maybe she was still in bed. That would be unusual. She was always up at the crack of dawn. But she was constantly in pain from her arthritis, and he figured he should talk to her about taking things a bit easier. Maybe get her extra help. No, he couldn't imagine her agreeing to that.

He pushed in the door to the kitchen. It appeared empty. Definitely nothing cooked for him. There was just a stale smell. Maybe it was from yesterday's food. Or the bin. It was his job to empty the rubbish into the outside bin. He'd do that first before he boiled the kettle, or maybe he'd have a cup of tea first. He went to the corner where the kettle usually sat. No kettle.

'Brigid?'

His voice echoed back at him in the stillness of the house. He backed out and glanced up the stairs. Her room was on the first floor. His, on the second, was an attic room, but he liked its quaintness and the privacy it provided.

'Are you up there?'

Silence.

He climbed the stairs and knocked on her door. No answer. He turned the handle and peered in. Her bed was made and the room was spotless. He went to the bathroom. The door was ajar. Water on the floor. He pushed the door in further. His hand flew to his mouth and he stifled a shout.

There was no point in going in to check. He knew death when he saw it. He dropped to his knees and blessed himself. He said a prayer for the dead before gingerly making his way back down the stairs to the phone in the hall.

He'd forgotten he could have used his mobile, such was his shock at what he'd seen.

56

Matt Mooney wondered how the likes of Detective Inspector Lottie Parker coped with murder. He supposed he'd had a sheltered garda life to date; murder was rare enough, though suicide was more prevalent. But who murdered innocent elderly ladies? He hoped she was innocent, because he could not contemplate Brigid Kelly being anything other than that.

He'd seen her naked body in all its distress lying in the bath of water. First he'd thought she'd merely drowned but then he'd spied the kettle and he knew that Brigid Kelly had been scalded to death. Or perhaps, if God was good, she'd died of a heart attack before that torturous pain was inflicted. He couldn't help noticing the similarities to Assumpta Feeney's body in the holiday cottage. There was no doubt in his mind. It had to be the same killer. But why? What the hell was the motive? He could not get his head around it.

Downstairs, he watched the priest, Father Lyons, being interviewed by a young garda. She was good with victims and families. He'd noticed the suitcase and shoes in the hall and the slippers on the priest's feet. Just returned from somewhere, or getting ready to leave?

'Father, I'm so sorry for your loss, but I have a few quick questions.'

The young garda closed her notebook and shook her head. She hadn't gleaned much from the distraught man.

He took her chair at the table and faced the priest.

'You found your housekeeper's body, is that correct?'

'Yes.'

'Where were you before that?'

'I was in Lourdes. Flew into Knock early this morning.' Father Lyons explained in detail about the road accident and going astray with the diversions. Very good detail. Was it all necessary? Mooney wondered. Was he overcompensating?

'Is that your suitcase in the hall?'

'Aye, I dropped it there, changed into my slippers and called out for Brigid. She wasn't down here where she usually is, so I went up the stairs and looked into her room and she wasn't there either. Then... I noticed the bathroom door slightly open and I pushed it in and...' He buried his face in his hands. 'May the good Lord have mercy on her soul, the poor woman.'

Mooney thought the priest's distress sounded genuine. 'You might want to take something for the shock, Father. A dram of whiskey could do the trick. We will need to take your finger-prints and a DNA sample. Routine procedure.'

'That's no problem.'

'My colleague will look after you.'

'Thank you. I hope you find who did this to Brigid. She had been through so much in her life. This is so not fair.'

'What do you mean? I'd have thought she'd have had a nice comfortable life here.'

'Before that. She went through hell in the convent.'

Tiny hairs on his neck stood up. 'Which convent was that?'

'The Sisters of Forgiveness. The laundry place. Shut down a long time now, but poor Brigid was born there.'

Now the hairs on Mooney's arms stood alert too. A definite

link between Assumpta, Mickey Fox and Brigid. The convent. Christ Almighty, what was going on?

As he turned to leave, he noticed a card on the table. A small business card. He turned it over with his gloved finger. For fuck's sake. What had she been doing here?

———

Mooney knocked on O'Shaughnessy's back door and walked straight into the kitchen, surprising Lottie. It seemed the back door was the main mode of entry in houses in the locale. It reminded her of her mother's house. Her phone call with Katie last night had comforted her that all was well with Rose. But she needed to talk to Chloe, because her younger daughter never sugar-coated anything. Chloe told it like it was.

The remnants of cigarette smoke misted around Mooney. She appraised his dishevelled appearance, strained eyes and fidgeting hands. She feared he was once again about to take Bryan away, and she felt helpless to prevent that happening. She had nothing to offer in his defence.

'This is a pleasant surprise,' she said, her voice laced with irony.

Grace stepped forward. 'You have no right entering this house like you belong here. Bryan has done nothing wrong. Nothing at all. He is a good man, and you...' she paused to point an accusing finger at him, 'you are trying to blacken his name by arresting him willy-nilly. I won't have it.' She stamped her foot. 'I won't have it at all.'

'I apologise for my intrusion, Ms Boyd, but it's Inspector Parker I want a word with, not Mr O'Shaughnessy.'

A bit worried by his formality, but at the same time relieved, Lottie stood and grabbed her cardigan from the back of the chair. 'We can talk outside so we won't disturb you, Grace.'

'If it's to do with my fiancé,' Grace said, 'I want to hear it.'

'It's nothing to do with him,' Mooney said. Then in a lower tone, for Lottie's ears only, 'As far as I know.'

He stood to one side to allow her to move out ahead of him.

'Do you want a cup of tea, Detective Sergeant? Coffee?' Grace asked, mollified.

'Maybe later, before I leave. Thank you all the same.'

Lottie walked across the back yard to the far wall. Grace was clever behind it all, she thought, offering Mooney tea or coffee so she could eavesdrop on the conversation.

'Are we safe out here from curious eyes and listening ears?' Mooney asked.

'She can see us but not hear us.' Sure enough, Grace was peering through the window over the sink. 'What's this about?'

'We have another body. Discovered this morning.'

'Oh no. Who?'

'Someone you met recently. Maybe yesterday.'

'You're the only one I met yesterday...' Then her heart dropped in her chest as she remembered. 'Please no. Don't tell me it's Brigid Kelly. Please don't...'

'I'm sorry. She was murdered in her bath.' He shook his head wearily. 'Probably scalded. The kettle from the kitchen was on the bathroom floor.'

'This is so terrible. Why, though?' Lottie felt a deep sense of regret and sorrow over the death of the little housekeeper. 'Why pick on her? She was such a nice woman. She was no threat to anyone. This is awful, Mooney. Can I visit the scene? See her body?' Her words ran into each other as she tried to get her head around the senseless act.

'No, you cannot. And I want to know why you visited her yesterday. I found your card on her kitchen table.'

'Did I draw the killer to her door? Was I being followed, do you think?'

'I don't know what to think, but I do need to know why you were there.'

'I wanted information about Robert Hayes. It was his old Galway address. Seems he used to be a priest. Your own people had already visited Brigid enquiring about him.'

'Oh, I'd forgotten about him. Shite.'

'Shite is right. Edie Butler, the Ragmullin victim, was scalded too, as far as I know. Her body dumped in a river. This is a mess, Mooney.'

'A mess? A right fuck-up, I'd call it. I better see which guards spoke with the housekeeper and what they found out.'

'They probably didn't get much from her. She was a spiky person. A lovely woman behind it all, though. I was with her for ages. God, when did she die?'

'We think sometime yesterday evening. We'll know more after the post-mortem.'

'I was likely one of the last people to see her.'

He leaned heavily on the dry-stone wall. 'What did you talk about?'

She paused, thinking before she spoke. 'I peeled potatoes and cooked a lamb chop for her. She was so grateful to have someone to talk to and to wait on her. I don't think she had many friends or visitors. She mentioned that the parish priest was in Lourdes but due home. Have you contacted him?'

'Father Lyons. Yes. He found her body.'

'Oh. Do you think he could have...?'

'No, we checked his story. He didn't fly in until this morning.' He paused, gathering his thoughts. 'I need to know what she told you and I want to know more about Robert Hayes. He is now my number one suspect.'

'And rightly so. I told you to talk to my colleague Kirby. Hayes is his suspect too. According to Brigid, he was a bastard – not her exact word, but you get the picture. He was chaplain at the convent, and Edie Butler was also there at one stage.' She was more certain than ever that the motive for all the killings would be found rooted in the past. 'The murders have to be linked, and we need to figure out who is next.'

'My bet is Imelda Conroy. That's if she's not the murderer. But if I can't locate her, then he might not be able to find her either.'

'Were there security cameras at the priest's house?'

'No, but there are some cameras around the church. I'm having them checked.' Mooney turned to look directly at her and she tried not to flinch. 'I need to know where Bryan O'Shaughnessy was yesterday afternoon and evening and last night.'

'He was in custody until you released him. He was here when I returned home and didn't leave the house afterwards. Didn't even go out to tend his sheep. Grace and Boyd did that with Tess. Tess is the dog, before you ask. You can scratch Bryan off your list.'

'You know I have to ask the hard questions.'

'Yes, but it wasn't him.' She pondered the dilemma Mooney was in. 'He told me about the DNA match you have.'

'It's undergoing further analysis, but it seems he is in some way related to Imelda Conroy. Do you know what that relationship could be?'

'I'm not sure, but it's possible she could be his daughter. You see, he asked me to find a girl he knew at one time who was pregnant and ended up in the convent. But everything is hearsay until you get the final analysis on the DNA and find Imelda.'

'One of my priorities.'

'Your main priority has to be to find Robert Hayes. The murder in Ragmullin is too similar to what's gone on here.'

'The sick bastard.'

'But you can't be blinkered. You don't know that he is the murderer; he's just a person of interest at this stage. Don't lose sight of the bigger picture.'

'And what's that?'

'I'm not sure, but as my mother used to say, don't put all your eggs in one basket.'

'You think there's someone else I should be looking at for these murders?' he asked.

'I don't know, but Bryan was here so he did not kill Brigid Kelly. Has anyone else come to your attention in the course of your investigation?'

'Not a one, though the possibility still exists that Imelda is on a killing rampage.'

'But why?' Lottie had met the girl in distress after Mickey Fox was killed. Could she be a killer? Anything was possible. 'What's her motive?'

'If she was born in the convent, that laundry, she could be avenging her mother's incarceration. Even her own birth. Shit, I don't know.'

'I'll try to find out more about her,' she said.

'You will do no such thing. Leave this to me and my team. I only told you about Brigid's death because I wanted to know what you'd been doing there. I'm warning you. Stay out of my investigation.'

'You could do with some help.'

'No, I don't need any more help because my bloody super is after calling in hotshots from Dublin, and that's all I fucking need. Apologies for the language.'

'No need to apologise. I'd be raging too if that happened to me.'

Mooney's body seemed to deflate, then inflate with anger again as quickly. 'Talking of my super, he's pawned fucking Councillor Wilson off on me. That man is now living in my frigging ear. When things seem bad, they're usually a whole lot worse.' He shook his head and took a pack of cigarettes from his creased suit pocket. 'I better go. I've to find that Hayes prick. Oh, and I've had your car brought back.'

Lottie watched him light a cigarette, button his jacket, smooth down his beard and walk off around the side of the farmhouse. She wanted to help him. Had offered her assistance. He'd rejected it. But that wasn't going to stop her. No way. This had to do with the convent laundry. Something had stirred a killer. She just needed to figure out what that was and she would be on the right path. And she had a feeling it was all down to Imelda Conroy and her blasted documentary.

'Lottie?'

Looking up, she saw Grace standing at the back door with a mug in her hand.

She made her way towards her. 'Coming.'

'I made the sergeant a coffee, but he seems to have left.'

'I'll take it, Grace.' Lottie held out her hand.

'Well I made it for him, so you can go in and make your own. And don't forget I have my final dress fitting in an hour. You have to come with me.'

Shit, Lottie thought. Stuck in a dressmaker's – that was all she needed.

The dressmaker worked out of a mid-sized cabin structure located beside a pub at the end of Spiddal village. Net curtains draped the one large window and the glass panel in the door.

'Aren't you cutting it a bit fine, Grace?' Lottie asked.

'I'm not cutting anything. The seamstress does that.'

She tried not to roll her eyes. 'I mean the wedding is this Sunday. What if the dress isn't right? You haven't much time to rectify it.'

'It will be grand. I'm just collecting the dress. I got it all sorted the other day when you were supposed to be with me but then you let me down.' Grace looked at her pointedly.

Without rising to the barbed remark, Lottie said, 'Why do you need me today if you're only collecting it?'

'I'm going to try it on and I want you to give me your opinion. I don't want to look a fool in front of Bryan.'

Taking a deep breath, she followed Grace inside and hoped she could keep her reaction in check. No way would she tell her the dress was anything but gorgeous.

The seamstress, dressed in jeans and T-shirt, stood to greet them in her cluttered space. She was as lean and as tall as

Lottie, and though she was beautiful, with glinting green eyes, her features were hard. Lottie hoped her own face was a little softer.

Rolls of material lined the shelves and the large work table held a sewing machine and other implements. A sheet draped over a mannequin made Lottie shiver. It looked like a cartoon ghost.

'Ladies.' The woman's eyes focused on Grace. 'Your dress is ready for you, young lady. Are you game for one final try-on?'

'Game?' Grace's eyebrows knitted in apparent confusion.

'Do you want to try it on for your... eh... friend?'

'This is my future sister-in-law, Lottie Parker,' Grace said. Lottie prayed she wouldn't say she was a detective. 'She's a detective inspector in Ragmullin and my brother is a detective sergeant. She's his boss.'

Lottie felt her cheeks flush, and the woman smiled awkwardly, holding out her hand in greeting.

'Pleased to meet you, Detective Inspector.'

Lottie shook the hand. It was as rough as sandpaper. 'Lottie will do.'

'Ann Wilson. Ann will do.'

'Pleased to meet you too,' Lottie replied, feeling like a parrot. Wilson? She wondered if she was anything to do with the councillor who had apparently become a thorn in Mooney's side.

'Grace,' Ann addressed her client, 'off you go to the fitting room. Your dress is all ready for you.' She pointed to the end of the cabin.

Lottie could swear Grace actually skipped behind the curtain that was hanging there.

The air felt too warm and there was no chair to sit on. She leaned against the wall and fanned herself with her hand.

'Are you okay?' Ann asked. 'Here, have my chair.' She led Lottie around the large table. 'Would you like some water?'

'Please. It's so hot in here.'

'I like the heat.' She extracted a bottle of water from a small fridge behind the table. 'But I keep hydrated. Sorry, I've no glass.'

'This is okay.' Lottie accepted the bottle gratefully, unscrewed the cap and drank.

'You're here for the wedding then?'

'Yes. Looking forward to it,' she lied. God, but she had no interest in it. Not now that she yearned to be involved in Mooney's murder investigations.

'I believe it's to be a small affair,' Ann whispered. 'Bryan is a lucky man. Wasn't always so. But he fell into luck... Then again, maybe he made his own luck.'

Lottie sat up straight and placed the bottle on the cluttered table, careful in case it toppled and spilled over the delicate material Ann had been working on. 'Oh, why is that?'

'I don't want to speak out of turn.'

'I won't tell anyone.'

Ann laughed. 'We sound like two schoolchildren conspiring in the playground.'

'I need help with these buttons,' Grace said from behind the curtain.

'Be with you in a second.' Ann picked up a pair of scissors. Noticed Lottie eyeing her. 'In case there's a loose thread.' She went off to assist Grace.

Lottie took a business card from a bundle stacked in a small box on the table. *Ann Wilson.* Again she wondered if she was related to Councillor Denis Wilson. No harm in asking. First, though, she had to fix her expression into one of joy for the dress she was about to see. She slipped the card into her pocket.

But when Grace emerged from the fitting room, Lottie found she did not need to fake her reaction. Boyd's sister looked radiant in an off-white calf-length dress of satin. One shoulder was bare and the other had a diamanté strap. The waist was similarly adorned, though the sparkling belt was wider. The skirt rippled around her body like a stream in a breeze. She had let her hair down, and with her pale skin, she looked like a Greek goddess.

'Wow!' Lottie gasped. 'My word, it's beautiful. *You* are beautiful.'

'Really? You like it?' Grace did a twirl, and Lottie grinned. She had never seen the young woman this happy. Then Grace's face dropped. 'You don't really like it. I think you're being insincere.'

'God, Grace, no. I love it. Honestly. It's fab on you.' She turned to Ann. 'It's amazing. You are so talented.'

Ann blushed. 'Ah, thank you. I love my work. I delight in transforming a bolt of material into a magical piece. And I agree. It looks fantastic on you, Grace. You bring the dress to life.'

'Thank you. Now I'll take it off and pay you what I owe. Then I need to go home to make the dinner.'

When the curtain dropped back and they were alone again, Lottie took Ann by the elbow and led her to the other end of the room.

'What did you mean earlier? About Bryan?'

'Oh, nothing. Don't mind me. It was just gossip anyhow.'

'I'd like to know. I don't want Grace getting hurt.'

'Grace is a beautiful, innocent human being. But we all get hurt. It's called living life.'

She heard a touch of bitterness in Ann's cadence. 'Please tell me what you know.'

Ann leaned against a shelf holding bolts of material. 'It's nothing really. Just that he wasn't nice as a youngster. That's what I heard. He was even sent to Knockraw for a time.'

'A lot of young men were sent to industrial schools through no fault of their own.' Lottie felt like she was trotting out a well-worn phrase, she'd used it so often in the last few days.

'From what I heard, it was his own fault.'

'What did he do?'

Ann glanced towards the dressing room. 'It's only hearsay.'

'Hearsay from whom?'

'My husband.'

'Is he the councillor?'

'Yes, Denis Wilson.'

'And he knows Bryan O'Shaughnessy?'

'Everyone around here knows Bryan.'

'So what did Bryan do?'

'I'm not saying. You can find out from someone else. But it's enough to know that what happened to his family was not nice. And now he has the farm and all that land.'

'Sounds like sour grapes to me.' Lottie said the words out loud without meaning to.

Ann pushed away from the shelving unit. It wobbled, but nothing fell from it. 'I've said enough.'

'I apologise. I was out of order. I'd like to know more.'

The fitting room curtain twitched. 'I can't talk now.'

'I have your card. I'll give you a call later.'

Grace emerged, still glowing. She handed the dress to Ann. 'I'd like to pay. How much is my balance?'

Lottie remained standing where she was and watched as the seamstress began to search for a suitable zip cover and hanger for the beautiful dress. She felt that the excitement of earlier was tainted. And once again, it was her fault.

———

The simple one is getting married to the monster. A dress fitting, no less. As if anything could look good on her. She does not deserve happiness, because she is getting married to him. And he definitely does not deserve to find happiness this late in his life.

The detective could cause me a problem as she is a bit of a mystery. I don't want her to detract from my mission, though. She is not on my itinerary. I need to get rid of the others first. All those who committed the sins of the past. And then I can rest easy in the knowledge that I will be the only one left who knows the truth.

58

When she found a few minutes to herself, Lottie and Boyd went for a walk up through the fields. She told him what the dress-maker had said.

'It's gossip,' he said.

'What if it's not?' She curved her arms around her body, feeling cold suddenly. Shit, she'd nearly passed out with the heat in Ann Wilson's cabin, and now she was cold.

'You don't know what she meant, so please, Lottie, leave it alone. I'm beginning to think there's some sort of conspiracy against Bryan.'

'But don't you want to find out now rather than when your sister is married to him?'

'It's her life, her choice. I realise that we can't interfere in fate.'

'We interfere with it all the time in our daily work,' she said, unable to mask sounding petulant.

'How so?'

'When a perpetrator thinks he or she is off scot-free, we catch them.'

'That's called following the evidence.'

'You know what I mean.'

'No, I don't.' He stopped walking. Turned to her. 'You need to leave all this alone and let Mooney do his job.'

'But this has nothing to do with Mooney. Ann mentioned Bryan's family. Something isn't right. Why didn't he look for his little sister? Why, after all this time, does he want to know about his old girlfriend?'

'Imelda Conroy resurrected the past for him. That's why. Now leave it be.'

He strode on ahead of her. She debated staying stock still in the field of gorse bushes, but in the end that would achieve nothing. She followed him.

'I'm going to phone Ann and find out what she was on about,' she said. 'Then I'll sit Bryan down and get the truth out of him.'

Boyd shook his head. 'You never listen to me, do you? You go off on one and ruin people's lives. I'm wasting my breath with you.' With longer strides he left her almost running to catch up.

'Hey, not so fast,' she panted. 'What's got into you?'

'More like what's got into you?' he shouted over his shoulder then waited until she reached him. 'I am asking you to leave well enough alone, Lottie. Please, for me. Do it just this once.'

But she knew that was not possible. 'I can't, Mark. I really can't leave it. People are being murdered. Older people. It must have something to do with their past. What if Bryan is a target? What if he's murdered too?'

'You don't really believe that, do you? You think he has something to do with all this.'

'Well I know for a fact he didn't kill Brigid Kelly. He was here all evening.'

'Oh, so that's the only way you can absolve him of guilt?' He snorted derisively. 'How do you know he didn't creep out in the dead of night? Were you up at the window looking out like a bloody nightwatchman?'

She didn't like his tone. Didn't like the way he was staring at her. And most of all she didn't like that he made her feel guilty of something she had not done. She only had Grace's interests at heart. But then again, that wasn't wholly accurate. She wanted to know the truth.

'I'm sorry,' she said at last, not wanting to fight with him.

'So you'll leave it? Move on from all this?'

She bit her lip, felt tears building. From frustration, repentance or guilt? She was not sure. But she could not stop the words leaving her lips.

'I can't walk away from it.'

59

Lottie was in such a temper by the time she returned to the dressmaker's cabin in Spiddal that she had to spend five minutes walking around the village before she was calm enough to talk to the woman without making a show of herself.

She took off her cardigan and slung it over her arm. No point in fainting with the heat inside. She knocked on the door and entered when Ann called out to come in.

'Oh, you're back.' Ann stood up from her table and hurriedly covered whatever she'd been working on.

'I hope I'm not disturbing you.' Lottie's tone was too formal. Acting like she was on the job. She'd have to tone it down.

'You are, actually. I've an order to finish today.'

'I won't delay you. I want to pick up the conversation we were having earlier.'

'It wasn't a conversation, and I don't want to talk about it.'

'Ann, please tell me what you were implying about Bryan O'Shaughnessy. It's important.'

'I told you already. I have nothing to say. I don't want to disrupt the wedding. Grace deserves to be happy and she seems besotted with him. So let fate make its own way.'

Jesus, had Boyd phoned Ann? She sounded just like him.

'You must tell me if there's something Grace should know about Bryan. You already intimated as much.'

'I don't have to tell you anything. I'd like you to leave.'

'Maybe I'll ask your husband.' Now she was being a right bitch. Didn't stop her, though. 'You did say it was him that mentioned it to you.'

Ann came around the table so quickly Lottie took a step back.

'Do not go near him.' There was venom in the spittle flying from Ann's lips. 'I'm warning you. You have no authority around here, so please leave it. Leave me alone.'

Lottie was in full fighting mood now. 'So be it. I'll inform Detective Sergeant Mooney that you have information pertinent to his investigation. You can talk to him.'

'I don't have to...' Ann's face lost all its anger in an instant as realisation seemed to strike her. 'What investigation?'

'The murders of three people this week here in Galway, quite possibly linked to one in Ragmullin.'

'That's ridiculous. What I was saying has nothing to do with murder.'

Lottie leaned her head to one side sceptically. 'How can I be certain of that while you are withholding information?'

Ann leaned back against the table before sitting on the edge of it. 'I should have kept my mouth shut.'

'Maybe, but you didn't.'

'No, and now you're going to drag me into a murder investigation. Denis will kill me.'

'Really? Is he violent?'

'Jesus, woman, it's a figure of speech.'

'But you look scared.'

'That's because I am. I built up this business on my own, without help from anyone else. And you seem hell-bent on destroying it all.'

Lottie threw up her hands in confusion. 'Ann, I have no idea what you are on about.'

'No, you don't.'

'Tell me then.'

'I can't. I'm sorry I ever said anything about Bryan O'Shaughnessy, but I can't go there. I won't go there.'

'Is it about his time in Knockraw?'

'That. And more.'

'I don't understand...'

Ann began to cry. Deep sobs racked her body. Lottie moved to comfort her, but Ann held out her hand, warding her off. 'Don't. Don't touch me.'

'I want to help.'

'You're not helping,' she sobbed. 'You're making everything worse.'

Lottie was at a loss to know how to handle this. She wanted information, but she didn't want to distress Ann any further. She waited while the woman composed herself.

Ann said, 'You could never understand what I went through.'

'Try me.'

'No, I want you to go.'

'Okay. But I will find out what it is that's upset you so much.'

'You can't leave it alone, can you?'

Lottie closed her eyes and felt shame rush to her cheeks. The same words Boyd had used not a half-hour earlier.

'No, I can't, and I'm truly sorry.' She moved towards the door.

'I was there.' Ann's voice was soft and trembling. 'I was in the Sisters of Forgiveness laundry. And I don't need you, nor my own buried memories, bringing me back there.'

. . .

Following Ann's directions, Lottie drove them over to the seaside resort of Salthill. She had to circle to find a parking spot and then wait until someone pulled out of a space.

They walked along the promenade, making small talk. About the weather. How busy the area was. Young mothers with buggies, people walking dogs, men and women jogging and a host of speed-walkers. All sorts enjoying the good weather and the sea breeze. Apparently without a care in the world. And Lottie figured that was how she and Ann looked to the unobservant eye.

Pausing at the entrance to the strand, Ann slipped off her sandals. 'I love to feel the sand on the soles of my feet and between my toes. It grounds me.'

Lottie groaned inwardly. She hated sand. It got everywhere. But she wanted to hear what the woman had to say, to keep her onside, so she removed her own shoes and followed. The sand was surprisingly warm but scratched her feet. Ann walked straight down to the water's edge and began to stroll along it, leaving a trail of wet footprints in her wake. Lottie remained as best she could on the dry stuff.

The dressmaker's voice was soft as she began to speak. 'We were always in the laundry, down in the basement. The heat, the steam, the sweat... it was unbearable. But we were forced to venture into it every single day. Teenagers, young and pregnant. And children. Child labour? Call it what you want, but to us it was inhumane and torture.'

'I've been to the convent. I've seen the remains of the laundry. I can't begin to imagine what it was like back when it was operational.'

'No one can. You'd have to have experienced it. Our clothes, thin shift dresses, were useless to protect us. We got burned and scalded more often than not. One day, I've no idea of the date nor the year, this young girl arrived. Maybe seven years old. I was about fourteen or so. She looked frail and scared. Fragile. But she wasn't really. She had a determined attitude. Reminded me a little of myself, if I'm honest. In the beginning, she tried her best to please the nuns. She did every single thing that was asked of her, until one day she didn't.'

'What do you mean?'

'The sheets often got stuck to the inside of the large washing machine drums. And this is the awful thing...'

Lottie waited, holding her breath.

Ann continued slowly, her voice trembling. Breaking.

'The nuns usually got the smallest child to climb inside and extract the offending article. They picked on this wee girl. She was a wisp of a thing. Anyway, on this particular day she was taking too long in the machine. The poor mite was terrified. Wide-eyed. Her whole body was one long tremor when she crawled out with her knee bleeding. The nun roared insults at her, the girl shook her head frantically and made the mistake of talking back and then the nun whipped her across the face with the large crucifix of her rosary beads.'

Lottie felt nauseous. 'That's horrific. What did you do?'

'I did nothing. We were all frozen like useless statues and did absolutely nothing. We were terrified.'

'I can understand your fear.' Lottie thought there was no way she could fully appreciate the horror of what they'd experienced.

'The worst thing was... No. I can't bring myself to speak of it.' Tears were streaming down Ann's face like torrential rain. Unstoppable. She grabbed Lottie's arm and linked her, leaning her head against her shoulder. 'The murders this week, I think they have to do with what happened in the laundry back then. I really believe that.'

'Why is that so?' Lottie waited for Ann to elaborate, for the woman's tears to abate.

'Because... because I heard the victims this week were scalded with boiling water. Is that true?'

'I'm not involved in the investigation. I can't say.'

Ann pulled away from her. 'Oh for God's sake. I know it's true. Denis told me, and he heard it from the superintendent.'

'Okay, okay.' Lottie reached for her, but Ann marched ahead. She caught up. 'I'm sorry, Ann. Please continue your story.'

'It's not a frigging story! It's the truth. It's my life. My old life. I was sent there because my mother died and my father hadn't the will nor the means to rear me. It was the same situation for that wee girl.'

'What was her name?'

'The nuns gave us new names, usually saints or angels. We only knew her as Gabriel.'

'What became of her?' Lottie asked, though she wasn't sure she wanted to know. She recalled Brigid Kelly mentioning that name too.

'The nun was shouting. The poor thing was in hysterics, getting blood from her face all over the sheets wrapped around her. Then... Oh my God, I can't go back to that moment...'

'Please, Ann. It might help me save someone else.'

With a deep, troubled breath, Ann exhaled what she'd seemed hesitant to utter a moment ago.

'Then Robert appeared.'

'Robert Hayes?' Lottie scrunched her brows in confusion.

'Yes. The very one. The devil incarnate. Huh.' Ann swiped at her tears, and a steely anger flashed from her eyes. 'He was some sort of deacon then, but he became a priest afterwards. Bastard. He worked at the convent and also at Knockraw. He wanted to know what all the commotion was about. I believe he understood what was going on. And as if he was possessed by the devil himself, he pushed the nun out of the way, saying he knew how to sort the errant girl. He threw her in, slammed the drum door shut and turned the dial, and the machine roared into life.'

No longer just nauseous, Lottie felt she wanted to be physically sick. 'Oh my good Lord God.'

'The good Lord did nothing to help. None of us did. Robert didn't even wait to see his handiwork. Just strode out as quickly as he'd arrived. Another nun, a young novice, was standing there open-mouthed with shock, like we all were. She did her best to turn off the machine, but she twisted all the wrong dials. It seemed an age before she got it to stop. When it did, the silence was unbearable, a deathly quiet that I will never forget. The first nun backed away, fell to her knees and prayed. The fucking old bitch. As if that was going to save poor little Gabriel.'

'What happened to the child?'

'What do you think happened? She was bruised, bleeding and blistered. A wee slip of a thing couldn't survive that. She died shortly afterwards. They didn't even call a doctor! Her body was taken out and buried somewhere, probably in the grounds, and we weren't allowed to mention her or the episode ever again.'

Lottie kneeled in the sand at the edge of the sea and splashed her face with cool water. She sensed Ann kneeling close to her and welcomed the physical presence by her side.

'What has this to do with Bryan O'Shaughnessy?'

'He abandoned her. He never looked for her. You see, I believe that wee Gabriel was his innocent little sister.'

Both of them were silent as Lottie drove back to Ann's shop. Shocked was too light a word for what she felt after what she had heard.

Outside the cabin, she idled the engine. 'How did you keep going in the convent, after what happened?'

'It was what I had to do. I had nowhere else to go. When I was eighteen, I got out. The only skill I had learned was sewing.

So that's what I did. For the rest of my life. Every single day. My work brought me solace.'

'How did you meet Denis?'

'It was a friendship first, then developed into a sort of love. We have no children, before you ask. I could not bring a child into this horror of a world I grew up in.'

'I am so sorry this has happened to you. Where is that old nun now?'

'Long dead, and good riddance.'

'And the other one, the novice?'

'I've no idea where she is.'

'You heard Brigid Kelly was murdered? In the house where Robert Hayes lived for a time as a priest.'

'I heard.'

'She was in the laundry too. Why do you think she may have been targeted?'

'I don't know. Isn't that the guards' job to find out?' Ann opened the car door. 'Goodbye, Lottie.'

Lottie felt immense guilt at having pressed the woman for her story. She now knew why Ann detested Bryan. Because he did not try to find his little sister. But was there something more? Could Bryan be the killer Mooney sought? Was he avenging his sister's death? If so, he'd have to have known what had happened to her. She was confused, but she'd still put her money on Robert Hayes.

60

On the drive back to the house, Lottie thought of all the questions she should have asked Ann Wilson. What did she know of Assumpta Feeney, Brigid Kelly and Mickey Fox back in the day? And did she know Edie Butler? Ann could shine a light on their roles in the convent. The laundry. The hellhole. She would have to tell Mooney, and it was up to him to ask the pertinent questions. After all, she was not involved in the actual investigations. Then again, she had inadvertently become embroiled in it. Boyd would have something to say, but she could handle him. He never stayed mad for long.

As she pulled up in the yard, she noticed a familiar car parked out front. She rushed round the side and into the kitchen.

'Look what the cat dragged in,' she said, instantly happy to see Kirby sitting at the table, a mug of steaming coffee in his hand.

'Hello there, boss. There's been a development in my case and that brought me here in person.'

Grace was sitting beside him. 'He's telling me all about how Sergio is getting on with Amy. You know, Detective Kirby, you and Amy need to have children of your own. Have you been doing anything about that?'

Lottie smiled at the young woman's directness, a trademark of Grace Boyd.

Kirby's mouth dropped open, but he quickly recovered. 'Ah, no kids. Not yet. We're not long enough together to be making such plans. You know yourself.'

'I don't know,' Grace said.

Reddening, Kirby said, 'It's early days.'

'You must make an honest woman of her soon, Detective Kirby.'

Lottie cringed at the old-fashioned mindset. It was easy to forget that Grace was only in her mid thirties. She'd lived with her mother, just the two of them, isolated for too many years after Boyd had left to join the guards.

'I'll chat to you in a minute, Kirby,' she said. 'I need to have a word with Boyd first. Is he upstairs? I'll go see him.'

Grace stood and picked up her own mug. 'That will be difficult. He isn't here.'

'Out with Bryan, is he?'

'No, he's gone to Ragmullin,' Grace said. 'And he better be back for my wedding. He has to give me away.'

'But...' Lottie struggled. 'Why?'

Grace tutted. 'He said he wanted to go see Sergio.'

Kirby patted his pocket. 'I'll go outside for a smoke if you want to join me, boss.'

'She is not your boss because she's not working,' Grace said. 'And smoking is bad for you. I'm sure you've heard that.'

'I hear it every day.' He chuckled and made his way outside.

Lottie followed, glad to escape Grace's scrutiny. She was still reeling from Ann's revelations, despite her good humour at seeing Kirby.

'Amy actually thinks I've given these up,' he said, lighting his cigar, 'so don't go telling her.'

She didn't care about his smoking. 'Do you know what's up with Boyd?'

'No. He was gone when I arrived.'

'I better ring him.' She struggled to get her phone out of her pocket.

'Don't you want to know what brings me here?'

'Oh, yes.' She gave up on the phone. 'Tell me.'

'It's about Robert Hayes.'

'God, I've just heard the most horrendous story about him. Sickened me to my stomach.' She paused for a moment. She didn't know what to say or how to say it, so she decided to let him tell her what he'd come to relate. 'Go on.'

'His car was found at Athlone train station. CCTV shows him getting on the Galway train. It's logical to assume he is actually here.'

'Galway is a big county, Kirby.'

'I know that. Did you have any luck tracing him for me?'

'I visited his last known address here. Turns out it's a priests' house out Moycullen way. He used to be a priest, if you can believe it. I spoke to the housekeeper, lovely lady.' She felt a sadness wash over her, clothed in guilt. Was Brigid dead because of her visit? She hoped not.

'Oh good. I'll call to her for a statement.'

'That's impossible.'

'Because of jurisdiction issues? Nah, my investigation has brought me here. The super okayed it and—'

'Stop, Kirby. You can't talk to her because Brigid Kelly was murdered yesterday evening. Sometime after I spoke with her. Her body was discovered this morning.'

'What? Are you serious?'

'I never joke about murder.'

'And do you know...? Shit. I don't know what to say.'

'Detective Sergeant Matt Mooney is the man to talk to. He's investigating the murders. Unfortunately, I believe there will be a task force or a new team taking over soon. You know how the powers-that-be work.'

'Holy Mother of God. Do you think... could Robert Hayes be involved here?'

'It's a strong possibility,' Lottie said. 'I suspect he could have killed Edie Butler in Ragmullin and then come here to murder more people. I need to talk to Mooney and so do you.'

'Okay. I can ring him and arrange to meet as soon as possible, if not before.'

'Sure.' Lottie felt empty. It was frustrating being consigned to the sidelines.

'Changing the subject,' Kirby said, 'what's up with you and Boyd?'

'Don't ask.'

'Rough waters?'

'Stormy enough.'

'Shit.'

'Yeah, Kirby, I agree. It's shit.'

He puffed on his cigar. Coughed a little before putting it away. 'Need to give up these bastards.'

'I agree.'

'You're no saint yourself.' He smiled, his eyes twinkling. 'You smoke too.'

'Only occasionally, and I haven't done so for a long time. Mainly when I'm stressed. Which is now.'

'Well you're not getting one of my cigars. Listen, there's something else I wanted to tell you.'

'Fire ahead.'

'It's to do with Bryan O'Shaughnessy.'

'Just what I don't need to hear.' She stifled a groan. 'Did you find something on PULSE?'

'No. It came to light while I was investigating Edie Butler's murder.'

'I've a feeling I'm not going to like this, Kirby.'

'Maybe or maybe not. Do you want me to tell you?'

'Jesus, you're here. Spit it out.' She realised she sounded contrary. 'Sorry. I've had a stressful morning.'

'Maybe you should buy a pack of Silk Cut purple?'

'Shut up.' She grinned, and some of the tension left her body.

'It turns out Edie Butler knew your Mr O'Shaughnessy. She used to live around here before she was married. Over twenty-five years ago or so. They were a bit of an item back then, according to the owner of the salon where Edie worked.'

'This gets weirder by the day. I don't know what to make of that nugget.'

'The thing is, I will have to talk to Bryan in relation to Edie's murder.'

'I'd say he was nowhere near Ragmullin. He spends all his time on the farm. Let me speak to him.'

'You can't do that formally. You're on leave.'

'I'll rescind my leave then.'

'Superintendent Farrell won't allow it if she learns the reason why.'

Lottie marched in a circle around Kirby, kneading her hands into each other. 'I have to do this. You can take the lead. You see, I've heard some terrible stuff this morning that may be relevant to the murders. Bryan is either wholly involved, or alternatively, he could be a target.'

'It never ceases to amaze me how you can confuse me.' Kirby scratched his curly hair. 'What did you hear?'

She decided to tell him. 'I spoke with a woman called Ann Wilson. She's a dressmaker in Spiddal. Her husband is a local councillor and a bit of a bollox, per Sergeant Mooney.'

She related some of the story without the grotesque imagery Ann had conjured.

'That's horrific,' Kirby said. '*Now* can I talk to Mr O'Shaughnessy?'

'We have to be careful. We can't upset Grace. Boyd already had words with me over it.'

'Oh, so that's why he went off in a huff. You were rocking the boat with his sister. Figures.'

'Why does it figure?'

'Don't take offence, but as much as Boyd loves and respects you, his sister is blood. His last surviving family member. I imagine she's as close to his heart as you are, if not closer.'

She felt miffed at this, but then reality hit her. Kirby was right. She held her children closer to her heart than anyone else. No one could break that bond, not even Boyd. It had come between them during her last case, when they'd discussed buying a house together. She'd felt they'd got over that hurdle, but her life was never straightforward. She negotiated one obstacle, and before she could catch her breath, another reared its head, blocking her path forward.

She'd overcome worse.

She'd overcome this.

61

'Grace, where can we find Bryan?' Lottie asked as nicely as she could manage, not wanting to rattle Boyd's sister more than she'd already done. She had warned Kirby to let her do the talking.

Grace was sitting at the table threading flowers, some dried, into a small wreath, possibly a headpiece for her wedding. Tiny green leaves and discarded colourful petals were strewn over the worktop. The kitchen smelled of a forest infused with a simple blossom scent. All it needed was a few butterflies and bumble bees and you could be outside among the trees.

She looked up warily. 'What do you want with him?'

'Just a chat.' Lottie squirmed under her steely gaze. Grace seemed to have a way of reading her mind, just like Boyd. 'Listen, Grace, he knows more about this locality than we do. We just want to pick his brain.'

'I'm from round here too, so ask me your question.'

'It's to do with the case that Kirby is working on back home.'

'Oh, so another top-secret mission.' Grace dropped the flowers and stood, shoving her chair noisily in against the table.

'It sickens me, you know. How you work. It's all a mystery, until it's not.'

'Huh?' Kirby said, sniffing loudly.

Grace ignored him, her eyes throwing daggers at Lottie. 'Mark has left you, hasn't he?'

'No, you have it all wrong,' Lottie protested, but Grace wasn't listening.

'He's my brother. My only relative. I love him, even more than he loves me. I know I'm not a very expressive person. Not a hugger or kisser like most people nowadays. When did all that malarkey start in this country? It was not long ago that a simple handshake was the norm.' She turned up her pert nose before a wave of hurt traversed her features. 'I can't bear it when I see Mark in pain. He nearly died from cancer, and you stood by him. I respected you for that. Now he is hurt in his heart and you let him drive off alone. He was in a terrible state after your walk with him this morning. What did you say to him?'

'Nothing.' Lottie wished she could sink through the flag-stone floor. She couldn't take much more of Grace's words, her piercing eyes, her loathing. 'Nothing of significance to cause him to get upset and leave.'

'Oh, for God's sake, I might look stupid to you, but I am far from it. I notice things. I pick up vibrations. In here.' Grace thumped her chest. 'I picked them up when he came back in after whatever argument you had. And do you know something else? I also picked them up between you and Ann Wilson this morning. So, Lottie Parker, don't treat me like I am an imbecile. You have run my brother from your life and you have also annoyed my fiancé.' She paused as if reordering her thoughts. 'Tell me this minute, what *is* going on with Bryan?'

Lottie had never heard Grace raise her voice in all the time she'd known her. But she didn't know Boyd's sister very well. She pulled out a chair and sat. Kirby remained standing, looking from one to the other, wordless.

'Sit, Grace.' Lottie pointed to the seat opposite.

'I am perfectly fine standing right here, thank you very much.' Grace picked up a tea cloth and wiped it over the counter before twisting it round her fingers. She was far from fine, Lottie noted. At last she gave in and sank into the chair.

'You should sit down too,' she said to Kirby. 'You're making me nervous standing there like a lost sheep.'

'Ah, I'm grand.' But he must have seen Lottie's pleading eyes, and he did as he was told.

'Now, what is all this palaver about?' Grace asked.

Lottie would have loved a coffee, a glass of wine. A pill. Anything to smooth the path for what she had to say. But she had to plough on without artificial fortification.

'You know Bryan was in Knockraw as a boy?'

'Yes, he told me. Only this week. I was annoyed with him, but I understand that he never wanted to revisit that part of his life. I respect him for that.'

'Do you know anything about his family?'

'Not a lot. He doesn't like to talk about that either. And I'm not nosy like you.'

'Okay.' Lottie thought it better not to mention Bryan's younger sister at this time. She gathered her thoughts and hoped she could make sense of it all for Grace. 'He had knowledge of the laundry and what went on there. And this week three people have been murdered in Galway and another in Ragmullin. It may have something to do with this Imelda Conroy and the documentary she was making. She spoke with Bryan a few weeks ago.'

'I know. He told me that too.'

'Right. And Ann Wilson, your dressmaker, she was in the laundry as a girl.'

'She never told me that. But she is a discreet woman. Unlike...' Grace looked pointedly at Lottie before recovering her poise. 'We had a purely professional relationship, me and Ann.'

'I know.'

'Then what has she to do with Bryan?'

'I'm just laying out facts. The woman who was killed in Ragmullin was called Edie Butler.'

'Never heard of her.' Grace shook her head, emphasising the fact.

'She was in the Sisters of Forgiveness laundry, according to Brigid Kelly, who was also there and was murdered yesterday.'

Grace gasped. 'The poor woman who was a priest's house-keeper? It's nothing to do with Bryan, though, and isn't that the point of this conversation?'

Lottie was beginning to believe that she had underestimated Grace Boyd.

'Detective Kirby has discovered that years ago... a long time ago,' she added, to take the harm out of it, 'Bryan knew Edie Butler.'

Grace didn't flinch. 'He knew her? So what?'

'He has to be spoken to about it. That's all.'

'You're making no sense. You have spouted stuff at me with no real connection to Bryan. A few very thin links, but nothing concrete.'

'That's why we need to talk to him,' Kirby said, finding his voice. 'To establish if he has information that can help us and—'

Lottie interrupted him. 'Sergeant Mooney believes the murders may link back to the Sisters of Forgiveness. To their laundry. There is a connection to that institution and at least two of the murders via a man called Robert Hayes.'

'You are trying to confuse me now.' Grace looked from one to the other.

'No, we are not,' Lottie said forcefully, immediately sorry for her raised tone. She'd alienated Grace enough as it was.

'You *are* confusing me. First you say Bryan has a link to it all, and now it's this Hayes man. Make up your mind.'

Lottie sighed. She knew she was skirting round the issue, but there was only so much she could reveal. 'Robert Hayes was a deacon, chaplain to the laundry and to Knockraw industrial school. Then he was ordained a priest. Brigid Kelly was his housekeeper.'

'Oh, I remember some scandal years ago about him.' Grace seemed to brighten as she said this, maybe thinking Hayes's misdemeanours would deflect attention from Bryan. 'It was rumoured he interfered with young children or something awful like that. Seems he was a very bad man.'

Her summation of Hayes sounded childish in the current horror show. But that was Grace for you, Lottie thought.

Kirby said, 'He worked as a chef and at some stage moved to Ragmullin, where he struck up a recent relationship with Edie Butler.'

'I still don't see anything to warrant you hounding my Bryan. He's a good man.'

'I'm sure he is,' Kirby placated. 'But he might be able to tell us more about Hayes, seeing as he was chaplain at Knockraw while Bryan was there.'

Grace turned back to Lottie. 'But you said Sergeant Mooney thinks the murders have to do with the nuns and the laundry. Now you are talking about the industrial school. You are not making any sense to me.'

Lottie felt bewildered herself. 'Nothing makes sense until we can see the whole picture. We think Bryan might be able to shed some light on it. He knew Edie Butler. He spoke with Imelda Conroy. He may have known some of the other victims.'

'Everyone knows everyone in a small community. That does not automatically make them a criminal.' Grace folded her arms indignantly.

'I get that. Did you know them?'

'No, but... You mentioned my dressmaker, and I picked up some tension between you two when I was showing you my dress. Did Bryan know her too?'

'That's one of the things we need to establish,' Lottie said, hoping Grace didn't dig any further. The time was not right to reveal Ann's news about the little girl who might have been Bryan's sibling.

Grace stood and slapped the tea towel down on the table. 'I think my brother is right.'

'In what way?'

'Mark said that you are a hard, unfeeling woman.'

'He never said that.' Lottie felt the shock register on her face and bit her lip to keep from saying something she'd regret. How was this happening?

'He did so. You are trying to stop me having any happiness in my life because you don't have it yourself.' Grace paused, closed her eyes, then opened them. She'd made up her mind. 'I don't want you under my roof tonight, Lottie Parker. I'd like you to leave. Now. You can go and find a hotel for yourself. You are no longer welcome here.'

62

Kirby went off to meet Mooney. He said nothing to Lottie concerning Grace's outburst. Just patted her arm to show his sympathy for her predicament. The only thing she'd said to him was to not tell Boyd that Grace had evicted her. He promised he wouldn't, but she knew they were buddies so she couldn't count on him.

Bryan had not returned to the house while she packed her case. She got on the phone and found a room in a hotel between Spiddal and Salthill. Google Maps showed it overlooking the sea. Maybe she could jump out a window and disappear in the water. She sniffed away her tears and sat on the bed, phone in hand, Boyd's name and number open on the screen.

Was this really the end for them? Had she been that bad a partner? Wasn't he the one who was disagreeable? Surely he had to accept that she could not walk away from a crime, or a supposed crime. It had yet to be determined if Bryan was involved or not. At the very least, he was guilty of not searching for his little sister or trying to find out what had happened to her. Likewise regarding his old girlfriend and baby.

The images from Ann's story about what had occurred in

the laundry decades ago caused her to shiver violently. How could anyone be that cruel to a defenceless child? And it seemed the crime committed in Ragmullin in recent days bore some similarity to those that had occurred in Galway. No matter which way she looked at it, she could not see Bryan as the sort of man who would scald and burn people. It had to be Robert Hayes. But what had Imelda Conroy learned from Bryan? Why had she sought him out initially?

And then there was that DNA Mooney had mentioned. Shaking her head slowly, she put her phone away. Would her pursuit of the truth deny her her own happiness? Possibly. She zipped up her case and made her way down the stairs.

She exited using the front door, not wishing to encounter a distressed Grace. By the time Lottie and Kirby had left the kitchen earlier, Grace was crying into her hands, childlike. And that was why she felt so protective of the young woman. She was trusting, loving, a prime candidate to be taken advantage of. To be hurt. Lottie could not bear for that to happen. But at the very least, Grace was entitled to know the truth, and she was determined to find it. Even if it put paid to the impending wedding. She was right, wasn't she?

She extracted the phone from her pocket again, pressed the number. Listened to it ring before voicemail cut in. She hung up. She didn't know what to say to Boyd on a voicemail. She had no idea of how to fix things. Not now. Not yet. She could work on him once she either discovered the truth or let go of her need for it.

The hotel was luxurious and she didn't even look at the price. A few nights would not break the bank. She hoped. She took a long, warm shower, just because she needed to feel the power of water after three days of dribbles. Drying herself, she marvelled at the softness of the big towel.

When she was dressed, she stood at the bay window and concentrated on the whitecaps on the sea. She couldn't hear a thing because of the triple-glazed windows, but the sound was echoing in her ears from all the time she'd spent outdoors at Bryan's house.

Kirby had texted her to say he had a meeting scheduled with Mooney and the sergeant had specifically said it would not happen if Lottie turned up. So be it, she thought. It wasn't going to stop her doing her own investigation.

First, though, she phoned Chloe.

'Yeah, Mam, Gran is good. She's knitting and ripping and knitting. Her friend Betty calls in every day.'

'How is Louis doing?' She was missing her grandson more than her own children. That made her smile.

'He's pining for Sean. I think it's more that he misses the PlayStation. I never knew my brother could have that much patience with a child. I think he should be a teacher.'

'I believe he is aiming for something more in the tech world. But you never know. And Katie? How is she?'

'She's being a pain in the arse. We have a rota for caring for Gran this week, especially when I'm at work. And what does Katie do the other night? She goes out on a date. Selfish wagon.'

'Did she leave Rose on her own?' Lottie gripped her phone tighter, horrified. Chloe was employed in Fallon's, a local pub, and she worked most evenings.

'She wrangled Betty to stay. She has a new boyfriend. God knows who he is, given her track record. My sister's a piece of work.'

'At least she didn't skive off and abandon Rose. Give her some credit.'

Chloe groaned. 'Katie can do no wrong in your eyes, Mam.'

Lottie could hear the plea in her daughter's voice. 'You are my star, Chloe. I can depend on you so much more than the others. You know that.'

'Whatever. But thanks, Mam. We'll see you at the wedding. Betty confirmed again that she'll stay with Gran.'

'That's great. Chat you soon.'

After the call, Lottie wondered if her girls would still be welcome at Grace's wedding. Would she herself be welcome? Would there even be a wedding?

———

Ann was unable to finish her sewing work after her conversation with Lottie Parker on the beach. She was annoyed with herself. Why had she been so open? Revealing things she'd only spoken aloud to one other person in her life. On the other hand, she hadn't told the detective everything. A frisson of guilt caused the shake in her hands, and she decided to abandon her work for the day.

Hopefully Denis wouldn't notice her anguish when she arrived home, though she suspected he would. He was very astute. That was what made him an ideal county councillor. His constituents loved him. He was a fighter, too. Fought tooth and nail for the children's playground located outside the village. He'd even completed the funding application for the local community group, and in the end the council had carried out most of the work.

She tidied up the fitting room. Put away the material she had been working on. Stowed the cash Grace had paid in the floor safe. Plugged out anything that was connected to a socket.

At the door, she took one last look around and found all was in order, but the tremor had moved from her hands to her entire body. She suddenly felt cold, as though ice was flowing through her blood. The terrible memories she'd resurrected refused to abate. Home to a hot bath and a glass of wine and she'd be fine.

She held the shop keys in her hand and switched off the

light. As she reached for the latch, a knock on the door made her jump backwards. The door opened.

Her hand flew to her chest. 'You scared the living daylights out of me.'

'Are you leaving early? I could see you through the window tidying up.'

'What if I am? I'm my own boss.' Where was she getting this courage from? 'I'm sorry, but I'm finished for the day. I'm heading home now.'

A hand clasped her shoulder as the person walked in, pushing her backwards. 'We need to talk. And I will decide when and if you can leave. Got it?'

She stayed silent, not trusting what words would come out of her mouth.

The ice in her blood froze solid with fear.

63

Galway Garda HQ would have taken Kirby's breath away if he hadn't already been coughing after a hastily sneaked cigar before entering the main doorway. He couldn't remember ever seeing such a modern garda station. Ragmullin station had undergone an extensive renovation a few years back, but despite that, over half of the building was still a 1930s structure.

'That inspector of yours is something else,' Mooney said, clearing files from one side of his desk to the other.

Kirby wasn't sure if he was complimenting Lottie or ridiculing her, so he didn't comment on it.

'Thanks for seeing me,' he said. 'I believe we may have a crossover on our respective investigations.'

'Robert Hayes, you mean?'

'Yes, but also the woman who was murdered in Ragmullin, Edie Butler. Though I don't have any proof, it appears she was in the Sisters of Forgiveness laundry at some stage in her life. My boss got that information from Brigid Kelly.'

'Yes, I know about that. Nevertheless, as you say, we have no way of verifying it. We contacted the bishop, and he says there are no longer records from that institution. Claims the nuns took them all when they left. But I'm wondering if old Mickey Fox had access to them. He had been burning papers before his body was found. We sent the fragments and scraps, mainly ash if I'm being honest, to a specialist forensic lab, but I wouldn't hold my breath.'

'That's a shame. Have you made any headway in locating Robert Hayes? We know he got on the Galway train.'

'We have him on CCTV exiting Ceannt station in the city. After that, it's like a needle in a haystack. We're checking CCTV around that locality and whatever we can get our hands on out in the Moycullen area where he used to be the parish priest. So far, nothing.'

'At least the CCTV footage can prove he is in Galway.'

'All it proves is that he got off that train. God only knows where he went after that, and he's had days of a head start.'

Kirby was not to be discouraged. 'Is there anything in his background that could lead us to where he might be?'

'All we know is that he spent time as a deacon before being ordained a priest. The bishop reluctantly handed over a file that he had prepared about allegations of abuse of a minor.'

'I didn't see any record of it on PULSE,' Kirby said.

'It was never reported to the gardaí. The bishop now says he shelved it for lack of evidence. God Almighty give me patience. Hayes got kicked out of the clergy but was left to his own devices to roam the country and settle in Ragmullin.'

'The Church has a lot to answer for.'

'You're right there,' Mooney said. 'How did he come to meet Edie Butler?'

'Well, he said he originally knew her in Galway in the eighties.' Kirby had yet to get to grips with Edie's life story. He felt he was jumping all over the place. Two steps forwards, one step back. What he'd learned from her son was that Edie was like a wounded bird. Noel had been sure she'd carried some early life trauma in her heart. 'Hayes may have sought her out if he learned she was living in Ragmullin, or he may have bumped into her. Ragmullin isn't like Galway. It's a small enough town in a smaller county.'

'Still, of all the women he could meet...'

Leaning back in the comfortable chair, Kirby patted his shirt pocket, as usual craving a smoke. 'You're right. Something or someone could have led him to her.'

'Was she ever featured in the local papers for anything? He may have seen a photograph of her.'

'From what I can gather, talking to the salon staff where she worked, and her son, she was a private person. Not involved in anything in the community, as far as they could tell me. Liked her alcohol, though, and Hayes worked in a pub as a chef, so he could have spotted her there.'

'What about a husband?'

'He died in an accident right before her younger lad was born. She has two sons. Noel works as a mechanic, the other, Jerry, is a student. He's just flown back from an end-of-school trip abroad. Such a sad time for them both.'

A knock came on the door and it was opened without Mooney answering.

'Sarge, Councillor Wilson is downstairs spitting fire.'

'That's all I need. What's his problem this time?'

'It's about his wife. He says she never came home from work and she's not at her shop.'

'Maybe she went to the pub for a drink. Met a friend. Went shopping or something. Fob him off.'

Kirby eyed Mooney. 'I wouldn't be so quick to do that if I were you.'

'You don't know Wilson like I do. If there's a day without his puss in the paper or his voice on the radio, he blames us. A fucking head-the-ball, he is.'

'My boss told me that she spoke with her today. Something about a disturbing conversation. And if she really is missing...'

Mooney rubbed his beard, tightened his tie and stood.

'What has Lottie Parker done now? God give me strength. Seems I better give the Pope his audience then.'

'What are you doing to find my wife?' Wilson exploded before Mooney hardly had his toe across the threshold. He noticed that the councillor was without his customary cravat.

'You'd better sit down and explain it all to me,' he said, keeping his voice as low and even as he could muster.

'I told that other guard. He wrote it down. I want to know what you're doing about it.'

'We have three murders to investigate, Mr Wilson.' He refused to call him Councillor. 'Unless you can show me some proof that your wife has been harmed or is missing, you must wait a few more hours.'

'Proof she's been harmed? You want me to bring you her body?'

'No need for theatrics.'

'You have three people murdered and no one charged. You arrested that prick O'Shaughnessy and then you let him go. Do you even know what you're doing? Are you waiting until my wife turns up dead as number four?'

'Not at all. Have you checked the pubs and—'

'My wife does not drink in public houses. You are insulting me now, Sergeant.'

'Maybe she went for a drive. Is her car at her work or at home?'

Wilson looked momentarily confused. So perhaps he hadn't checked, Mooney thought.

'It's not at home,' he said. 'It's not at her shop either. But if she went anywhere, she'd have told me. She'd have phoned or texted me. She never, I repeat never, goes anywhere without telling me.'

'Did you know she met and spoke with Detective Inspector Lottie Parker today?'

Wilson squinted at him, head to one side. 'Who the fuck is she?'

'She's from Ragmullin and is here to attend the wedding of Grace Boyd and Bryan O'Shaughnessy.'

Wilson shifted on his chair, hands fidgeting. 'And I'm supposed to know her?'

'Do you?'

He shook his head. 'Her name doesn't ring any bells, but I'll be sure to check her out.' He paused, as if trying to get some normality back into his cadence. 'What was my Ann talking to a detective about anyway?'

'That I don't know, but it seems Mrs Wilson had something upsetting to relate. Perhaps she needed some time to herself afterwards.' Mooney made a mental note to contact Lottie as soon as he got rid of Wilson. 'Does your wife's shop have CCTV?'

'Are you joking? Have you seen it. A glorified cabin at the tail end of Spiddal. But it keeps her happy.'

'Okay. Give it a few more hours, and if she's not home then, I'll put someone on it.'

'There's a bloody maniac going around murdering people, and now my Ann is missing and you don't seem to give a damn. I want your best team out looking for her! Do you hear me?'

'I have three investigations on the go and I can't spare any more personnel unless it's absolutely necessary.' Mooney crossed his fingers. He would most likely be sidelined tomorrow by the arrival of new detectives. Maybe then he could go look for Ann Wilson, if she was still missing. Perhaps she'd seen sense and left her bully of a husband. At least he hoped that was all it was. He ran a finger along the inside of his shirt collar, suddenly sweating.

'I'm going straight to your superintendent to report you for insubordination and neglect of your duties.' Wilson shoved back the chair as noisily as he could and left the room, banging the door behind him.

Mooney breathed out a sigh of relief, which was closely followed by a surge of panic. What if Ann Wilson was another victim? He needed to talk to Lottie Parker.

Lottie was sitting on a wall outside the hotel, gazing out at the sea, which in the late afternoon was placid and mirror-like.

'Can I join you?' Mooney asked.

She kept staring at the mesmerising water without looking at him. 'You're here and it was a free country last time I checked. How did you locate me?'

'Larry Kirby told me you got kicked out of O'Shaughnessy's house and gave me the name of your hotel.' He sat on the wall beside her. 'Listen, we have a bit of a situation. Well, it's not a situation yet, but it could be.'

'And everyone says I'm the one who talks in riddles.'

'Not the time, Lottie. I know you met Ann Wilson earlier today. I need to know what you two spoke about.'

'And why would you need to know that?'

'Her husband seems to think she has disappeared. That's what he claims, anyhow.'

Lottie turned to look at him for the first time since he'd joined her. 'Really?'

'He's full of blather, but I don't go seeking out a detective inspector who is on her holidays for the good of my health.'

'Shit.'

'Yeah, shit,' he echoed. 'Thing is, I'm not sure she is actually missing. Denis Wilson is a pumped-up eejit who likes making a drama out of a molehill. He claims she never came home from work and isn't at her shop.'

'Did you check?'

'Where would I get the time for that with three mur—'

'You had the time to find me.'

'That's because I want to know what Ann Wilson talked to you about.'

'You think it's relevant?' she asked.

'Might be.'

'In what way?'

'Don't. Please. Just tell me.'

'It was confidential.' She felt unexpectedly sorry for Mooney and didn't like the sense of unease that squeezed something tightly in her chest. 'What you need to know is that she spent time in the laundry. During her years there, she witnessed a particularly vile attack on a child. I think that could have put her in the cross hairs of the killer.'

'Oh my good God. What happened?'

She ignored his question. 'Did you find Robert Hayes?'

'No, but we traced him getting off the Galway train on Monday evening. He has to be around somewhere.'

'He was involved in the incident Ann witnessed all those years ago. And he knew Edie Butler who was found murdered earlier this week in Ragmullin. He is very dangerous.'

'What exactly did Ann witness?'

'A young child was shoved into one of the washing machines. Hayes locked her in and turned the machine on. She died shortly afterwards. Ann claimed the child was Bryan O'Shaughnessy's little sister.'

'Fuck.'

'Yeah. Fuck.'

'This could mean that it's O'Shaughnessy going around killing those he deemed to be involved in his sister's murder.'

'Possibly, but I think it's more likely Robert Hayes who is killing witnesses.'

Mooney lowered his head, tugged his beard and sighed long and hard. 'Where is Bryan O'Shaughnessy now?'

'I have no idea. But he doesn't know what Ann told me. I haven't spoken to him yet. I've been kicked out of the house and I seem to have fucked up my relationship with Mark Boyd. All in a day's work, even though it's not my work. I just wanted to uncover the truth. It's up to you to follow the evidence and nab the killer.' She paused, listened to the purring of the Atlantic Ocean. 'I can't stop thinking about that child and what happened to her. And I can't stop thinking about Brigid Kelly. Just as defenceless as the child.'

'Was Brigid involved back then?'

'She was born in that convent.'

Mooney stood, shoved his hands in his pockets and sighed long and hard. 'Is it the same person doing all this?'

'I suspect it is. Have you found Imelda Conroy?'

'No. She's in the wind too.'

'She could be more of a suspect than a victim in all this,' Lottie said quietly. 'Did you get the advanced DNA results?'

'Nothing's back yet. You know as well as I do that this type of analysis takes time.'

'Have you found out any more information on Assumpta Feeney?'

'Just that she entered the convent at eighteen, but by the time she was twenty she'd left the Sisters of Forgiveness and was studying to be a nurse.'

Lottie stood. 'It's likely that she was in the convent at the same time as Ann and Edie, even Brigid.' She felt a perverse sort of excitement that they were getting somewhere. 'Mooney, you have a serial killer on your hands and it's more than possible that the motive relates to the incident with the child that Ann told me about. This killer won't stop until everyone who witnessed it, or took part in it, is dead.'

'She told you that Robert Hayes locked the child in the machine. I need to elevate him from person of interest to a serious suspect in all the murders.'

She didn't want to state the obvious again, but felt she had to. 'Don't forget that the little girl was possibly Bryan O'Shaughnessy's sister.'

Mooney looked around wistfully. 'There's that too. What do I do?'

'Find Ann Wilson before it's too late. She can tell you who else was there that day.'

'What if you're wrong about this?'

'What if I'm right?'

64

By the time Bryan returned to the house, Grace had made three floral wreaths, though she needed just one. She heard his jeep drive into the yard, but it was another five minutes before he ventured inside with the dog at his heels.

'Where were you?' she asked, sounding like a nagging wife, even though she hadn't meant to sound like that and she was not yet his wife. Might never be. That thought filled her with sadness.

'I drove around.' He filled the dog's bowl, then plugged in the kettle. 'There's so much going on, I don't know what to do with myself.'

'You could have stayed here and talked to me.'

'With your brother and Lottie around? Impossible.'

She found herself smiling conspiratorially. 'You don't have to worry about them for the time being. Mark went back to Ragmullin to get Sergio. He won't return until tomorrow. And I sent Lottie Parker away.'

'Sent her away? Where?'

'I think she went to a hotel. I honestly don't care where she is. I couldn't stand having her in our house any longer. She is a pain, that woman.'

'But—'

'She thinks you are a murderer. Can you believe that, Bryan?'

'I don't blame her, to be honest. Things don't look good for me.'

'Why would you say that?' She twisted round on the chair to look up at him.

'I've been interviewed by the guards twice, arrested once. They'll be back for me.'

'If you've done nothing wrong, what have you to be afraid of? And take off those boots. You're trailing muck over the floor. I mopped it fifteen minutes ago. Where were you, to get in such a state?'

Grace surprised herself with how she was able to talk to him. Usually she was a listener, and it had served her well over the years. You could learn a lot by just keeping your ears open and your mouth shut.

'Told you, I just drove around, and then I walked the fields with Tess and along the beach. My head is in bits, Grace. I'm so afraid.'

'Why would you be? You've got a good solicitor. The guards can go and shite.'

He laughed.

'What's funny?'

'That's so un-Grace-like.'

'It's time I stood up for myself and for you. People will walk all over us if we let them.'

She felt his hands wrap around her neck as he leaned into her back where she sat. She could smell his sweat, the odour of the sheep and the fields, even the sea. He kissed her hair.

'What are you making there?' He was looking over her shoulder, his voice a little too harsh in her ear.

'Attempting to make a wreath for my veil. But I'm not sure...'

'Not sure of what?'

'If we should get married at all?'

He released her and sat on the chair beside her. 'Why not?'

'Because people are getting murdered and you are a suspect.'

'I didn't kill anyone.'

'I know that.' She twisted round to look at him. 'But how do we convince other people?'

'I shouldn't have to convince anyone. Grace,' he took her hand in his, 'I honestly don't know what to do.'

'You need to eat,' she said, 'but I haven't cooked anything.'

'Don't worry about it. We can go out somewhere.'

'We can't do that. I can't face people staring at us.'

'They won't stare.'

She pulled her hand free of his. 'They will. Until you can clear your name. Have you told me the truth about that DNA?'

'I told you the reason for it. I did some work at that cottage. So it's perfectly legitimate that my DNA would be found there.'

'No, I mean you being some sort of relation to Imelda Conroy.'

'I really don't know what it means. I told you all this the other night.'

'You did. Could she be the sister you told me about. Your younger sister?'

'I'm not sure the age works.'

'Maybe a daughter of your sister then?'

'Anything is possible,' he said. 'I lost all contact with my family until I inherited the farm from my brother when he died. My father had bequeathed it to him.'

'You could try some of those sites. I read about them. Ancestry something or other.' She suddenly felt excited.

'The thing is, Grace, I really don't want to find anyone. I'm content with my life here with you. I can do without the compli-cations.'

'What complications?'

'There's something else I haven't told you.'

She felt stuck to the chair, frozen in place, with an irrational urge overtaking her. She wanted to smash the three little floral wreaths she had made. 'I am not sure I want to hear what you have to say.'

'But I have to tell you this. There is another possibility for the DNA. I was hoping Lottie could find out something for me, and I would have told you then. But events have surpassed all that now.'

'I'm not liking this, Bryan O'Shaughnessy,' Grace said, 'and you haven't even told me yet.'

He took her hands again, and she felt the callused skin press against her soft flesh. She could hear Tess barking furiously outside.

'The thing is, *mo ghrá*, a lifetime ago I had this girlfriend—'

A knock came on the door, interrupting him, before it was pushed in.

'Bryan O'Shaughnessy, you are a fucking murderer and I want to know what you've done with my wife.'

Grace looked on in horror as Denis Wilson grabbed Bryan by the collar and hauled him up from the chair. Tess circled them, barking.

Bryan was bigger and stronger than the other man. With one punch he landed Wilson back out the door he'd just come in through.

And she didn't know whether to laugh or cry.

65

'I need your help.' That was what the young woman had said to Ann, and for some reason she could not explain at the time, she had believed her. There was something pathetic and strangely beguiling about her, and she could see that she'd been physically hurt.

'Why do you think I would help you?' she'd asked, surprising herself at how calm her voice sounded despite being totally petrified.

'Because you are in danger. We need to go someplace else. It's not safe here.'

'Of course it's safe. This is my haven, my shop and studio. The only place I can find peace of mind.'

'You have to believe me, Ann.'

'How do you know my name?'

'For one thing, it's over your door outside.'

Of course it is, Ann thought. Still she hesitated.

The woman grabbed her sleeve, tugging her. 'Please. Come with me. We have to leave now.'

Full of misgivings, Ann found herself locking the door and leading the woman to her car. Her hands still shook, but there was something else too. It was as if a surreal mist had descended. As if her childhood nightmare was nearing an end, and she welcomed it.

They drove all the way out to Clifden. It took well over an hour, and the woman slept fitfully, her head pressed against the side window. When she stopped the car, Ann suggested a pub to get food and a drink.

'Do the people around here know you?'

Ann thought about that. They'd know her husband, so in turn it was realistic to assume her face would be familiar to some.

'Maybe.' She drove on down to a secluded cove, parked the car and removed her seat belt. 'Tell me who you are.'

'You don't need to know that. It's better actually that you don't, because everyone I've been in contact with over the last few months is now dead or in danger. I fear it's all my fault.'

'That's reassuring.' Ann tried to be light-hearted when inside all she felt was turmoil.

'No need for the sarcasm. I'm serious.'

'So am I. I want to know who you are.'

'Imelda Conroy.'

Ann had half expected that answer, so the shock was not immense, but it did make her shiver. 'You started all this with your stupid radio documentary thing.' Anger now replaced her fear.

'I wanted to tell a story. I was trying to make a living. I didn't mean for... all this murder.'

'Huh? How can it be your fault, then?'

'I opened up old wounds, wounds that cannot be repaired. They run too deep.'

'I don't follow.'

'I talked to people who would rather forget their trauma. In doing so, I believe a killer took matters into their own hands and began to wreak havoc.'

'And you think I am one of those carrying around a trauma?'

'Yes, I know it. I saw the convent records. Mickey Fox had them. The old bastard.'

Ann had heard he'd been murdered. 'Did you kill him for them?'

'Me? Good God, no. But someone got to him. I think he was burning the records at his caravan and then he was... attacked. I fled.'

'But there were hundreds, if not thousands of women who were thrown in the convent and forgotten about. Do you really think they are all going to be killed?'

'No, not all. Only those who were present the day a little girl was murdered.'

Ann held her breath, shocked that Imelda had learned of the tragedy. She didn't want to reveal her personal knowledge of that terrible event. Not yet.

'A lot of girls and babies died in there. Mainly from neglect and torture. Some of those deaths could be classed as manslaughter, if not murder. So who are you referring to?'

'You know exactly who I'm talking about. A little girl the nuns renamed Gabriel.'

Ann inhaled so suddenly she thought she might pass out. 'How do you know who was there that day?'

'It was logged. Those who were working in the laundry room. Whoever visited the convent. All that.'

She had no memory of anyone keeping a note of events. 'Who made the log?'

'A young novice named Assumpta Feeney.'

'That's the name of the woman who was murdered in the cottage you were renting.' The fear returned in waves. Had Imelda killed Assumpta?

'I know what you're thinking, but I did not kill her.'

'You were renting the place and then you disappeared. Makes you look guilty as hell.'

Imelda slammed her fist on the dashboard. 'No, no, no. You have to listen to me. Assumpta knew who locked the little girl in the machine.'

'And who was it?'

'A man called Robert Hayes.'

Ann felt the air release from her body. So Imelda knew.

She leaned back in the seat. Then she got out of the car, the atmosphere suddenly stifling in the confined space.

The sea looked so peaceful while she was churning around inside. It was all too much. Too much in a short space of time. She'd been transported back to the horror and she knew she had no choice but to face it. Stand up to it. First of all, though, she needed to discover everything Imelda Conroy knew and what she was after.

66

Kirby had driven out to the priest's house near Moycullen. The crime-scene tape was in place and the house was well guarded. The SOCOs' van was in the driveway and he visualised the work they were doing inside. Would Robert Hayes return to the scene of the crime? Probably not. He was more than likely off hunting for his next victim.

He looked at the printout that Mooney had given him. It contained only broad details of the murders. He reversed the car, made a three-point turn and headed for O'Shaughnessy's house.

He arrived just as a man came flying out the back door, landing on his back on the paved yard. He stood quickly, dusted himself down and pointed an accusing finger at the man standing in the doorway.

'This is not the last of it, O'Shaughnessy,' he yelled, gesticulating wildly. 'I'm going to have you arrested. For assault. For murder.'

He turned and jumped into a shining white SUV and sped off down the narrow lane.

Kirby approached as Grace joined Bryan at the door. A black and white dog ran around in circles.

'You're back, Detective Kirby,' she said.

'Heel, Tess,' Bryan said, then turned to Kirby. 'You're the guy from Ragmullin, are you?'

'Yep, that's me. And I'd murder a cup of tea.' Then he felt his cheeks flare. 'Sorry. Wrong turn of phrase there.'

But it seemed to defuse the situation. Grace smiled and brought him inside. Bryan followed them in after he'd calmed and secured his dog.

While she busied herself with mugs and tea bags, Bryan brought Kirby into a musty-smelling living room.

'This is my den. Grace has the rest of the house looking like a new penny, but I like to retain some of my old life in here.'

Kirby thought the room could do with a window being opened now and again. However, he welcomed the smell of cigarette smoke. A kindred spirit.

'I'm not here to judge the decor or to judge you, Mr O'Shaughnessy, but I do have a few questions.'

'It's Bryan. Do I need my solicitor present?'

'That's up to you.' Kirby was surprised by the question but recognised the wary look in O'Shaughnessy's eyes.

'You see, I've been questioned twice already and arrested once before being released without charge.'

'I heard. I understand.'

'Where are my manners? Please, sit.'

Kirby took the couch and almost sank to the floor. He thought he felt a spring twang, then buckle beneath him. Bryan sat on the recliner armchair.

'You've lived here all your life then?' Kirby tried to not look as uncomfortable as he felt.

'On and off. The land was left to me by my brother when he died.'

'And you're all set to be married now. Grace is a lovely woman.'

'She is one in a million.'

'Have you had other relationships over the years?'

'That's an odd question, if you don't mind me saying so.'

'The thing is, I'm investigating a murder that occurred this week in Ragmullin.'

Bryan visibly bristled. He puffed out his chest, and even though he was sitting, his height seemed to stretch. 'I don't believe this. While Mooney is trying to pin three murders on me here in Galway, you think you can make me responsible for another one?'

'Not at all. I'm just after some information.'

'Who am I supposed to have murdered this time?'

'I did not accuse you of anything.' The way the man was acting, Kirby felt like adding a *yet* to that statement.

'Fire ahead, but I warn you, I am at the end of my tether with all this.'

'The woman who was murdered in Ragmullin, in the most vicious way, was named Edie Butler. Did you know her?' He watched for a reaction.

Bryan raised an eyebrow, leaned his head to one side then shook it. 'Can't say that I did.'

'It appears, and this is hearsay, that you dated her for a time when she lived down this way. She was originally from Salthill.'

'Have you a photograph of her?'

'I do.' Kirby scrolled through the photos on his phone, then stood, with difficulty, and handed it over.

'Shit. Yes. She looks different, but I did know her. Long time ago. She was Edie Martin back then. And she's dead?'

'Murdered.'

'Good God. May she rest in peace.'

'Tell me about your relationship with her.' Kirby returned to sit on the couch.

Bryan rubbed a hand over his eyes and down his cheek. 'What is going on?'

'I don't know, but I want to know about you and Edie.'

'I can hardly remember it. It was a long time ago. There's not much to know. A fling. We met a few times. For drinks and food and... She was a lovely woman. But what I remember about her is that she was never comfortable in her own skin, if you get my meaning. Always on edge. Then one day she said she had to leave. She wanted to spread her wings. That's what she said as far as I recall.'

'She seems to have only got as far as the midlands.'

'Was she happy, do you know?'

'I don't know that. She worked in a hair salon. She had two sons. Her husband died.'

'How did you discover I used to know her?'

'It came up in one of our interviews. A colleague of hers at the salon mentioned your name. Seems that Edie had really liked you. Apparently yours was the only name she mentioned from her past.'

'How? It was so long ago. I wasn't in love with her or anything. I had the farm to take care of. I was busy. And truthfully, I was happy on my own.'

'Until you met Grace?'

'Aye, she made me realise that there's more to life than raising and selling sheep.'

'Grace is a lot younger than you.' Kirby worried he might just have overstepped the mark. But Bryan smiled back at him.

'Stating the obvious, detective.'

'Sorry. None of my business.'

'But murder is, and I'm sorry I can't help you. Edie was a troubled woman when I knew her, but I haven't seen her in decades. I did not kill her.'

'That's grand, so.' Kirby knew Bryan's DNA was already on file in Galway, and he would make sure it was checked against what they had in Ragmullin.

'How did she die?' Bryan asked.

'She was found in a river. The final post-mortem report isn't in yet, but she was scalded so badly that she had a heart attack from the shock. It seems the murderer kept pouring boiling water over her until she died. Boiled to death.'

The sound of smashing crockery filled the room as Grace let the tray she was holding fall out of her hands.

Neither man had heard her enter.

67

Sitting in her beautiful hotel room, almost going insane staring at the four brightly painted walls, Lottie phoned Kirby and asked him to join her. When he arrived, he had a bottle of wine in one hand and a corkscrew in the other.

'I know you're off the sauce,' he said with an apologetic smile, 'but I need a drink, so I booked a room for the night. It was either the wine or brandy from the bar, and no way was I paying for a bottle of brandy.' He busied himself with the cork.

She fetched two glasses from the bathroom. 'I'll have a small one.'

'Stop right there. I won't be responsible for you falling off the wagon.'

'I have no intention of getting drunk. I just need a drop to drown my sorrows.'

'If you insist.' He poured the wine into the tumblers, filling his to the top and tipping little more than a dribble into hers.

'You're a bastard, Kirby.'

'I've been called that countless times.' Grinning, he sat by the desk situated under the wall-mounted television and took a long, thirsty gulp before refilling his glass. 'A bit warm, but it's thirteen per cent alcohol, so I won't say no to it.'

She figured he should have got himself two bottles, or perhaps forked out for the brandy. She pushed her own glass away untouched and sat on the bed, stretching out her jeans-clad legs before crossing them at the ankles and resting her hands behind her head.

'This case is a bit of a mess,' she said.

'What case? You're on holidays. You don't have a case. Well, maybe your suitcase there on the floor.'

'Funny ha-ha,' she said glibly. 'I feel like I'm in hell, not on a holiday. Tell me what Mooney has. He isn't sharing much with me.'

'He hasn't got a lot, from what I can gather. I was provided with a synopsis of his investigations, but the evidence seems to be sparse.'

'Let us assume the killer is a he for argument's sake. He is slick and must be working to a plan.'

'What plan would that be?'

'If I knew that, I'd be able to get ahead of him. We have to figure it out before he kills again. Because I'm certain he won't stop until he gets them all.'

'Gets who?' Kirby looked askance, scratching his head of curls.

'Whoever is next on his list. My theory is that he got his hands on the nuns' records, or else he has a photographic memory. He spent years locating all his victims, maybe even keeping an eye on them, but when Imelda Conroy started her documentary, he knew he had to act.'

'She could be the killer.'

'She could be, but... I don't know, Kirby.' She looked around the room. 'I wish we had an incident board.'

'I can go buy a set of Sharpies if you want,' he said, following her gaze around the white-painted walls.

'God, no. I just mean it makes it easier to follow when things are visible.'

'It'd be easier if you were legitimately working the investigations.'

'Tell me something I don't know.'

'Okay, I will,' he said. 'Ann Wilson was reported missing by her husband this evening.'

'Sure I know that. Mooney told me. I should ring him to see if she has turned up. She was in the convent back then too, when Gabriel was murdered.'

'Who is Gabriel?'

'I told you already about what Ann told me on the beach.'

'Oh, right. All these names are new to me.'

'I have an idea. I just remembered I have Ann's phone number.'

'Mooney and her husband would have called it numerous times.'

She found Ann's card and tapped the number into her phone. 'No answer.'

She got off the bed and took the glass with the drop of wine Kirby had poured for her. She sniffed at it, hoping to relish a fine grape aroma, but a stale odour wafted to her nose. 'How are you even drinking this shit?'

'Needs must.'

Just then, her phone rang and Ann's number appeared on the screen. 'It's her. Thank God. She must be okay.' She put down her glass and answered the call. 'Hello, Ann.'

'Who is this?'

'Lottie Parker. We spoke earlier today. Ann, are you okay?'

'I'm not Ann. I just have her phone.'

A trickle of dread tracked a cold line down the length of Lottie's spine. It was a female voice, one she could not place. Still, she had a feeling she'd heard it before. 'Who are you? Where is Ann?'

'Too many questions at once. I can't think. You're confusing me.'

Lottie thought she heard a sob, and her training kicked in. She could not alienate this person who was in possession of Ann Wilson's phone. 'Don't be upset. Please talk to me. I want to help in any way I can.'

'No one can help me. Are you the detective Ann spoke to?'

'Yes.'

'Then you have to do something before someone else dies.'

'How can I do that? Do you have information that can help?'

'Find out all you can about Assumpta Feeney. She has to be the key to it all. She was first to die.'

A thought raced through Lottie's mind. 'Is this Imelda?'

The call went dead.

She looked at the phone in her hand. 'I think that was Imelda Conroy. Why has she got Ann Wilson's phone?'

'Holy Mother of God,' Kirby exclaimed. 'I better call Mooney.'

'Wait a minute. Let's think this through.'

'What did the caller say? You look puzzled.'

'She said Assumpta Feeney is the key to everything. But Mooney said Assumpta lived abroad for years. How can we find out about her? Is there anything on those printouts he gave you?'

He opened his jacket and extracted a wad of very creased pages.

'Jesus, Kirby, you need to get a man bag. Or an iPad.'

'Nothing wrong with an inside pocket.' He flattened the pages out on the narrow table. Lottie leaned over them. He was right, they were sparse. She realised why Mooney hadn't told her much. It was because he really hadn't got anything. Loads of DNA with only one hit, Bryan O'Shaughnessy.

'Did Bryan ever know Assumpta Feeney, I wonder.' She put a finger under his name.

'We could go out there and ask him, I suppose,' Kirby said, 'but I don't think I'd be welcomed.'

'Why?' She looked at him pointedly. 'What did you do?'

'Nothing. Why do you always think I did something wrong?' He must have caught her look, because he said, 'Okay, I get it. Anyhow, I only asked Bryan about Edie Butler and if he had a relationship with her. He didn't remember her at first, but then he did. Said she always seemed to be on edge and left him suddenly.'

'And that was enough to get you barred from the house?'

'Not that, no. I was telling him about the awful way Edie had died just as poor Grace arrived with tea on a tray, which she dropped. Tea and crockery all over the floor. I made my excuses and left. But honestly, I don't want to bother her again. I'd say this week has been hell for her.'

'It has been worse for the victims of these awful crimes. I better ring Mooney.'

It felt like she'd hardly finished the call when Mooney arrived.

'How did you get here so fast?' Lottie asked, opening the door.

'I was in the vicinity. I received a call from Denis Wilson wanting to press charges against Bryan O'Shaughnessy. I'm on my way to the Wilson house now. Probably another storm in a teacup for me to listen to when I should be in my office reviewing the evidence or out searching for his wife, if she really is missing. I sincerely hope she's just upped sticks and left him.'

'Come in. You've met Detective Kirby.'

'Care for a drink?' Kirby said.

'No thanks, I'm still working. God knows, I hardly put my head down all week.'

Kirby offered the weary detective his chair and went over to the window to lean against the ledge.

Mooney asked, 'What's this about Ann Wilson's phone?'

'Like I told you, I tried ringing her,' Lottie explained. 'I had her number from earlier today. It went unanswered. Then, a few seconds later... It was only a few seconds, Kirby, wasn't it?'

'Yep.'

'I got a call. Ann's number was on the screen. When I answered it, it wasn't Ann. I'm certain it was Imelda Conroy.'

'Why would she have Ann Wilson's phone?'

'Because she abducted Ann, perhaps?'

'I doubt that.' Mooney looked sceptical

'You said her husband reported her missing,' Lottie insisted.

'I did, yes, but Denis is a fucking drama queen.'

'Maybe this time it's not drama,' she said. 'Why else would Imelda have Ann's phone?'

Mooney yawned and shook his head. He looked so exhausted that Lottie almost offered him the bed to lie down on. 'What did she say? This caller you think might be Imelda Conroy.'

'She told me to find out about Assumpta Feeney. That she's the key because she was the first to die.'

Kirby piped up then, coming alive. 'But Edie Butler was first to die if we connect all the murders.'

'Maybe she was just the first to be found,' Mooney said. 'What's the link between them all?'

'Their history and the method of killing,' Lottie said. 'They were scalded with boiling water, Mickey with toxic fluid. And little Gabriel was murdered decades ago in the convent in a big old washing machine. Robert Hayes has to be the killer.'

'But you have no evidence of him being anywhere near any of the crime scenes.'

'Not yet,' Kirby said. 'But we'll find it.'

'Like I said, the modus operandi is similar,' Lottie said, 'and he used to be in and out of the convent.'

'I need hard evidence,' Mooney said. 'All I have so far is DNA tying Bryan O'Shaughnessy to the cottage where Assumpta was murdered, not to mention him being in some way related to Imelda Conroy. And you vouched that he couldn't have killed Brigid, the priest's housekeeper.'

'True. We have to find Imelda.'

'You do know you have nothing to do with this investigation?'

'Well, you keep contacting me.' She realised she sounded childish. 'I received the call from Ann's phone.'

'And I will investigate that.' Mooney sounded adamant. 'I better see Wilson and take details of this complaint he wants to make.'

'You should get uniforms to do that.'

'He insisted on me. Anyway, it will be good to have a look around his house. If his wife is actually missing, there might be some clue there. Goodnight to you both.'

When Mooney had left, Kirby stood and saluted the closed door. 'He's a bit out of his depth, isn't he?'

'I agree. He seems to be collapsing under the pressure. I feel sorry for him.'

'I better be off to my own room before I collapse from tiredness. I'm heading back to Ragmullin early in the morning. Will I take that with me?' He pointed to the almost empty bottle.

'No, leave it. I think you've had enough. I'll pour it down the sink.'

'You're the boss,' he said with a wink, and left the room.

68

It was fully dark by the time Ann arrived home. After the journey from Clifden, she'd had to drive into the city to drop Imelda Conroy in Eyre Square. The young woman said she'd be safer in a crowd. Ann had pleaded with her to go to the guards, but she was adamant that she could not. They could not protect her, she'd said.

When she put her key in the front door, Denis almost collapsed out on top of her.

'Where the fuck were you?' He grabbed her shoulder and hauled her into the hall, shoving the door shut behind them.

'Slow down, Denis. You're hurting me.'

'I want an answer.' He shook her with his hands on both her shoulders. 'I've been out of my mind with worry. I even went to the guards. Do you realise you've made a fool of me?'

She wanted to say he'd made a fool of himself, but bitter experience made her pause. Then she noticed his bulging, damaged eye.

'What happened to you?' she asked, incredulous, though secretly impressed by whoever had done it.

'It's nothing. A skirmish. Don't worry, the bastard will pay for it. I'm making a formal complaint. If they won't lock him up for murder, they can lock him up for this.' He stabbed a finger to his eye and scowled.

'Who did it?'

'Doesn't matter. Where were you?'

'I had a particularly taxing day, so I went for a drive.'

'A drive? A fucking drive? Without telling me? You're so stupid.' He shook his head, and it must have hurt because he gingerly patted his eye socket. His tone reduced a notch. 'You know there's a murderer out there, Ann. I really thought you would turn up dead. I was terrified for you.'

'Don't fret. I'm here now, and as you can see, I am very much alive.'

'Are you being smart with me?'

'God, no. I'm trying to reassure you that I'm fine.' She made to pass by him in the hall, but he caught her arm.

'Why didn't you ring or text?'

'I just needed some head space, Denis.'

'You had no regard for *my* head space and what you've put me through.'

'I said I'm sorry. What more can I say?'

'Give me your phone,' he demanded.

She sighed and searched through the detritus of her handbag. 'I must have left it in the car.'

He snatched the bag from her hands and upended it. Everything fell out on the hall floor. No phone.

She bit back a *told you so* and said, 'I'll go out for it.'

'Doesn't matter.'

Leaving the mess on the floor, he took her by the elbow and led her into the living room. She noticed a smear of dust on the mantelpiece that she must have missed, and hoped he didn't see it. He was upset enough.

'Tell me exactly what you did today,' he said. 'Who you saw. Who you spoke to. The works.'

With a sigh, she extracted herself from his grip and sat on a hard armchair. He preferred sturdy furniture. Said it was better for his back. No thought for her comfort, but she'd learned to live with it.

'Really, Denis, this is getting too much for me. I need to have some space to myself. You are crowding me out.'

'You know it's because I love you. I'm trying to protect you.'

Protect yourself, more like, she thought. 'It's too much. You're smothering me.'

'For fuck's sake, woman. Answer what I asked you and then we will sit down with a nice cup of tea or a glass of wine. Maybe a whiskey. Yes, I need a strong one.'

'I'll fix the drinks.'

'Not until you answer the question.'

She wondered which question he meant, but dared not antagonise him further. Plus she feared she might not be convincing in her lies. Then again, she'd been lying to him her whole life, so she should just about manage this.

'I had a wedding dress fitting.'

'Not for that Boyd woman, I hope?'

'Actually, yes. Grace came into the shop with her future sister-in-law. Lottie Parker.'

'Mooney mentioned her. What has she to do with you?'

'Nothing. She's just here for the wedding.'

'What had Grace to say for herself?'

'Nothing much. Just that she loved my work and would recommend me to everyone she knew.' She had done no such thing, but Ann wanted to divert his attention from her own subterfuge.

'What was so taxing about all that? Did this Parker woman question you or something?'

'No, it's just that Grace is fussy. She wanted the belt raised and the strap tightened. And as it was the final fitting, I had to do the alterations with both of them there looking at me. You know I find it hard to work under scrutiny.' She hoped he didn't see through her lies.

'I have to work under scrutiny every day. It's a pain in the hole, but if I want to get into government, I have to suffer the eejits around here.'

'You love it, Denis. I know you do. But I prefer working in the shadows.'

'You will have to come out of the shadows once the election is called. I'll need a dutiful wife by my side. There will be interviews, soundbites, canvassing, hand-shaking, baby-kissing.' He paused, and smiled at the image he was creating. Then he frowned. 'I'll have to hire someone in PR to tutor you for your new role.'

'That won't be necessary. I can act as good as the next one.' Shit, maybe she'd gone too far. 'I'll make those drinks. I'll have a whiskey myself.'

'No, you need to put on some food. I'm starving and I can't have you half cut. You might poison me.' He laughed.

She thought it wasn't a bad idea at all.

69

At the Wilson house Mooney had to leave his car on the road outside the closed sliding gate. He hopped over it, caught his trousers on a splinter of timber and ripped a hole down the knee.

'Bad luck follows bad luck,' he said aloud. Had he got the quote right? Didn't matter. He was having a shit few days, that was all he knew.

He looked up at the imposing house and thought that there must be money in the radio business, because he didn't think councillors got paid much. But what did he know? Not a lot, if his lack of progress on the murders was anything to go by. And now he had to take a statement about an alleged assault and find the missing wife of an obnoxious prick.

He rang the bell and waited. He noted there was no shrubbery or flowers. Resin driveway and a cobbled step. Low-maintenance.

The door opened. Ann Wilson stood there.

'Yes?' she said.

'Mrs Wilson?'

'That's me.'

For a moment Mooney was speechless. 'I thought you were missing.'

'Seems like I've been found.' Her voice was strained, he noted.

After introducing himself, he said, 'Your husband asked me to call round. Something about a complaint he wanted to make.'

'Oh, and I thought you were looking for me.'

'I was, I am, but now I'm not.' Jesus, he was making a hash of this. Ann Wilson was a striking-looking woman, though she looked as tired as he felt. He could see a tough history written in her face, and he wondered what it was that had her on tenterhooks.

'Come in. Please. Don't mind the mess. I was looking for my phone, but I must have left it in the car.'

'When did you have it last?' Hadn't Lottie Parker said she'd had a call from Ann's phone? She'd thought it might have been Imelda Conroy. Was Ann lying?

'I can't recall. I've had such a busy day.'

He saw how flustered she was and decided not to mention Imelda Conroy just yet.

'Denis is in the living room.' She bent to retrieve her personal stuff from the floor, furiously shoving it all into a large open handbag. Mooney figured it would be easy for someone to steal a wallet or a phone from it. He was about to ask her where she'd been to make Denis think she was missing, but she looked up at him, an unspoken plea in her eyes, just as Wilson appeared in the doorway.

'Detective Sergeant Mooney. At last. Come in here where we can talk in peace.'

Mooney noticed Ann exhale in relief behind her husband's back. He was sure that was what it was. Relief. There seemed to be a strange dynamic going on, and he needed to be alert. He followed Wilson into his living room.

'Nice house you have.' He was useless at small talk.

'See this?' Wilson pointed to his eye. Mooney thought it would take more than a bag of frozen peas to reduce the swelling. 'That gobshite O'Shaughnessy punched me. A totally unprovoked attack. I want him arrested and charged.'

'Can I sit down?'

'Of course. My apologies.' Wilson smirked and sat on a straight-backed armchair. Mooney took the other. It felt like he was sitting on a board. It would help keep him awake.

'Could you explain what happened?'

'Are you not going to write this down?'

'I just want to get the basics tonight. You'll have to make a formal complaint at the station at your convenience.'

'For fuck's sake. It's the likes of you that has the country the way it is.'

Mooney stared him out. No way was he rising to the bait for a row at this hour. He silently congratulated O'Shaughnessy on his precision punch.

'So what happened?'

Wilson exhaled. 'I thought he had taken Ann. He's a murderer after all. But he just lashed out. Didn't give me a chance to defend myself.'

'Did you provoke him?'

'Are you for real? See this?' He jabbed a finger at his eye and winced. 'This is assault. No extenuating circumstances. And that mongrel of his needs to be put down. I'm lucky it didn't bite me.'

'But surely the man didn't do this to you in his own home for no reason?'

'I'm telling you, he did.'

'Did it happen outside the house?'

'I... I was inside, in his kitchen. Or as near inside as I got before he hit me.'

'Did he invite you in? What did you say to him?'

'You're unreal, you know that? If you want to know, I asked

the prick what he'd done with my wife, and he launched at me and punched me in the face.'

'Were you invited into his house?' Mooney asked again, but he was getting a clear picture of what had happened. He knew the likes of Wilson. Jumped up, full of their own importance. No regard for anyone other than themselves.

'No, but you'd already arrested him. He is guilty.'

'Guilty of what?'

'Of murder. Of hitting me. Of abducting my wife.'

'But your wife is here. She looks perfectly all right to me.'

'That's beside the point.' Wilson stood and went to the dresser, pouring himself a generous finger of whiskey. He sat again without offering Mooney anything to drink.

'You entered a man's home.' Mooney adopted the most officious tone he could muster through his exhaustion. 'You threw accusations at him. He may have felt threatened by you and was protecting himself and his property.' He had no idea if that was true or not, but he figured he was close enough.

'Why haven't you charged him with murder?'

'It's an ongoing investigation, which I have no intention of discussing with you.' He stood. 'Call to the station tomorrow morning if you want to make your complaint.'

'I'll make a complaint about your incompetence, Sergeant.'

'That is your prerogative as a civilian. I'm glad your wife wasn't actually missing.' At the door, he paused and turned around. 'Do you know where she was?'

Wilson's face flushed a red-hot fire. 'That is none of your business.'

So Wilson had no idea where Ann had been. But Mooney wanted to know. He had to find out if she'd met Imelda Conroy. And if so, why.

.   .   .

He closed the living room door and found the hallway empty. He spied a light coming from a room to his right, so he walked towards it and stuck his head around the door.

'This is some kitchen,' he said, which was true. 'It's like stepping into a ...' He struggled to find a word to describe the clean lines and meticulous spotlessness.

'Thank you. I like it,' Ann said. 'Denis had this extension built. It's a bit big for just the two of us.'

Mooney was about to ask if they had children, but then thought it might be a sensitive subject. 'I'd like to know where you were today. Your husband reported you missing.'

She stared at the door, her green eyes wide and fearful.

'Don't worry, Ann. Denis is nursing a tumbler of whiskey and his bruised ego.'

'All the same, I don't think it's any of your business, or his.'

'We got a call from your phone.'

'My phone? A call?' She failed to mask her surprise. 'It's in the car. I must have dropped it in the footwell.'

'Or someone took it. Did you give anyone a lift?'

'No, I... I'd like you to leave,' she said, her tone a desperate plea. He noted she had dropped her eyes, unable to meet his gaze.

'Ann, we are hunting a murderer and looking for a missing woman. Not you, I'm glad to see. But this missing woman made a call from your phone. Care to explain.'

'I can't... I must have lost it, or maybe it was stolen.' She bit her lip, hands trembling.

'Where might it have been stolen from you?'

'I don't know.' She lowered her voice. It was laced with desperation. 'Please. Leave me alone.'

'I can't, I'm sorry,' he said. 'Where is Imelda Conroy?'

She slumped onto a chair and brought her hands to her face. 'I dropped her off in the city.' Her voice was just a whisper. 'She must have taken my phone.'

'Where in the city?'

'Eyre Square. I don't know where she is now. That's the truth. Please leave me alone.'

'You will have to explain it to me.'

'I did nothing wrong.'

'You aided a fugitive.'

She looked up at him, tears in her eyes. 'That's not true. She accosted me at my shop. She got in my car and made me drive her all the way to Clifden and back.'

'What did you talk about?'

'Nothing.'

'Ann, I've had a long, exhausting few days, and I'm afraid you may have committed a crime.'

'Please leave me alone. Denis will kill me.'

'Why would he?'

'I don't mean it that way, but if you think I committed a crime and arrest me, it will be a bad image for his public relations machine.'

Mooney smiled, and Ann did too. He pulled out a chair and sat with her.

'His public relations?'

'He reckons the general election will be called soon.'

'I get the feeling you know something that can help my investigation, and it's nothing to do with an election. Tell me everything.'

'Not here. I'm serious. If he believes I'm mixed up in this, he'll go berserk.'

'Do you think that's what happened at O'Shaughnessy's? He went berserk?'

'Probably. But I can't talk now.'

'Okay. When can you speak to me?'

'Tomorrow. In the morning. Give me your number and I'll phone you.'

'You don't have your phone.'

'I'll call to the station then. Where are you based?'

'Garda HQ. Renmore.'

'I'll be there by nine.'

'Are you sure you don't know where I can find Imelda Conroy tonight?'

'I left her in the city. She could be anywhere.'

70

Alone at last, Lottie opened the window and looked out at the dark night. The tide must be in, she thought, because the sound of the waves crashing on the shore was loud, albeit soothing. The hum of the city traffic in the distance brought a little reality to the scene.

Turning back to the room, she picked up the two glasses and stowed the bottle under her arm. She looked around the space that was hers for the night. She missed Boyd. She should ring him. He probably wouldn't answer. And she would not be able to sleep with that hanging over her. No, he'd be back in Galway tomorrow. They could have a proper talk then, face to face. Iron out their differences. Everything would be fine. She hoped.

The room smelled of the two men who had left. Stale cigars and body odour. They could both do with a shower, she thought. Then there was the fusty wine perfume from the glasses. It was so strong she could almost taste it. She emptied what was left and put the bottle in the bin, then ran her finger over the glass that contained the small drop Kirby had poured for her. She tasted it. No, God no. It was vile.

After pouring the remains of the wine down the sink, she had a long, cool shower, brushed her teeth and got into bed.

Her body had chilled, but her mind was on fire.

Even the sound of the waves breezing through the open window could not lull her to sleep.

THE PAST

Gabriel had no idea how long she'd been in the convent, but one Christmas and one Easter had passed. No one from her family had visited her in all that time. She'd been abandoned. This felt even worse than when her mother had died. At least then she had family around her. She had a purpose. She'd cared for her father, brothers and the new baby. But in this horrible place, she was nobody. Nobody's child, they called her. Well, she was somebody's daughter once, but it seemed that now they were right.

There was still no sign of the education she was supposed to get. She needed to learn more reading and writing. She wanted to. But she never once saw a classroom. She depended on the others to sneak books to her and help her with big words. But that wasn't an education. She supposed the real education she'd been getting was one in cruelty. It hardened her heart and destroyed her soul. And she was only a little girl.

One day, she slid into the big machine to scrape the sheet off the sides of the drum. Her hands were torn and the calluses started to bleed. She could feel tears bubble, but she had a job to do.

'Will you hurry up, or I'll switch the machine on with you in there,' a nun shouted.

The words echoed deep inside her and she hurried to get the sheet unstuck. No way did she want to be inside if they closed the door and boiling water spurted in. Climbing out, she scratched her knee on the rough bit of steel where the door shut, and she hesitated, terrified the blood would get on the sheet. The old nun standing in front of her was new. Gabriel hadn't seen her before.

'Well, if it isn't the midget,' the nun roared. 'Heard all about you. You are like a weasel burrowing in where no one else can fit. Do you know why that is?' She didn't wait for a reply. Gabriel didn't have one anyhow, because she had no idea what the nun meant. 'It's because you are a sneaky bitch.'

Gabriel stood with the sheet draped across her arm and her hands and knee bleeding. Some internal alarm was sending signals to her brain to be careful. This nun was unlike the others. She was ancient, big and plump. Most were skinny and scrawny, like the girls themselves. But this nun was well fed, and she had a nasty twist to her mouth, her lips curved downwards as if she had never learned to smile. Her hair was wild and bushy, bursting out of the veil, and her eyes... they were the darkest eyes Gabriel had ever seen. She had never encountered anyone with such piercing blackness pulsing from their soul out through their eyes. She felt as if she was staring evil in the face.

'And what do we do with sneaks?' the nun bellowed.

'I... I don't know.' Gabriel ignored the alarm bells and somehow got the words out.

'You don't know?' The nun shook her head. 'You are an evil child.'

It was then that Gabriel realised all work had stopped. The slow hum of the machines was like a radio switched on low in the background. The girls were standing frozen in the act of ironing, lifting baskets, folding. A tableau of inactivity. Of fear. She spied the young novice at the door. She had befriended Gabriel, *brought her books to read, helped her with her writing. Was she going to run for help? Or was she just ready to run?*

'I'm sorry, but I don't know what you mean,' Gabriel said. Bravery overcame fear for an instant. A fatal instant, as it turned out.

Without warning, the nun hit out with her crucifix, cutting into Gabriel's cheek, then wrenched her arm with the sheet and tugged the cotton from her. She twisted it around Gabriel's body, and even as she struggled, she knew she could not win over the woman's size and strength. She was like a mummy, with only her face visible. She felt she was about to die.

'No!' she cried.

'Come here, someone help me,' the nun roared.

No one moved.

Then someone else came into the room. Footsteps stomping on the concrete-slabbed floor. A man's footsteps.

The mechanical hum of the machines seemed louder. Breath was held in the air. A stagnant silent fear permeated the steamy room.

The nun's eyes blazed as she acknowledged the man who had entered.

She felt weak and strong simultaneously and prayed to her mother to save her. She didn't believe in God any more, but she believed her mother was waiting for her on some higher plane. But she'd deserted her too. Deserted her own daughter.

'No, stop. I don't want to go in there.'

Ignoring her cries, the man lifted her and threw her bodily into the large drum. He slammed the door shut. Gabriel's hands and legs were bound tight by the sheet. As she struggled to free herself, she knew it was fruitless.

The drum started to move. To turn. She went with it. Her stomach roiled and fear turned to terror. She was trapped. She was going to die, the second the boiling water came through the tiny holes in the drum.

The first shot of water hit her between the eyes. And then her nose and cheeks. She coiled in horror as she was twirled around, the water rising with the heat. The heat.

The drum turned faster and faster, and before she succumbed to the swirling water, darkness overcame her. She would not see the light again.

71

RAGMULLIN

SATURDAY

The next morning, Kirby reached his home in Ragmullin shortly after 7.30. He was delighted with himself for having had a good night's sleep and being on the road before six.

Amy was still asleep, so he crept up the stairs, took a shower and pulled on clean clothes. Then he went downstairs to make coffee. Probably created too much noise, because she woke up.

'Good to see you home, Larry,' she said, entering the kitchen and wrapping her arms around him.

'You too. Toast? I've the kettle on.'

'Are you working today?'

'Unfortunately.' He put two slices of bread in the toaster, mentally making a note to buy a bigger one. 'It was a bit of a shit show in Galway.'

'Boyd told me some of what was going on. He picked up Sergio yesterday. He's an amazing kid, though he did miss his dad.'

'How is Boyd?'

'Hard to know. He said he and Lottie had a row. Between

the lines, I think he's broken up with her. You should talk to him.'

'And I think we should stay well away from that drama.' The bread popped up and he began buttering it.

'Ugh.' Amy ran from the room.

'What did I do?' Confused, he looked around as he heard her slam the bathroom door.

He knocked on the door. 'Amy pet, what did I do?'

'Nothing. Sorry.'

'Are you okay in there?'

'Give me a minute.'

He thought he heard her retch. A knot of anxiety twisted in his gut.

'Are you sick?'

Stupid question. He could hear her and hoped he didn't catch whatever she had. No, he was fine, but he worried about her ongoing health issues. Having been badly injured during the course of a murder case a while back, she still attended physio for her damaged leg. Could there be something much worse than that going on?

'Amy, please answer me.'

'The door isn't locked.'

He entered the confined space. She was sitting on the edge of the bath.

'Will I call a doctor?' He knelt in front of her as she wiped her mouth with a towel. He took it from her and held her hand to stop it shaking.

'Are you proposing?' she said with a grin.

'What?' Then he realised the image she had before her. Him on his knees, his hands on hers.

'God, no.' He saw her expression fall. 'I don't mean it like that.' He wondered if perhaps he should ask her the pertinent question. He loved her. Both of them had a troubled past and they were able to share experiences – and, he added in his mind, he really didn't want to live his life without her.

'It's fine,' she said. 'Don't look so worried.' Her face was strained as she tried to make light of her faux pas.

'I'm thinking that maybe it's not such a bad idea.' He noticed her scrunched brow. 'To get married. You and me. Tie the knot. You know?'

Her face lit up. 'Do you mean that?'

'Amy, I never meant anything like it in all my life. Will you marry me?'

He nearly toppled backwards as she threw her arms around his neck, leaned down and whispered in his ear, 'This is the most unromantic proposal ever, in a bathroom with me puking my guts up, and I love you for it.'

'Is that a yes?'

'Of course it is.'

A swell of happiness rushed from his head to his toes as he stood, taking her with him. Then he felt her pushing him away and dashing to lift the lid of the toilet again.

'You're right, Amy. This is not the most romantic place to ask you to marry me,' he said, holding her hair back as she retched.

72

CONNEMARA

As the sun rose on the horizon, Lottie was back standing at the window, a cup of Nespresso in her hand. The spacious room seemed a waste without having Boyd with her. The sea was rough, and the blue skies of the previous few days had been replaced with troubling black clouds.

Imelda's words swirled around in her head, consuming her. Mooney had phoned her at a godawful hour that morning to tell her about his chat with Ann Wilson the night before. She was glad to get his updates and wondered if he did this to keep her from investigating on her own or to get things straight in his mind. Probably a bit of both, she concluded. Her own mind was full of questions.

Why was Imelda in hiding? Why did she say Assumpta was the key to everything? She must have discovered something crucial while researching her documentary. That had to be it. Then there was the link to Bryan's DNA. Was Imelda his daughter? It seemed likely and could yet prove to be critical.

Her brain was still racing when her phone rang. Putting down the cup, she checked the screen.

Mooney. She hadn't expected to hear from him again so soon.

'There's been another murder,' he said without preamble.

'Imelda?'

'No, and I'm only telling you because you'll hear about it. I want you nowhere near this. I need you to know that the shit is properly going to hit the fan today. But I'm warning you. Stay away.'

He hung up.

She tapped into the news app on her phone, fingers trembling at what new horror she would find.

Her breath caught in her throat as she started to read.

Ignoring Mooney's instruction to stay away, she drove over to the crime scene but could not get close. An avalanche of media trucks had descended on the small, seemingly select community of houses where the Wilsons lived. The pack was held back at the end of the road, but she guessed the prominence of Denis Wilson and his radio station, not to mention his role in local politics, had catapulted the murder to the top of the national news.

Mooney must have blacklisted her name, because there was no way anyone was allowing her to get close to the house. Irritation clawed beneath her skin as the first drops of rain fell on her face. She craned her neck to see over the shoulders of the reporters in front of her. No joy. She didn't see any sign of Mooney either. He was probably inside the house.

She made her way back to her car, digging her nails into the palms of her hands in frustration. She hated this outside-looking-in lark.

As she approached the car, a hand reached out from behind her, tugging her sideways.

'Hey, what the...?' She paused when she saw who it was. An

ashen, harried face. A tattered and torn blue fleece with the hood up.

'Imelda?'

'We need to talk.'

'You're right about that,' Lottie said as the rain came down in earnest. 'Get in the car.'

'I'm not going to the garda station with you, if that's what you're planning.'

'Okay. But I'm getting soaked out here and I need you to get in before those reporters recognise you.'

'How would they?'

'Your photo has been all over the news and social media. You're easily recognisable.' Though Lottie had to admit to herself that the unkempt young woman looked nothing like the photo that had been circulated. 'You're a suspect in a series of murders. Don't you know that?'

'Of course I do. But you have to believe me, I did not kill anyone.'

How many times had she heard that in her career? Too many to count. 'Why are you here?'

'I thought I might have got Ann into trouble. I wanted to apologise to her. I reckoned I'd get her on her own when he left for work, but this circus was in full flight when I arrived. What's going on?'

'Get in the car.' Lottie opened the door and waited.

Imelda furtively scanned the area before complying.

Lottie also looked around to see if anyone had noticed them, but all eyes were on the Wilson house. She knew she should ring Mooney about Imelda showing up, but he'd told her to stay away. He was going to be replaced by other detectives soon, so she decided to handle the young woman herself. Once she'd heard what she had to say, then she would bring her in.

God, it felt good to be in control again.

73

RAGMULLIN

Boyd rang the doorbell a second time. He felt guilty calling so early, but he needed to get on the road.

'Sergio forgot his iPad,' he said when Kirby eventually opened the door to him.

'You're up bright and early,' Kirby commented.

'I'm heading back to Connemara this morning.' Boyd followed his colleague into the living room. 'The wedding is tomorrow. Grace would never forgive me if I missed it.'

Kirby picked up the tablet from an armchair. 'This it?'

'Yeah, thanks. And say thanks to Amy from me. She was a tower of help this past week. Sergio loves her.'

'And she loves the lad. She's got a bit of a tummy bug this morning. I sent her back to bed.'

'Give her my good wishes.' Boyd made to leave, then paused. 'You're looking like the cat that got the cream. Spill.'

'Can a man not be happy nowadays?'

'Course he can. But you are unusually bubbly.'

'Let me tell you,' Kirby said, 'you don't look too cheerful. What's up?'

'You know yourself. Woman trouble.'

'Lottie?' Kirby asked, and Boyd could see he was trying to feign ignorance.

'Who else could it be?' He moved his son's tablet from hand to hand. It didn't come naturally to talk about his personal life, even though he and Kirby had been friends for a long time. 'She can be so obstinate and belligerent at times. A lot of the time, if I'm being honest. I don't know what I ever saw in her.'

'Ah, come on. Don't be like that. You still love her, don't you?'

'Sometimes love isn't enough, my friend. Not nearly enough.' He clasped the tablet to his chest in an effort to stop fidgeting. 'I better head off.'

'I met with Lottie yesterday. Just give her space to do her thing.'

'That's exactly the point.' Boyd shook his head. 'It's not her thing. Not her investigation. She can't keep her nose out of things that don't concern her. She's going to cause my sister heartbreak.'

'How do you figure that out?'

'Because of Bryan... you know, the murders...' Boyd bit back an irritated expletive. 'I can't begin to think what will happen to Grace if he... if he actually killed someone.'

'I'm sure he didn't do anything wrong.'

'But his DNA was at one of the murder scenes.'

Kirby put a hand on his arm to reassure him, but Boyd felt its weight. A weight of words he did not want to hear.

'Listen,' Kirby said, 'stop thinking about things that haven't happened yet. And if the worst does happen, I'm sure Grace is stronger than you give her credit for. If she calls off the wedding, it will be her choice.'

'That's the thing, it should be her choice, not Lottie's.'

'Come on. You're being too black and white here. Lottie hasn't done anything wrong. You're overreacting.'

Boyd sighed, knowing he hadn't the will to fight his friend.

'What do you think about the murders? You've been involved in one here.'

'It's the same guy, I'd bet my pension on it.'

'Then it couldn't be Bryan, could it?' A moment of elation replaced his suspicions.

'We believe Edie was abducted on Friday, but her body wasn't found until Monday morning. We're attempting to check Robert Hayes's movements for the weekend and I'm praying for a definite time of death soon. The pathologist suggests it's somewhere between twenty-four and thirty-six hours before the body was found. If Edie had been in the river any longer, she'd probably have been discovered before Monday morning. I think, alive or dead, she was kept somewhere for that intervening time. I haven't really looked at your future brother-in-law as a suspect yet and I'm not even sure if it's the same killer for all the murders, but Lottie said Bryan couldn't have killed Brigid Kelly, the priest's housekeeper, as he was at home all night.'

Shifting from foot to foot, Boyd knew his intake of breath gave away his unease. He shook his head slowly.

'What?' Kirby asked.

Boyd saw the realisation dawn on his colleague's face before he told him what he knew. But he had to spell it out, if only to clear his own mind. 'The thing is, Bryan wasn't home all that night. I heard him go out. Heard the engine of his car. Lottie slept through it.'

'Well, holy God.' Kirby ran a hand through his still damp mop of hair. 'Does Grace know?'

'Probably. Maybe not. I don't know.'

'Shit.'

'Yeah. Shit.'

Kirby was quiet for a moment. 'What are you going to do?'

'Not my circus. I'll let the local detectives do their job.'

'I meant what are you going to do about Lottie? Your relationship?'

'It's finished. I'm done. This time it's for real. I can't live with her inconsistency, her obstinacy and her disregard for my feelings.'

'I thought you understood her and how she works.'

'I thought so too. Seems I was wrong.' He opened the door and stepped outside, feeling decidedly sorry for himself.

'Want my advice?' Kirby held onto the door, and Boyd could see the compassion in his friend's eyes. He was only trying to help.

'Not really, I've my mind made up, but I suppose you're going to tell me anyhow.'

'All I'll say is take your time. Don't make any rash decisions. Not now when emotions are high. Let the dust settle.'

'Whatever that means.'

Boyd waved as he walked to his car, believing no one could say anything to rescue his and Lottie's relationship. No amount of dust settling could change his mind.

It was over.

His heart felt empty.

Totally empty.

74

CONNEMARA

Mooney made his way up the stairs, decked out in his white protective clothing. The booties over his shoes were making him slip, and even though he wore gloves, he forced himself not to grab the banister. The two SOCOs stood back as he moved into the bathroom.

The sight of the body caused his stomach to turn. He felt a lurch of unease. Should he have done more last night? Taken Ann Wilson to the station? To get her to talk. To take her out of harm's way. To get her husband out of harm's way. But he was well aware that there was no point in mourning what he should or shouldn't have done. It was all too late now. The ravaged body in the bath bore testament to that.

Ann had been scalded. Her skin looked like it was ready to peel off. Her face was twisted in anguish. She had found no relief in death. A callous and cruel murderer had seen to that. Mooney itched to run back down the stairs, to tear off the white suit, to scratch his own skin raw. He had failed the woman, and he suspected she had been failed all her life.

'Where's Denis?' he asked the SOCO nearest to him.

'He said he'd be back. Doctor came to give him some sedation, but he headed for his car. Said something about knowing who had killed his wife.'

'Oh, for fuck's sake,' Mooney said, and raced down the stairs.

———

Lottie drove around the unfamiliar roads, unsure of where she was going or where she could park so that they would be undisturbed and unseen. At least the rain had cleared, and the clouds were making way for a blanket of blue sky.

'How did you get out to the Wilson house, Imelda?'

'Bus. Ann gave me twenty euros for food and stuff.'

'Where's your car? It wasn't at the cottage.'

'I had to use it to escape a fucking murderer, didn't I? Then I abandoned it in a housing estate because he might know what I was driving and find me.'

Or the police might know, Lottie thought. She had a host of questions, but instead asked, 'Any ideas where we should go?'

'We're nearly in Salthill now. It might be a good place. It's always busy.'

This surprised Lottie. 'I thought you'd want seclusion.'

'More chance of being seen when you're trying to hide. In a busy seaside resort I can blend in.'

Lottie glanced at her passenger. No way could Imelda Conroy blend in anywhere in her current state. She looked haunted. Her clothing, face and hands were filthy.

'Where did you stay last night?'

'I walked around the city for a bit before bunking down in a shop doorway. A couple of homeless guys kept me company.'

'Were you not scared?'

'I'm more afraid of whoever is trying to kill me.'

This caused Lottie to grip the steering wheel tighter. She

wasn't yet sure if she had a killer in her car or a victim. 'Who would that be?'

'I have my suspicions, but I don't want to say anything yet.'

'Why not?'

'Because I'm not sure.'

Lottie scanned the area for a parking spot. 'I think you are.'

Imelda kept her head down. 'Leave it for now, okay?'

'Okay,' Lottie relented. 'But you should have gone to the guards on day one.'

Imelda was quiet for a few moments before asking, 'Do you know how Ann Wilson is?'

'What do you mean?'

'I saw all the guards and news vans at her house. She killed her husband, didn't she?'

'Imelda, do you not know?'

'Know what?'

'It's Ann who's dead.'

'No!' A fractured sob escaped Imelda's mouth and she pressed her hand to her lips.

Lottie waited while someone exited a parking space, and then pulled in. 'Have you eaten?'

'How could anyone eat at a time like this?'

She switched off the engine. 'You need to eat. You look like you haven't had a bite in a week.'

'I can't face food at the moment.' Imelda paused, staring out the window, before glancing over at Lottie. 'Is it all my fault?'

'The murders?'

'Ann's death.'

'Why do you say that? Do you think you're responsible for hers but not the others?' Lottie decided to say what had been lurking. 'I think it's time you explained your role in all this.'

'I should have known you'd think I'm a murderer,' Imelda snorted, her voice laced with derision.

'You have done nothing to convince me otherwise.'

She put her head in her hands and sobbed. 'No one understands.'

'I'm willing to try,' Lottie said, unsure if the tears were genuine or manufactured. She found it difficult to get a handle on the real Imelda Conroy. 'Let's walk and get some air.'

'I'm not sure I can move.'

'The fresh air will do you good, and then if you feel up to it I'll get us some food. A cup of tea.'

Once out of the car, Lottie looked down along the promenade, at the strand where only yesterday she'd walked with Ann Wilson. Now Ann was dead.

She let her gaze wander over to Imelda, who in her current state was sure to attract attention. From the boot of the car she fetched a navy fleece jacket. It had *GARDA* emblazoned across the back, so she turned it inside out and Imelda put it on.

Once attired, the woman seemed unsteady on her feet. She took Lottie's proffered arm and clung on.

'Why did you decide to make this particular documentary?' Lottie asked.

'I wanted to tell a story. But the story became bigger than anything I could ever have hoped for.'

'Start at the beginning.'

'We haven't time. You need to stop him. Did you look into Assumpta Feeney's background?'

'Imelda, if you know something that can prevent more murders you need to talk to the Galway detectives. Detective Sergeant Matt Mooney is a good man. I can bring you to speak to him.'

Imelda's fingers tightened on Lottie's arm. 'No, I can't do that. I'd be arrested and charged and locked up.'

'If you've done nothing wrong, you won't be.' At least not initially, Lottie thought.

'The thing is... I don't know if I have or not. What if my documentary caused all this?'

'How? It hasn't even aired yet.'

'That's because I haven't finished it. But I asked questions of people and I must have unsettled someone so much that they feared their long-held secret would be outed.'

Lottie had already mulled over this scenario. She had thought Imelda could be the killer. Now she didn't know what to think. 'Who did you talk to?'

'All of them.'

'All of who? You need to tell me.' An empty bench was up ahead, so Lottie brought Imelda to it. They sat.

'The sea can be beautiful but also rough, intimidating,' Imelda said. 'Just like my work.'

'What do you mean?'

'When I started this project, I was excited, happy even. I was invigorated, but then I felt threatened and that scared me. I should have stopped, but it made me more curious to discover the truth.'

'The truth about what?'

'What happened to Gabriel all those years ago.'

Okay, Lottie could understand that. Gabriel was the little girl she'd heard about from Ann Wilson. She turned on the bench to watch Imelda. 'You investigated Gabriel's death?'

'Her murder, you mean. I knew nothing about it when I began my research. But I was told about it and then I felt I had something tangible. I had access to witnesses, those who were around when the horrific event occurred. And as macabre as this seems, it excited me. Does that make me a bad person?'

Lottie reserved her judgement until she knew more. 'What went wrong?'

'I talked to the wrong person.'

'Who?'

'I don't know, but one of them had to have been put on alert by my probing. Assumpta was one of the first people I talked to, that's why she could be the key.'

'I don't think she was the first to die, though, and I don't know if Mooney has found out much about her yet. She was abroad for years, wasn't she?'

'She was a novice nun at the Sisters of Forgiveness convent in the eighties before she suddenly left. She then studied to be a nurse.'

'Did she tell you why she left the convent?'

'Not in so many words. But I figured it was shortly after the killing of the little girl.'

'What did she tell you about that?' Lottie was intrigued to know the version Imelda would relate.

'Not a lot.' The woman seemed to retreat into herself.

'Let's walk,' Lottie said, and they stood and set off along the promenade. 'Did Assumpta tell you who locked the girl in the machine and turned it on?'

'She mentioned a Robert Hayes.'

Bingo. This matched what Ann had told her. 'Did you interview him?'

'No, but I did some research on him. He was a priest for a time before being kicked out of the clergy. Something to do with child abuse, but it was all vague. No garda involvement. A cover-up by the Church if ever there was one.'

'He became a chef after that. He lived in Ragmullin, where I work. He could be the killer.' Lottie crossed her fingers, because she still had a sense that Imelda was not an innocent in all this.

'But why?' Imelda said quietly.

'To silence witnesses and to stop you investigating further for your documentary.'

'I'm still alive.'

'There's no one left to corroborate your story, though. They're all dead. They can't talk.'

'That's not strictly true.' Imelda looked straight ahead as they walked.

Lottie sensed the young woman felt sad in her company. But was she really sad? Was there something else at play here?

'How is that so?' she asked.

'I can listen to their voices, their stories. I have the recordings.'

'You have?' She stopped sharply and turned to Imelda. 'Where?'

'Safe.' Imelda walked on slowly.

Lottie decided to leave that line of discussion for now. She didn't want to spook her any further.

'Bryan O'Shaughnessy. How do you know him?' She wondered if she should tell Imelda about the DNA, but it wasn't conclusive and she had no idea if the further analysis had been finalised. She'd have to ask Mooney.

'I don't know him,' Imelda said, keeping her eyes cast downwards. 'Not really. I spoke to him early on. His name came up.'

'Who brought it up?'

'I'd rather not say.'

'There's a lot you're not saying, Imelda. Why is that?'

'I need to have some bargaining power.'

'With Mooney?' Lottie paused as Imelda turned to face her.

'No, with the killer.'

Mooney was relieved to see that Denis Wilson had been taken to one side by the Dublin detectives. Thank God, he thought. At least he hadn't been allowed to leave the premises.

He walked around the outside of the Wilson house, pulling at his beard, rubbing his head, tugging his ear lobe, generally baffled and more than a little annoyed with himself.

Last night Ann had said she'd talk to him in the morning. Tell him about Imelda and maybe a whole lot of other stuff. Now she couldn't tell him anything, because she was dead.

What had she to say that she didn't want her husband to hear? And how or why had Imelda come into possession of Ann's phone? What did Imelda mean when she said that Assumpta Feeney was the key to it all?

He was being sidelined, he got that. He hadn't succeeded in securing an arrest or a quick result and people were still being murdered. The powers-that-be on the top floor with the huge windows overlooking the bay had not given him time to get his feet under the table let alone analyse the information his team had gathered. But the murders had come so close together, he had hardly time to draw a breath, never mind draw a clear image of who he should be investigating.

He could not rid himself of the fear he'd seen in Ann's eyes the previous night when she spoke of her husband's anger. That made him think of the altercation that had occurred earlier that day between Denis Wilson and Bryan O'Shaughnessy. He should warn the farmer, because as sure as night followed day, Wilson would be gunning for the man Mooney had arrested and released without charge.

He also wanted to determine if O'Shaughnessy had been anywhere near the Wilsons' house last night. He'd have loved to interview the councillor straight away, but that had been taken out of his hands. Damn.

Had he missed something yesterday? Had the killer been lurking in the trees? Had Robert Hayes been following him? Watching the house, watching the Wilsons, watching Mooney leave? A shiver travelled up his spine and down his arms.

He hoped to God he hadn't led him to Ann's door.

75

The promenade was getting busier. Lottie retraced their steps knowing she had to say something to move things on before they reached the car. Imelda had said Assumpta Feeney could be key to it all, and she now wanted to know more about the novice who had left her vocation.

'Do you know where Assumpta lived?' she asked.

Imelda looked at her, a raised eyebrow in her thin face. 'Yes. Why?'

'I want to go there and see if there's anyone, a neighbour, who knew her.'

'I can tell you what you want to know.'

Lottie shook her head. 'You want to keep me going round in circles, Imelda. But listen to me. Too many people have died. I don't want another person on my conscience. You have directly involved me, so I need to be proactive.'

'Okay. I'll show you where she lived.'

'Maybe I should call Sergeant Mooney to meet us there,' Lottie said quietly.

'And maybe I should destroy my recordings.' Imelda's tone had taken on a sinister cadence.

Lottie said nothing as she unlocked the car. Imelda was showing signs of instability. And one thing was for sure, she did not want those tapes destroyed in a fit of rage.

'I'd like to hear what you've recorded. I need to get a handle on what this is all about.'

Imelda considered her over the roof of the car. 'I don't trust you.'

'I don't trust you either. But I haven't turned you in yet. Shouldn't that allow you to have some level of trust in me?'

She could see the woman turning this over in her mind, biting the inside of her cheek.

'We'll go to Assumpta's house first, then I'll decide.'

Fuck you, thought Lottie, but she just nodded.

Assumpta had rented a narrow pebble-dashed house on the outskirts of the city. A sprawling new housing estate arched up and behind the little terrace. It made Lottie wonder if the residents had refused to sell up to the developer. Good on them, she thought.

'Number six,' Imelda said.

After parking a little way down the road, they walked back to the black-painted door. There was no evidence of crime-scene tape, but Lottie hadn't expected it. SOCOs would have completed their examination of the house quickly. The true crime scene was the holiday cottage, so that was where they would have concentrated their efforts. She remembered poor Assumpta's scalded, blistered body, and shivered.

Imelda extracted a key from a zipped pocket in her fleece.

'How the...?' Lottie stared, mouth agape. 'You have a key?'

'I took it from Assumpta.'

Snake-like apprehension stalled Lottie. 'You killed her.'

'That's getting old. I told you I did not kill anyone. Not

directly, but my work may have been a factor. That's my only crime. Are you coming in with me or not?'

'Yes, I want to see what we can find.'

They entered directly into a small carpeted living space.

Lottie closed the door behind her. It was immediately clear that SOCOs had been very discreet in their work.

The room was small but elegantly furnished. What she noticed was that which she could not see. No photos or personal effects. The surfaces were naked of any knick-knacks. Clean and polished. The fireplace was pristine, as if a fire had never graced the grate. No items of clothing hung from the back of chairs, and the small kitchenette was neat and tidy. She opened a wall cupboard to find clean crockery, and in another the non-perishables were sorted by jar size. The refrigerator was well stocked, though the milk was now out of date. There were a couple of bottles of wine too, but no evidence of who Assumpta Feeney had been.

'Have you been here before, Imelda?'

'Yeah. To initially interview Assumpta about a month ago. I wasn't here for long.'

So she had a ready excuse if her DNA was found here, Lottie thought. 'Why was Assumpta at the holiday cottage?'

'She came to talk, and maybe to warn me. I hadn't been expecting her. Someone must have followed her.'

'Warn you about what?'

'That I was in danger.'

'But you escaped and she didn't,' Lottie said. 'How did you manage that?'

'I was lucky. I was in the kitchen, heard her scream, and when she was dragged to the bathroom, I grabbed what I could and fled. Coward's way, but I was petrified.' Imelda eyeballed her as if challenging her to comment. 'What are we looking for here?'

'I want to get a feel for the woman. I only saw her in death.'

Lottie waited for a beat to see if Imelda would query her explanation, but she didn't. 'Her body had been so badly damaged, I could not even determine her age. What can you tell me about her?'

'Assumpta was a troubled woman, but I found her to be genuine. I believe she wanted to atone for events in her past. But someone else wanted to shut her up.'

'What did she tell you?'

'Later. Do you want me to search here or not?'

'I'm confident the investigation team have been through the place. I doubt we will find anything.'

'Seeing as we're here, I'll start upstairs,' Imelda said. 'You can search down here.'

'Not so fast.' Lottie wasn't about to let the woman find something pertinent and then destroy it. She did not trust her, nor did she believe her. 'We stick together.'

'I'm not going to steal—'

'Imelda! Just stay with me and don't touch anything.'

'You really are a piece of work.' Imelda slouched into a beautifully upholstered Queen Anne chair like the surly teenager she might once have been. 'I am trying to help, you know.'

'If you wanted to help,' Lottie said, 'you'd have handed yourself in.'

'Isn't that what guilty people do?'

'You are a person of interest. You need to provide the guards with whatever information you possess. Including all your recordings.'

'I can't do that. Not until—'

'Not until the documentary is ready to broadcast?' Lottie tried to dampen her anger at the woman's obstinacy. 'Is that what you were going to say?'

'Something like that.'

'Imelda, there have been five murders in less than a week.

Assumpta Feeney, Mickey Fox, Brigid Kelly, Ann Wilson and Edie Butler were sadistically killed. All were in some way involved with the convent and its brutal laundry. You can't keep evidence from the guards.'

'You mean six murders. You forgot about little Gabriel.'

'Do you even know who she was?'

'Yes, I do. But come on, we're wasting time.'

'You sit there and I'll scout around. I mean it, Imelda. Don't move.'

A sound from the stairs that led down directly into the living room made Lottie look upwards. She heard Imelda gasp.

A pair of black-booted feet stomped threateningly into view, followed by denim-clad legs, before the full figure appeared. He wore a dark bomber jacket over a checked shirt, and his greying hair was tied back at the nape of his neck. But what really caught her attention was the long carving knife he held in his hand.

'What a nice surprise,' he said in a gravelly voice.

Lottie recognised him from the photo Kirby had shown her.

'Robert Hayes, I presume.'

76

Bryan O'Shaughnessy was sick to death of Detective Sergeant Matt Mooney, and when he saw the detective's car pull into his yard, he felt like sprinting for the hills. Instead, he remained standing at the wall, spade in hand, ready to use it if his temper was ignited.

'The very man,' Mooney said.

'What do you want *this* time?'

'I wanted to congratulate you for punching Denis Wilson in the eye, but that doesn't seem appropriate now, in the sad circumstances.'

'What sad circumstances do you mean?'

'Ann Wilson is dead. Murdered.'

'What...?' Bryan looked one way then the other, conflicted at Mooney's news. 'I'm sorry to hear that. Grace will be so shocked. But it has nothing to do with me.'

'I think it does. Whether directly or indirectly, you assaulted Denis yesterday afternoon, and now his wife is dead. Where were you last night?'

'Do you get off on this, Mooney? Accusing innocent people day in and day out. No wonder you haven't found the killer.

You're too busy hounding me. Read my lips. I did not harm anyone. But if it saves you time, I admit I hit Wilson. He deserved it. I certainly did not kill his wife. I don't believe I've ever met the woman.'

'Your bride-to-be met her. On numerous occasions.'

'Grace? You are a fucker, Mooney. Grace got her to make her wedding dress. She paid for it and collected it yesterday. You think that's a motive for murder? As far as I know, she was happy with Mrs Wilson's work.'

'I don't believe Ann's death has anything to do with Grace, but it may have something to do with you.'

'You are clutching at the proverbial here, Mooney. I was at home all night. Grace can vouch for me. Now fuck off and find someone else to blame.' Bryan tightened his grip on the spade.

'Calm down. I'm not blaming you. I will have to interview you shortly, but my priority at the moment is to warn you to be careful. Denis Wilson will be like a loose cannon now...'

'He's always been a loose cannon.'

'... and he may well target you for revenge.'

'Revenge for what? Clocking him yesterday?'

'For his wife's murder.'

Bryan lifted the spade and took a step forward. 'I told you, I was nowhere near his wife. Not yesterday, not ever.'

Mooney stood his ground. 'You will have to offer proof of that at the station. Wilson knows you were arrested and released without charge. He believes you murdered all those people. He will definitely think you killed his wife. I'm here to warn you and your lovely Grace to be careful.'

'I suppose you're going to provide me with protection as well as an empty warning.'

'Just be vigilant, Mr O'Shaughnessy. Call into the station later today. I need details of your whereabouts for the last twenty-four hours.'

Bryan watched the detective get back in his car and drive off. Grace came out to the yard.

'What's going on, Bryan?'

'I wish I knew.'

As Mooney's car disappeared around the corner, another drove into the yard.

'Mark, Sergio!' Grace cried, running towards them. She bear-hugged the boy.

Boyd raised an eyebrow. Bryan shrugged. Grace didn't do hugs. Not normally. She took her nephew by the hand and led him into the house, talking about hot chocolate and marshmallows.

'Was that Mooney driving out?' Boyd asked.

'Yeah,' Bryan said. 'The fucker now thinks I murdered Councillor Wilson's wife. It seems that if someone sneezes around here, Wilson will want my ugly mug pasted on wanted posters.'

Boyd studied his future brother-in-law, reading the worry etched in the deeply furrowed lines around his eyes. 'Has Mooney got cause to suspect you?'

'Maybe.' Bryan leaned on his spade. His dog circled his legs before lying at his feet protectively. 'You see, I thumped Denis Wilson yesterday. The bastard arrived here shouting and roaring at me. I'd had enough abuse at that stage, so I drew out. Got him good and proper.' He smiled fleetingly at the memory before the grave look returned, dragging down his expression. 'It was a mistake. I shouldn't have let him vex me so much. It's just... at a time that should be the happiest of my life, I feel the world is against me. I know Grace is hurting and I haven't a clue how to deal with any of it.'

'Maybe you need a holiday.' Boyd struggled to find the right thing to say. 'Have you a honeymoon planned?'

'I don't even think there will be a wedding. How can I marry your sister with all this suspicion hanging over my head?' Bryan paused to take a laboured breath. 'Will you see if Lottie can talk to Mooney on my behalf?'

Boyd cringed. He didn't want to tell Bryan that she was one of those who was sceptical of his innocence. 'I'm afraid Lottie and I aren't on speaking terms at the moment.'

'Oh, I forgot. Grace told me she asked her to leave. Sorry about that.'

Boyd squinted through the misty sun. Bryan seemed to have aged considerably over the last few days. 'I didn't know that had happened. God, now Lottie will be furious at me. Why did Grace do that?'

'I think they had words. Lottie is staying at a hotel. Go talk to her.'

'No, I'm done with talking. She's bull-headed, and when she gets on her high horse, there's no talking her down.'

'I'm so sorry. All this is my fault. I should never have asked her to get involved in the first place.'

'Don't worry about it. I know Lottie. She'd have found some way to get involved. Trouble has a habit of following her.'

77

'Sit down,' Robert Hayes said, brandishing the knife in their direction. 'Both of you.'

They did so, not having any choice. He was the one holding the long-bladed knife.

Lottie seethed, but kept her eyes directed on the weapon. 'Perhaps you should get rid of that. We're not going to harm you. You have no reason to protect yourself from us.'

'Is that so?' His mouth curved into a sneer as he pointed the knife at her. 'You're a cop. I'd smell one a mile away. You're that Lottie Parker detective, aren't you?'

'I'm on holidays and I'm not involved in any role with the murder investigations. Despite that, I believe you've been following me. Killing anyone you think might be able to rat on you.'

'Rat on me?' His face twisted into a knot of confusion. 'About what?'

Was he playing stupid?

'You know full well what this is about, Robert. What I don't understand is why you didn't just disappear. There was no need to kill so many innocent people.'

The knife wavered in his hand. 'I have no idea what you're talking about.'

'Why are you here then?'

'I... None of your business. Why are *you* here?' He twisted her question back on her.

'You know why.'

He sat then, keeping them both directly in front of him. 'Is it something to do with Edie?'

'Edie?' Lottie paused, letting him believe she had to think for a moment. 'She's the woman you murdered in Ragmullin.'

'For Christ's sake, I didn't murder her. I loved her, actually. But then...' he pointed the knife in Imelda's direction, 'you and your stupid documentary put the wind up her.'

'What are you talking about?' Now it was Imelda's turn to look confused. 'I never talked to anyone in Ragmullin.'

'Of course you did. And you tried to smoke me out too.'

Imelda shook her head. 'Smoke you out?'

The man was delusional, Lottie thought. And Imelda was demonstrating instability too. Great combination.

'Yeah,' he said. 'Coming into the pub where I worked, asking questions. Phoning my manager. Scaring the life out of Edie. She even broke up with me over it all. You killed her.'

Lottie looked over at Imelda, who seemed genuinely puzzled. She turned her attention back to Robert. The hand holding the knife was shaking and his knee jiggled up and down.

'Robert, why do you think it was Imelda?'

'It's obvious, isn't it? She's the one making the documentary. Digging up the past. Turning over lives and—'

'Okay, okay. I admit I tried to find you,' Imelda interrupted him, defiance written all over her face. 'I didn't succeed, though. And I knew nothing about any Edie. Her name didn't come up in my research. Not so far anyhow.'

'Of course it was you,' he said. 'Who else could it be?'

The tiny, uncluttered room felt overcrowded with the three of them in it. Lottie felt the lies bouncing off the walls. 'This was Assumpta's home. Why are you here?'

'I heard about her death.' He pointed the knife at Imelda again. 'I knew about the documentary you were making and I assumed you'd come here after she was killed. Maybe hide your research notes or backup files here.' His shoulders slumped. 'Honestly? This was my last hope of finding you.'

'You need to be calm,' Lottie said evenly. 'Take a breath and we will try to make sense of it all.'

'You're stalling.' He stood and gawked out the small net-curtained window. 'Have you called for backup?'

She realised then just how unhinged he was. That made him dangerous and susceptible to carry out an unprovoked attack. She had to talk him down.

'Robert, there's just us three here. I'm not on duty. I haven't called anyone. That's the truth.' She realised then that no one knew where she was, and she cursed herself for her impetuous decision to take Imelda with her that morning. 'Let's talk it out and see what we can do to help you.'

'No one can help me,' he muttered. 'It will all come out now and I'll be ruined. I thought things were bad when I got kicked out of the priesthood, but this is a whole different level.'

'What do you think makes this worse?'

'Because it's about murder.'

Was now the time to say it out loud? Probably not, but she said it anyhow. 'A long time ago, you killed a little girl. She was named Gabriel by the nuns. Why did you do that?'

He lunged, the knife pointed at her. She held her breath for a moment, but remained seated upright. He could fuck right off if he thought he was intimidating her.

'Don't you dare try to lumber me with another murder. I killed no one. I don't even know who you're talking about.'

'Not true, Robert.' Defiance flowed unhindered through her

blood. 'Remember the laundry at the Sisters of Forgiveness convent? A little girl called Gabriel was used by the nuns to clear sheets and pillowcases out of the big washing machines. One day you arrived to a row between Gabriel and a nun. You helped the nun throw the little girl into a machine and switched it on. Utter cruelty. She died. That makes you what you are, Robert. A murderer.'

His colour heightened as she spoke and his eyes turned darker and bulged in their sockets. 'The two of you are stirring up shit you know nothing about. You don't understand a thing.'

She lowered her voice, tried to make it sound soothing, to make him talk. 'Help us to understand.'

His shoulders slumped as he sat down again. 'It wasn't me, not really me, that's all you need to know.'

'Oh, are you trying to say that your body was inhabited by an evil spirit who told you to kill a defenceless child?' Had she gone too far? she wondered.

'You are close to the truth,' he snorted, an ugly hue shrouding his face.

'I'd like to know the whole truth.'

'Assumpta knew the truth. She could have told you. But now she's dead.'

'So you killed off anyone who could point the finger at you?'

'Why would I kill the one person who could explain what really happened back then?'

'To bury the story,' Imelda said.

'Shut up, you.' He waved the knife again and Lottie glared at Imelda, hoping she got the message to keep her mouth shut. Some hope.

'I won't be silenced,' Imelda said.

Brave? Lottie wondered. No, she was reckless.

'Imelda, leave this to me,' she warned, infusing her voice with steel.

'No, I won't. He says I started all this and I want to hear his side of the story. I'm only raging that I have no phone or anything to record his lies.'

Lottie was certain Imelda still had Ann Wilson's phone but didn't mention it.

'You won't be around much longer, either of you,' Robert sneered. 'I've had enough.' He stood abruptly and thrust the knife towards Imelda. 'I was doing grand. My life was trundling along nicely. I was on the verge of proposing to Edie, and then you fucked it all up.'

'I want to hear your side of things,' the young woman repeated.

Gutsy, Lottie thought. Definitely foolhardy. But Imelda had been through a lot over the last week, so maybe she was entitled to have her say. As long as it didn't get them both killed. She knew she'd be able to overpower him if he attacked Imelda, but if he went for her first, that would have an unknown result.

'You think you know it all,' Robert snarled. 'But you don't know the whole truth. Did you find Assumpta's notebooks?'

'Notebooks?' Imelda asked. 'No.'

'I've searched the house and can't find them.' He appeared flustered now.

Lottie said, 'The guards and SOCOs have searched here. If there was anything to be found, they'd have it. What sort of notebooks are you talking about?'

'She recorded everything that happened in that place. Kids who were born and kids who died. Mothers who died. She kept records of the whole lot.'

'Mickey Fox had all those,' Imelda said. 'He burned them shortly before he was murdered.'

Lottie looked over at her, but before she could speak, Robert was talking again.

'No, he probably had the nuns' official records. I'm talking about Assumpta's own personal notes.'

'Personal notes?' Lottie said. 'Why would she do that, and how do you know about them?'

'She was meticulous. Studying to be a nun. A novice. But... me and her, we had a... friendship back then. I would never kill her.'

'But you killed the child. The little girl.'

'I didn't think she'd die, did I? I was forced to do it. I had no choice. I was young and stupid. I thought they'd let her out in time. I meant no harm. It was a prank.'

'No it wasn't. She was just a child. Don't try to cover up the truth,' Imelda said.

'I heard an eyewitness account of what happened,' Lottie said. 'You were not that young. Early twenties? It was deliberate.'

'Okay, I admit the action itself was deliberate, but I was forced to do it. The outcome was unintended.'

'Explain.'

Lottie wondered where her bravery was coming from. A killer was holding a knife on them and she was conversing with him like it was an afternoon tea party. Her training? Perhaps. Or was Imelda's pluckiness rubbing off on her? Whatever it was, she did not fear Robert Hayes as much as she should, and that worried her. Being complacent was dangerous. But she had to hear what he had to say.

He sat back heavily and pulled at his hair. His ponytail came loose and the grey strands fell about his face in a greasy mess as he began to talk.

78

The interview room was large and airy, but the air-conditioning unit was on too high and Mooney felt his skin prickle from the cold air.

'I'm sorry for your loss, and thanks for coming in, Councillor Wilson,' he said.

He was trying, he really was. He might not like the man, but Denis Wilson had lost his wife in a brutal attack, so he had to demonstrate some sympathy. The detectives that the powers-that-be had drafted in had allocated him the task of interviewing Wilson. They were of the opinion that a serial killer was their target, not a grieving husband.

'I had no choice,' Wilson said. 'Those detectives at my house said I had to talk to you. Anyway, I want someone to arrest and charge the man who did this to my Ann. I know who killed her. I just need to convince you.' He fixed Mooney with a stare before straightening his cravat.

The detective wondered how a grieving man kept himself so neat. Then again, Denis Wilson always had his appearance just so. The bruising around his eye was the only thing that pointed to all not being rosy.

'Who are you referring to?'

'You know right well I'm referring to Bryan O'Shaughnessy. You should arrest him. This time charge him with multiple murders, including that of my precious Ann.'

'Did you see him enter your home?'

'No, but it *has* to be him.'

'Why has it to be him?'

'You wouldn't have arrested him for the other murder if you didn't have something on him.' Wilson flicked his cravat and a tiny diamond sparkled in its centre.

'If I had something on him, I would have charged him. Denis, you need to stop this vendetta.' Mooney had to get the man back on track. 'Where were you last night?'

'I went home after that prick punched me. Ann wasn't there. I thought she was missing. I shouldn't have reported that, because she was just late. She came home and you arrived after that. You know all this.'

'What happened after I left?'

'I got drunk as a skunk, if you want to know. I passed out on the couch. Never heard a thing. All O'Shaughnessy's fault.'

'You look fine this morning. No hangover?'

'My wife is dead. I'm in shock. I don't know which way to turn. This...' Wilson pointed to his suit, his shirt, his cravat, 'this is what I do well. Image. Projection. Inside I'm dying, second by second. You need to find her killer.'

Mooney found it difficult to muster any sympathy for him. 'Your wife was murdered while you were at home. I need you to give me a timeline of last night. What did you and Ann do?'

'I told you, I got drunk.'

'I'm sure you remember some of the evening. Did you eat?'

'This morning? No.'

Was he being deliberately obtuse? 'I meant last night. What did you both do after I left?'

'I didn't eat. Ann probably did. I don't know. I marinated

my brain in whiskey to stop me from jumping into the car and driving out to take the head off O'Shaughnessy.'

'Drink-driving wouldn't look good for your PR machine.' Mooney couldn't help himself.

'What are you talking about?'

'Ann mentioned something about your PR people and how you didn't like anything derailing a well-oiled machine.' Mooney was well aware she hadn't said all that, but Wilson didn't need to know it.

'She looked out for me. She is... was a stellar wife.' Wilson seemed to realise what he was saying. 'I looked out for her too.'

There wasn't a hint of a tear in his eyes. Not a touch of emotion. It was like he was reciting a prepared script. Mooney wouldn't put it past him to have got one of his PR people to draft his words for this interview. Stop, he warned himself, he was being unduly cynical.

'When did you realise things weren't right? That there was something wrong?'

'This morning. I woke up on the couch and she wasn't hovering over me. Usually she'd wake me with a cup of coffee.'

'Did you *usually* drink yourself into oblivion and end up sleeping on the couch?'

'You are twisting my words, Sergeant. There wasn't a sound in the house. Just the tick of the stupid clock on the mantel. I dragged myself up the stairs to have a shower. I thought she must have slept in or maybe she'd left for work. I know she's really busy with the wedding season and all that.'

'So now you are upstairs.' Mooney tried to visualise Wilson in a state of intoxication, but it was impossible. The man was always so prim and proper. 'Where did you go first?'

Denis closed his eyes for a moment. 'Into the bedroom. She wasn't in bed. The sheets were rumpled and I figured she was up and gone to work even though it was so early.'

Mooney noted that Wilson seemed to have a problem calling his wife by her name. 'How did that make you feel?'

Denis dropped his head, looking down at his perfectly manicured fingernails. 'I thought she was mad at me for getting drunk. I decided to have my shower and then I'd phone her to tell her I was sorry.'

Wilson didn't strike Mooney as a man who would lower himself to apologise to anyone, least of all his wife. 'Go on.'

'I grabbed a towel from the cupboard and had my shower. In the en suite.'

'Okay.' Mooney thought it was convenient for him to have showered. No evidence to be gathered from his body or skin. Not that he was a suspect, according to those in authority on the case. And just because Mooney didn't like him didn't make him a killer either. He needed to get the facts and move on. 'When did you go to the main bathroom?'

'I showered, shaved and dressed. The main bathroom door was ajar. I hadn't noticed it on my way up. We hardly ever use that bathroom. Not since we had the en suite installed. Used up a spare bedroom for that. She was a bit put out about it at the time. Not that it matters now.'

'Right, so you noticed the door open. Why did that strike you as odd?'

'We keep all the doors shut to conserve the heat in the house. Not that we have the oil on in this weather, but it's a habit. I went to shut the door and something caught my eye. That's when I saw her there. In the bath. God, I will never get the image out of my mind. It was horrific. How could someone do that to another human being?'

'A psychopath or sociopath, perhaps?' Mooney thought that Wilson was displaying characteristics of both. Or maybe he just wanted that to be the case, such was his distaste for the man.

'It was awful. I never want to see anything like that again. I will be traumatised for life.'

Selfish bastard, Mooney thought. 'Did you move or touch anything in the bathroom?'

'What? No. I went in and checked if she was breathing, but I knew, I knew she was gone.'

'How did you check? Did you touch her?'

'Of course I did. I held my fingers to her throat, but there was no pulse. No one could survive the burns she'd got.'

'We didn't find the source of the boiling water in the bathroom. How do you think she was scalded?'

'Isn't that your job to figure out?'

Tears were now lodged in Wilson's eyes. Maybe Mooney should reassess his assumptions about the man.

'Can you remember anything else that might help us?'

'Not at this time.' A single tear rolled down his face. His PR team would be happy, Mooney thought, though he might have a heart after all.

'There doesn't appear to have been any evidence of a break-in. Do you lock the doors at night?'

'I told you I passed out drunk. Maybe she forgot to lock up.'

It was on the tip of Mooney's tongue to tell the man that his wife's name was Ann. He thought of what she had spoken to him about in her kitchen last night. She was to come in this morning to tell him about Imelda Conroy. And Imelda had Ann's phone. Who was to say she hadn't the keys to Ann's house too?

Shit.

SOCOs had been given free rein in the Wilson house, Mooney noted when he returned. The other detectives had retreated to the incident room in HQ to assess what they had. Mooney preferred to be hands-on. The niggle he'd felt about Imelda having the Wilson house keys had flared into a full-blown rash.

Though his skin wasn't red or itchy, he still found himself scratching his arms under the protective clothing.

He examined the locks on the doors, now blackened with forensic dust, but found no evidence of forced entry. He'd already known that, but no harm to double-check. He could do with having Lottie Parker here with him. She was a shrewd detective and her investigative prowess was renowned, but she was a bit of a loose cannon. He was lucky to be allowed in himself, so having her around was a non-runner.

In the kitchen, SOCOs had found hidden at the back of a cupboard a prescription bottle for Ann containing five anti-anxiety pills. The script was for six. What good were six pills? He backed out and entered the living room.

He went to the drinks trolley. The whiskey bottle was three quarters full. Was there an empty bottle somewhere? Looking through the cabinets, he found no more alcohol. In the utility room he noticed two bins, one for rubbish, one for recycling. Nothing of interest in either, the SOCO told him. On the counter beside a basket of washed laundry there were two empty wine bottles. No whiskey bottle. And he was informed that SOCOs hadn't removed any bottles.

Had Denis lied? Possibly. But why? That was the question burning a hole in his brain as he looked around for Ann's door keys. In the hall on a pottery dish he saw a single Toyota car key. She drove a Toyota. No house key. SOCOs had not come across it either.

There were too many things not making sense right now and he had few answers to his questions. The one thing he knew for sure was that last night Imelda Conroy had had Ann Wilson's phone. She'd made a call to Lottie Parker. They needed to locate that phone.

He called the office and organised a young garda, dubbed a computer nerd, to do whatever he needed to do to find the phone. It might just lead him to the elusive Imelda Conroy, which in turn might give him the answers he craved.

Then again, Imelda had phoned Lottie, so maybe he should talk to the inspector again.

That thought did not fill him with the joys of life.

79

Lottie listened with mounting doubt as Robert told his story in halting words. Was he reinventing the past to suit his present situation? She had no option but to hear him out. After all, he was the one holding the knife.

'You see,' he said, 'when that Kirby detective told me Edie's body had been found blistered and scalded, it brought me right back to the laundry and what had happened that fateful day.'

'That's because you made it happen,' Imelda said.

'Do you want to hear about it or not?'

'Go on,' Lottie said, throwing Imelda a look to keep a lid on it. Imelda's cheeks flared but she remained mute. Thank God.

'I wondered if someone was sending me a warning. Or taunting me. I thought it had to be someone who knew what had happened. That made me think of Assumpta. Beautiful, young and bubbly. She had told me what the girl's body looked like when they took her out. Blistered and scalded. That tragedy in the laundry soured our friendship.'

'You had a relationship?' Lottie asked quietly, not sure if interrupting him would make him stop or continue.

'It wasn't a relationship. She was too devout for that. But

she caused me to have thoughts about leaving the priesthood even before I was properly ordained. I was a deacon, a chaplain, but only a few years in the seminary.'

'But the events of that day did not make you leave the priesthood, you fucker,' Imelda said.

'Stop! For God's sake, stop.' He raised the knife, pointing it at her, his eyes even darker now, his complexion wan. Lottie sensed he was at his most dangerous when challenged. Not good.

'You locked a tiny defenceless child in a washing machine.' Imelda smothered a sob.

He sighed and ran his free hand over his eyes. 'I was compelled to do it. You wouldn't understand that. When I next saw Assumpta, she attacked me. Fists flying. But her verbal assault was worse than anything physical.' He lapsed into silence.

'What did she say to you?' Lottie pressed.

'She told me she had recorded the whole incident in her notebook. That's when I told her the truth. But it was no good. She said that if I ever came back to the convent, she'd destroy me.'

'And did you go back?'

'She left soon after. I still had to do my chaplain duties. But she was gone and I was heartbroken. Years later, I met Edie. I realised that she'd been there that day too. She believed me when I told her how I was forced into the act. You see, she already knew the man who'd forced me.'

Lottie had been thinking Hayes had meant a higher force, not a human one. This was interesting. 'Who was he?'

'I can't say.'

She'd had enough of his reminiscing and lies. 'I heard that you ferried young girls over to Knockraw. That you and others abused them.'

'What? No, that was not me.'

'Maybe you were "forced" to do that too?' Imelda sneered.

'Shut up, you little bitch,' he snarled. 'You have ruined me all over again. You and your stupid documentary.'

'You don't have to worry about that now,' Lottie lied. 'Imelda has lost all her research and recordings.'

'I did not—' Imelda shut up quickly when she realised Lottie's ploy.

'Where is it?' Hayes asked, having caught her words before she'd stopped.

When Imelda next spoke, Lottie was glad the woman could think on her feet.

'Mickey Fox took it and burned it, along with all the convent records.'

'How would you even know that?' Robert asked.

'I was there. After he was murdered.'

'Are you sure you didn't murder him?' His voice rose in a shriek.

He'd asked the question that had been simmering within Lottie all this time. She sensed Imelda was not an innocent in all that had happened. But had she been the facilitator or the perpetrator? That was the burning question of the day.

THE PAST

Mary Elizabeth was in so much pain she could not even utter her own name. When the old nun came for her, she was sure she was being brought to a doctor, being aware enough to know she needed medical attention. She also knew she would never see her baby and might just die of heartbreak before any internal wounds killed her.

She'd seen the black car before. And the man who drove it. The chaplain. Was he tasked with bringing her to the doctor? She slid into the back seat. There were two other girls there. They were timid, silent.

He slammed the door and started the engine. 'Keep your mouths shut. I don't want to hear any moaning, not now, and definitely not afterwards.'

She could not remain silent. 'Where are you taking us? Is it to Knockraw?'

'What did I say about silence?'

'You are a man of God and this is a mortal sin.'

He did not reply, and Mary Elizabeth knew she had needled him. The pain in her abdomen abated slightly and she took this as a sign she was right to ask questions.

'Why are you doing this?'

'I have to.' His voice was barely audible above the rattle of the engine. 'He makes me.'

'God is making you?'

'No, the devil himself.'

She had no answer to that and lapsed into silence.

When the car pulled up at the back door to Knockraw, she felt a stab of pain sear through her body. She wondered if it was physical, or telepathic for what was to come. She had no time to think about it because she was dragged out of the car and in through the door to hell.

80

The coffee tasted as good as it smelled. Boyd took a good gulp in an effort to remain calm now that Detective Sergeant Mooney had returned.

'Thanks, Grace,' Mooney said, cradling his mug. 'You don't know how badly I need this.'

'Just say what you've come to say,' Bryan said irritably.

'Then you can leave us in peace,' Grace added.

Boyd looked at all three. 'What's going on?'

Mooney inhaled before speaking. 'You know Ann Wilson is dead. She was murdered last night in a similar way to the other victims. There are new detectives working with me now and they're privately saying it's a serial killer and that—'

'Bryan is not a serial killer,' Grace said, indignation lacing each word, 'so you can put that in your pipe and smoke it.'

Mooney smiled at her use of the old adage. 'I'm not saying any such—'

'And he was with me all last night.'

Boyd shook his head at Grace to keep quiet. He said to Mooney, 'What do you want? This is your second visit today.'

'I'm looking for Inspector Parker. She's not at the hotel. I thought she might have come back here.'

'Likely story,' Bryan said.

'You could've just phoned her,' Boyd said.

'Believe me, I've tried. No answer. It's not switched off, just rings out.'

'She may have it on silent,' Boyd said, but his hand holding the mug shook. Lottie rarely had her phone on silent, especially when she was away from her family.

'It's possible.' Mooney took a sip of his coffee. 'I thought I'd find her here, seeing as you're here. Saw your car arriving as I left earlier. Will you try ringing her? She might answer you quicker than she would me.'

Boyd doubted that, but he took out his phone and, though he wasn't yet ready to talk to Lottie about their situation, tapped her number. It rang out. 'No answer.'

'When did any of you last see her?' Mooney asked.

'Yesterday,' Grace said, 'when I asked her to leave.'

'I'm sure you've seen her since then,' Boyd said pointedly to Mooney. 'She seems to be very much taken with your investigation.'

'I admit I wanted her input and experience at the beginning, but I warned her not to become involved.'

'Did she listen to you?' Boyd asked. 'She sure as hell doesn't listen to me any more.' He blushed at his own words. He'd meant to think them, not speak them. Too late to retract.

Grace's head bobbed furiously. 'That's just it. She keeps poking her nose in where it's not wanted.'

'It's more my fault than anyone's,' Bryan said softly. 'I asked her to find out something for me from my past. And it had nothing to do with Imelda Conroy.'

'So what was it?' Mooney asked.

'That's none of your business,' Grace said, surprising the

three men with her vehemence. 'You need to find the killer before he comes here for Bryan.'

'Why do you think he'd come here?' Mooney put down his mug.

'You keep turning up at our door. You could be leading him right to us. Did you stop to think of that?'

'Papa?' Sergio stood at the door. 'I need the Wi-Fi code, please.'

'Sure.' Boyd followed his son and pulled the door shut behind him.

After he'd set the code on Sergio's tablet, he ventured up to the room he'd shared with Lottie and felt a swell of sadness wash over him. Their relationship was floundering and he wasn't sure he could rescue it. But hearing that Mooney was unable to get hold of her moved something in him. He'd never be over her. He had to talk to her, and to do that he had to find her.

He tapped Kirby's number.

'Did you get back okay?' Kirby asked. 'All set for the big day tomorrow?'

It took Boyd a moment to realise his colleague and friend was talking about Grace's wedding.

'It's just going to be a small affair and it's taken a back seat with all that's going on.' He hesitated before continuing. 'When did you last see Lottie?'

'In her hotel last night. Had a nightcap and went to my own room around ten. I left early this morning. Why?'

'She's not answering her phone. Did she give you any idea of what she would be up to today?'

'Not a dicky bird.'

'What were you talking about last night then?'

'Imelda Conroy phoned Lottie from Ann Wilson's phone. And I heard this morning that the Wilson woman was murdered. This Imelda appears to be MIA, so my bet is that Lottie went off looking for her. Talk to Mooney.'

'He's here. He can't reach Lottie either.'

'Oh shit. Can't he track her phone? Find her location?'

'I'll mention it to him. I'm worried, Kirby.'

'She'll be grand. And if you don't mind me saying this, because I've not got the world's best track record, you two need to talk. Rescue your relationship. Don't let a good thing die.'

'I'm not sure there's much good left to rescue.' Boyd found himself shaking his head in the empty bedroom. 'But thanks for the advice. First, though, I need to locate her and find out what she's up to.'

'Good luck, and if I hear anything my end, I'll contact you straight away.'

Boyd walked Mooney to his car.

'What's this about Imelda phoning Lottie from Ann Wilson's phone?'

'Lottie contacted me about it last night and I went to talk to her and Detective Kirby.'

'What did Imelda say in the call?'

'That Assumpta Feeney was key to it all.'

'The woman who was murdered out at the holiday cottage,' Boyd said, reminding himself. 'And what did you do about that?'

'I spoke with Ann Wilson last night. She was nervy and anxious. She said Imelda had made her drive around half of the county. Ann had something to say, I'm sure of it, but she didn't want her husband to overhear anything. She promised she'd come to HQ this morning to talk to me. But as it turned out, she didn't make it. Poor soul.'

'What could she have known that got her killed?' Boyd ran

the toe of his shoe over and back on the gravel yard. 'Did you mention Assumpta Feeney to her?'

'No, but Ann had told Lottie about a child being pushed into a washing machine in the convent. She blamed Robert Hayes. He was a young chaplain at the time.'

'And was Assumpta there then too?'

'She must have been. I'm finding it hard to tie in why they are all being killed now.'

'Someone doesn't want what happened back then to emerge. The only person that can be is Robert Hayes. We have to find him.'

'We?' Mooney raised an eyebrow. 'I've had enough interference from your fiancée, so you stay out of it.'

'You asked her in on day one.'

'True. I did.'

'Well, you better find her. And I can help.'

'Do you want to get me sacked?'

'Do you want the wrath of Lottie Parker raining down on you?' Boyd said.

'Okay.' Mooney capitulated, his shoulders drooping. 'Where would you look?'

'If Imelda said Assumpta Feeney is key to it all, that's where I'd start. Where did she live?'

'God, I hope I'm not making the second-biggest mistake of my career.' He unlocked the car. 'Hop in.'

'And what was the first-biggest mistake?'

'Meeting Lottie Parker.'

As they drove, Mooney took a call on his hands-free. He had earlier asked for a trace to be put on Ann Wilson's phone, before he'd asked for the same thing on Lottie's. Now they had a location for Ann's phone.

'It's at Assumpta Feeney's house,' Mooney said. 'I'll ring it and see if she answers.'

Boyd put out a hand to stop him. 'Wait. Think. If Imelda is involved in these murders and she still has the phone, you could be alerting her to the fact that we know where she is.'

'How would she figure that out?'

'Because she is most likely a techie nerd and will put two and two together.'

'If she's that techie, she would have dumped the phone or turned off its location.'

'True,' Boyd said. 'Up to you.'

'Fuck it, we'll be there shortly, so I'll ring.' Mooney took his phone off the hands-free and handed it to Boyd. 'I saved Ann's number in the contacts. You call it.'

Boyd found the number, hesitated, then tapped the screen.

81

Bryan couldn't take much more interruption in his life. He wanted to herd his sheep, feed them. Walk his dog. Hold Grace in his arms. Marry her. And for everyone else to leave them alone for the rest of their days.

Grace was in the living room, taking it upon herself to scrub it from top to bottom. He hadn't the will to ask her not to do it. It was his space. He had to remember that it would soon be their space. The little boy, Sergio, had his head in his tablet and seemed to be no trouble to anyone. Bryan's trouble was the memory of a life he'd spent trying to forget.

He needed to be outside. The walls were enclosing him and he felt claustrophobic.

He left the house and walked across his fields. The sound of the waves, usually a balm to his soul, now seemed to intrude on his thoughts. The smell of the seaweed rose from the rocky shore, and his sheep grazed on the hard, barren ground where little grew other than heather and gorse. Maybe he should buy a few goats.

At the wall that held the sheep back, he stood and leaned his arms on the stones. Memories came rushing back to him. His home. His poor mother, his sorry father. His brother and his little sister. He rarely thought of her and suddenly he felt ashamed.

The girl had tried to be a mother when their mam died. He had been a teenager then, a boyo. Causing trouble. Ending up in Knockraw. Getting Mary Elizabeth pregnant. He had been so caught up in his own delinquent ways he forgot about the sister who had fed them and tended to the baby. The baby who had entered the world as their mother took her final breath. He had little memory of that child. What type of brother did that make him?

Big fat tears rolled down his cheeks. His sorrow arrived with full force, years late. He did not deserve to spend his life with someone as good and beautiful as Grace. He had abandoned his family. He had gone about his life doing whatever the hell he'd wanted, but his sister had done nothing wrong. She was a gem and he'd ignored her.

Feeling sorry for himself made him ashamed all over again. But crying wasn't going to solve anything. It would not absolve him of his many sins. He needed to look forward. To Grace and the life they were about to make together. He had to man up and be truthful.

Bryan O'Shaughnessy had never been fully truthful in any part of his life.

He wasn't sure he could be now.

82

Somewhere in Assumpta's house a phone rang, and all three heads swung around.

Lottie took her chance and leaped from the chair, tackling Robert Hayes in an effort to dislodge the knife from his hand.

Imelda screamed.

Hayes refused to loosen his grip on the knife as Lottie struggled with him.

Imelda screamed again.

Lottie fell to the floor, Robert on top of her. She had to get the knife out of his hand. He held fast, too strong for her, twisting around and thumping her head down on the hard boards.

Her world converged in a sea of fog.

Then total darkness.

A massive headache pounded in her skull when she came round. Imelda handed her a damp cloth to hold to the bump on the back of her head.

'What happened?' Lottie asked, then it came back to her. 'Where is Hayes?'

Imelda was now holding the knife and Hayes was sitting on the armchair, his head in his hands.

'I'm sorry,' he said. 'I didn't mean for any of this to happen.'

'Prick,' Imelda said.

'Was I out for long?' Lottie asked, dragging herself upright.

'A minute, maybe less. Thirty seconds. You'll have a whopper of a headache, but I doubt there'll be any permanent damage. Hard to kill a bad thing, eh?' Imelda laughed, then her expression turned dark as she studied Robert. 'I should just stick this in you and be done with your vileness.'

'How many times do I have to tell you?' he said. 'I did not kill anyone.'

'You are a liar.' Imelda wasn't for changing her opinion, Lottie concluded.

'Imelda,' she said, gingerly touching the back of her head for damage. It was tender and sore. No blood came away on her fingers. A good sign, at least. 'I heard a phone ring somewhere, before this all kicked off. Where's my handbag?'

'It wasn't your phone. You left that in the car. It was Ann's.' Imelda took it out of her jeans back pocket. Waved it in front of Hayes. 'And I got your confession recorded in full, arsehole.'

'I did not confess to anything. What are you even talking about?'

'Shut up while I think what to do next.'

Lottie's eyes were unfocused, looking from one to the other. 'Imelda, Ann is dead, so who was calling her phone?'

'Unknown number. I hadn't time to answer it seeing as I was helping to keep you from being stabbed by this prick and—'

A loud knock on the door cut off Imelda's words.

'Open it,' Lottie said.

'I have to watch him. You open it.'

Lottie stood, then bent over in pain. Robert must have

landed a punch to her stomach at some point. She reached the door and unlocked it.

Mooney, followed by Boyd, entered the cramped space.

The Galway detective looked shell-shocked. 'Holy Mother of God, what's going on here?'

'That's Imelda Conroy, and he's Robert Hayes,' Lottie said. She eyed Boyd, who quickly looked away. She yearned for him to hold her, to ease her pain. But he was standing close to Mooney, avoiding making any eye contact with her. So that's the way it's to be, she thought sadly.

'I've his confession recorded.' Imelda handed Mooney the phone. He also took the knife from her and slipped both into evidence bags he'd extracted from his jacket inside pocket. It reminded Lottie of Kirby, and she wanted to cry.

'I did not kill them. You've got it so wrong.' Robert Hayes had at last removed his hands from his face, and Lottie noticed the tear tracks down his cheeks. She found it difficult to figure out if he was telling the truth or was just in denial.

'Are you okay?' Mooney asked her.

'I'll be fine.'

Silence fell over the small group standing around the tiny living space, until it was broken by Mooney calling for squad cars.

When he'd finished, Lottie watched him appraise Imelda. Was he having the same doubts that she had about the woman's innocence in all that had happened?

'I'll have to take you in,' he said. 'We were scouring the countryside for you all week.'

'Are you arresting me?' Imelda demanded.

'If I have to.'

'What charge?' Defiance lit a fire in her eyes.

'I'll think of something, but I'd rather you came willingly. I need you to fill in a lot of blanks.'

'Okay, I can do that. But the second it gets awkward, I'm calling a solicitor.'

'I'd advise you to get one in any event,' Lottie said. 'I heard Norah Ward is good.'

Mooney glared at her. 'You need to be seen by a doctor.'

'I'll be fine.' She didn't feel fine but wasn't in the mood to acknowledge any weakness.

Mooney looked at Hayes. 'I'm arresting you for assaulting a member of An Garda Síochána.'

Before he could launch into his legal spiel, Imelda said, 'No need for pussyfooting, detective. Arrest him for murder.'

'That will come later,' Mooney explained. 'Assault is a tangible charge.'

'I hope you know what you're doing.'

'I do. But I'm not at all sure that you took the wisest course of action in absconding from a crime scene and then leading us on a wild goose chase. Why do you have Ann Wilson's phone?'

'She gave it to me.'

Lottie suspected this was a lie.

'Where's your own?' Mooney asked.

'Gone the way of all my recording equipment. He probably dumped everything in the Atlantic Ocean.'

'I did nothing wrong,' Hayes murmured. All fight seemed to have deserted him.

Two uniformed gardaí arrived at the door. Mooney walked Hayes outside. He was back a few minutes later, Hayes having been whisked off to Garda HQ.

'Now, do either of you care to tell me why you are here and what the hell happened?'

Imelda seemed to be waiting for Lottie to speak, but she felt too dizzy to talk.

'You need to take her home,' Mooney told Boyd.

'Come on,' Boyd said. 'I'll drive your car seeing as I came with Sergeant Mooney. I can drop you at your hotel.'

83

Outside on the pavement, Lottie stood with Boyd and watched as Mooney put Imelda into a squad car. A small crowd had gathered on the opposite side of the road, but quickly dispersed as if they were well used to gardaí calling to disturbances.

Mooney turned to her once the car had been driven off. 'What brought you here?'

'I wanted to get a feel for Assumpta when she was alive. Imelda had a key to the house. Don't ask, because I don't know how she came to have it. I find her hard to believe.'

'Okay,' Mooney said. 'And then what?'

'Robert Hayes was already in the house. Upstairs. I'd say he most likely broke in the back door or a window. You need to check it.'

'What was he even doing here?'

'Looking for notes that he says Assumpta kept about her time with the Sisters of Forgiveness. Personal notes, written in notebooks. Not the official records, which I think Mickey Fox burned.'

'Why did Fox burn them?'

'How would I know?' she said, sharper than she'd intended, then softened. 'But I suspect he may have been threatened.'

'Did Hayes find these mystery notes?'

'No. And the thing is, he claimed vehemently, numerous times, that he did not kill anyone.'

'They all say that. Innocent until we can prove otherwise.'

'But... I don't know, Mooney. What if he's right? What if Imelda is lying? I don't trust her. You need to keep a close eye on her.'

'Don't you worry your sore head about her.'

'Before I leave,' she chanced, 'is it okay for me to have a look around? I might find those notebooks.'

'This place was thoroughly searched by my team and SOCOs. If there were any to be found, we would have found them.'

'All the same...' She wasn't giving up that easily.

'You need to get your head seen to.'

'My head is fine. I've had worse knocks.'

'You are a tough nut, Inspector Parker. And a dangerous one,' he added with a smile. 'You'll get me fired.' He rubbed a hand around his bearded chin. 'Okay then. We'll give it five minutes, and if we don't find anything, I'm locking up and going back to HQ to interview the two people of interest in this series of murders.'

'I'll help too,' Boyd said to Mooney, ignoring Lottie.

She forced herself not to look at him as she climbed the stairs to begin her search. Two could play his game.

While Mooney searched the living room, Boyd followed Lottie upstairs into one of the two bedrooms.

'At least we know Hayes is locked up,' he said. 'No one else can be murdered.'

'Are you making an effort at small talk?' she asked.

'Don't start, Lottie.'

She relented. 'Imelda is hiding something from us. From Mooney, I mean. She knows more than she's letting on. I wish she'd told me where she'd stashed her documentary recordings. She probably has them on a USB somewhere. The answer to everything could be there. And if we find Assumpta's notes, they should throw further light on what went on in that laundry.'

'It must be related to Gabriel's death,' he said. 'Hayes has to be covering his tracks in relation to it.'

She felt warm inside, being in close proximity to Boyd after all that had happened between them. Maybe their relationship could be rescued.

With one bedroom unfurnished, they split up the other room between them to search. A double bed sporting flower-patterned sheets, one locker containing two pill bottles, vitamins and rosary beads. The only other furniture was a built-in wardrobe.

'It appears to have been recently decorated,' Boyd said.

'Not to my taste,' Lottie said, shielding her eyes from the floral decor on almost every surface. 'Where would she hide something that was precious to her?'

'A lock box at a bank?'

'I doubt it. If Imelda thought the notes were here, then I think Assumpta mentioned it to her.'

'We should ask Imelda. Save ourselves time.'

Lottie looked under the bed then sat back on her hunkers. 'She was anxious to get up here, just before Hayes walked down the stairs.'

'Do we pull up the carpet and lift floorboards?'

'Not a bad idea, but Mooney would kill us.'

She moved to the wardrobe. The clothing appeared to be all washed and clean. Hung neatly by type of item, then size. She pushed the dresses to one side and felt around the back of the wooden frame. Nothing movable. After a fruitless check of the pockets of jackets and jeans, the clothes swaying over her head, she leaned down and ran her hand over the flooring. 'Boyd, I think this board is loose.'

He joined her. 'Yep, it is. Will I get Mooney to come up?'

She wanted to see for herself, but knew Mooney was the one to do it in case they found something that provided evidence. Chain of custody was crucial.

'Yeah, do.'

She sat on the edge of the bed and waited.

'The back door was shimmied,' Mooney said when he shuffled into the small bedroom. 'I think it's time you two left this to me.'

'We'll move out of your way,' Lottie said reluctantly, hating not to be the one to do this.

'I've never met a more persistent person in my life.'

He pressed hard on the loose timber and it sprang back. He lifted the board to reveal a small opening. 'Better not be a mouse nest,' he said.

Lottie shuddered. 'Better not or I'm out of here.'

'Ah-ha. Now I know how to get rid of you,' Mooney said. He shone a thin flashlight into the opening. 'I'll be damned, you were right. These must be Assumpta's notebooks. I'm not touching or removing them until I get someone to take photos.'

'I can take photos on my phone,' Lottie chanced.

'You could, but you won't.'

Lottie didn't want to leave until the SOCOs arrived. Irritated at not being allowed in on the find, she launched into a rant.

'It's not fair. I want to know what she wrote,' she said, marching around outside on the footpath.

'Forget it.' Boyd took her car keys. 'Let's go to Grace and Bryan's place.'

'You do know I'm not welcome there?'

'For fuck's sake, Lottie, will you do what you're told for once in your life?'

'Jesus, you'd think I was a five-year-old.'

'You're bloody well acting like one. Get in.'

'I'd rather just go to the hotel.'

'You'll do what you're told or I'm calling a taxi for myself.'

'Fine, then.'

She got in without further protest and opened the glove box. She found a packet of paracetamol and took two, then rested her head on the side window and closed her eyes.

When the car stopped, she was jolted awake outside the farmhouse. She was raging with herself for having fallen asleep.

'This is going to be awkward,' she said.

'Never stopped you before.'

'God Almighty, you're like a broken record.' She got out of the car and slammed the door, the noise reverberating in her skull. Ouch.

A scream came from inside the house.

84

When Bryan returned to the house after his walk through the fields, there was an SUV parked in the yard. Denis Wilson. Good God, he'd forgotten all about Mooney's warning that the grieving husband might seek him out again.

He ran the last hundred metres and burst into the kitchen. Wilson was sitting in his shirtsleeves, his jacket over the back of the chair, drinking coffee at the table. Grace was peeling potatoes at the sink.

'We need to talk,' Wilson said, rising. 'Thanks for the coffee.'

'No problem,' Grace said. 'Again, I'm sorry for your loss.'

He pointed to Bryan, then the door. 'Outside.'

Bryan backed out, glad to get the man away from Grace. He didn't like Wilson, but he felt he had to humour him, despite Mooney's warnings. They walked towards the barn.

'We can talk in here if you'd like, though I've no idea why you need to speak to me.' He knew full well that Denis Wilson saw him as a murderer.

'An apology for hitting me yesterday would be a start,' Wilson grunted.

Bryan didn't want to apologise, because he'd meant every bit of the force of his punch, but then the man's wife was dead. He was bigger than his pride. 'I apologise. I was out of order.'

'You were.' Wilson sniffed and turned up his nose. 'This place smells rank.'

'It's a farmyard barn, it's supposed to smell.'

He ran a finger under his nose as if that could minimise the odour, then leaned against a stake with chains and nooses. 'What are these for?'

'They're not used any more. It's just ancient stuff that's not needed.' Bryan shifted from foot to foot. Wilson was making him uneasy by not getting to the point of his visit.

'I think you should confess to the guards,' Wilson said at last.

'About old farm equipment?'

'Don't be smart. I know your type. You think you're the salt of the earth. You prance around the village like Farmer Muck when you should be going to church and confessing your sins.'

Bryan thought the councillor was a dab hand at the prancing bit but thought better about mentioning it. 'We all have sinned.'

'Maybe, but the thing is, I know your secret.'

'I don't have any secrets.' Bryan bristled, memories flooding his brain. What could Wilson mean? Surely he didn't know about Mary Elizabeth or his little sister.

'All those years ago, out in Knockraw and the convent. I know what went on.'

Bryan scratched his head. 'I really have no idea what you're talking about.'

'She died in the laundry. Your Mary Elizabeth. Did you know that?'

Bryan felt the blood drain from his brain and felt faint. He staggered and held onto a wooden rail. After a moment, he gathered his wits and righted himself. 'What?'

'Ann said she was fiery, not that it did her much good. I'd say she's in an unmarked grave now. And if you want that secret to remain hidden, I guess you can bypass confessing to a priest and confess to the guards.'

'Grace knows about my relationship with Mary Elizabeth, so it's not a secret. Is there something else you're talking about?' Bryan shook his head as if the action could imbue him with knowledge of what the councillor was referring to.

'The sexual assaults. At Knockraw. I can spin it to put you in the frame. If it ever comes out.'

'I really don't know what you're talking about, but I'll tell you this, you're a twisted bastard.'

'I'm leaving now, but if you haven't been arrested and charged by this evening, I'll be back. And mark my words, Miss Grace Boyd will not be impressed.'

85

Detective Sergeant Mooney was fairly thick-skinned by nature, but the content of Assumpta's notebooks raised the hair on the back of his neck. What kind of a society did he live in? The events she had documented happened not in the dark ages but in the recent past. He could not stomach some of the descriptions. It verged on debauchery. He turned the page.

I watched the two girls being manhandled into the back of the black car. Would they return? I supposed they would, like the others before them. Broken and terrified.

Mickey Fox was standing among the trees, watching. Useless. But I can't blame him. He once tried to rescue a girl from this place but he didn't get far. The only surprise for me is that he kept his job. Perhaps the nuns felt safer having him under their watchful eyes rather than him mouthing off to all and sundry in the town. Who knows the way those witches think.

Robert is driving the car to Knockraw tonight. I don't know how I ever thought of abandoning my vocation for him. I will renounce my vows in order to find another path for myself. He

*is a stupid man, easily manipulated, which makes him danger-
ous. I'm glad I saw the light, but I am so, so sad that it took the
death of little Gabriel for me to see him for who and what he is.*

*Tonight he is taking three girls. One of them, Mary Eliza-
beth, has just given birth. How cruel can the nuns be? For one,
they get money out of these sordid transactions. Greed. And
two, I believe there's a more sadistic reason. Mary's baby was
taken from her when she had barely gulped her first breath of
air, leaving the girl's healing slow, both physically and
emotionally. Poor soul.*

*I feel powerless to do anything. I am inadequate. A lone
voice among the fearful. The only thing I can do is document
what I see and hear, and hope that one day I will be brave
enough to tell their story. At the moment, I am a coward.*

*Mary Elizabeth is sobbing as I watch from my window.
Robert takes her by the arm and bundles her inside the car. The
girl called James is crying, but Ann is stoical and resigned.
This is Mary's first time to be brought on this journey, but I'm
sure she knows where she is being taken; the girls talk, and she
will realise what awaits her. Mickey told me about it. Made me
swear not to breathe a word. But I spoke with one of the girls,
and the things she told me about what goes on over there, with
those men, terrified me. Men – priests, brothers, deacons – who
have vowed celibacy see this as a way to fulfil their primal
needs. They do not view the girls as human beings, otherwise
they would not do it. How can I live in a society that treats
young girls as subhuman?*

I must be careful.

*What happened to Gabriel could happen to me, to anyone.
The little one did nothing wrong. It broke my heart to see her
abandoned by her family and thrown into this place. I tried to
make her life easier, but all she wanted was to learn, to go to
school, to return to her family, and she never stopped talking
about the baby she had cared for after her mother died.*

Mooney raised his eyes heavenward, trying to make sense of it all. He wanted to read more, to find out what it was that had someone murdering innocent people. Those who had been damaged and abused by others entrusted with their care. He wanted to go out and burn the convent to the ground. To travel over to Knockraw and similarly destroy the crumbling ruins. But the only legal thing he could do was find the killer and bring them to justice.

He looked down and focused on the words in Assumpta's notebook.

His heart almost stopped when he came to the next entry she had documented.

I am writing this a week after my last entry. I was sickened to my stomach by what I was told happened that night and I could not hold a pen, let alone write. I could not even pray, so I know now for sure that my religious vocation is at an end. I will instead train to be a nurse. I want to help heal visible wounds because I realise I cannot heal anything within a person's heart or soul. I am a failure, a coward. But I want to try to make amends. Somehow.

Mary Elizabeth is broken, in body and spirit.

The three girls came back in the car driven by Robert. Two are survivors. Ann and James, whose real name is Edie. The other poor soul, Mary Elizabeth, will not survive.

I bathed and dressed the visible cuts and put a tincture on her bruises. She is bleeding a lot, which is understandable as she recently gave birth. I think it is more profuse than it should be. Perhaps something is ruptured. Mother Superior will not allow the doctor to come to examine her. I even went out to Mickey Fox and asked if he knew a doctor in the village where we could secretly bring the girl. But his sad eyes and shake of the head told me more than any words could.

'Mary Elizabeth,' I whispered in her ear, 'please try to be strong. I will care for you.'

But the girl smiled weakly and held my hand. 'No one can save me. You need to get out of this place. It's not good. Save yourself.'

Her voice was weak, and I had to lean close to hear what she had to say.

'I know I will never see my baby. I hope it is with a good family who takes care of it. I beg of you to tell everyone what happened in here, and over there... in that awful place. You have to do something...'

'Who abused you?' I asked. 'Do you have the name of the ringleader?'

I felt sure she would say Robert's name and braced myself. But it was not his name that she whispered to me. In that instant, I knew I had to do something. I might be a coward, but I was furious enough to seek revenge.

This morning, Robert came by with another young man. He was tall and gangly and extremely handsome. I estimated he was no more than eighteen or nineteen. He carried himself well and seemed to have some hold over Robert, though Robert himself is no angel.

He stayed by the back door while the younger man went down to the laundry. I think he had some perverse interest in seeing where little Gabriel had been killed. This incensed me. So much so that I sinned. I am not sorry. I had to do something. I enlisted the help of some of the others. We filled a steel bucket with boiling water, and when he was bent over looking into the machine, two of us held the bucket high and poured the water down his back.

His screams did nothing to assuage my guilt, but at the same time, I felt a surge of exhilaration.

He tore at his shirt, stripping skin off his back as he tugged the cotton away. We hastily filled another bucket and *poured more water over his naked skin. He was so intent on helping himself that we were able to melt away into the background. Later I realised I had blisters on my arms from the splashes.*

I was sure he would never know which of us had carried out the revenge attack on him. And if he did find out that I was the main culprit, then I would be ready to face him.

This was the last entry from Assumpta's time in the convent. But she had made a new entry recently.

I returned to Galway.

I know I made a promise to myself that I would never set foot in the city again. But I was drawn back by a call from a woman making a documentary. She said her name was Mel, and she was insistent. I wondered how she'd got my name. But that did not concern me too much, because I knew it was time to tell my story.

What I didn't expect was to see him. The man who had been with Robert that day. The man who had violated and abused young, vulnerable women. Tall and elegant, neatly dressed. The woman by his side appeared drawn and subdued. But still very beautiful. And she was with the man who had abused her and a host of others decades previously. I was stuck to the pavement. How could she? But then I knew how she could. He was a brute, while at the same time a sweet-talker, a master manipulator.

I wanted to run over and drag her away from him. To shout words of sense at her. But I knew that would never work. I knew his sort. He had moulded her into a person he could control in entirety. God only knew what coercive power he had over her. I could imagine he forced her to believe that it had all been her own fault. Bastard.

Then I suspected there was a better way to bring him

down. I could reveal what I knew, all that I had witnessed back
then, to a wider audience. To an unforgiving audience.
   I called Imelda Conroy.

Mooney knew who the killer was. A man who had so much to lose if even one person talked about his past.

A man who had been humiliated and possibly scarred by the boiling water being thrown over him. A man who was ruthless and vengeful. He had proved that. He had manipulated Robert Hayes all those years ago. And while Robert was guilty of the crime against the little girl called Gabriel, Mooney suspected he had nothing to do with the recent killings.

But his problem was that the author of the notes, Assumpta Feeney, was dead. He had no proof to link the man she'd written about to any of the crimes. Everyone who could speak up was dead, except Robert Hayes. And it was possible he would not incriminate his one-time friend and exploiter.

He'd have to talk to Imelda and get her to reveal what she knew. And he wasn't at all sure she would want to disclose her information, as she had now asked for a solicitor. She probably wanted to broadcast her documentary and make a ton of money. He could force her to talk, threaten to charge her with impeding an investigation. With obstructing the course of justice. That would take time. What else could he do in the short term?

He needed Lottie Parker's help. He had already crossed enough lines to tarnish his reputation, one more to add to the list wasn't going to make much difference to him, but it might help catch a brutal killer.

He sent a text to Inspector Parker. Then he sent it to DS Boyd.

86

The scream that Lottie and Boyd had heard came from the kitchen. They rushed in to find blood dripping from Grace's hand. A knife lay on the floor.

'What happened?' Boyd ran to her side.

'I cut myself,' Grace said, as if it was blindingly obvious. She turned on the tap and waited for the water to run cold.

'How did you do that?' Boyd asked.

'I was peeling spuds. I couldn't find the potato peeler. I know I have it somewhere... I used the little knife. It's too sharp.'

He held her hand under the running water.

'Where's Bryan?' Lottie asked.

Grace pulled her hand free. Blood-infused water splashed around and dripped to the floor. 'What are *you* doing here?'

'I want to apologise and—'

Her phone beeped with a text, and Boyd's did so a second later. They both checked their screens.

'Mooney,' they said simultaneously.

She read the start of the message on the locked screen.

'Shit, Boyd.'

'Double shit,' he said.

She looked over at Grace. 'Where is Bryan?'

'He is not your concern and I want you to leave this house. You upset everyone.'

'Please, Grace...' Boyd said.

Grace ignored Lottie and directed her answer to her brother. 'He's outside, Mark. Councillor Wilson called round. I hope they apologise to each other. I can't bear it when good people don't get on.'

Lottie wondered where that left her, but she didn't dwell on it.

'Whereabouts outside?' she asked.

'What did Wilson want?' Boyd asked.

'I don't know,' Grace said, Lottie wasn't sure which question she was answering. The distressed young woman continued, 'I hope Bryan doesn't hit him again. I don't like violence.'

'And Sergio, where is he?' Lottie asked, and saw a stricken look cross Boyd's face.

'He's in the living room.'

Boyd raced past Lottie to go find his son.

'I'm sorry for all the upset, Grace,' Lottie said.

She was met with silence. With no time to mend bridges, she hurried outside, the words of Mooney's message sparking alarm in every step.

Outside the house, trying to decide where to look first, Lottie breathed in the fresh air, which was tinged with the scent of the sea and a strong farm-related odour. She reread the text from Mooney. As she did so, two men walked out of the barn. Denis Wilson, she presumed, along with Bryan. Thank God. She exhaled a breath of relief and made her way towards them.

'I'm Detective Inspector Lottie Parker,' she introduced herself. 'You must be Denis Wilson. It's so sad about poor Ann. Please accept my condolences.'

'Thank you. And you'll be pleased to know I have the killer right here. I need to call Sergeant Mooney to take him in. This time I'll make sure he's charged.'

She noticed blood seeping from beneath Bryan's greying hair at his temple. He had his head low, his demeanour one of defeat. Wilson was gripping him by the arm.

'Do you know Bryan O'Shaughnessy well, Denis?' she asked, winging it.

'I'm Councillor Wilson to you.'

His arrogance stalled her momentarily, but she was used to that from her superiors, so she infused her tone with steel. 'Councillor, do you know Bryan well?'

'Well enough. He murdered my wife and all the others.'

'The thing I'm grappling with is why? Why would he do that?'

'Because he's a bloody psycho, that's why,' Wilson said, a smug grin plastered on his face. Delighted with himself. Give me a break, Lottie thought.

'As far as I'm aware,' she said, 'Bryan has nothing to gain by killing those people.'

'Of course he has. He was in Knockraw as a youngster, and that documentary was going to expose his past crimes.'

'The crime of stealing a few groceries? I don't think that holds much fear for him. Definitely not enough to embark on a killing spree of innocent people.'

'They were not innocent.' Wilson seemed to realise what he had said, the politician in him catching up with his misspoken words. 'My Ann was an innocent. I don't know about the others. But I do know this. Bryan O'Shaughnessy killed them all.'

'Why are you so adamant that he is the murderer? Are you trying to deflect the investigation away from yourself?'

'From me? What do you mean? I am an upstanding citizen. I do my utmost for the community, and when I am elected to government, this whole area will prosper and flourish. And let me tell you, it will all be down to me.'

'I suppose as a grieving widower you will appeal to the masses,' she said as nonchalantly as she could fake. Inside, a hot rage boiled.

'I am insulted by that statement. I loved my wife.'

She had to keep him talking. She needed Bryan to move away. But he seemed to be stuck in a stupefied state. A knot of doubt twisted in her gut. Had Mooney got this all wrong?

'Then I am sorry for your loss,' she said.

'You don't sound like you mean it.'

'I do. I met and talked with Ann. She was a lovely woman, but she was damaged.'

'What do you mean? There was nothing wrong with her.'

'You spent a lifetime controlling her,' Lottie said, 'but was she really the best person for you by your side going forward?' She hated belittling Ann, but she had to poke for a reaction.

'You are out of line,' Wilson said, looking around. Was he searching for a way out of the conversation or a way out of the yard?

Just you wait and see how far out of line I can go, she thought.

'That may be so,' she said, 'but I think you are obsessed with your image. And maybe Ann was not the most suitable person to be a parliamentarian's wife. She was beautiful, but she was nothing more than a dressmaker. Wouldn't stand up to scrutiny at Dublin Castle tea parties, would she?'

Bryan, move, she silently implored, but he kept his head lowered, immobile.

'I will have you dismissed from the force.' Wilson's face turned puce. Not a pretty sight. It matched his stupid cravat.

'Others before you have tried,' she said with half a laugh, 'so I wish you luck with that.'

This incensed him. She could see him working to keep his

temper in check. The air seemed to drop low around them, shrouding them from reality.

'Are you purposely trying to get fired?' he said.

'No, I'm trying to help you own up to your actions.'

'Are you mad?' he spluttered. 'You are a spiteful bitch, that's what you are. You can't bear to see anyone do well for themselves.'

'Mr Wilson, I don't know you, so I have no personal grudge against you. But I don't like people who get others blamed for their actions.' Time to end this charade. 'Do you know a man called Robert Hayes?'

His face paled. Good. She appeared to have wrong-footed him. His confused expression was fleeting before he righted it.

'I've heard of him. He was a local priest out Moycullen way,' he said. 'Got kicked out of the clergy. Rumour had it that he interfered with children.'

'I can't say if that was true or not, but I'm referring to incidents much further back. The Sisters of Forgiveness,' she said. 'The convent laundry. Knockraw industrial school. Now do you know Robert Hayes?'

He leaned his head to one side, appraised her with a quizzical gleam in his eye. 'I really think you have lost the plot.'

His grip on Bryan must have loosened, because the farmer suddenly twisted and with an extended arm landed a punch to the councillor's stomach. Wilson bent over in two before regaining his equilibrium. Bryan caught hold of his shirt collar and tugged him backwards. The shirt ripped, came away in his hand. Wilson turned around, sparring with his fists, and knocked Bryan to the ground.

Lottie stood open-mouthed, staring at the burn scars streaking across the skin on the councillor's back. Bad burns. Deep and old. Decades old.

She shook herself out of her stupor and leaped forward, grappling with him, but she had no cuffs to restrain him, no weapon to impair him. He flung her off, then turned, spittle dripping from his lips.

'You are one fucking bitch,' he snarled, curving his hand into a fist, ready to make contact with her face.

She heard footsteps rush around the side of the house as she prepared to fend him off.

Mooney grabbed Wilson's arm and twisted it up his back.

'I've been dying to do this for a long, long time, *Councillor*. You are under arrest for the murders of Assumpta Feeney, Mickey Fox, Brigid Kelly and Ann Wilson.'

87

Grace dressed Bryan's head wound with a handful of plasters while Lottie made a fresh pot of tea. Boyd stayed with Sergio in the living room. Wilson had been taken away in a squad car. Mooney remained to tell her some of what he had read in Assumpta's notebooks. When she had the teapot and cups on the table, Grace took over and Lottie and Mooney went outside.

'It was pure greed and gross negligence on behalf of the nuns,' he said grinding his teeth in disdain. 'She wrote that they got paid for the girls by those in power at Knockraw. How low can human nature sink?'

'It was criminal, that's what it was.'

'What I can't get my head around is that so many people seemed to know what was going on but no one stepped in to stop it.'

'Our recent past does us no favours as a nation,' she said. 'All we can do is highlight what went on. And that's something Imelda can do with her documentary.'

'She won't be allowed to broadcast it any time soon.'

'I get that, but she will in time. So did Robert Hayes kill

Edie Butler?' Lottie asked. 'I noticed you didn't mention her name when you arrested Wilson.'

'I don't know yet. Hayes is still adamant he didn't.' Mooney blinked, his eyes tired. 'I've asked Detective Kirby to track Wilson's SUV. I gave him all the details. Now that he knows what he's looking for, it should be a simple exercise to eliminate Wilson if he didn't kill Edie, or confirm that he was in Ragmullin last weekend when she disappeared.'

'He'd have had to keep her from Friday until at least Sunday night,' she said. 'Could he have done that?'

'I will follow the evidence. There's a long and twisty road ahead of me to uncover everything.'

Lottie looked at the sky, trying to digest all that had happened.

'Imelda is not totally blameless in this either.' Mooney interrupted her thoughts. 'She had information that she should have shared with us. We may have been able to prevent Ann's death at least. I suspect that having talked with Imelda, Ann was about to reveal her husband's past. And after I left her home last night, she was either provoked by Denis or got up the nerve to accuse him and he had to shut her up. He will tell me what actually happened, because he is arrogant enough to blurt it out. Eventually.'

'I feel sorry for Imelda. I think she found herself in a difficult situation and didn't know which way to turn, or even what was the right thing to do.'

'I didn't think you were one of those people,' Mooney said with a small grin.

'What people?'

'Those who allow others the benefit of the doubt.'

'Don't forget, I was on the outside looking in on this one. I could afford to be totally neutral and objective.'

'Isn't that what we have to be at all times?'

'Yes, but I found it different when not running the investigation.' She paused and noted the weariness in his eyes, a sort of sadness. She knew what had caused it. 'Can I read the notebooks?'

'I'm sorry, but no. They're logged into evidence. And in all honesty, you don't want to know what's in them.'

'I can imagine, which isn't a good thing either. Is there any mention of Bryan?'

'No.'

'Of his girl, Mary Elizabeth?'

'Yes. She'd just had a baby, who was taken from her. Then she was brought over to Knockraw with other girls, where Wilson and God knows who else abused, violated and injured her. She died not long afterwards. Assumpta left the nuns then and went on to be a nurse.'

'How could she walk away?'

'She wrote in her notes that she was a coward. But I think she was traumatised and scared. When she returned and saw Wilson strutting around the city, she knew then that she had to do something, and Imelda's documentary was just the vehicle to tell her story.'

'If she had told her story to Imelda, why didn't Imelda warn Ann?'

'Imelda believes Assumpta came to the cottage that night to tell her everything, but she was murdered before she could do so.'

'How did Imelda escape?'

'She ran out the back door when she heard the commotion. She said Assumpta had had a few drinks. She doesn't rightly know what happened, but she had Assumpta's bag in the kitchen with her, something about biscuits being in it. Her car keys were in the kitchen too, so she was able to flee. She says she didn't see the attacker but thought she'd heard someone outside a few minutes earlier.'

'I presume Wilson destroyed her equipment, laptop and phone.'

'I'd say you're right.'

Lottie said, 'You need Imelda to hand over her research and her recordings.'

'She claims they were all taken that night. Presumably by Wilson. She reckons he dumped it all in the sea.'

'I think she is being economical with the truth. She told me she has them hidden, but wouldn't say where. She probably had everything on a USB. I bet she's waiting until the right time to launch her documentary.'

'She better not or she may well interfere with our case against Wilson. We have very little physical evidence to tie him to any of the murders. I'm hoping for a confession.'

'The chances of that are—'

'Slim to none. I know.'

'I'll talk to Imelda.'

'No, she's a witness. Don't interfere.'

'Me?' Lottie said in mock shock. 'I'd never do that.'

He groaned. 'I'm so glad I don't work with you, Lottie Parker. You'd put me in an early grave.'

She laughed then. 'You are a good detective, Matt. Let me know how things progress.'

'I might, and then again, it might be safer not to.'

'What do you mean?'

'Look, I shouldn't tell you this, but with those notebooks and that DNA familial match for Bryan... No, I better shut up.'

'For God's sake, don't leave me hanging on that.'

Mooney sighed, relenting. 'I have reason to believe that Imelda may be Bryan's sister.'

Lottie leaned her head to one side in disbelief. 'No, she can't be. His sister was murdered in the laundry, wasn't she?'

'I'm not talking about the wee girl known as Gabriel.'

'Mooney, you better tell me what you suspect.'

'Look, you can't say anything to him until it's verified, but I think Imelda was the baby that was born when Bryan's mother died in childbirth. Assumpta wrote as much in her notes. Which means she's his youngest sibling.'

'Holy shit.'

'Yeah. Holy shit.'

Mooney walked off with a slow wave of his hand behind him.

88

RAGMULLIN

Kirby was working late. He and Martina were updating the incident board with facts and timelines. Now that he had a description of a car to search for, it made for a much easier job. They knew the make, model, colour and registration number.

McKeown first found Wilson's SUV on the M6 toll booth CCTV on the Friday, travelling east. Dash-cam footage from a taxi caught it going past the carwash facility down the road from Edie's apartment at 16.00 hours on the same Friday. This was the last day Edie Butler had been seen alive.

'There it is,' McKeown said.

'Great work,' Kirby said with grudging respect. 'Keep trawling the footage. We should be able to place his car in Ragmullin on Sunday night also, as that's when we believe he dumped Edie's body in the river. If he disposed of her earlier than that, she would have been found before Monday. But check each day.'

'Where did he keep her for the weekend?'

'God only knows. Probably somewhere in Galway. Hopefully Detective Sergeant Mooney gets a confession out of him.'

McKeown was ace at CCTV, and he soon called to Kirby

again. Kirby leaned over his shoulder to look at the toll footage: Wilson's car heading west at 19.00 hours on the same Friday. Then returning to Ragmullin late on Sunday, 22.05 hours, before heading back west at the toll before midnight.

'The bastard,' Kirby said. 'Speeding too. Keep digging.'

'I've ANPR on his car as well. He's not going to talk his way out of this one.'

'It's obvious now that Edie Butler was the first to be murdered then he went back to Galway. I think his intended target was Imelda, but he found Assumpta. He was some fucker.'

'What did Edie do that got her killed?' McKeown asked.

'She had to have been in the laundry the day the little girl was murdered. That made her a target.' Kirby thought about it and added, 'I wonder why Ann married him. According to Mooney, she was afraid of her husband. She must have known what he was like and what he'd done. He had abused her, after all. She was one of the girls trafficked, for want of a better word, to Knockraw, according to Assumpta's notes.'

Garda Martina Brennan turned from the incident board. 'He got inside her head. Made her feel it was all her fault and he was her saviour. She was like the abused partner in domestic violence cases, controlled and too frightened to leave. He must have given her a way out of the laundry. It has to be that. He offered her a different life and she snatched it with both hands. Little did she know that living with the devil for the rest of her life doomed her to a worse fate.'

'You don't know all that as fact,' McKeown countered. 'It's hogwash from your course. Ann may have had a perfectly good life with him.'

Kirby spoke up before the two started a sparring match. 'We may never know what went on between the two of them.'

'Is his car being examined?' Martina asked.

'Yes, forensics have it in Galway, and they'll also examine

his house and his office at the radio studio where he worked. They have Edie's DNA profile, which I'm certain will show up in his car.'

Kirby's phone rang.

'Hello, Matt,' he said, and mouthed 'Mooney' to the others. 'Really? Yes, send it over. You don't think it belongs to Ann, do you? In his car boot? Okay. We'll have a look. Thanks. I'll get back to you straight away.'

His email pinged and he turned to the computer to access the attachments Mooney had sent.

'Martina, have a look at these snaps. The items were found wrapped in a towel, beneath the jack in the boot of Denis Wilson's car. Anything familiar?'

She looked back and forth between the images on screen and the photos pinned to the board.

'I have those photos scanned,' McKeown piped up. 'I can run them side by side on the screen.'

'No, it's okay,' Martina said. 'I'd swear on a stack of bibles that the items are the same.' She looked up at Kirby. 'This jewellery belongs to Edie. She wasn't wearing any when she was found dead, but in all the photos we have of her she wears similar silver stud earrings, a thin silver bracelet and a silver chain with a small cross. All are an exact match for what was found in Wilson's car boot.'

'Why would he be so stupid as to leave them there?' McKeown asked.

'Men are stupid,' Martina said. 'And arrogant.'

'Not all men,' he countered.

'Well, you are,' she said.

'Stop it, the pair of you.' Kirby was tired, he had a headache and he needed a smoke. But most of all he wanted to go home to Amy. She'd texted to say she had something important to tell him. 'I'll let Mooney know that he now has physical evidence tying Wilson to at least one murder.'

'You should talk to Edie's sons,' Martina said. 'They need to know about this development.'

'I'll do it in the morning.'

'You have a wedding in Connemara tomorrow,' she reminded him.

'So I have.' He turned to McKeown. 'Will you speak with them?'

'I've a ton more CCTV to get through. I want to nail this bastard to every road he drove over the weekend.'

'Five minutes out of your time,' Kirby said.

'Can't you do it on your way home?'

'Can't you?'

'I'll go,' Martina said. 'But I'll need a senior officer with me.'

'Okay, okay.' McKeown threw his arms heavenwards. 'I'll go with you.'

'Fine, but keep your mouth shut and your hands to yourself on the drive over,' she warned. 'I've your wife on speed dial.'

'Thanks, guys,' Kirby said, and made his escape.

89

CONNEMARA

The sky was darkening quickly, with a mist rolling in from the sea. Lottie shivered, clutched her hands to her arms and turned to go back inside. Boyd was walking towards her holding a mug of tea.

'That looked like a cosy chat,' he said.

She smiled, glad he'd brought her a drink. Then he raised the mug to his own lips and drank. Oh-oh, she thought, this is not good. Like sister, like brother.

'He was just filling me in on what Assumpta wrote in her notebooks.'

'You've been spending a lot of time with Matt Mooney this week. A lot more time than you've spent with me.'

'Are you jealous?' She knew she shouldn't have said it. Too late now.

'For fuck's sake, Lottie. What's going on with you?' He tipped the mug, intentionally spilling the remainder of his tea.

'Nothing's going on. I'm not the one who's jealous.' She felt a slow white fury build in her chest. He was out of order. She prayed he'd stop now, rather than making things worse. But of course he kept talking.

'You insisted on putting yourself in danger when there was no need for it, for Christ's sake.'

'Mooney asked me for help on day one. Then he was struggling, so I helped where I could.'

'He got assistance from Dublin. He didn't need your "help".' Boyd even did air quotes, and this incensed her further.

'You are a pain in the hole when you're like this, Mark Boyd. There's no talking sense to you.'

He sighed. 'I really think we are done, Lottie.'

She heard the finality in his tone. Her lips quivered as her rage quickly died. This was not good.

'We were going to buy a house together,' she said. 'We were to get married. Blend our families. Live happily ever after and all that. What happened to us?'

'You. You happened. You can't help yourself. You have to get involved even when it's nothing to do with you.'

'That's unfair.'

'Is it?' He walked in small circles and turned to face her, waving the empty mug. 'Can you deny it?'

She couldn't. Not really. Her shoulders slumped. 'I do what I have to do. Surely you know me by now?'

'I thought I did, Lottie. I really thought I knew the real you. I thought you were able to prioritise me and your family, but no. I was wrong. The only thing you prioritise is your work. Do you want to know what I think?'

'I suppose you're going to tell me.' She was resigned to whatever nail he was about to put in their relationship coffin.

'I think it's all a throwback to when Adam died.' Spits of anger flew from his mouth as he spoke. 'You buried your husband and then proceeded to bury yourself in the job.'

She was struck speechless for a moment before the words exploded from her lips.

'How dare you! How bloody dare you, Mark Boyd! You've crossed a line, bringing my dead husband into this argument.

That is the lowest you've ever sunk. For fuck's sake.' Her tears came then.

Much as she wanted to be strong, to stand up to him, she felt herself crumble. Fuck. No. She was not that person. Not the person he spoke of. She was not!

As he strode back to the house without another word, she calmed a little, wiped her tears and felt her breathing dip a notch away from hyperventilation. In the clarity of that moment, she had to admit there was a film of truth running through Boyd's words. And that enraged her even more.

She turned away and headed out into the dark fields, to be swallowed by the descending sea mist.

90

Armed with the CCTV evidence he'd received from Detective Kirby, Detective Sergeant Matt Mooney strode into the interview room feeling lighter on his feet than he had all week. He'd even had a shower, changed his suit and trimmed his beard. At last he had something tangible with which to wipe the arrogance from Wilson's face.

He did the introductions for the recording and sat back, his finger tapping the manila folder on the table. Everything he needed was digitised, but a file helped to unsettle a suspect.

Norah Ward was the solicitor, now that Bryan O'Shaughnessy was no longer her client. Mooney outlined the arrest sheet, keeping his eyes firmly on Denis Wilson. The man never wavered, his eyes pinned to a spot above the detective's head.

'What have you to say for yourself, Mr Wilson?'

'It's Councillor,' Wilson said, unable to stop himself.

'A conviction will soon see you lose that title, and any hope of running for the Dáil will be gone.'

'I did nothing wrong.'

Mooney slowly opened the folder, flicked through a few

pages and closed it again. 'Care to tell me where you were last weekend?'

'Home.'

'All the time?'

'What's it to you?'

'Take any trips?'

Wilson glared at his solicitor, who had her head down, then back at Mooney. 'What's this about?'

Mooney was glad to see Norah Ward had little interest in her client. Good. 'Did you take a trip to Ragmullin last Friday?'

'If you're asking, you must know that I did.'

'What was that trip for?'

'Business.'

'On a Friday afternoon?'

'I work every hour God gives me.'

'Still believe in God, do you?'

Wilson swerved around on his chair, almost falling over as he spat out words at his solicitor. 'Will you stop this farce? He can't prove I did anything wrong. I should not be here. Do something, woman.'

'Why don't you listen to what the detective has to say.' Norah inclined her head towards Mooney. 'I'm sure you have something more than conjecture to impart, otherwise you wouldn't have arrested my renowned client. Is that correct?'

Mooney heard the implied slur on the word 'renowned'. Good woman, Norah. Beaming, he extracted two CCTV stills from the folder. 'Mr Wilson, your white SUV shines up lovely and bright for the cameras. Does it have a PR engine too?'

'You're a bollox, Mooney,' Wilson said. 'It's my car, you know it's my car, so what?'

'This is you in your car in close proximity to Edie Butler's apartment complex.'

'Who the fuck is Edie Butler?' Wilson was all bluster, but

Mooney could see he was rattled. The tremor in his voice was a true giveaway.

'Edie was murdered last weekend. On Friday afternoon, she was taken from her apartment by force and—'

'There was no force. She...' Wilson paled, realising his faux pas.

'Please continue.' Mooney worked at keeping a neutral expression painted on his face. Inside he was dancing a jig. 'She went with you willingly, did she?'

Wilson exhaled loudly and licked his lips, contemplating the CCTV image on the table. No denying it was his car, him behind the wheel, the diamond on his stupid cravat catching the light. See if you can talk yourself out of this one, Mooney thought.

'She contacted me.' His voice was low.

Mooney asked him to repeat what he'd said.

'You heard me. She contacted me.'

'Why would she do that?'

'That Conroy woman was harassing her. Wanted her to go on the record for her stupid documentary.'

'And?'

'And nothing. Edie was distraught. I told her I'd go to Ragmullin to talk to her. That's all. We talked and I went home. End of story.'

'How did you first meet Edie Butler?'

'No comment.'

Mooney took a moment to align his information. He'd secured it from the bishop, who still had possession of the Knockraw industrial school admission records, eager to help, now that it suited him.

'You were put into the Knockraw institution by your mother when you were a young boy. Ten years old. Your father had died and she couldn't handle you along with your four younger siblings. You stayed on after your time to leave because you became invaluable to those who ran it. You became a real-life pimp. Isn't that true, Mr Wilson? Isn't it also true that you met Edie – who was then known as James – through your crimes while you were in Knockraw?' This last bit was conjecture based on Robert Hayes's statement, but he delivered it as a fact.

'No comment.'

'Here are a few more CCTV stills,' Mooney said, to disconcert the suspect. 'Take a good look at them.' He spread the images out on the table. A tableau of Wilson's movements the previous weekend laid bare before him. 'You returned to Ragmullin on Sunday evening. Why was that?'

'She called again. Hysterical. What could I do? I went back to calm her down.'

'That's not strictly true, though, is it?' Mooney was enjoying seeing Wilson squirm. After all, he was a cold-blooded murderer.

'What do you mean?'

'According to the final post-mortem results, the assistant state pathologist has determined that Edie Butler was murdered either late Saturday night or Sunday morning. So you could not have spoken with her on Sunday evening.'

Wilson bit his lip, and Mooney visualised the cogs turning in his brain. He hoped they were rusty.

'No comment.' He folded his arms.

Taking another image from the folder, Mooney slid it across the table. 'These were found hidden beneath the floor of your car boot. Recognise them?'

'Must belong to Ann.'

'She has her own car. Why would she hide them in yours?'

'How would I know?'

Another page made its way across the table. 'This is Edie Butler wearing the exact jewellery.'

'I'm sure there are a lot of people with similar jewellery.'

'Perhaps, but no one else would have that same jewellery containing Edie's DNA.'

'Is there a question there?' Wilson dropped his eyes.

'I also have proof that your wife was at a bridal expo in Birmingham last weekend and did not arrive home until Monday morning.'

'So?'

'So, you had the house to yourself. Did you have a nice time catching up about the old days with Edie? Before you filled her with drugs, as per her post-mortem toxicology results. Before you killed her?'

'You can't prove a thing.'

'Do you know something? I can. Edie's fingerprints were lifted from the mantelpiece in your living room. Hair has been recovered from your bath drain with her DNA. You killed her in the same bath in which you later killed your wife.'

'You're delusional.'

'No, Mr Wilson, you are if you think you can talk your way out of this. But I would like to know why.'

'Why what?'

'Why did you have to kill all those women?'

'If you're so smart, you should know.'

Mooney felt his heart surge in his chest and his eyes went to the machine to double-check it was still recording. Wilson had as good as admitted to the murders.

'You were the mastermind behind what went on between the convent and Knockraw. What age were you then? Nineteen? Twenty? So clever at such a young age.'

'That wasn't me. It was all Robert Hayes.'

'He has a slightly different take on it.'

'I'm sure he does. The lying weasel.'

'What do you think he lied about? Killing the wee girl in the convent?'

'He did that, not me.'

'Ah, but he was under your immense influence. You were such a strong character and he just did what you told him to do.'

'He couldn't even do it right. Got me blamed. Did you see the scars I still have to this day? Those bitches were as delusional as you.'

Mooney tapped the folder again. He had copies of pages from Assumpta's notebooks. But he didn't want to show them to Wilson if he didn't have to.

'I can kind of understand why in your warped mind you felt you had to kill Assumpta. She was going to land you straight in the shit. She, Ann and Edie were all in the convent, and I believe Edie told you she wanted to tell her story to Imelda Conroy. And Brigid Kelly, she'd been in the convent too, and she'd later worked with Robert for years. You couldn't risk her talking either. Then poor old Mickey Fox. He knew too much. Knew it all. You made him burn the records he'd stolen, then you came back and murdered him.'

'And why on earth would I do all that?'

'You had too much to lose with a general election coming up later this year. An old murder and abuse of vulnerable girls would not look great on your CV.'

Wilson was silent for a few moments, and when he spoke, his voice was so low Mooney had to strain to hear him. He hoped the machine picked it up.

'I should have just killed Imelda Conroy. That would have saved me a lot of fucking bother.'

'Why didn't you?'

He looked up from beneath his eyebrows. Eyes dark as his soul. 'Why do you think I went to the cottage that night? It was her I wanted. Didn't even know who the other bitch was until she blurted out how she knew me and that she and others were going to destroy me. That was when I knew I had to get rid of them all.'

'Let me get this straight,' Mooney said. 'You were still on a high that Sunday night, thinking you'd got away with killing Edie by dumping her body in a Ragmullin river to keep her murder from being traced back to you. But you still didn't know what information Imelda Conroy had amassed for her documentary. So that same night you decided to go after Imelda, whom you suspected might cause you the most damage.'

Wilson chewed his lip. Said nothing.

Mooney was satisfied he had enough with the forensics and the interview. But one thing puzzled him.

'Why not kill Robert Hayes while you were at it?'

'Bastard disappeared. He even called to Edie in the hair salon on Friday evening to warn her not to talk to Imelda. If I'd found him, I'd have forced him to do the deeds. And I'd have kept my hands clean. Robert could never say no to me.' Wilson made to flick his cravat, only to find he was wearing a garda-issue grey tracksuit. His lips curled in disgust. 'I should not be here. It's all his fault.'

'I'm getting tired of hearing you blame everyone else. I think it's time you answered for your sins, *Mr* Wilson.'

Mooney looked over at Norah and caught the curve of a smile on the edge of her lips.

91

CONNEMARA

SUNDAY

The day dawned, and Lottie felt the pain of loss deep within her body. Every inch of her flesh blared with aches, and she wanted to turn over and bury her head under the pillow. But no, that wasn't her true self. She had never shied away before and was not about to do so today. Grace and Bryan's wedding day. She would stand strong and resolute.

She showered and found the lemon-coloured chiffon dress that Katie had told her to buy online. She hadn't even tried it on, and it would be her luck if it didn't fit. But it did. Neat and snug to her body on top and floating away from her hips reaching her ankles. She tied up her hair and plastered on eyeshadow, mascara and a swipe of lipstick. She couldn't see that it made any difference, but her girls would be incensed if she turned up with a naked face. After slipping on a pair of silver gladiator type sandals with heels, belonging to Chloe, she did a twirl in front of the hotel bedroom mirror.

'You'll have to do.'

She practised a smile to use throughout the day. Hopefully

she could keep it in place and her feet in the sandals. Which would she abandon first? With weariness and an ever-increasing void in her heart, she set off for the little stone chapel that was no longer consecrated but was used for civil ceremonies.

It was going to be a long day.

Chloe jumped from the car outside the chapel and ran to her mother. Lottie smiled. She'd missed her family.

'You won't believe it, Mam.' She hugged Lottie tightly, squeezing the breath from her. 'The best thing ever has happened. I bet you won't believe it.'

'Try me, Chloe.' Lottie extricated herself and held her daughter at arm's length. 'I can believe just about anything at this moment in time.'

'It's great news, honestly it is.'

A skein of apprehension wended its way through Lottie's veins. She hated being kept in the dark and she knew Chloe was a dab hand at subterfuge. 'What's your news?'

'I got accepted. Can you believe it? I'm over the moon. Totally. It's just amazeballs.'

'Accepted? For what? Where?'

For the first time she noticed a flutter of doubt pass over her daughter's face.

'I didn't want to tell you before now, not until it was official, because I knew you'd stop me, and don't say you wouldn't have because I know you, but anyway, I start in August.'

'Start where? Chloe, I know I got a bang on the head yester-day, but I don't think it impaired me that much. I haven't a clue what you're talking about.'

'I got accepted into Templemore Garda College. Mam, I'm going to be a guard. Just like you.'

Words deserted her, and she let her hands drop away from

her daughter. Chloe was right, she would have stopped her. One guard in the family was enough for anyone.

'Aren't you going to congratulate me?' The girl looked crestfallen.

'Well done, pet,' Lottie said flatly, her head filled with a myriad of scenarios. None of them good. Chloe had blindsided her. A guard? God, no. To turn out like her? Please, no. Especially as she was still reeling from Boyd's damning words about her priorities. 'How did you...? When did you apply?'

'Oh, a while ago. Boyd was great. He helped me with the application and even wrote a reference for me.'

Lottie swung round to glare over at where Boyd stood with Sergio. He'd interfered with her family, and committed the ultimate betrayal by keeping her in the dark about it. Still, she couldn't help noticing how handsome he looked in his white shirt, blue suit and tie. She mentally kicked herself for that thought.

Turning back to Chloe, she forced a smile to her lips. 'Can we talk later? We have to go into this wedding, today preferably.'

Her grandson, Louis, ran to her and she lifted him up. He wrapped his arms around her neck and his legs around her waist, hugging her tightly. She hugged him back, and felt like crying at his innocent demonstration of his love for her.

She watched as Katie helped Rose out of the car. She turned to look at Chloe.

'Why did you bring your grandmother? I thought we agreed that Betty would stay with her.' Her tone was rising and she was unable to calm it. 'You know this is not a place for her. She will—'

'Don't worry, Mam, she'll come home with us tonight,' Chloe said. 'It's good for her to get out and enjoy a bit of scenery.'

'It will only confuse her.' Lottie tried to comprehend how

she was going to cope with her mother for the rest of the day, along with the swirling emotions already threatening to swamp her. Her head was splitting and she craved a drink, but she knew from experience that would not solve her problems. Still, the thought was enticing.

Chloe laughed. 'Gran will be grand. Sure she can't be any more confused than she is already. The sea air will be good for her.'

'She'll get a cold... or something.' Lottie felt like crying. God, she was turning into a whinger, a wreck.

'Lottie, for God's sake,' Boyd said, appearing at her side. 'Leave them alone.'

'It's none of your bloody business,' she snapped.

Chloe stood open-mouthed as Boyd walked away. 'Mam? What's going on?'

'You really don't want to know.' Lottie gritted her teeth in an effort to keep her anger locked in place.

'Actually, I really do.'

'Later, then.'

'Okay. Whatever.'

'Yeah, whatever.' Lottie moved towards the car, still carrying Louis, and took Rose's arm from Katie. 'Great to see you, Mother. Did you have a nice trip?'

Rose squinted up at her, struggling to place her own daughter. 'Katie said there's a wedding. Are you getting married?'

'No, not me. Not ever.'

Katie looked at her, and then over at Boyd's retreating back as he made his way to the gate to await his sister's arrival. She gave Lottie a sad, knowing look. 'Let's get you inside, Gran. You might like to meet the priest.'

'I hate them bastards. They killed my boy. My only son.'

A moment of lucidity in Rose's dementia gave Lottie cause for a genuine smile. 'You're right there, Mother. But this is no longer a consecrated church, and the ceremony is being conducted by a woman.'

'A woman?' Rose said. 'What is the world coming to?'

Lottie laughed then.

Louis lifted his head from her shoulder and asked, 'What's so funny, Nana?'

'Everything,' she said. 'You know what, Louis? Sometimes if you didn't laugh, you'd cry.'

The almost four-year-old let himself down from her arms. 'That doesn't make any sense, Nana.'

She watched him join her family. He grabbed hold of his great-grandmother's hand and they entered the ancient stone building together, without her. She looked over at Boyd. He'd been watching them. He turned away quickly and held tightly to his son's hand as Bryan drove up in his Range Rover. It had been washed and polished to a bright sheen.

Grace climbed out, a wreath of wild flowers in her hair and Ann Wilson's hand-made dress snug to her body. She looked beautiful and serene until she latched eyes with Lottie, who flinched under the frosty glare. It seemed Grace had not bothered with the tradition of arriving separately from the groom. Bryan jumped out and flashed Lottie a sad smile.

With Boyd and Sergio on one side and Bryan on the other, Grace sailed past Lottie, her head held high in the air.

She could not bring herself to go into the chapel. Instead, she sat on the little wall that surrounded the old building, wishing she'd stayed in bed and kept her head under the duvet.

Another car crawled up the narrow road. She saw Kirby's bushy hair before she saw him. He always made her smile.

He helped Amy out of the car. She gave Lottie a hug. Kirby beamed beside her.

'Nice to see you, boss,' he said. 'Are we late?'

'They've just arrived.' She pointed to the old wooden door in the thick stone wall.

'And you're not going in?'

'Not yet,' she said. 'In a while. Maybe.'

'You look sad,' Amy said.

'Don't mind me.' Lottie attempted a laugh, but failed. 'Things are a bit shite at the moment.'

'Hey, we've got news that will cheer you up,' Kirby said.

'McKeown is leaving?' she said hopefully.

'No, but we're engaged, and we are pregnant! Me and Amy. Well, Amy is, I'm not...'

Lottie hugged him, then Amy. 'That's the best news I've heard in ages. Congratulations to you both. I'm thrilled.'

'Thanks, boss. Come on, Amy. We'd better hurry.'

As the glowing pair went inside, leaving her alone again, Lottie felt her heart swell with happiness for them. It was good to see love and joy come to two people who absolutely deserved it. Things didn't always work out that way, so when they did, it was extra special. Then a crest of loneliness settled on her shoulders. Did she not deserve some happiness in her life?

'Penny for them.' The voice came from behind her. She'd been deep in thought and hadn't heard the car approach.

'Matt.' She stood. 'What brings you here?'

'I have another guest for the wedding party, but she's a bit shy. Could you talk to her?'

'I'm not sure I'm the best person to talk to anyone today.' A cool breeze swept around the side of the church, fluttering the leaves in the trees, swirling Lottie's dress around her legs, and she clutched her arms tighter to her body.

The young woman approached, head low, arms also hugging herself. She was dressed in a flowered cross-over cotton dress with flat leather sandals. Her hair hung loose around her shoulders and it shone in the morning sun.

'Imelda,' Lottie said, unwinding her own arms.

'I'm so sorry for all the sorrow I've caused. If I'd never started my documentary, those people would still be alive.'

'You can't blame yourself.'

'But it was a catalyst for all that happened.'

'Maybe so, but the only one to blame is Denis Wilson – his past, his ego and the evil in his heart.'

'Maybe.'

'That's what I told you,' Mooney said. 'You are still a vital witness for us.'

'Any confession forthcoming from Wilson?' Lottie enquired.

'One interview in and I'm delighted to say he is beginning to panic. The jewellery belonging to Edie Butler in the boot of his car and forensic evidence at his house and the other crime scenes will all help to convict him. Plus, Robert Hayes is singing like the proverbial canary. His testimony corroborates Assumpta's words written in her notebooks.'

'That's a result so.' Lottie then addressed Imelda. 'Have you talked to Bryan?'

'I wanted to wait until the wedding was over.'

'He will be delighted to get to know you.'

Imelda inclined her head to one side. 'I'm not so sure about that.'

'Can I ask if you knew he was your older brother?'

'I didn't know, not really. I was taken away by an aunt on my mother's side. I wasn't even a year old. I heard bits and pieces over the years. Enough to know that something awful had happened in the past. But I was led to believe I had no surviving family. It was only in recent years, when I went through my aunt's belongings after she died, that I learned I once had a family in Galway.'

'Why didn't you approach Bryan directly about your relationship?'

'I wasn't sure of the whole truth. I had discovered that one of the family had been sent to the laundry, and it seemed right for me to try make a documentary about it. That's my job. I hoped my research would open up my own past. Instead, I brought a murderer into the mix.'

'Don't fret. What's done is done,' Lottie said. 'Come into the chapel with me. We'll sit at the back. Take it one step at a time. How does that sound?'

'Sounds good.' Imelda smiled, and Lottie saw something of Bryan O'Shaughnessy in the girl's eyes and the curve of her mouth. Sometimes you didn't need DNA evidence for proof. It was right in front of you.

THE PAST

Nadine O'Shaughnessy thought all her problems were about to be solved when her Auntie June arrived. Her aunt had been in living in England. That was what her daddy said.

The door was open and her daddy was pushing her out, even though she hadn't the buckle fully shut on her shoe. Clarks red shoes. She loved them, though they were too small for her. But she hadn't told her mammy because she knew her daddy never gave Mammy enough money. Now she was dead and Nadine had to wear them because no way could she tell her daddy that she needed new shoes. But then she thought maybe if she was going to get educated, she'd get a new pair. She was about to open her mouth to ask when her auntie turned up.

'Is it yourself?' Daddy said.

'Sure is.' Auntie June was young. Maybe only about twenty years old, though Nadine wasn't sure. She glanced down at the little girl, then back up at him like he was a bit of dirt on her shoe. 'Where is the young one off to, all dressed up?'

'I'm getting an education,' Nadine said, realising she sounded a bit doubtful. Her big brother Bryan had gone somewhere to get an education. That was what she'd been told, anyway. But he never came home and her other brother was always out in the fields. She rarely saw him.

She heard the baby crying then, in the back room. Her daddy hadn't given her time to change her nappy, and she could smell it. She turned to go back in, but he took a hold of her shoulder and made her face the door. Like he was using her as a shield for himself against her auntie. Or something like that.

'She's going to the convent, June. It's what your sister would have wanted,' he said. 'I'd like you to get out of the way and leave us be.'

'And why would I do that? I'm here to help with the young ones.'

'Don't need no help,' he said. 'But you can change that brat's nappy while you're here.'

Nadine could see red blotches appearing on her auntie's cheeks and noticed she was wearing make-up. Cool.

Her daddy's fingers pressed harder into her shoulder and his other hand gripped the scruff of her neck. She'd have a bruise there. Maybe Auntie June would give her some of her make-up to hide it. She wasn't to know that nothing could hide the bruises she was yet to get.

But in that moment, she was happy that her aunt was there to care for her little baby sister, Imelda.

92

Bryan took Tess for a walk around the village before the wedding meal. He needed head space to process what had been revealed about Imelda. His heart was broken into tiny, miserable pieces of shame. He had no idea how to handle it.

He wished it was dark so that he could get in his car and drive to the ocean. He loved doing that at least once a week in the dead of night. No one knew about it. At least he didn't think anyone did. It was his escape, for himself, by himself.

Just to listen to the sound of waves thundering against the rocks was a balm to his soul. An insignificant human being met with the force of nature. Threatening, but simultaneously soothing. It usually brought him peace from the demons haunting his soul. But now he had an abiding shame to overcome. Shame because he'd abandoned his sisters; he hadn't searched for them. Shame that maybe he could have saved Nadine's life. Shame that he might have known Imelda sooner and perhaps those people would not have been murdered. He also had to mourn Mary Elizabeth and the child he would never know. A family he'd lost because of his selfish need for his own survival.

And regret. So much regret.

He wiped away a stream of tears. Tess whimpered.

Then he shook himself.

No, he must stop feeling sorry for what had happened in the past. He had to celebrate the now, the future. His new life with Grace, and getting to know Imelda.

But then there was the conversation Mooney had had with him that morning. About the old rumour that he'd had something to do with his father's death decades ago. Just a rumour, Mooney had said. Bryan smiled to himself. Some problems you just had to deal with yourself. Like he'd dealt with his bastard of a father. That was the truth but he'd denied all knowledge of it to the detective. Some truths were best left in the past.

He patted Tess, who growled a welcome for his touch. 'Come on, girl. We better get back before we're missed. I've missed too much in life already.'

The wedding reception was held in a local pub, which had a small function room at the rear with tables on a back lawn. The guest list was small and intimate.

After the delicious meal of roast lamb, and baked Alaska for dessert, Lottie saw Imelda and Bryan deep in conversation. She hoped Imelda could forgive her older brother for abandoning his family. For the fate that had befallen their sister, Nadine, known as Gabriel in the convent. But none of it was really his fault. He'd just been a teenager trying to survive in a shit show of a world. They'd all suffered in different ways, at the hands of a country ruled by fear, by church and state. She wondered when the full story of life in those institutions would ever be told. Every month there seemed to be some new horror unfolding.

She held her grandson on her knee; he was sleeping with his head in the curve of her shoulder. Her hair had come loose and she'd kicked off her sandals in some corner. Her forced smile eventually fell away as she spied Boyd, the traitor, dancing with Grace. Sergio sat with Chloe, his head buried in a book for a change.

Rose was sitting beside her, eyes closed though she wasn't asleep, her head resting on Lottie's other shoulder.

'Let her, Lottie,' she said, opening her eyes.

'Let who what?' Lottie said softly so as not to awaken Louis.

'Chloe. Let her do what she wants with her life. Don't stand in her way.'

This awareness from her mother stunned Lottie. Maybe the sea air was good for her after all.

'I won't stand in her way,' she said. 'I just fear for her.'

'And what good will that do? Life is too short. We don't know what fate awaits us. My old brain has let me down and I struggle to remember things sometimes.' Rose let out a wry laugh. 'All the time. I find it hard to remember who is alive in my life and who has left it. But I do know this. None of us know what the morrow will bring. None of us can predict what will happen to us or know what lies ahead. So let her be herself.'

Stunned, Lottie shifted on the chair, and Louis groaned, his bare feet swinging against her legs. But it was only a restless movement in his sleep. She shushed him and caressed his hair. She adored having him in her life. She cherished all her family. Her eyes wandered and lingered on Boyd.

'What about me and Boyd, Mother? What will I do without him?'

'Who are you talking about?' Rose had lapsed once more, but Lottie wanted to talk.

'I loved him. I do love him. But we're a mess. I keep fucking it up.'

'Language, missy.'

That made her smile. A sad smile. She felt a little piece of her heart had been chipped away. She wasn't sure if it was because she was losing her mother, or because she had lost Boyd. Mary Elizabeth had once loved and lost her man, before losing her baby to another family and then her life at the hands of evil. If she'd known what had lain ahead of her, would she have done things differently? And Bryan's younger sister, poor little Gabriel, whose real name she'd learned was Nadine. A name that meant hope. An innocent who at seven years old had only wanted to care for her baby sister, Imelda, and be with her family. Instead, she had suffered unimaginable torture and death.

This brought tears to Lottie's eyes, and she wondered why this case above any in her recent memory made her so emotional. Was it because she was out on the periphery of the investigation? Was it because she could be more human when not caught up in following a killer's trail? Perhaps.

She was tired. Tired of fighting. Tired of struggling. But she could not allow Boyd to diminish the one thing that had kept her sane through all the heartache of losing Adam. Her work.

At the same time, she had to admit that Boyd was right. Of course he was. She had immersed herself in the job. Without it, she did not know who she was. Now her family was growing up; even her youngest, Sean, was managing just fine on holidays in Lanzarote with his friends. But her husband was dead and her mother was suffering from dementia, and Lottie didn't know how much longer she would have with her.

She'd seen how important family was to Imelda Conroy. How far she'd been willing to go to uncover the truth and how much her fight had cost her, and others. She wondered if she could muster that fight within herself. To save what she'd once had with Boyd.

She looked out across the dance floor and caught his eye over his sister's shoulder. The dip of his head, in acknowledgement perhaps, and his sad smile.

Maybe there was hope for them. But she knew today was not that day.

Like her mother had said, no one knew what lay on the path ahead. And she allowed that to comfort her as she held her sleeping grandson tighter and kissed his soft hair, her heart brimming with love for him.

She wished she could live in that moment for ever.

Safe and unconditionally loved.

With her family.

After all, family was everything.

A LETTER FROM PATRICIA

Dear reader,

Thank you so much for reading book fifteen in the Lottie Parker series. I hope you enjoyed *Hidden Daughters*; if you did, I'd be so pleased if you could post a review on Amazon or on the site where you purchased the eBook, paperback or audiobook. I'm so grateful for all the reviews received so far.

If you would like to keep up to date with all my latest releases, just sign up at the following link:

www.bookouture.com/patricia-gibney

Your email address will never be shared, and you can unsubscribe at any time.

If you have already read the other Lottie Parker books, *The Missing Ones, The Stolen Girls, The Lost Child, No Safe Place, Tell Nobody, Final Betrayal, Broken Souls, Buried Angels, Silent Voices, Little Bones, The Guilty Girl, Three Widows, The Altar Girls* and *Her Last Walk Home*, I thank you for your support and reviews. If *Hidden Daughters* is your first encounter with Lottie, I hope you will find time to read the previous books in the series.

You can connect with me on my Facebook author page, Instagram and X.

Thanks again for reading *Hidden Daughters*.

I hope you will join me again for book sixteen in the series.

Love,

Patricia

facebook.com/trisha460
instagram.com/patricia_gibney_author
x.com/trisha460

ACKNOWLEDGEMENTS

It is eight years since *The Missing Ones*, my debut book in the Lottie Parker series, was published. In those eight years, I have written fifteen books in the series.

All of this would not be possible without the support of my readers, who continue to want to read more about Lottie, Boyd and the team. And it is a team that keeps me going and working on this series. I want to thank all at Bookouture who do such professional work in getting my books out to you the reader. Imogen Allport, Mandy Kullar, Alba Proko, Sinead O'Connor, Peta Nightingale, Occy Carr, Sarah Hardy, Noelle Holton, Jess Readett. Special thanks to Kim Nash for your support since day one.

I want to express my thanks to my copy-editor, Jane Selley, for her attention to detail and for getting what I'm trying to say. I'm delighted that she continues to work with me.

I especially want to thank my editor, Lydia Vassar Smith, for her valued input to all my novels and for her kindness to me, especially when things get tough.

My agent, Ger Nichol, put her faith in me on day one with *The Missing Ones* and has been with me since. I could not do all this without her, so thank you.

Thanks to Michele Moran of 2020 Recordings for her excellent narration and bringing my books and characters to life.

Thanks to Hannah Whitaker at The Rights People for securing foreign translations of my books.

Thank you to my sister, Marie Brennan, for assisting me with edits and proofreading. Her friendship and help are essential to me.

Writing can be a solitary and lonely craft to pursue. I am indebted to my friends in the writing community for their support and for checking in on me. And thanks to my friends Antoinette and Jo for all the coffees.

Special thanks to Ger and Danny Mulvihill.

The importance of libraries and bookshops cannot be taken for granted. To all the librarians and booksellers, thank you.

My family is growing up so quickly, I can't believe how fast time is passing. I write for them, and I could not do it without them.

So a special word of thanks to my daughter Aisling and her husband, Gary, and my grandchildren Shay, Lola and Sonny.

To my daughter Orla and her husband, Darren, and my grandchildren Kal, Daisy and Caitlyn.

And to my son, Cathal and his girlfriend, Kate.

All of you keep me on my toes and fill my heart with joy.

I dedicate *Hidden Daughters* to some of the teachers from my time in school, all of whom had a positive effect on me throughout my life. My secondary school English teachers, Fionnuala Aherne, Mary Casey and Joan Farrell. Also my primary school teacher Yvonne Keaveney. Even though I probably broke your hearts in school, you all still continue to support me. Thank you.

This book is a work of fiction. Some locations are real, but I've taken literary licence with them, as I do with police matters, to make them fit into the story. All the characters are products of my imagination.

Thank you dear reader and I hope you will join me for book sixteen in the series, coming soon.

PUBLISHING TEAM

Turning a manuscript into a book requires the efforts of many people. The publishing team at Bookouture would like to acknowledge everyone who contributed to this publication.

Audio
Alba Proko
Melissa Tran
Sinead O'Connor

Commercial
Lauren Morrissette
Hannah Richmond
Imogen Allport

Contracts
Peta Nightingale

Cover design
Tash Webber

Data and analysis
Mark Alder
Mohamed Bussuri

RAISING READERS
Books Build Bright Futures

Dear Reader,

We'd love your attention for one more page to tell you about the crisis in children's reading, and what we can all do.

Studies have shown that reading for fun is the **single biggest predictor of a child's future success** – more than family circumstance, parents' educational background or income. It improves academic results, mental health, wealth, communication skills, and ambition.

The number of children reading for fun is in rapid decline. Young people have a lot of competition for their time, and a worryingly high number do not have a single book at home.

Our business works extensively with schools, libraries and literacy charities, but here are some ways we can all raise more readers:

- Reading to children for just 10 minutes a day makes a difference
- Don't give up if children aren't regular readers – there will be books for them!

- Visit bookshops and libraries to get recommendations
- Encourage them to listen to audiobooks
- Support school libraries
- Give books as gifts

Thank you for reading: there's a lot more information about how to encourage children to read on our website.

www.JoinRaisingReaders.com

Made in the USA
Monee, IL
30 July 2025

22220901R00270